Soft Fo...

Matt waited until the set had cleared before moving next to Ellie. She could feel the heat of his body as he leaned towards her. 'I want you to make love to that camera,' he breathed softly. 'I want to look into your eyes and see the same expression I'd see if I was going to fuck you. I want to see your nipples rock hard beneath that dress, and I want you liquid by the time I take a photograph. Fuck me through that lens, Ellie.'

As Matt began to take pictures, she felt herself vibrating with an excitement and energy she'd never felt before as she stared into the lens. Matt shot roll after roll of film without pause, refusing to allow the usual tinkering with hair and make-up. As Romi adjusted the lighting and logged each spent roll, she too found herself responding to the sexual charge in the studio, her breasts tingling as waves of desire swept over her. With a few words, Matt had changed the whole atmosphere in the studio; he hoped the pictures he was shooting now would possess exactly the element of untamed, sensual power he'd wanted.

Tess Stimson was born and brought up in Sussex. After graduating from Oxford University, she worked for four years as a Producer with ITN, before emigrating to Cyprus to write her first novel. She is married to Brent Sadler and lives with her husband and son in Rome, where she is currently working on her next book.

TESS STIMSON

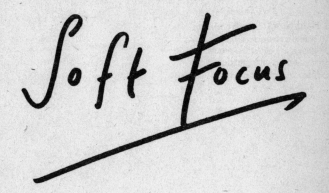

Soft Focus

Mandarin

Soft Focus is a work of fiction.
Names, characters, incidents and
places are either the product of
the author's imagination or are
used entirely fictitiously.

A Mandarin Paperback
SOFT FOCUS

First published in Great Britain 1995
by Mandarin Paperbacks
an imprint of Reed Consumer Books Ltd
Michelin House, 81 Fulham Road, London SW3 6RB
and Auckland, Melbourne, Singapore and Toronto

A CIP catalogue record for this title
is available from the British Library
ISBN 0 7493 1593 8

Typeset by Deltatype Ltd, Ellesmere Port, Wirral
Printed and bound in Great Britain
by Cox & Wyman, Reading

For my son,
Henry Louis Brent

*without whom this book would have
been finished in half the time.*

Acknowledgements

I owe a deep debt of gratitude to my editor, Louise Moore, whose skill and patience have made this book far better than I could have hoped to do alone.

My thanks, too, to my agent, Mark Lucas, for both his friendship and advice. His time-keeping I forgive.

So many people gave away their secrets to help me write this book, and there are some I wish to thank in particular: my friend Alastair Blair, for his insights into the design world; CNN's Elsa Klensch, for sharing her expertise with me and engineering my access behind the scenes at the fashion shows in Milan; designers Amy and Grace Li for their kindness and advice; Romy Godwin for much expert information; model Susannah Lindsmeer, make-up artist Carol Brown and photographers Sam Brown and Fergus Greer for sharing the secrets of their work; Gail Rolfe, of the *Daily Mail*, for allowing me to join a fashion shoot and giving me the benefit of her experience; Ian Griffith at the Kingston School of Fashion for his sound guidance; Sue Bingham, for her introductions and superb covers.

It is with particular gratitude I thank my family and friends: my mother, Jane, for always being right (I forgive the freckles) and my father, Michael, for letting her; my mother-in-law, Ruth, for being such a loyal friend; my sister, Philippa, for her invaluable research; my brother, Charles, and step-daughter, Nic, because they wanted to be mentioned too; and Kelly Evans, for giving me some sleep for which I will be forever grateful.

My most heartfelt thanks go to Henry, my son, who had the good sense to be born exactly twelve hours after I finished this manuscript.

But most of all, to Brent, always my hero.

Rome, February 1995

Book One

1970–1976

One

Nova Esperancia, Rio de Janeiro, Brazil
Monday 7 December 1970
2.20 p.m.

At first no one realised that the earth was moving.

The rain had been falling for many hours now. In the beginning, the parched soil had seemed to welcome the unexpected rainfall, the water quickly disappearing into the wide cracks networking sun-baked earth that cried out thirstily for more.

But the water had nowhere to go. The forest that had once covered the hills behind the shanty town of Nova Esperancia had long since gone, the trees felled and the land cleared by the ever-expanding population of the *favella*, desperate for more room and the space to raise a few scrawny chickens or a half-starved cow. The impoverished villagers didn't realise that it had been the trees which had held the hills together. In a few seasons, the rich, absorbent topsoil, deprived of the tree roots to which it had clung, had been washed away. The clay that lay beneath could not absorb the rainfall. Instead, the water slipped through the cracks in its surface and ran, unchecked and unseen, down the hill towards Nova Esperancia.

Half a mile from the village, Maria Manuela straightened

up from the chipped porcelain sink beside the *favella*'s lone water standpipe, and cocked an ear towards the hills.

'Juanita?' She frowned. 'Did you hear that?'

Her daughter was attempting to wring the dirty water from the faded shirt she was washing. It had rained for so long that they'd given up waiting for sunshine in which to do the laundry. She half-turned towards her mother.

'Did I hear what?'

'Listen!'

The two women stood motionless beside the sink, straining to hear beyond the steady thrumming of the rain on the corrugated roofs of the tin shacks of those who lived in the *favella*. After a long moment, Juanita shook her head and turned back to her washing.

'It's nothing. Just the rain.' She gave the last shirt a futile squeeze and dumped it in the bucket of clean clothing beneath the sink. 'I hate this weather.'

'You'll long for it when the wells run dry again and you're forced to clean yourself in the river in front of everyone,' Maria said. 'Rain is a gift from God, whenever it comes.'

She bent to pick up the heavy bucket of washing, shouldering it easily as Juanita gathered the basket containing her sleeping baby and sheltered his face from the rain with the hem of her skirt. Abruptly the rain intensified, and the two women bent their heads against the downpour as they walked swiftly along the narrow dirt alley that served as the main street for the inhabitants of Nova Esperancia. Thunder rumbled in the distance. Their feet squelched in the mud as they tried to avoid the more noisome rubbish that had risen with the water level. Juanita swerved to avoid the rotting carcass of a dead cat, blocked from floating out into the street by the rusty sign that had once adorned the *favella*'s first – and last – health clinic. Nova Esperancia, New Hope. Some hope. Within weeks of its much-publicised opening by one of

Brazil's senior High Court Judges, Fernando Moreno, the clinic had been reduced to an empty shell, the shining instruments and newly stocked drug cupboard ransacked by villagers to whom food meant more than clean syringes or penicillin. Now not even the doors or window panes remained.

A group of ragged children played in the puddles, oblivious to both the teeming rain and the effluent from the sewers that floated around their ankles. Juanita barely registered the teenage couple locked together in the shelter of a side alley, drenched by the rain, the girl's face expressionless as her lover pumped half-heartedly into her. A *putana*; or perhaps just a young girl who was desperately looking for an escape from the poverty and misery of her life, and had fooled herself into thinking the young man could provide it. Neither of them could be more than fourteen. The same age as Juanita herself had been when she had had the same dream, and her first child, exactly nine months apart.

'Grandma! You're back! And Mama!'

Juanita ignored her eldest son as he ran out of the shack she shared with Maria, her husband and her two younger sisters. She shifted the basket containing her baby in her arms, the muscles in her back protesting. The child within her kicked its own rebellion.

Maria stopped and crouched down, putting aside the bucket of damp washing and stretching out her arms towards her grandson. '*Querido!*' She scooped the three-year-old boy into her arms and held him tightly against her pillowy chest. 'Well, Claudio, what have you been doing?'

The child wriggled in her arms. 'The giants are coming, Grandma.' He stared at Maria, his dark eyes wide. 'We heard them in the hills.'

Juanita ducked her head as she entered their two-roomed

shack and put the baby down in the corner. Maria followed, carrying Claudio. 'The giants, hmm?'

'Oh yes, Mama. Their footsteps made the earth shake.'

Juanita turned to the little girl sitting in a corner of the shack. 'You felt them too, did you, Elizabetta?'

The little girl nodded her head, her expression grave. 'They sounded angry. I didn't like them. I don't want them to come here.'

'It's your mother who will be angry, Eliza, if you don't get home before dusk.' Maria stroked Elizabetta's dark curls affectionately. 'You know she needs you, with the new baby coming so soon. You can't spend all your time here, playing with Claudio.'

Eliza nodded and jumped off the wooden crate which served as a stool. 'Because I'm a girl. Boys are so useless.'

Juanita suppressed a smile. 'Indeed they are.' She felt a flicker of sympathy as she glanced across at the little girl. Elizabetta reminded her of herself as she had once been, before life and poverty had ground her down. The child was still confident, still certain that her life would be different from that of her mother and her sisters. At four years old, Elizabetta had yet to learn that the few meagre opportunities life offered were not meant for a child who had had the misfortune to be born a girl.

Claudio twisted angrily in his grandmother's arms and turned to face his mother. 'They are not! Girls are no good for anything but having babies. Father Lucio said so.'

'Juanita,' Maria warned, raising her voice to be heard over the noise of the rising storm. 'Not in front of the little ones ...'

Juanita never had the chance to reply.

The thin layer of loose topsoil on which Nova Esperancia had been built had absorbed the rain for as long as it could. Its wells had been filled, its sewers swamped, its homes flooded. The whole town had become a giant crumb floating on a soup of water, gravel and dirt. A low, terrible roar like the rumble of thunder echoed through the hills as the upper layers of the *favella*, wrenched free of their fragile foundations, slid downwards towards the valley on a deadly slurry of mud and rocks. The flimsy shacks constructed from iron, cardboard, plywood and cloth collapsed before it like a deck of cards, trapping people beneath their weight. Those who were not instantly crushed to death were smothered by the mud as it bore inexorably downwards. In a matter of seconds, streets and houses concertinaed on top of each other, half a mile of the *favella* crushed into a few jagged feet of iron and blood.

Maria clutched at the fragile wall of her home, unable to do anything as a sheet of corrugated iron detached itself from the roof and neatly decapitated Juanita where she stood. Claudio ran towards his mother and was felled instantly by a second sheet of metal as the walls collapsed inward. He did not get up.

'Under the bed!' Maria screamed, shoving Elizabetta to the floor. 'Get under the bed and cover your head!'

She ran towards the door to gather the baby from its basket. In the street outside, even as she watched, a gaping crack twenty feet wide split the ground open and swallowed half a dozen homes before snapping shut again as the hillside gave another convulsive heave. Of the teenage lovers she could see nothing. The alleyway in which they had stood had disappeared. A woman, her legs trapped inside the earth as it closed around her, struggled desperately to free herself, her hands clawing frantically as the rubble of the town rushed towards her. Screaming, she threw up her arms to ward off the avalanche that buried her cries beneath tons of mud and metal and rock. Three feet away from her, a water pipe twisted upwards as the ground convulsed around it, knifing through the stomach of a child standing frozen in shock. He collapsed without a sound. Maria watched as people hurtled past her, hopelessly trying to outrun the landslip, tumbling forwards

7

and disappearing as the tide of rubble and mud caught up with them and swept on past. The *favella* had been home to over 20,000 people. How many would survive this terrible onslaught?

Maria looked behind her. Nothing remained of her home or her family. She had seen Juanita and Claudio die. The bed was gone, Elizabetta with it. Tears flowed unheeded down her cheeks to mingle with the rain. She sank to her knees, the baby in her arms.

'*Ave Maria, gratia plena,*
Dominus tecum,
Benedicta tu in mulieribus,
Et benedictus fructus....'

Death, when it came, was almost a relief.

Two

Avenida Rio Branco, Rio De Janeiro, Brazil
Monday 7 December 1970
3.25 p.m.

Fernando Moreno eased back in his chair and rested his elbows on the mahogany desk in front of him. His eyes were closed. To his left, a deep green telephone burred, its receiver neatly placed beside it on the desk. His gold fountain pen lay idle on the blotter. The door to his secretary's office was wide open, but that scarcely mattered since she was currently beneath his desk, her wide lips clamped firmly around his cock. He shoved his pelvis forward, forcing himself further down the girl's throat, heedless of her discomfort as she was forced to accommodate him. He felt the sharp talons of her fingernails as she reached into his trousers to stroke his balls in an attempt to hasten his ejaculation. Aware of what she was trying to do, Fernando deliberately opened his eyes and allowed his gaze to travel across his office, filling his mind with trivia in order to dampen his arousal. He didn't give a flying fuck if the girl was enjoying it or half-choking to death. He'd come when he was ready and not before.

His eyes slid past the silver frames on his desk. This was not the time to think either of his mother or Annabel, his beautiful, blonde English fiancée. *Ex*-fiancée. He must remember to throw the photograph away. After all, she was dead now. There was no use living in the past. She had lost any right to be remembered when she had killed herself.

He stared at the heap of files that were piled across his desk and overflowing on to the floor. Applications for identity papers, work papers, adoption papers. Appeals for clemency, mercy, pardons. Cases of industrial injury, wrongful dismissal, rape, theft, fraud, murder. As one of Brazil's most powerful and influential judges, in his time Fernando Moreno had seen it all. Most of those pleas for help would be ignored. To Fernando, justice was a valuable commodity, and like all such commodities, it had its price. One very few ordinary Brazilians could afford.

He felt the girl shift beneath his desk, her throat convulsing around his cock as she tried not to gag. She was one of the lucky ones. Her brother might just get his pardon, thanks to her. Fernando reached beneath the desk and twisted his hands in her long, dark hair, forcing her to suck him harder in her desperation to get him to come before she suffocated.

Fernando smiled, enjoying her helplessness and humiliation as much as her manipulative tongue. Power was his aphrodisiac. Every decision he ever made, every aspect of his well-ordered life, revolved around his need to control and subjugate. Money, fame, pleasure – these were just pleasant by-products. Even his closest friendships were based on his need to control. Friendship created trust, and trust made people vulnerable.

He thought briefly of Roberto. His closest friend. And perhaps his most bitter enemy.

From the moment Fernando had been introduced to the Italian Ambassador at an embassy party just under three years ago, he had been consumed by an unreasoning envy that almost bordered on hatred. Roberto Cerreni had been born with everything Fernando had ever wanted – good breeding, impeccable connections, and a debonair charm that had won him a beautiful wife who obviously adored him. And yet Roberto treated them all so carelessly, as if to him they didn't even matter.

Fernando's own life had been so different. His father had died in a street brawl over a woman when he was only two; his mother had immediately dumped him with his father's mother and had never returned. His grandmother had treated him well, but on her death the rest of the family had thrown him on to the streets. Not quite ten years old, he had survived the only way he knew how: by selling his body to the rich and powerful men who cruised the streets of Rio by night, looking for boys desperate enough to do anything for the price of a meal. He had swallowed his pride and endured their abuse, vowing that one day he would be in a position to exact his revenge.

His moment had come when he had turned sixteen and had approached one of his customers, a Justice Minister anxious to avoid a scandal. In Fernando's eyes, the man had got off lightly: the price of his silence had been no more than the opportunity to exercise his formidable intellect in the corridors of power.

One chance had been all he had needed. In a few short years, he had risen from lowly clerk to senior High Court Judge, ruthlessly overtaking and deposing all those who had once paid for his favours. Now, at the age of forty-two, Fernando Moreno could mix with the cream of Brazilian society as their equal, but the insecurity had never gone away. Simply by the fact of his existence, Roberto Cerreni reminded him of everything he could never be, no matter how hard he worked. Overnight, his need to prove himself against the Italian had become an obsession he couldn't control.

He had tested the waters by asking Roberto for one or two slightly questionable favours, slowly involving him deeper in his illegal machinations as the Italian proved receptive. His inner triumph had mounted as Cerreni had moved further and further into a maze of corruption and intrigue. It hadn't been that Fernando wanted to destroy him; he had simply needed to know that he could.

And then suddenly he'd realised that Roberto hadn't been fooled for a moment. Cerreni's position had undeniably been compromised by what he had done for Fernando, but the Italian had been far from in his thrall. It was as if Roberto had been indulging the darker side of his nature for his own entertainment, following a Machiavellian agenda that had had nothing to do with Fernando. He could have broken free whenever he chose.

And then Fate had intervened so that Fernando owned Roberto, body and soul.

The memory was enough to make him come. He bucked in the chair as he poured himself into the girl's throat, gripping her head with his hands so she could neither back away nor swallow. A thin sheen of sweat filmed his sallow features, his pleasure flushing his cheeks and slackening his narrow jaw. With his thick, dark hair and strangely luminous amber eyes, Fernando exercised a fatal fascination over most women; but his preference was for those who didn't fall under his spell. It was more fun breaking them.

Abruptly he withdrew from the girl's mouth and showed his chair away from the desk. He stood and turned his back on her, staring out of the window as he zipped his trousers so that he didn't have to see her struggle awkwardly from beneath his desk. Through the smeared glass he watched the heavy drops of rain hissing down on the pavements below. The rainy season didn't start for months; by rights, it should have been thirty-five degrees out there. He shrugged. So much for summer.

He waited until he heard the door shut before sitting back down at his desk and reaching for his appointments diary, the girl already forgotten. He was due for re-election in less than two months. All but the most prominent and sympathetic engagements had been ruthlessly excised from his schedule. Fernando didn't doubt that he'd win a third term of office at the High Court. The right gifts had found their way into the pockets of the right people, and he was a vociferous supporter of the ruling military junta, who always looked after their own. But at the end of the day, it never did any harm to make sure. Whilst technically it was his peers who re-elected him, having the popular support of the people made it that much harder for them to change their minds if someone else offered a more – generous – incentive. In Fernando's lexicon, an honest politician was one who stayed bought.

He glanced briefly at his schedule for the next day and pressed the intercom button on his desk. 'Anna, who the hell is Angelo Ricci? And why am I having dinner with him tomorrow evening?'

There was a pause before his secretary responded. 'Signor Ricci is the new Italian Consul.' Fernando smiled slightly. He knew his secretary hated him, but he was also aware that she didn't dare show it. 'He arrived when Signor Cerreni returned to Italy last month. You haven't met him yet.'

'I am aware of that,' Fernando said drily.

'If you want me to reschedule –'

'No, no. It has to be done, I suppose.' Briefly Fernando wondered if Angelo Ricci would be Roberto's successor in all things. 'But find me something else to do at around ten o'clock. I'll need a good reason to escape.'

'At ten o'clock in the evening, Senhor Moreno?'

'Just do it.'

Fernando flicked the intercom off and thoughtfully smoothed his moustache with his thumb and forefinger. His strange eyes held an unreadable expression as he reached for the telephone and flipped open his address book. He punched

13

in the numbers and waited, calculating the time difference. It was ten to four in Rio. That made it around ten to eight in the evening in Rome. He was certain Roberto would still be in his office. The Italian had no reason to hasten home. After all, his young wife didn't have quite the allure she'd once had. Not now.

'*Pronto?*'

'Roberto?'

'*Si. Chi parla?*'

'Roberto. My old friend.'

There was a brief silence. '*Attenda all'apparecchio.*'

Fernando smiled, savouring the moment as Roberto changed telephones, presumably to a more secure line. When he returned, the Italian spoke in English, his voice guarded. 'Fernando. What can I do for you?'

'What makes you think you can do anything for me?' Fernando asked genially.

'Nothing, nothing.' There was a pause. 'It's just … it's been a while.'

'Oh, only a few weeks,' Fernando laughed. 'What's a few weeks between friends?'

'Yes. Of course.'

'I hear you arrived back in Italy with style,' Fernando continued conversationally. 'A position in the Foreign Ministry, I'm told. You've come a long way in such a short time. Next step, Prime Minister, hmm?'

Roberto's laugh sounded forced. 'If you say so, Fernando. You always seem to know these things before anyone else.'

'I just listen to what I'm told, that's all. A little here, a little there – you know how it goes.'

'Yes, I know how it goes.' Even across the transatlantic static, Fernando could hear the distaste in Roberto's voice. 'Fernando, it's nearly nine o'clock already –'

'I know, you have to get home, of course.' Fernando's voice was like silk. 'Tell me, how is Joanna?'

There was a pause before Roberto replied. 'Fine. She's fine.'

'And your daughter? She's well?'

'Yes, yes. Beautiful. She's six weeks old now. We called her Alexandra, you know. Alix. After my mother.'

'Charming. A delightful name for a delightful child.' Fernando smiled as he delivered the *coup de grâce*. 'A beautiful baby, yes? I'm sure she'll grow up to look just like her father.'

The words hung between them in the tense silence. Fernando could sense Roberto trying to control his fear and anger, and felt his cock harden in response. Power. This was what life was about. Pure, unrefined, intoxicating power.

Suddenly he heard the sound of raised voices outside his office, and looked up in irritation as a small, swarthy man bundled his way past Anna, an expression of self-importance inflating his doughy features. 'Senhor Moreno, I'm sorry, I tried to tell him you weren't to be disturbed –'

Fernando's erection deflated as he recognised the man as Carlos Silvera, one of the Justice Ministry's gofers who was also in his pay as an informant.

'Roberto, something's come up. I have to go. But do give my regards to Signora Cerreni and little Alix. I must remember to send her a christening gift.' He ran his tongue along the inside edge of his teeth, tasting the other man's humiliation. 'Oh, and Roberto?'

'Yes?'

'Keep in touch.'

Fernando replaced the telephone and swung round to face Silvera, not troubling to hide his annoyance at the interruption. He would have enjoyed baiting Roberto a little longer. 'So. What is it this time?'

Silvera assumed an expression of sorrow. 'I wouldn't be interrupting you if it wasn't important, Senhor Moreno. I know how busy you are. But I thought I should come straight to you with such tragic news –'

'Oh, spit it out, Silvera.'

Silvera bristled but complied. 'It's Nova Esperancia – one of the *favellas* on the outskirts of Rio –' He glanced at Fernando for confirmation that the Judge knew the place he was talking about.

'Yes, yes, I know it. I opened a health clinic there six months ago. Total waste of time and money.' He waved his hand at Silvera. 'Go on.'

'There's been a terrible mudslide in the hills, Senhor. It's all this rain, the rescue officials said. The water gathered underneath the *favella* – no drains, of course – and literally washed the place away.' Silvera spread his hands expressively. 'The whole place just collapsed. It's disappeared. Gone.'

'Gone? It can't have gone. There were 20,000 people there. It was a mile wide. What do you mean, it's gone?'

Silvera's expression was mournful, but his eyes gleamed with ghoulish relish. 'At least 10,000 dead, according to initial reports. It would've been even more, but it happened mid-afternoon so half the population was down in Rio, begging and thieving I should think.'

'Ten thousand dead?'

'According to first reports, Senhor. It may be more.' Silvera eyed the Judge speculatively. 'Shall I call your car round, Senhor?'

Fernando thought rapidly. This was a big story. He was well aware of the distorted judgement of Western news editors around the world; in their parochial minds, a hundred Third World deaths were approximately equal to two dozen East Europeans or one slightly offended Englishman. But

10,000 Brazilian peasants – mostly women and children – brutally crushed to death beneath tons of mud and gravel would merit headline coverage from even the most xenophobic news organisations. Quite apart from Brazil's domestic coverage, there would be television crews and journalists heading to Rio from all over the world. The BBC was probably already there, and the other news agencies wouldn't be far behind. It was a gift of a PR opportunity, and Fernando Moreno wasn't about to look it in the mouth. Thirty seconds on the World Service or a soundbite on an American TV network would be worth a hundred times more to his bid for re-election than months of gruelling campaigning and thousands of dollars in bribes.

Fernando stood up and put on his $2,000 Pavesi jacket. Thank God it was television-friendly: he wouldn't have to go home and change. 'Any survivors?' You couldn't comfort corpses for the cameras. A few photogenic orphans would be perfect.

'Some. Not many. A few houses on the western ridge were spared, but that's all,' Silvera answered, struggling to keep up with the Judge as he headed towards the lifts. 'Put an earthquake and a tidal wave together, and you get some idea of what's happened. Those who managed to survive their houses collapsing on top of them got drowned in the mud.'

Fernando glanced quickly in the mirror as he entered the lift, running his hand back through his dark hair and smoothing his moustache. 'Anyone else there yet? Apart from rescue workers and do-gooders, I mean.'

'I don't know. I came to you first.'

'Of course you did. That's what I pay you for.'

It was only as he walked out of the building that Fernando remembered that Father Lucio had been due to collect some more merchandise from Nova Esperancia today.

Three

Piazzale Farnesina, Rome, Italy
Monday 7 December 1970
8.00 p.m.

Roberto Cerreni stared unseeingly at the telephone receiver long after he'd replaced it. He'd spent the last month trying to pretend the events in Rio had never happened, but one call from Fernando Moreno brought them all back. In his heart, Roberto knew that he would never be able to forget them.

In the gloom of his darkened office, he leant on his desk and put his head in his hands. For the rest of his life, he would be living a lie, never knowing when the truth might come out.

He knew Fernando well. The Brazilian was a man who found his pleasure not in the act of destruction, but in the waiting game. He was like a cat playing with a mouse, allowing it to run but never to escape. Roberto was probably safe for now; Fernando could wait years before he struck. But from now on, every step Roberto took along the road to success, he knew, would bring him that much closer to annihilation.

He pushed back his chair and moved to the window, parting the dusty venetian blind with his forefinger and staring out into the dark street below. Cars rattled over the cobbles, their headlights illuminating his office for a few seconds as they turned the corner into Via Paolo Boselli. He heard a church bell strike eight, and slowly let the blind fall back into place. He couldn't put off returning home any longer, however much he dreaded the inevitable confrontation that seemed to have become the pattern of his marriage in the past few months. The Cerrenis were giving their first party since returning to Rome this evening; their guests would be arriving at 9.30, and he still had to get home to shower and change.

And deal with Joanna.

Roberto turned back to his desk and slid a pile of papers into the top drawer, carefully locking it and pocketing the key. He changed the lock himself every month. He knew it wouldn't stop a determined thief, but it would circumvent the routine spying that went on between departments. It was certainly more secure than using the office safe. Even the cleaner had the combination for that.

He picked up his raincoat, still damp from the morning's rain, pushed open the heavy mahogany double doors and started in surprise to see his secretary still sitting propped at her desk, half-asleep, a heap of yellow telephone messages in front of her.

'Juiliana! I thought you'd gone home hours ago! Today is your half-day, isn't it?'

His secretary jumped, knocking her papers to the floor. 'Signor Cerreni! I'm sorry, you frightened me.'

'I'm not surprised. You must have been sitting there for hours. Is something wrong?'

'No, no – I just had some papers to finish – the Swedish Embassy need them by tomorrow morning,' Juiliana stammered, leafing through her files to hide her confusion. She could hardly tell him she had been waiting all afternoon, despite her half-day, just to be able to say goodnight to him. 'And you had a couple of messages I wanted to give you before you left; I thought you might miss them if I just left them on my desk.'

Roberto smiled. 'You're right, I probably would have done. I admire your dedication, but you didn't have to wait all night for me to leave. You could have just come in and given them to me.'

Juiliana blushed. 'I'm sorry, Signor Cerreni. I thought you didn't want to be disturbed.'

'Never mind. Next time you'll know. So, what were the messages? Anything important?'

'The Foreign Minister says he'd like to see you tomorrow at around ten to discuss your visit to New York, if that's convenient,' Juiliana said. 'You haven't got anything in your schedule, but I thought I'd check with you before I agreed.'

'No, no, tell him ten is fine. What else?'

'A journalist from *Elan* magazine called, a Miss Stephi Kay. She says she'd like to do an interview with you for her column as soon as possible, preferably the second week in February.'

Roberto frowned. '*Elan* magazine? Do I know it?'

'It's an American fashion magazine, but it's also got a number of European editions,' Juiliana said, pleased that he had asked a question she could answer with authority. 'I could bring you in a few back copies, if you like – I usually get it every month. It's a bit like *Vogue*. Stephi Kay's quite new, I think, but she has her own column, sort of gossip and news. She writes mainly fashion pieces, but her interviews are terribly good. I remember she did one with the British Prime Minister, Edward Heath, for the UK edition last month. It made headlines in the British tabloids.'

'Edward Heath?' Roberto raised an eyebrow. 'I'm surprised she's interested in me.'

Juiliana shrugged. 'Well, last month's *Newsweek* did tip you as one of the ten men in Europe to watch. And after all, you are a Cerreni.'

'Your loyalty is utterly undeserved, but much appreciated,'

Roberto said. 'I'm not sure about an interview. I don't really think I can give her enough colour to spice up the political side of things. Let me sleep on it and we'll discuss it again tomorrow.'

Juiliana nodded, privately thinking that Roberto Cerreni didn't need any spicing up at all. He was the most fascinating and handsome man she'd ever met. She'd only worked for him for six weeks, but already she was half in love with him. She had no doubt that this American journalist would feel the same. What woman in her right mind wouldn't?

Despite grilling every other secretary in the Foreign Ministry pool, Juiliana had been able to learn little more than was known to every gossip columnist writing about Italian politics, although she could supplement it with the evidence of her own eyes. At thirty-seven, Roberto Cerreni was an attractive man who bore more than a passing resemblance to his Roman forebears. A thick wave of strong, black hair swept back from a broad forehead, his large, aristocratic nose giving his handsome face character. The eyes that looked out from beneath heavy brows were clear and so dark they seemed almost bottomless. Only in his full lips was there a suggestion of the sensuality that lurked beneath the patrician surface.

Juiliana knew that before his marriage, Roberto had been among the most eligible bachelors in Italy. He came from one of the country's oldest and wealthiest families; for centuries, the Cerrenis had been at the heart of Italian politics, contributing no less than fourteen Cardinals to the early Church before switching their allegiance to the state and providing two Prime Ministers in half a century. After completing his education at Oxford, Roberto had followed in the steps of his father and grandfather, cutting his teeth first in the Ministry of Information before entering the diplomatic corps and joining the Italian Embassy in Yugoslavia. Three years later he'd become Italy's youngest Ambassador when he'd been appointed to Brazil at the age of thirty-four. Already he was widely tipped to succeed the current Foreign Minister when he retired; beyond that, who knew how far he might reach.

Juiliana watched him surreptitiously from beneath her fringe as he buttoned his raincoat. It wasn't just his success or his family connections that made him so attractive; it wasn't even his good looks, arresting though they were. It was something else, some quality she couldn't define; a subtle aura of danger and promise wrapped around him like a cloak. When she dared to glance directly into his eyes, Juiliana found herself remembering that he did not just number churchmen amongst his ancestors but assassins and seducers as well. If Roberto was aware of this fascination with his darker side – or even that it existed – he gave no sign. For Juiliana, as for so many women, this only added to his attraction.

'Juiliana? That's everything?'

Juiliana realised she had been lost in her own thoughts. Hiding her embarrassment, she flicked hastily through the pile of telephone messages. 'Oh yes, there was one other call. Signor Pavesi.'

Roberto frowned. 'Giulio Pavesi? The designer?'

'Yes, I think so. He called twice, but didn't leave a message.' She looked up. 'Why? Is there something wrong?'

'What? Oh, no, no.' Roberto picked up his briefcase and walked towards the door. 'Good night, Juiliana. I'll see you tomorrow.'

He did not see Juiliana's puzzled expression as he marched past the bank of lifts, and started down the stone staircase that led directly to the courtyard below. His thoughts churned as he emerged into the piazza and climbed into the ministry car waiting for him. He settled back into the soft leather seat of the Mercedes and stared grimly out of the window at the murky waters of the River Tevere as the driver headed south through the city along the Lungotevere della Vittoria. First Fernando, now Giulio Pavesi. What the hell was going on?

The vicious pounding between Joanna Cerreni's temples intensified, the cruel pain extending around the base of her skull like a vice. Miserably she pinched the bridge of her nose between her fingers and stared out of the nursery window, willing her headache to go away. Knowing that it was just the result of nerves didn't help.

She'd been dreading this party. Joanna knew that, despite herself, she'd be the centre of attention. She and Roberto had left Italy for Rio de Janeiro so soon after their marriage that Italian society had not had a chance to meet her and tear her to pieces, as would normally have been their privilege after she had dared to steal one of Rome's most eligible bachelors from under their noses. She had no doubt that they would be eager to make up for lost time.

She glanced down into the cot at her sleeping daughter, wishing that she could change places with the baby. How uncomplicated Alix's life was, how simple. She only existed to eat or sleep.

Right from the beginning of their marriage, Roberto's mother had been certain Joanna wouldn't be able to cope with the demands of being his wife and had made absolutely certain that everyone knew it. Now Joanna wondered, for the first time, if her mother-in-law was right.

When she'd married Roberto three years ago, she'd had no idea of the vital role she would be expected to play in his political career. She'd been so young, barely nineteen, anxious to escape the shadow of her four brilliant older sisters. She'd watched each of them do the London Season and catch an array of chinless, titled young men, dreading her own turn and longing only to be free to pursue her secret dreams of becoming an artist. Roberto had been fifteen years older than

23

she was, attractive, successful, and apparently madly in love with her. She'd never even stopped to think if she loved him in return. She'd thought that by marrying him she'd not only earn the approval of her parents – who had never struggled to hide their disappointment in her lack of accomplishments – but be free to follow her own secret desire to paint.

But instead of spending leisurely days studying the Old Masters in Rome, as she'd expected, she'd found herself stranded in the pampered but restricted world of Rio de Janeiro just weeks after their wedding. She'd spent her days playing tennis, sunbathing on the beaches of Copacabana or simply reading, her evenings battling to overcome her shyness and be the perfect hostess as Roberto concentrated on his career. Somehow she'd survived in the relative backwater of Brazil, but now that Roberto had moved back into the centre of Italian politics, her role as his wife would become more demanding. If she couldn't handle an informal reception such as the one this evening with Roberto at her side, how on earth would she cope when she had to host dinner parties for a hundred and fifty people, her husband far away at the end of the table? She still didn't even speak any Italian, despite Roberto's best efforts to teach her.

It had taken her the whole day just to decide what to wear. Even now, she was supposed to be downstairs organising the flowers and the caterers. Instead, she was cowering in her daughter's nursery using her migraine as a pretext to escape, and leaving her overpowering mother-in-law to deal with everything. She smiled bitterly. At least her incompetence had pleased one person. There was nothing Roberto's mother liked more than being proved right.

Joanna twisted the material of her dressing gown nervously in her hands. Oh God, it was all so unfair. All her life she had had to cope with her parents' and sisters' well-meaning attempts to help her shine in public. She'd only ever wanted to fade into the background, to be left in peace to draw or read. And yet it had been she who had married a man whose career had propelled her to the centre of the stage. She had tried so hard to be what he expected. She wanted to sparkle and glitter for Roberto's sake as she had never done for her own. She knew she had the physical beauty to turn heads if she could only summon up the courage to step out from the shadows. She longed to have just a little of her sisters' confidence, to be able to talk to someone whose face she had only ever seen before in a magazine or newspaper, and feel as though she was their equal. Desperately she wanted Roberto to be as proud of her as she was of him. If he could respect her, perhaps it might open the door again to the love they had shared in the beginning.

She left the nursery, shutting the heavy wooden doors behind her, ignoring the baby's wails of protest. Alix probably wanted feeding yet again. Or changing. It seemed that was all she ever did these days.

Joanna glanced involuntarily at her watch: 8.20. Their guests would be arriving in just over an hour and she still hadn't even showered.

In the marbled bathroom she shared with Roberto, she let her négligé fall to her feet and stepped under the shower, turning up the pressure so that the sound of the water sluicing over her body drowned out the noise of Alix's wails. Slowly, rhythmically, she started soaping herself, her hands running across her skin with unconscious sensuality. Soothed by the water, she started to undulate with the movements as if dancing to music only she could hear, stroking her skin with the tips of her fingers and closing her eyes as the water played across her face, her erotic performance reflected in the mirrored tiles around the bathroom. She gazed at her reflection and smiled sadly at herself.

'Have I changed that much? Am I so very different from the

woman he married?' She cupped her firm breasts in her hands and stared defiantly at her image. 'He wanted me then. What's wrong with me now?'

With one hand she reached up to gather her hair, its whiteness darkened by the water, and held it on top of her head for a moment. 'I still have a waist, don't I? My legs are still beautiful. He's always loved my legs.' She turned to the side so that she could survey her stomach, running her hands down over her firm belly. 'No stretch marks. No fat. I haven't let myself go. I'm only twenty-two. I'm still young, aren't I? Still desirable? So what have I done wrong?'

Slowly she sank down in the shower until she was kneeling, turning her face upwards in despair so that the falling water mingled with her tears. It was so ironic. Roberto hadn't been able to get enough of her at first, but she had held back, uncertain even as she married him if she was doing the right thing. By the time she'd realised how much she loved him, it was too late. His obsession with her had barely outlasted their honeymoon.

Whereas she had fallen more in love with him with every day that passed.

She pulled a pale peach towel out of the linen cupboard and wrapped it around her wet hair, pulling on a matching bathrobe before padding silently into the bedroom. Throwing open her wardrobe, she studied her clothes, automatically considering Roberto's response to what she'd wear. She riffled through her clothes and came to the cream silk Pavesi dress she'd selected for this evening. It was Roberto's favourite, though she'd always hated it. She thought it made her look like a child, but he'd bought it as part of her trousseau. Perhaps it would please him if she wore it today.

The baby was screaming now, so loudly she couldn't ignore her any longer. Roberto's mother might hear. Joanna knotted the tie of her robe about her waist and slammed the wardrobe door shut as she left the bedroom.

She entered the nursery and picked Alix up, cradling the baby against her shoulder. She was so tiny, not yet two months old. How could anyone fail to love such a helpless scrap?

Secure in her mother's arms, the baby's cries subsided, and Joanna smiled. Roberto adored his daughter. Perhaps she'd been wrong. Perhaps the baby would bring them back together, if she gave it time. In a sudden flare of optimism, all her doubts about him faded. She must have been crazy to think that he would ever be unfaithful to her. He'd promised her he would never leave her, and he wouldn't break his promise. She'd given up everything for him, even her painting. He couldn't let her down now. If he betrayed her, she'd have nothing left.

She glanced at her watch again and her happiness disappeared as quickly as it had come. It was almost nine o'clock. Their guests would be arriving in less than half an hour. Where was Roberto?

Almost roughly she put Alix back into her cot. She knew exactly where Roberto was. There could only be one explanation for him being so late, tonight of all nights.

He was with another woman.

Roberto heard the church bells chime the hour as the Mercedes eased through the narrow arch of Porto San Sebastiano and into the Appia Antica. He prayed Joanna wouldn't put him through another of those scenes which inevitably ended in tears and recrimination. He did not have the energy to deal with his wife on top of everything else.

A Fiat in front of them braked suddenly and swerved on to the soft verge that bordered the narrow road. Roberto smiled to himself as he watched the Fiat come to a halt and cut its lights. Already the verge was crowded with parked cars, wedged in amongst the 2,000-year-old ruins that lined the ancient paved road leading south out of Rome. Their steamed-up windows were papered over with cardboard and newspapers as the occupants sought the privacy they could not find at home amidst their extended families of grandparents, uncles, aunts, cousins, parents and siblings. It was no coincidence that Italians, as a race, were not tall, Roberto thought wryly. Fiats were difficult cars in which to pass on genes for long legs.

Five minutes later, the Mercedes turned into an overgrown drive. The driveway and gates were exactly the same as they'd been when Roberto had lived here as a child, the weathered boulder on the ground at the foot of the drive bearing a house number rendered unreadable by the years, the dilapidated gates wreathed in ivy which all but obscured the rusty post-box hanging from their railings. When he'd returned from Brazil and reopened his old family home, Roberto had resisted the urge to install the latest in electric gates, entry phones and security cameras that adorned the driveways of so many of his wealthy and paranoid neighbours. He reasoned that an atmosphere of neglect and emptiness would protect him against thieves and terrorists more effectively than any complicated security system could.

At the end of the drive, the porch lantern gleamed brightly in the darkness. A wave of memories swept over Roberto as the car drew to a halt outside the front door. Everything was at once familiar and strange. He still couldn't get used to coming home and not finding his mother sitting at her card table, cheating at Patience, while his father dozed in front of the fire and pretended to be listening to the wireless. In some ways it seemed like yesterday, although it had been nineteen years now since his father had died. His widowed mother had retired to the Cerrenis' dowager apartment in the Piazza Borghese, where she still lived surrounded by the hundreds of mementoes and *objets d'art* with which she could not bear to part. The sprawling villa on the Appia Antica had remained untenanted for almost two decades, too large for Roberto – his parents' only child – to occupy alone. When he had been recalled to Rome, it had seemed right to bring his family back here, to breathe life into the lonely rooms at last, although he knew Joanna could never fill the space his mother had left.

Roberto watched the Mercedes' tail-lights diminish as the driver made his way back towards the main road, aware that he was delaying the moment when he had to go in. Finally, when he saw the car swing right out of the gates, he turned back to face the house. He opened the front door slowly and eased it shut soundlessly behind him, feeling uncomfortably like an interloper. He sighed as he heard voices and the chink of china coming from the direction of the kitchen as the caterers prepared for the evening's reception. He could have done without this party tonight.

As he crossed the hall, his footsteps echoing on the black and white marble floor, he had the uneasy sensation that he was being watched. He tried not to think of the half-million Christians buried deep in the Catacombs that extended below his house. He was almost relieved to find it was only his wife who was standing at the top of the stairs staring at him.

'Who was she? Tell me! I want to know her name!'

Roberto stared up at Joanna, stunned by the suddenness of the attack. 'Who was who?'

Joanna clutched the marble balustrade as she leant over it to face him. 'Oh, don't play games with me. I know where you've been. You were with some tart, weren't you? Some accommodating little secretary or waitress, I suppose. Don't think I don't know. Give me some credit, Roberto, I'm not a complete fool.'

Roberto sighed, weary of the accusations. 'Joanna, you're being ridiculous.'

'*I'm* being ridiculous? I'm not the one chasing every girl in sight!'

'Do we have to go through all this yet again?' Roberto said, trying to keep his temper. 'You know where I was, you have the telephone number. All you had to do was ring the office.'

'How do I know you weren't doing it right there, in your office, on your desk? It wouldn't be the first time, would it?'

'What the hell are you talking about? I've never been unfaithful to you, never even looked at another woman since I met you!'

'It's easy for you to say that now,' Joanna sobbed. 'Why should I believe you? How can I possibly trust you now?'

'Do you imagine it's been easy for me?'

A sudden silence fell as they stared at each other. Roberto felt as if he were on the brink of a precipice. Briefly he wondered where the cool, controlled woman he had married just three short years ago had gone. The unhappy woman in front of him now was a stranger he barely recognised. Breathing deeply, he tried to defuse his anger; it was a luxury he could no longer afford.

He tried to sound conciliatory. 'Look, Joanna, I admit we've had a hard few weeks, moving countries, settling into this house, looking after a new baby. I know you're nervous about this party. It all takes some getting used to. But it *will* get easier, I promise. We just need to take one day at a time.'

Joanna trailed slowly down the staircase, clutching her silk dressing gown together with one hand. 'That's all it is?' she whispered forlornly. 'It'll get better? You promise?'

Roberto concealed his relief that he'd managed to deflect her tirade. It wasn't unknown for these arguments to go on for hours as she trailed him around the house, shouting accusations until two, three, four in the morning. Despite himself, his heart twisted as he gazed into her eyes, washed almost colourless by her tears. He reached up to stroke her hair, tucking an ash-blonde wisp behind her ear. 'Sweetheart, it'll all seem better in the morning, once this party's out of the way. Tiny babies are exhausting, you know that.'

'Sometimes I wish we'd never had her,' Joanna muttered. 'We don't seem to have time for each other any more. You don't spoil me like you used to –'

'Only because you always seem to be so tired,' Roberto said softly. 'Having Alix hasn't changed the way I feel about you. You're still my wife, I still care about you. Alix just needs more of our attention at the moment, that's all. She's so tiny still.'

Joanna smiled tremulously, and with a pang Roberto was reminded of the girl she had been when he had first met her. 'I do love you, Roberto, you know that, don't you?' she said earnestly. 'I couldn't bear it if you left me. I wouldn't want to live without you.'

'Ssh, *cara*, don't be so dramatic,' Roberto said, leading her towards the stairs as if she were a child. 'I'm not going to leave you, now or any time. I promise you that. But you have to learn to trust me, Joanna.' He sighed. 'I can't face this kind of scene every night when I come in.'

Slowly he helped her up the stairs and into the bedroom they shared, slipping the dressing gown off her shoulders and gently brushing her long hair as she sat passively in front of her dressing table. Her anger had faded as quickly as it had flared, leaving her drained and empty. Roberto gazed over her shoulder at her reflection, feeling a sudden flash of pity. She was so young. She'd had no idea of what she was taking on when she'd married him.

Roberto knew now that he'd been so desperate to have her he hadn't stopped to think of the consequences of taking an inexperienced nineteen-year-old as his wife. He felt a sudden surge of guilt. If she was hysterical and insecure, it was because he had made her so. When they had first met, she'd seemed so controlled and self-contained. It was falling in love with him that had made her vulnerable.

Ever since he'd been a teenager, Roberto had been aware of the effect he had on women; without bothering to analyse it, he had exploited it to the full, skilfully eluding any suggestion of marriage. Some women had been passing fancies, his interest disappearing after only one or two nights. Others had endured for months, even years, yet had come no nearer to possessing his heart than those whose names he had never even bothered to learn.

And then, in the summer of 1967, as he'd wandered around Rome making his own private farewell to the places he loved before departing to take up his post as Ambassador in Rio, he'd met Joanna Davenport, and everything had changed.

From the moment he'd seen her staring up at the ceiling of the Sistine Chapel, Roberto had been determined to have her. He'd never seen a woman like her. Her classic features were unspoilt by the fashionable pancake make-up he hated, her fair waist-length hair parted simply in the centre of her head and left to fall naturally around her face. Unusually for a teenager in the sixties, her clothes had been unprovocative and elegant, almost dull. From her appearance, he would have said she was only a child; yet the intelligent woman who had toured the Vatican Museum with him had seemed very much his equal. Bored by countless partners too anxious to please him to contradict a word he said, Roberto had been intrigued and fascinated by this distant English beauty who was not afraid to articulate her views on art.

For the first time in his life, Roberto had neglected his political duties, pressing as they were, to spend time with a woman. Knowing he had only a few weeks in Rome, he had determined to get her into bed before he had to leave for Brazil. With every other woman he'd ever known, his desire had waned almost as soon as it had been satisfied; he'd been

32

certain it would be the same with this strange child-woman who somehow exerted such power over him. But Joanna Davenport had remained remote and unattainable despite his most strenuous efforts. Far from wanting him, she'd seemed almost indifferent to his pursuit. By turns she had intrigued him, fascinated him, frustrated him, eluded him. Driven to a frenzy of wanting, Roberto had managed to convince himself he'd fallen in love with her.

Six weeks after they'd met, utterly obsessed and desperate to sleep with her, Roberto had asked Joanna to marry him. The wedding had taken place three days before they'd had to leave for Brazil, in the tiny church of Saint Ignatius where his family had been christened, married and buried for genera-tions. Four days after the simple ceremony, Roberto had carried his young wife over the threshold of their new home in Rio, believing that he held all that he could ever want in his arms.

He hadn't understood then that her mind was even more fragile than her body.

Four

Nova Esperancia, Rio de Janeiro, Brazil
Tuesday 8 December 1970
6.20 a.m.

The darkness was all around Elizabetta, smothering her. With a sob, she fought against it, as if by force of will she could make it retreat. Still she could see nothing, but gradually she became aware of herself as separate from the blackness. She was trapped on her side, her knees curled up against her chest, her arms wrapped around them. She tried to move, but the darkness held her fast. Around her, the earth shifted with her movement and automatically she froze and screwed her eyes shut in fear. She could hear the mud creak and slither, but it did not press any closer.

She was aware of a cold trickle of water running along the side of her neck and down her back, and tried to move away, but there was nowhere for her to go. With her fingers she followed the thin stream of water back to its source until she touched a circle of metal, its wet edge sharp. A rivulet of water ran down her fingertips and along her bare arm, dripping off her elbow and forming a small puddle beneath her knees.

The silence around her was as solid as the darkness itself. Her left side had grown numb, and arrows of pain shot through her legs and arms. She had to change position, and finally shifted her arms and legs against the walls of her prison, her discomfort outweighing her fear. She gained a few inches, but not enough. Exhausted and afraid, her mind drifted in and out of consciousness. She wondered if she was already dead. She'd seen dead people put into the ground; Mama said the angels came to get them when no one was looking. Had the angels forgotten her? Surely they wouldn't have left her behind. It was getting so hot and airless that she could barely breathe. She had no idea how long she had been here – days, perhaps, or was it only a few minutes? Did the angels even know she was here? Perhaps they just couldn't find her, buried so deep in the darkness. Maybe she was supposed to let them know where she was?

She wrestled with the problem for a few moments, then murmured her own name into the darkness. Her voice sounded weak and quiet, even to her. She called out again, this time a little louder, wondering if the angels would be able to hear, or if they were even listening.

'*Aqui! Por favor*, here!'

'Dad? Did you hear that?'

Christopher Logan rocked back on his heels and stared at his son.

'You heard something, Matt?'

Matt nodded, his green eyes troubled. 'I'm not sure. It sounded like someone calling, maybe a child, but it was so faint. It might be nothing. The wind, or something.'

Christopher studied his young son for a moment, then stood up and signalled towards a gaunt, dark-haired man standing to one side of the area of gravel and mud that a group of rescuers were currently searching. 'David! Over here!'

David Conto turned and ran towards them, holding out his arms for balance as he made his way around the steep edge of the landslip. 'You've found something?'

Christopher frowned. 'I don't know. Matt thinks he heard

35

someone calling, perhaps a child, but he's not sure. I don't like to hold up what you're doing, but on the other hand, if there is a child down there, alive …'

David undid the tight plastic strap of his hard hat. 'We've been here twelve hours now, and we haven't seen a single sign of life since we started. If Matt thinks he's heard something, it has to be worth following up.' He turned to the twelve-year-old boy standing beside them. 'Matt? Where did the sound come from?'

'It seemed to be right beneath my feet, kind of near those pipes there, you see?' Matt pointed to a tangle of metal protruding about eighteen inches from the mud and rubble. 'It was very faint. I only heard it because I was bent down next to the pipes. It seemed to come right out of them.'

The two rescue workers exchanged looks over Matt's head. 'If there's an air pocket down there, those pipes might be providing enough oxygen to breathe. Someone could be alive,' Christopher said quietly. 'But whoever he is, he won't have long now. His air must already be running out.'

'In that case, we'd better be quick,' David said. 'I'll get the team over here.'

'Dad? Could someone still be alive underneath all that?'

Christopher squeezed his son's narrow shoulders in answer as they watched David run towards the cluster of rescue workers on the other side of the landslip. Both understood there was nothing they could do without the equipment that would shore up the unstable earth whilst the rescuers dug. Christopher thought of all those tons of mud and rocks pressing down, with someone still alive beneath them. At least for most of the residents of Nova Esperancia it had been quick.

He watched as Matt moved over to the tangle of pipes and bent down beside them. 'We're coming!' he called. 'Don't give up! We're coming!'

His son shouldn't be here, going through this, Christopher thought angrily. None of them should be here, least of all the pitiful victims. This whole tragedy could have been avoided, *should* have been avoided.

Christopher Logan had become used to witnessing disaster on a vast scale. As a representative of the charity *Children First*, he'd spent most of his life trying to alleviate the horror of famine, war, poverty and disease, at times frustrated, but never defeated, by the enormity of the task. But avoidable accidents, born of carelessness and neglect, angered him as natural disasters did not. A simple programme of education on the importance of looking after the environment, and a decent drainage system in the *favellas*, would have prevented this tragedy.

His brief, ten-day trip to Brazil had been *Children First*'s final attempt to lobby the government on this very subject. For once, he had managed to persuade his wife to join him, along with their youngest son, by presenting the trip as their last family holiday before Matt was sent to St Francis' to board in the New Year. It had not been easy. Even after thirty years of marriage, Caroline Logan's genteel distaste for her husband's work had not mellowed.

Over the years there had been many who had wondered what on earth had lead the vivacious, aristocratic ex-débutante to marry an impoverished, idealistic young man who had come to lobby her father about his tenants' rights. Caroline and Christopher Logan differed on almost every moral, ethical and social plane. Intelligent and compassionate she might be, but Caroline was also very much the product of her class; to her, charity meant village fêtes and raffles, not grubbing around in disease-ridden slums halfway across the world. The only daughter of a wealthy gentleman farmer, Caroline Bower-Mitchell had fully expected the charming, penniless young man with whom she'd fallen in love to become her father's surrogate heir once they married. But although Christopher had been poor, he had also been determined to be his own man. To her lasting chagrin, he had refused to give up his work with *Children First* even after her father had died and they had inherited the vast family manor in Sussex.

In the early days of their marriage, there had been some spectacular rows, but gradually they had developed a *modus operandi* that seemed to suit them. Christopher had ceased to upbraid his wife for spending upwards of £15,000 a season at Pavesi's or Valentino's, and she had given up trying to persuade him to replace his worn jeans and ancient Volkswagen Beetle with the latest in couture clothes and designer Range Rovers.

The only real source of dissension between them was their youngest son, Matt. He had been born when Christopher was already well into his forties, long after both he and Caroline had resigned themselves to the fact that their elder son, Hugh, had seemed destined to be an only child. The sixteen-year age gap between the two brothers had meant that the bond between them had never been close, particularly as Caroline had always made it clear that she doted on Matt. She cherished fond dreams of Oxford, an Honourable wife and a successful career in the City. Christopher doubted they'd ever be fulfilled.

Matt was already fascinated with his father's work, an interest Christopher encouraged despite his wife's vehement opposition. When his son had begged to be allowed to join the lobby team as they had made their final, futile bid to alter the mindset of the Brazilian government, Christopher had agreed, thinking it good experience for Matt. They had been in the middle of a meeting with the Brazilian Finance Minister when news of the disaster at Nova Esperancia had reached them.

38

Matt had followed his father as the team had raced to the stricken village to help the rescue effort.

Now, despite his pain at seeing his son's anguish, Christopher couldn't help a sense of pride in the boy. He had displayed an understanding and compassion that went beyond his twelve years. He watched Matt studying the rescue team as they began to shore up the loose shale and gravel directly above the tangled pipes. The boy was pale and shocked, but Christopher guessed he was determined not to leave if there was a hope that someone might be alive. Matt knew as well as his father how slim that hope was.

The entire disaster area was eerily quiet. Instead of the cries and pleas of the injured that they might have expected, the team had been met with a grim silence. Their response had been equally muted, with none of the conversation and mutual encouragement that normally accompanied such rescue efforts. By some miracle, a narrow swathe of homes along the western ridge of the mountain had been saved from the lethal tidal wave. The rest of the hillside was an open wound of raw earth. Nothing remained to show it had once been home to thousands of men, women and children. So far the rescuers had pulled fewer than fifty survivors from the ruins at the bottom of the mountain.

Christopher glanced up as David joined him. 'How's it going?'

'We have a problem.' Conto nodded towards the rescue workers struggling to widen the narrow gap they had forced in the hillside. 'The ground is so loose, it collapses inwards every time we try to dig deeper. We could get round it by shoring up all the sides as well as the roof, but if somebody is alive down there, they're on borrowed time as it is. I just don't think we can make it.'

'So what are you telling me? We just leave them to die?'

'If you have any suggestions, Chris, I'm happy to hear

them. We've dug in about eighteen feet, which is as far as we can go, but the shaft is just too narrow. If we make it wide enough to allow someone to get down there, we risk the whole thing collapsing. Fortunately the line we're digging is almost horizontal rather than vertical, but it's still too dangerous to put someone in without reinforcing the roof and walls. The only other way is to clear the whole mountainside, and that'll take days.'

'Couldn't you make the tunnel smaller?' Matt asked.

David smiled sadly at him. 'We could, but then no one would be able to get in there anyway. And whoever it is stuck at the bottom probably can't get out without our help.'

'But would a smaller tunnel be safe?' Matt persisted.

'Safer, yes, but there are still no guarantees.'

Christopher ruffled his son's brown curls. 'It wouldn't help anyway. Matt. None of these men can get down it.'

'I could.'

Christopher stared at his son for a long moment. 'Matt, these are trained rescue workers,' he said at length. 'There are all sorts of hazards involved, things you know nothing about. I don't like this any more than you do, but we'll just have to wait for them to do it their way.'

'But that person will die if you wait any longer!' Matt cried.

'Your father's right, Matt,' David said gently. 'We couldn't risk you.'

'But can't I go down a little way?' Matt pleaded. 'At least I could tell you if anyone is alive. You never know, they might be able to follow me out. You can't just leave them there to die!'

'It's just not safe, Matthew,' Christopher said, exasperated. 'Look, why don't you let me take you back to the hotel now? There's nothing more anyone can do right now.'

Matt took a deep breath. 'Dad, you always say we have to stand up and be counted if we want to make a difference, and that sometimes we have to do things we don't want to do because it's the right thing. Well, this is something I can do to help.' He gripped his father's forearm. 'Dad, I have to try. Don't you see? Otherwise I'll always wonder if I could have saved someone's life.'

Christopher stared at his son, suddenly ashamed. Matt was right. He couldn't teach his son principles he wasn't prepared to allow him to follow through. He just prayed Caroline would never need to know. 'Matt, are you sure you want to? You realise that there's probably no one alive there anyway?'

'Let me try, Dad. Please?'

Christopher returned Matt's steady gaze. 'OK, if that's what you want to do.'

'David?'

David nodded. Without another word, Matt ran towards the rescue workers. Christopher watched as they helped his son into a harness and tightened the buckles to fit his slight figure, then ran through the instructions for the various signals he could give by pulling on the rope attached to his harness. He knew he should never have agreed to let Matt go down, but he was only too aware of what it felt like to be driven to do something you believed to be right, no matter what the consequences. He realised with mixed feelings that his own sense of justice burned very brightly in his son. He knew from experience it did not make for an easy life. Swimming against the tide was never simple.

David handed Matt his hard hat and switched on the lamp fixed to the front of it. Matt peered into the narrow aperture, fear clutching at his belly as he stared into the darkness. It was all very well talking about it, but it was another thing to stare into this black hole and know he had to go down into it by himself. He thought of a child perhaps waiting for him at the bottom, scared and alone. Gathering all his courage, he turned to give his father a wave over his shoulder and plunged into the gloom.

He hadn't realised how hot it would be inside the mountain, how much the walls and ceiling of the narrow tunnel would seem to press down on him. The weak beam of the light on his helmet penetrated no more than three feet in front of him. Matt felt his way slowly along the sloping passage gouged out by the rescue workers' equipment, pausing every few inches to scrabble at the earth that had already fallen inwards to block the restricted passageway. Within a few feet it had narrowed so much that his shoulders rubbed along its sides, and he had to flatten himself completely as he moved further down the tunnel. He tried to block out the fear that the whole mountain would collapse on top of him, burying him like all those other people.

He was about twelve feet into the hillside when his fingers met cool metal, and in the light of his lamp he saw the glint of a pipe running along the floor of the passageway in front of him. The earth around it was soft and loose. As he squirmed forwards, a lump of clay detached itself from the roof and struck his helmet, knocking his lamp sideways. Matt cried out in fear, and froze. He waited motionless for what seemed like hours, but in reality was no more than half a minute, before straightening the lamp and crawling slowly on. The blood pounded in his head as the angle of the tunnel grew steeper, and the passageway narrowed so that he had to turn his face sideways in order to move forwards. The air was thick and hot around him and he coughed as he breathed in a cloud of dry earth. Wetting his lips with his tongue, slowly he groped his way forward, his left hand following the cool pipe. Suddenly he stopped, his ears straining in the darkness. For a moment, he had thought he'd heard a sound. He was about to move on, then he heard it again. Hope rose inside him as he used the glass face of his watch to tap the water pipe, one, one-two-three-four, one-two.

This time there was no mistaking the faint cry that echoed along the tunnel.

'Hold on! I'm coming! Please, just hold on!'

Frantically Matt wriggled forwards, ignoring the scattering of soft earth that fell on his back as he burrowed his way towards the sound. He'd moved no more than two feet when the tunnel ended. His head still twisted to one side, he dug at the earth wall in front of him, working as quickly as he dared. Within minutes he broke through into empty air. He paused, trying to see into the black hole in front of him by the light of his lamp.

Suddenly a small, warm hand gripped his so tightly he gasped in shock and pain.

'It's all right, I won't leave you!' Matt cried, clinging to the tiny hand. 'It's OK, you're going to be safe now! Can you move at all? I want you to follow me out, but we have to widen the gap a bit.'

In the darkness, a high, childish voice gabbled something in Portuguese that Matt couldn't understand. With his free hand, he scrabbled at the side of the narrow opening in the wall of earth behind which the child was trapped. 'We have to make the tunnel bigger,' Matt panted. 'It's OK, I'm not going away. But you need to let go of my other hand for a moment.'

The little girl seemed to understand what he was trying to do and released his hand. He heard her working from the other side of the earth that separated them, and clawed at the mud on his own side, praying she was uninjured and small enough to slip through into the tunnel without having to disturb the earth too much. After a few minutes she grasped both his hands with her own, and Matt guessed she could fit through the gap. He looked up and saw her eyes shining in the darkness. Without letting go of her, he reached for the rope around his waist and pulled it twice, then paused, then pulled again three times. Almost immediately, he felt himself being dragged backwards up the tunnel, the earth scraping against his bare skin as his jumper was rucked up around his chest. His arms ached as he clung on to the little girl.

Just as he thought he couldn't hold on to her for a moment longer, a breath of cool, fresh air swept over him and he was yanked out into the daylight. Before he realised what was happening, his father had swept him up into his arms, tears spilling down his cheeks. Matt watched numbly as rescue workers wrapped the muddy little girl in blankets, gently asking her in Portuguese if anyone else had been trapped with her. They shook their heads in answer to Christopher's silent question.

Suddenly the little girl spoke, her luminous dark eyes on Matt. 'Senhor?'

Matt broke free from his father and walked towards the little girl as the rescue workers strapped her into a stretcher for the rest of the journey down the mountain.

The four-year-old girl shyly held out her dirt-streaked hand. 'Elizabetta Ferreira.'

Matt smiled at her dignified formality and took her hand. 'Matthew Logan.'

They stared at each other.

'We must get her back to the medical centre now, Matt,' David Conto said. 'I'm sure you can see her later, if you want to.'

Matt watched as she was carried around the edge of the landslip, her tiny form dwarfed by the stretcher. He saw her turn towards one of the rescue workers, and their progress suddenly halted.

'Senhor? Matt?'

Matt took a step forward.

44

The little girl smiled, her whole face illuminated with happiness. '*Muito obrigado, senhor anjo!*' she yelled.

Matt turned towards his father. 'Dad? What did she say?'

Christopher smiled and hugged his son. 'She said thank-you, Mr Angel.'

Five

St Francis' Boys School, Somerset, England
Saturday 13 February 1971
10.00 a.m.

As soon as he entered the gymnasium, Matt could hear the chanting. He stopped and listened, trying to make out the words, but the voices were too muffled. The sound seemed to be coming from the equipment room at the far end of the gym, and Matt walked nervously towards it, his plimsolls squeaking on the polished wooden floor. As he drew closer the chanting intensified, and he heard shouts of laughter and the scrape of something heavy being pulled across the floor. He chewed his lip as he stood outside the equipment room, not wanting to get involved. He had a fair idea of what was going on behind the heavy wooden door and hovered uncertainly outside, wondering what he should do.

He couldn't just walk away. Someone was having a miserable time in there, and if he didn't do something about it, no one else would. He'd managed to overcome his fear and crawl into the centre of a landslide in Rio to rescue a little girl barely two months ago. Nothing he had to face here could be as difficult as that.

Suddenly he heard a second noise, this time right behind him. He whirled around, his eyes raking the gym, but he could see nothing but the ropes and apparatus already set out for the afternoon's inter-House competition.

'Mmm, mmm, aaaah!'

Matt hopped from one foot to another. The gym seemed completely empty, and yet he knew with absolute certainty that someone else was in there with him. He hoped uneasily it wasn't a trap. The initiation ceremony had been bad enough.

A thought occurred to him and he edged quietly out into the centre of the gymnasium, staring up at the visitors' gallery that ran around three sides of the room. Perhaps the acoustics were playing tricks on him; maybe the strange sound was really coming from upstairs. Slowly he turned in circles, his head craned back as he scanned every inch of the elevated seating. The urgent message for the games master which had brought him to the gym in the first place was completely forgotten.

He gave a cry of fear as something thumped him hard in the small of the back, and he tried and failed to keep his balance. He just had time to realise that he'd accidentally backed into the wooden horse in the centre of the gym before the momentum of his fall carried him forward and he tumbled hard across the box. His weight and the force of the collision knocked the top off its mountings and Matt fell with it on to the floor, where he lay, winded.

Fervently he prayed that the noise of his fall hadn't been heard by the other boys. To his intense relief, the chanting continued unabated, occasionally interspersed with shouts and cheers. Gingerly he tested his arms and legs, staring with morbid interest at the dark liquid staining the grey wool knee of his trousers. He prodded it experimentally and felt the blood trickle down his calf.

'I say! Are you all right?'

Matt jumped as a tousled blond head appeared from inside the horse.

'Logan? You did come a cropper, didn't you?'

'It didn't hurt,' Matt said swiftly, pushing the top of the wooden box out of the way and righting himself. 'I'm fine now, honest.'

'You've bashed your knee,' the boy said, staring at the bloodstained patch on Matt's trousers. 'You sure you're all right?'

Matt recognised the boy as another third-former from his own House, Blaise. 'Look, Yeates, I told you I was, didn't I? Don't go on.'

'I tell you, you didn't half give us a shock.'

Suddenly the peculiarity of the situation asserted itself and Matt peered past Yeates into the box. He saw a small, ginger-haired boy from Junior House hunched in the corner, his eyes closed as he pulled frantically on his small penis, apparently oblivious to what was going on around him. Yeates shook him by the shoulder and the boy opened his eyes, then blushed furiously as he saw Matt.

'What on earth are you doing in there together, anyway?'

Yeates groped around his knees, trying to pull up his trousers. 'Nothing.'

Matt shrugged. 'It's up to you. I don't care. But it must be flippin' uncomfortable in there for two of you. Couldn't you find anywhere else?'

'It was perfectly fine before. After all, we weren't expecting someone to crash into us,' Yeates said indignantly. He turned and nudged his companion, who was still cowering out of sight inside the box. 'Come on, Benson. Let's get out of here.'

Without meeting Matt's eyes, the two boys clambered self-consciously out of the wooden box and picked up the top section, puffing as they manoeuvred it back into place. After they'd finished, Yeates turned to Matt and shuffled uncomfortably from one foot to the other. 'I say, Logan, you won't tell anyone about this?' he asked anxiously. 'Benson's not even supposed to be out of Junior House, and I'm already gated for writing notes in prep. My parents will have a fit if they hear about this.'

'What do you think I am, a snitch?' Matt asked. 'Of course I won't tell anybody.'

Yeates grinned weakly and started to edge towards the door. Matt was about to follow him when he heard a series of sharp cries coming from the equipment room. He grabbed Yeates by the arm as Benson vanished outside. 'What's going on in there?'

Yeates looked uncomfortable. 'The usual. You know.'

'Initiation?'

Yeates nodded.

'But why's it taking so long? They sound like they're giving whoever it is a pretty rough time.'

The other boy looked unhappy, and Matt pushed him. 'Come on. Who've they got in there?'

'Tambo,' Yeates said reluctantly.

'But that's not fair!' Matt exclaimed. 'They've done him already! And two challenges, which he took right on the chin. Why pick on him again?'

Yeates shrugged and pulled away from him. 'None of my business. And if you've got any sense, you'll just get out of here and keep quiet.'

Matt watched as Yeates scurried out of the door, wanting to follow the other boy but unable to bring himself to leave. He turned and stared uneasily at the equipment room door, his conscience and his common sense pulling him in opposite directions. If he interfered, the chances were they'd turn on him, and he'd had enough of their attention to last him a while. But on the other hand, poor Tambo was really getting it badly. He couldn't just leave him there.

A sick feeling spread through him as he realised it was up to him. Summoning all his resolve, he thumped hard on the door. The chants and catcalls suddenly ceased.

A voice spoke inside the equipment room. 'What the fuck was that?'

'I don't know. Open the bloody door and find out.'

Matt backed away as the door opened. Through the narrow gap he could see Luke Tambo's naked body strapped by the wrists to the iron radiator on the opposite side of the equipment room. A tall, handsome boy with dirty-blond hair was standing beside him, a stiff-bristled brush in one hand. In the other he held an open can of black boot polish, half of which had already been roughly applied to Tambo's exposed genitals. The young black boy was clearly in pain; even from this distance Matt could see blisters forming on the inside of his arms where they had been pressed against the hot radiator, and bright speckles of blood from the harsh bristles dotted his genitals and the inside of his thighs. Matt was shocked. The brutal ritual was part of the initiation ceremony every boy had to endure at some time or other during his first term at Senior House; but Matt had never heard of it being inflicted at such length or with such severity.

The boy who had opened the door stared at him. 'Yes? Logan, isn't it?'

Matt nodded silently, suddenly terrified of what he'd started.

'What's going on out here?' The boy looked around the empty gym. 'Is someone coming?'

'I – I was looking for the games master. Mr Barlow,' Matt said stupidly. 'Um. Is he here?'

The tall boy with the brush and boot polish pushed his way forward and lounged against the door frame. 'What do you think, Logan?'

Matt's heart sank. Simon Derby-Lewis was the last person he'd wanted to see. The sixth-form senior prefect had a well-deserved reputation as a sadistic bully, who exploited his position over the younger boys in Blaise House to make their lives miserable. In his brief time at St Francis', Matt had already learned to avoid him whenever he could. Derby-Lewis never forgot a grievance.

'Well? Cat got your tongue?'

'Um. I thought I should warn you.' Matt mumbled. 'I think Mr Barlow is supposed to be here soon. Father Benedict sent me to find him.'

'Is that right?'

Matt glanced at Tambo, then looked away. 'Couldn't you – can't you – perhaps you could just let him go now? Before anyone comes?'

Derby-Lewis affected amazement at his daring. 'Did you hear that?' he said mockingly, turning to the group of boys now clustered in the doorway. 'Logan here says we should let Tambo go now. He's worried someone might come. How very, very thoughtful of him.' He turned back to Matt, a cold gleam in his pale blue eyes. 'You volunteering to take his place?'

Matt felt a surge of fear, but it was too late to stop now. 'No, of course not. But it's not – it's not fair to keep picking on Tambo. It's just not –'

'Cricket?'

Matt flushed. 'Well, it isn't. He's done his initiation, hasn't he? I just think he's had enough, that's all.'

'Oh, is that right?' Derby-Lewis said. 'And what makes you think you're such an authority on what's fair and what isn't? Daddy run the United Nations, or something? That what makes you such a nigger-lover, is it?'

'It's better than being a damned Nazi!'

Derby-Lewis laughed coldly. 'Nigger-lover!'

Taking their cue, the other boys circled slowly around Matt. 'Nigger-lover! Nigger-lover! Nigger-lover!'

51

Matt saw the ugly expression on Derby-Lewis' face and guessed he'd made a serious mistake by insulting him in front of everyone. Now, he'd turned it into something personal, and there was no way Derby-Lewis was going to back down.

'I think it's time we taught young Logan a lesson,' Derby-Lewis said menacingly, straightening up.

Matt turned round, ready to run, but the other boy was too fast. His hand grabbed Matt's hair and yanked his head backwards so sharply that tears sprang to the younger boy's eyes. Amid shouts and laughter, Matt found himself being dragged towards the equipment room despite his frantic attempts to wriggle free. Fervently he wished he'd never been sent to the gym with that wretched message in the first place. He was no hero, and he knew exactly what was in store for him now.

'Hey! You boys! What's going on down there?'

'Shit! It's Barlow!' one of the boys hissed. 'Let's get out of here!'

Matt felt a vicious tug on his left ear. 'Don't think I'll forget this, Logan,' Derby-Lewis whispered. 'I'll be seeing to you later.'

Abruptly he let go of his hair and Matt fell forward on to his face. Around him the floor reverberated with the sound of running feet. Stunned, he pushed himself up on his hands and knees and glanced round at the black boy, who had been hastily freed from the radiator and was busy pulling on his trousers and shirt.

The games master pulled Matt to his feet, an expression of concern on his face. 'What's going on, boy?'

Matt shook his head. 'Nothing, sir.'

'Didn't look like nothing to me.'

Matt said nothing, and the games master shrugged. 'It's up to you. Now go on, get out of here.' He gestured to Tambo, hovering in the doorway. 'You too. It's time for prep.'

52

The two boys fled. Without stopping to speak, they ran straight across the main quad, behind the science wing and up the long flight of stairs towards the Blaise House dormitories. Staggering into Matt's dorm, they collapsed heavily on to two beds at the far end of it, their chests heaving as they tried to catch their breath. After a long moment, they lifted their eyes and stared at each other.

'You all right?' Matt asked.

Luke nodded. 'I'm fine.' He paused. 'You didn't have to do that, you know. Thank you.'

Matt stared down at his feet, embarrassed. 'Forget it.'

'No, I mean it.' Luke touched his shoulder. 'No one's ever stood up for me before. You were a real friend. You ever in trouble, I want to be a friend like that to you.' He smiled, his white teeth gleaming against the rich chocolate of his skin. 'Any time. I mean that.'

'Not you again, Logan? How many times is it this week?'

Matt gazed at his shoes. 'Four.'

The prefect sighed, taking Matt's punishment slip and writing his name in the detention book. 'You never put a foot wrong last term. These days I seem to see your ugly mug every evening. Is there a problem?'

Matt shook his head, avoiding the prefect's eyes.

The prefect's expression softened. 'Look, Logan – Matthew, isn't it? – Matthew, it's up to you. You don't have to tell me anything if you don't want to.' His eyes were sympathetic as he handed Matt his detention attendance paper. 'But if I were you, I'd try to avoid Simon Derby-Lewis for a while. He's not a good person to cross, unless you plan to spend the rest of your school life stuck in detention.'

Matt gave a lopsided smile. 'I know.'

David Cameron watched the younger boy as he slid wearily into his seat on the other side of the classroom. As head prefect, David had a fair idea of what was going on; Matt's confrontation with Simon Derby-Lewis three weeks ago had been repeated with relish up and down the refectory tables. Derby-Lewis' retaliation had been characteristic. Time and again Matt had been caught in legitimate infringement of the school rules, and though David strongly suspected Derby-Lewis' involvement somewhere along the line, he was powerless to interfere without proof. Matt was just going to have to ride it out until Derby-Lewis either got bored or found another victim to torment. In David's opinion, the older boy should never have been made a prefect in the first place. Derby-Lewis lacked the character to deal with power or authority, and in his hands it had become spiteful tyranny.

Wearily Matt opened his Latin grammar and started his prep, wondering how much more of this he could take. Derby-Lewis showed no signs of letting up. Each morning he had Matt up at five o'clock to sound reveille in the quad outside, and kept him standing there shivering for so long that he missed breakfast and his fingers literally froze to his brass bugle. Every spare moment of Matt's time was spent writing the sheets Derby-Lewis had set him, painstakingly filling each line of the A4 paper with the prescribed twenty words. Every minor or imagined infringement earned him another dozen pages. In the past three weeks he'd been set so many that despite the help of his friends, and particularly Luke Tambo – who had his own quota of punishments from Derby-Lewis to deal with – he couldn't keep up with them during the day and had had to resort to finishing them under the bedclothes after lights out, his torch clutched between his teeth as he scribbled. Even then, Derby-Lewis had been one step ahead of him, catching him red-handed and assigning another two dozen sheets as punishment. Matt's school work had begun to suffer, and he'd been hauled up before Father Benedict twice in the last ten days for poor marks and inattention. Once he'd even fallen asleep in the middle of his maths class. If it got any worse, he thought he might be in serious danger of expulsion.

It was the first time he had ever had to deal with anything like this alone. He knew it was something he could never have shared with his mother. She wouldn't have understood the unwritten code of honour which meant he couldn't sneak on Derby-Lewis, however severe or unfair the punishments he received. She would have marched straight down to the school and confronted Father Benedict, earning Matt the undying contempt of his friends as well as his enemies. He could have told his father if he had been able to reach him, but Christopher was away in Mozambique, working on a famine-relief project in consultation with the UN. It seemed he was always away these days.

Over the years, Matt had grown used to his father's prolonged absences. They only ever came together as a family in the summer, which they always spent at the villa in Sicily that his mother had inherited from her father. Caroline led her own life when Christopher was away, smoothly combining a glittering social round in London with the efficient running of the estate in Sussex which had been owned by her family for more than three centuries. When he had been younger, Matt had been terrified that his parents would divorce. But gradually he had learned that beneath the constant battles, they both loved and needed each other.

The bell sounded for the end of prep and Matt closed his books, stumbling out of the classroom and along the corridor to his dormitory. It was deserted; apart from Luke Tambo, the rest of his form were on a school trip to London and wouldn't be back until midnight. Like Luke, Matt's impressive quota of demerits had meant he'd been barred from joining them. He shoved his books into the locker beside his bed and headed towards the bathroom. At least he'd be able to shower and brush his teeth without having to wait his turn. At this moment, all he wanted to do was sink into bed and sleep for ever.

He walked into the bathroom and froze.

The room looked as if it had been torn apart. Clothes and damp towels littered the floor, soap had been smeared across the mirrors, and the two baths had been filled with the contents of the waste disposal unit and what appeared to be soil and foliage from smashed plants. Soggy tissue paper blocked the toilets and sinks, causing water from the running taps to overflow on to the tiled floor, which was already swimming with cigarette ends, sweet wrappers, half-eaten sandwiches and sheets of paper from a ripped exercise book.

Matt kicked off his shoes and socks and waded across the bathroom to pick up the soggy book. His heart sank as he saw it was his history project. The ruined clothes scattered around the room were also his. His bare feet crunched on something brittle as he walked towards the sink, and he looked down to see the remnants of the photograph of his parents and older brother which he usually kept on the locker next to his bed. The silver frame had been stamped on and bent out of shape, the picture torn into a thousand tiny pieces.

Fighting back tears of anger and frustration, Matt turned off the taps and began unblocking the sinks, his feet splashing as he moved across the floor and started mopping up the water with towels. He knew he had to tidy up the mess; thanks to Derby-Lewis, the bathroom was his responsibility, and if it was not spotless in time for morning inspection, he would only gain another clutch of demerits, not to mention fines. Matt had a strong suspicion that his pocket-money was single-handedly keeping Derby-Lewis in alcohol and cigarettes.

He rocked back on his heels and stared at the chaos. It would take him hours.

'What on earth happened here?'

Matt glanced up and saw Luke Tambo standing in the doorway. 'I give you three guesses.'

'Derby-Lewis?'

'Who else?'

Luke slipped off his shoes and socks and waded into the room, heading for the two toilets. Grimacing, he plunged his hand into the nearest one and came up gripping a fistful of soggy tissue paper.

'You don't have to do that,' Matt said. 'It's up to me. Go on, you'd better get back to your dorm. You'll only get in more trouble if someone finds you here.'

'It's my fault you're in such a fix with Derby-Lewis,' Luke said stubbornly. 'The least I can do is help you clear up some of this mess.'

Wordlessly the two boys started piling the rubbish into the waste-paper bins, their feet squelching over the damp towels Matt had laid on the floor. Two hours later they stood in the centre of the bathroom, their arms sore and aching, their fingers scraped raw from scrubbing the baths and mirrors clean.

'It's not going to get any better,' Matt said. 'Everything's just too wet. All we're doing is pushing the mess round and round. I'll have to get up before reveille and try to polish it off a bit after the floor's had time to drain.'

'It's not that bad,' Luke said encouragingly. 'By the time everyone's been in here to wash and brush their teeth after they get back from their trip, it'll just look like normal. Father Benedict won't expect it to be perfect tomorrow morning, what with everyone going to bed so late.'

'Yes. But Derby-Lewis will,' Matt muttered.

The two boys stared at each other. 'How long is he going to keep this up?' Luke asked.

Matt had no idea.

David Cameron walked slowly up the great staircase leading to Father Benedict's study. In his left hand he held the detention and demerit books which recorded each boy's infringement of the school rules and the punishment set. Matthew Logan's name appeared almost four times more frequently than that of any other boy in his House.

Over the past seven weeks, David had become more and more concerned as Matt had continued to appear every evening for detention, his face growing more pinched and drawn by the day, heavy black circles appearing under his eyes. What Derby-Lewis was doing amounted to nothing less than persecution. He was literally hounding the boy out of the school.

The overbearing prefect was one of Father Benedict's own appointees, and David knew him to be amongst the headmaster's favourites. Of the six Houses that made up the school, Blaise was currently the least disruptive and difficult to manage. Truancy and breaking bounds under Derby-Lewis' regime were almost unknown. But, David was aware, the House was also the most unhappy.

He had known that there was no way the headmaster would accept his accusations without proof. So with the patience and skill of a seasoned investigative journalist, David had collected the evidence he needed to persuade him. For the last month, instead of throwing away the various punishment slips Matt handed in to him each evening during detention, he'd kept them. Every one had been signed by Derby-Lewis, and not one of them had been witnessed by any other prefect. Derby-Lewis was vicious, but he was also stupid. He'd left a paper trail a mile wide.

David knocked quietly on Father Benedict's door and opened it, his attention focused on the detention book in his hand. He didn't take in the scene before him for several seconds, and when he did, he was too shocked to move.

Simon Derby-Lewis was bent at right angles across the priest's burnished mahogany desk, his fingers gripping the far edge so tightly that his knuckles were white from the pressure. His eyes were closed, his face contorted into an expression of exquisitely mingled pain and pleasure. His shirt and blazer were rucked up around his shoulders; from the chest down he was naked, his trousers and underpants tangled around his ankles. Standing between his spread legs was Father Benedict, his black habit caught up around his waist, his heavy gold pectoral cross flapping against his chest as he plunged his erect cock between the young boy's naked buttocks. His bony fingers gripped Derby-Lewis' narrow hips tightly and his breathing was heavy and laboured as he pumped into the boy again and again, his face red with exertion and excitement. From the wordless synchronicity with which the two moved, David knew immediately that this was something they had done together many, many times before.

And, despite his horror and revulsion, he also knew he'd found a way to save Matt.

Six

Nova Esperancia, Rio de Janeiro, Brazil
Thursday 11 March 1971
3.40 p.m.

The woman's breathing was shallow and rapid as she tossed against the straw mattress, trying to find a comfortable position. Her olive skin was sweaty, her lips cracked and dry. With an obvious effort her eyes tried to focus on the two figures standing beside her bed. She muttered something so faintly that they had to strain forward to hear.

The old priest bent towards her and held his ear inches away from her mouth. After a moment he turned and nodded to the midwife, standing at the foot of the bed.

'She wants some water.'

Already the woman was so weak she could barely swallow, the water running out of the side of her parched mouth and dribbling down her chin. Gently the midwife laid her head back down on the rough square of foam that served as a pillow and moved a few feet away from the bed, nodding at the priest to follow her.

As soon as they were out of earshot, he turned to her. 'Is the child still living?'

The midwife nodded. 'For the moment. I can feel its heartbeat quite strongly. But if it's not delivered soon ...' She shrugged. 'The poor woman can't last long now. And the child isn't yet ready to be born, although its time is near.'

Father Lucio frowned. The child had to live; that was the reason the Judge had sent him here. He couldn't go back to Fernando empty-handed, not after the mudslide three months ago had claimed so many. 'At all costs, we must try to save the life of the child, even if the mother is lost to us. As one life ends, so another begins.' He glanced at the woman on the bed. 'I must tell her she's dying. She must make her confession and have the last rites.'

He crossed the dark, airless room and knelt down by the woman's bed. 'Bernadette. It's Father Lucio. Can you hear me? Can you understand what I'm saying?'

The woman fluttered her eyes in acknowledgement. Father Lucio reached for her hand, as dry and brittle as paper in his strong grip. 'Bernadette, it's time to prepare yourself for the end. It won't be long now. Do you understand me?' He felt her squeeze his hand in answer. 'Our Lord is waiting for you, my child. You will not be alone in this. He is with you every step of your journey. You must not be afraid.'

The woman's eyes opened and she stared at Father Lucio, her gaze suddenly focused. 'My baby,' she whispered, her hand moving automatically towards her swollen stomach. 'Tell me –' A sudden fit of coughing racked her. 'Father, tell me. My baby –' She paused and coughed again. 'Who will look after my baby?'

Father Lucio sighed. 'My child, your baby is trying to come into the world, but it is weak. Bernadette, the life of your child is in danger. We are doing all we can, but we need your permission to save the child. You have to let us help the baby. Can you do that? Can you put your faith in God and ask Him to help you?'

Bernadette stared at him, and for a moment the priest wondered if she'd understood. 'Bernadette, I am going to hear

61

your last confession, and then I will anoint you with the chrism of Christ so that you will be able to travel to His arms ready for Him.'

The midwife watched as Bernadette whispered her last confession into the priest's ear. Her heart ached for the dying woman, but at least she'd soon be beyond all this. It was those poor mites who were left behind who would need sympathy.

She heard the door creak and turned round to see one of Bernadette's daughters standing in the doorway watching her mother, her dark blue eyes huge in her pale face. With a quick glance towards the bed, the midwife scuttled over to shoo the little girl out of the way.

'Elizabetta, you know you shouldn't be in here. Where are Carmel and the boys? You should be with them.'

'Is Mama going to die?'

The midwife was unable to reply. The solemn eyes remained fixed on hers, and she shifted uncomfortably. How could she tell this five-year-old girl that her mother was on the brink of death, that she and her brothers and sister were about to find themselves orphans? Elizabetta had already endured so much in her short life. She'd never even known her father, who must have been one of her mother's many customers – probably an American, judging by the child's startling blue eyes. She'd seen seven of her eleven siblings die before their fifth birthday. Most of her friends and extended family had been wiped out in the terrifying mudslide that had swept nine-tenths of the town away just before Christmas. Elizabetta herself had only survived by some extraordinary miracle, rescued from the carnage by an English boy who'd disap-peared before the family could thank him. Bernadette and her children had been lucky that time: their house had been amongst the few on the western ridge of Nova Esperancia to be spared the torrent of mud and rock. But it seemed they had withstood that tragedy only to suffer another now, just as terrible.

The midwife had no illusions about what would happen to the four orphans once their mother died. Elizabetta's older sister, Carmel, was only eleven, the two boys just three and six. Any cousins and aunts who might have taken them in had been killed by the mudslide. Sooner or later, she knew, the children would end up on the streets of Rio, destitute and despised, forced to live on the scraps of food they scavenged from dustbins and sleep in doorways and alleys at night. If they survived the brutal purges by the police and citizens' groups bent on cleaning up the streets, the girls would almost certainly end up as prostitutes like their mother, the boys thieving, pimping or running drugs. The midwife doubted any of them would survive much beyond their teens.

She gave the little girl a gentle shove. 'Go on outside, child. I have to go and look after your mother. I'll call you later, when you can see her.'

She turned and shut the door, moving swiftly to the woman's bedside and putting her ear against Bernadette's swollen belly, then looked up at the priest. 'You've given her the last rites?'

Father Lucio nodded.

'We can't afford to delay any longer. You'll have to hold her down. I can't risk her moving while I'm trying to deliver the child.'

Reluctantly, the priest leant across the woman's chest, holding her arms down firmly with his hands. Barely conscious, she didn't move or cry out. Father Lucio said a swift prayer, glad that he was unable to witness what the midwife was doing from his awkward position.

The midwife moved swiftly now that the moment had come. She felt the woman's belly again to determine the position of the child, then drew a knife from her bag, not troubling to sterilise it with boiling water. Bernadette was beyond either help or harm now. Taking a deep breath to steady her hand, the midwife sliced horizontally across the bottom of the woman's abdomen, her stroke firm and sure. Bernadette stiffened and screamed, a piercing, terrifying wail of agony as her child was ripped from her belly, blood and fluid gushing across the bed. Working quickly, the midwife pulled the baby clear and wiped the blood and mucus from its face, severing the umbilical cord with one quick, sharp cut. She wrapped the child in a scrap of blanket and handed it to the priest, then pushed him out of the way as she bent her head to listen to the woman's heart. Straightening up, she shook her head and made a quick sign of the cross.

'Will the child live?'

The midwife shrugged. 'The boy's healthy enough. But as to who will look after him –'

'You don't need to worry about that. As long as he's healthy, I'll be able to find a good home for him.' Father Lucio stared at the small scrap of humanity in his arms. 'At least some good will have come out of this.'

The midwife pulled the bloodstained sheet over the woman's face and covered her savaged stomach, trying to avoid the pool of blood that had gathered beneath the bed. 'What about the other children?'

The priest shook his head. 'I can do nothing for them.'

He glanced again at the baby in his arms. At least this time he'd got what he'd come for, and without having to pay for it or trouble with papers.

Fernando Moreno would be pleased, very pleased.

Seven

Via Appia Antica, Rome, Italy
Wednesday 24 July 1974
8.20 a.m.

Roberto heard Joanna enter the bedroom behind him, but did not look round. Wordlessly he concentrated on fastening his cufflink, turning his wrist inwards as he slid the gold bar through the stiff linen of his shirt. He knew she was waiting for him to turn and ask her what was wrong. Stubbornly, he refused to give her the satisfaction.

Joanna stared at his unyielding back for a few moments, then sighed loudly and sat down on the stool in front of her dressing table. 'I'm afraid that girl has got to go, Roberto. I really can't put up with any more of this.'

Roberto picked up his other cufflink. 'I take it you mean Katya?'

'Of course Katya! Roberto, I'm serious. She's gone too far this time. I want you to give her notice immediately; she can have a week's pay and leave tomorrow.'

'I really can't see why you need me to deal with it,' Roberto said. 'As I recall, you haven't had any problem getting rid of the last dozen nannies I've hired.'

Joanna swung round to face him, her eyes chips of flint in her pale face. 'This isn't a joke, Roberto! That damn girl claims to have yet another of her migraines – she won't even get out of bed this morning. I've got an important fitting at Pavesi's that I can't possibly cancel. What on earth am I going to do about Alexandra?'

Roberto's expression was unreadable. 'You could always take her with you.'

'Oh, for God's sake, Roberto! How can I possibly take a three-year-old child to a couture fitting? What am I supposed to do with her there?'

Roberto looped his tie around his collar and fastened it with deft fingers. Despite herself, Joanna felt a stab of longing as she stared at his taut, loose-limbed figure and quickly looked away.

'She's not a monster, Joanna. She's just a child. If you spent a little more time with her, you might realise that.'

'I don't need any lectures from you on how to bring up my own daughter,' Joanna snapped. 'I've got enough to think about today as it is. The Derbyshires are coming for dinner, in case you'd forgotten, and those magazine people of yours are supposed to be photographing the house this afternoon, though God knows it's hardly ready for them. The last thing I need is a fractious child dragging at my heels.'

'I would have thought she'd be an asset,' Roberto said coldly. 'There's nothing like an adoring, photogenic child for a little extra good publicity.'

'If you think comments like that will hurt me, you're very much mistaken,' Joanna said crisply, clipping a pair of discreet diamond studs into her ears. 'You were the one who was so keen for me to be a proper wife, to go to all the right parties and wear all the right clothes. You can hardly start complaining now because that's exactly what I'm doing.'

'I didn't intend you to do these things at the expense of spending time with your own daughter,' Roberto shot back.

Joanna stretched her lips wide to apply her lipstick. 'You should have thought about that before.'

Roberto felt a sudden surge of guilt and shame. When they'd returned to Rome three and a half years ago, he'd been far too preoccupied with establishing his own position back at the centre of Italian politics to think about Joanna. He knew now what it must have cost her to take her place by his side at the many parties and receptions which were such an important part of his life. She had always been painfully shy and insecure. If he'd stopped to think how much pressure he was placing on her, perhaps he could have lessened the burden somehow. As it was, she'd had to fight for acceptance by the same group of people to whom he'd belonged since birth, enduring the gossip and slights alone. Bereft of his love and support, she'd used the only weapon left to her: his cheque-book.

Her determination to prove to Roberto that she could be the wife he expected had enabled her to overcome her shyness, and to her surprise she had discovered that her parents' and sisters' social skills had not passed her by. Gradually her parties had become renowned for being more lavish and entertaining, her guests more rich and famous, than those of any of her rivals. Shrewdly she had realised the power of the press and had courted journalists assiduously; her name had started to appear on the best-dressed lists, she'd been featured in *Women's Wear Daily*, and once she had appeared – sleek, blonde and self-assured – on the cover of *Tatler*. In a matter of months, her critics had melted away as she'd become not just an accepted member of the A-list, but one of its main arbiters of taste and style.

Preoccupied with his work, bored with his wife, Roberto had paid Joanna's transformation little attention. He had simply been relieved that the hysterical, jealous rages had ceased, that finally she had seemed to be coming to terms with her role as his wife.

And then suddenly he'd become aware of what he'd lost. With Joanna's shyness and insecurity had gone her essence. He could find nothing in the cool, glittering socialite who shared his home and his bed to remind him of the vulnerable girl he'd once thought he'd loved. In public, she was the perfect politician's wife, attractive, solicitous and charming, but behind the immaculate façade they led totally separate lives. He was rarely at home these days, travelling back and forth across the continent in his role as Italy's junior Foreign Minister, while Joanna spent her days at lunches and fittings, her evenings at parties and premières. They were now virtual strangers, linked by nothing but convenience and a piece of paper.

It was his own fault. When they'd married, he had been the one with the experience: he should have recognised his own feelings for what they were. By mistaking infatuation and sexual need for love, he'd sentenced them both to a lifetime of unhappiness. He was only too aware that while he'd tired of Joanna almost as soon as he'd taken her to bed, her love for him had become obsessive. There was no room for anything in her life but her need for him; not even for their own daughter.

'Roberto, couldn't you take Alexandra with you today?'

'To a meeting with the British and American ambassadors?' he said incredulously. 'What is she expected to do, discuss the relative merits of Edward Heath and President Nixon?'

'It's no more ridiculous than me taking her to Pavesi's.'

'Joanna, you're her mother,' Roberto said through gritted teeth. 'If only you'd just stop thinking of her as a burden. She's your daughter. She needs you. Would it really be so preposterous for you to spend half a day with her?'

'It's easy for you to say that. She adores you. Daddy can't put a foot wrong.' Joanna swivelled round on her dressing-table stool to face him. 'Roberto, I'm not a natural mother, you know that, and so does Alexandra. She can see it.' She stared down at her hands, twisting her enormous diamond engagement ring around her finger. 'She's better off without me. It's not as if she wants me anyway. It's you she wants.'

Roberto stared at his wife. Joanna had always been so cool towards their little daughter, so remote. At first he'd thought it was the exhaustion of looking after a new baby, the shock of moving back to Rome. But as the months had passed and she'd shown no sign of picking Alix up or cuddling her, he'd been forced to conclude it was something more.

He had a sudden memory of slipping upstairs to his daughter's nursery when she was only six months old. He could still remember the ache in his heart as he'd stared down into her cot, fascinated by the gentle rise and fall of her tiny chest as she'd lain sleeping. Her hair had glinted auburn and gold in the sunlight, her long, dark lashes fluttering as she'd smiled in her dreams. He'd known then he'd do anything to protect her from her mother's indifference.

He'd tried to make up by loving Alix twice as much himself as he watched his daughter turn to her mother for the comfort and reassurance any child had a right to expect, only to be coolly pushed away towards a succession of nannies and housekeepers. One night, when Alix was about eighteen months old, she had crept into their bedroom, disturbed by something in her sleep – the wind rattling the shutters outside, or a nightmare. He'd woken to see her standing in her pink pyjamas at the end of the bed, too terrified even to call his name. As Roberto had leaped out of bed to hug and reassure her, Joanna had woken up and taken Alix from him without a word, marching her back to the nursery and depositing her in her cot. She'd simply insisted that Alix needed to learn the meaning of discipline.

Now, for the first time, he began to wonder if Joanna's dislike of Alix had something to do with his own patent adoration of the child. She was the centre of his world, however much he tried to hide it. Perhaps, given the circumstances of her birth, he should have been more circumspect, allowed Joanna to form her own bond with the baby first. But she was his daughter, for God's sake. What was he supposed to do – pretend that she didn't exist so that her own mother wouldn't get jealous?

'Alix only asks for me because she's so used to you pushing her away,' he said evenly. 'It's not that she doesn't want you. She's afraid of getting sticky fingers on your skirt, or hugging you when she's not supposed to.'

Joanna stood at the door, a cold smile twisting her perfect features. 'Well, you should be pleased about Katya. It looks like I'm stuck with Alexandra. For today, anyway.'

Roberto was left staring after her as she walked from the room without a backward glance.

Eight

Via Condotti, Rome, Italy
Friday 26 July 1974
10.30 a.m.

'Darling, yes, there, yes, oh yes!' The dark-haired girl thrust her bony hips forward. 'Oh God, Lindi, don't stop, please don't stop, I'm going to come, I'm going to come!'

Kneeling on the floor between the other girl's spread legs, Lindi suddenly stopped her skilful tonguing and looked up, a wicked glint in her wide grey eyes. 'Tell me how much you want it, *chérie*. Tell me what you want me to do to you, how much you need me to fuck you.'

The brunette wriggled in delicious frustration against the wall of the changing-room, her short black leather skirt rucked up around her narrow waist, her skinny-rib sweater pushed aside to expose her tiny, pink-nippled breasts. 'Oh God, you know how much I want it. You can feel how wet I am. Please, darling, please, don't make me wait any longer, I'm right on the edge, I'm desperate to come.'

Lindi trailed her tongue across the engorged clitoris. 'Say the words, *chérie*. Tell me exactly what you want me to do.'

'Jesus, Lindi,' the brunette groaned.

'Say it!'

'I want you to suck me off,' the girl whispered hoarsely as Lindi's tongue started to probe gently inside her. 'I want you

71

to squeeze my nipples and lick my clit and … Jesus, oh God, Lindi …. I want you to stick your tongue in my cunt and … I'm going to come, I'm going to make it … and I want you to fuck me, oh, God, fuck me, please, Lindi, please now!'

Lindi's tongue flicked deftly from the girl's swollen pink clitoris to trail delicate whorls of pleasure along the inside of her white thighs, moving slowly, infinitely slowly, down towards her cunt until she tasted the rich, musky sweetness of her. There was nothing she liked more than fucking a girl who'd only ever made it with men before; it was like having a virgin, only even sweeter. Once they'd done it with her, she was sure it was never as good for them with a man again. The girl shuddered uncontrollably, desperate to keep Lindi's skilled tongue exactly where it was, yet longing to thrust her hips towards the source of such exquisite pleasure. Reaching upwards, Lindi took the girl's tiny breasts between her fingers and rolled the nipples beneath her thumbs, her tongue still working the girl's clitoris, drinking her in. Suddenly the brunette screamed, her whole body convulsing.

'Jesus Christ, what's going on in there, you two?'

The brunette slid dazedly down the wall of the changing-room, her body still shuddering in orgasm. Lindi stood up and quickly straightened her clothes, running her fingers through her shingled white-blonde hair as she glanced in the mirror.

'Is that you, Janet?'

'Of course it's bloody well me,' the voice on the other side of the door said waspishly. 'You and Cheryl do realise we have a show to do in less than half an hour?'

Lindi sounded contrite. 'I'm sorry, Janet, really I am. We're just coming, honest.'

'That's what I'm afraid of,' Janet said. 'Two minutes, then I'm coming in, ready or not.'

'Two minutes, Janet. Promise.'

Janet glanced at her watch and sighed. She knew from past

experience that neither of the models would have been in the slightest bit embarrassed if they'd been caught *in flagrante* indulging in some sisterly cunnilingus, but both would be absolutely mortified if they faced the world with their make-up less than perfect. If Janet wasn't standing guard outside the door, they'd be an hour getting it right.

Briefly she wondered where rounding up sex-crazed models slotted into her job description as a fitter. Probably somewhere in between letting out waistbands for the girls who'd got themselves pregnant but hadn't yet decided which candidate to name as the father, and handing out tissues to those who had and had then found out he'd had a vasectomy three years before. After more than twenty years in the business, Janet had lost her ability to be shocked or even vaguely surprised by anything. There was nothing the *cabine* models could do that she hadn't seen before. It was no wonder everyone dreaded the day she decided to write her memoirs.

Lindi opened the door, her gamine face the picture of innocence. 'Where would you like us, Janet?'

Janet grinned despite herself. 'You don't want the answer to that one.' She turned and headed back down the long, narrow corridor towards the fitting-room, Lindi and Cheryl trailing behind. 'You two better not have put on any weight since last week, that's all I can say. If these clothes don't fit, you're both of you out of a job, house models or no.'

One eye on the clock, Janet walked briskly into the backstage fitting-room adjoining the main salon that Pavesi used both for couture customer fittings and for the small private shows like the one they'd be giving shortly. Unlike last week, the atmosphere backstage was relaxed, the models wandering around in various states of undress, chatting casually and slipping out into the corridor for the occasional illicit cigarette. Today – thank God – there would be no predatory journalists waiting by the catwalk when the models emerged, pens poised to rip Pavesi apart if the new season's designs were judged less than inspirational. Every outfit the models would be showing this morning had already been revealed to the press in last week's couture collection; thankfully, they'd emerged unscathed to suitably rapturous applause from all the major publications with the exception of *Elan*, whose fashion editor, Stephi Kay, seemed to have taken a permanent dislike to almost everything Pavesi designed.

The show today was for a selection of Pavesi's serious customers, those women who spent at least $20,000 on his clothes every season. It would include only the more wearable garments from the previous week's collection – those outfits that had been designed with real customers in mind, rather than newsworthy photographs. Every woman waiting in the main salon next door was there with the firm intention of decimating, if not halving, her husband's bank account: all Pavesi had to do was help them decide how to do it.

Janet scanned the fitting-room quickly, realising they were running short of time. At least when they did these private shows, they were able to get away with using their own house models; even allowing for Lindi and Cheryl's overactive libidos, they'd a fair chance of starting on schedule. Janet disliked the new fashion – to which Pavesi unfortunately subscribed – of hiring high-profile editorial models for catwalk collections in order to capitalise on the ready-made publicity they generated. In her opinion, editorial and catwalk work didn't mix. The faces that regularly appeared in gossip columns and on the cover of *Vogue* might attract plenty of publicity, but the girls themselves were intensely competitive and insecure, turning the atmosphere backstage from sleep-over-intimate to divorce-court-lethal. Despite their growing celebrity status and the ridiculous fees they commanded, many of them had as much idea of how to show a garment and walk a catwalk as a boxing promoter. Pavesi's five permanent house models, on the other hand, were both skilled and highly professional, yet were paid a pittance to perform the same show for private clients again and again, and in between to act as flesh-and-blood tailors' dummies for the fitters and seamstresses. But then, thought Janet, whoever said this business was fair?

She turned as one of the dressers edged wearily through the cluster of girls milling around the atelier. 'Janet, you haven't got a spare 13-amp fuse for the iron, have you? Patti got caught in the rain and her hair's gone all wavy. Dead straight hair, Pavesi said. He'll go mad if he doesn't get it.'

'The things we do for love.'

The dresser sighed. 'Tell me about it.'

Janet rooted around in the grey Tardis slung over her shoulder, locating the required fuse in triumph. Over the years it had become a point of honour that she could provide anything that could possibly be needed for a collection from the grey bag she never let out of her sight. It contained perhaps a hundred items from pliers and false eyelashes to Tampax and purple hearts. She'd only ever failed once: when a frantic model had asked her for a fire extinguisher with rather more optimism than logic.

A tall, slender redhead with bright green eyes bent languidly over the ironing board, casually filing a broken nail as the dresser covered her long russet hair with a linen towel and began ironing the kinks out of it.

'Just mind my ears this time,' the redhead said, extending her hand to examine the shape of her nail. 'Last time someone did this I couldn't use the telephone for a week.'

Lindi pulled off her crocheted minidress and wandered naked towards the narrow corridor that separated the fitting-room from the main salon. 'Just think what could have happened if it'd been a lingerie shoot.'

'I hate these private shows,' Cheryl complained as her dresser eased a pink chiffon kaftan over her dark head.

'Never mind that, have you seen the groovy young boy at the back?' Lindi interrupted, peering into the main salon, her naked bottom wiggling with excitement. 'I wouldn't mind doing a private show for him.' She turned and sashayed lazily back towards the others, her high breasts jiggling provocatively. 'I wonder who'll get to him first, Angela or Pavesi. He's sheer jailbait – can't be more than fifteen. Reckon I could get his phone number?'

Janet glanced briefly into the main salon as she dragged Lindi back towards the dresser. 'If it's any of your business, that's Caroline Logan's youngest son. Now get dressed, or I'll send you out exactly as you are.'

Little Alix gazed around the huge lobby with awe as they hurried through the front doors of the fashion house. Her short legs stumbling, she struggled to keep up with her mother's pale blue silk skirts, thrilled to be part of her world, if only for a morning. They passed through the workroom where dozens of women sat surrounded by bolts of material, more colours than Alix had ever seen. Uncomprehending but enthralled, the three-year-old absorbed the secret femininity, the muted rustle of silks and satins, the subtle fragrance of a thousand expensive perfumes, the aura of some divine mystery at work which could transform the life of anyone privileged enough to step inside its orbit.

Seeing her fascination, the young PR girl who was leading them towards the main salon slowed her pace and began to describe the rooms past which they were walking. 'These are the ateliers – the workrooms – where all the clothes are made,' she explained, smiling. 'A different thing is done in each room – that one there is where we do all the beading, and that's for embroidery, those two for the buttons and any appliqué. Some of the seamstresses have been doing nothing else for twenty or thirty years.' She paused by the doorway to a workroom larger than those they had passed, filled with tailor's dummies of all shapes and sizes. 'That's the *atelier frou*, where we make all the evening wear.' She sighed, unable to keep a note of longing from her voice. 'Where all the most beautiful, delicate garments are made. Everything is done by hand, from the first cut to the last stitch. That's why it's all so expensive.'

Alix nodded, understanding little of what was being said but utterly absorbed. She clung to the doorway of the *atelier frou*, unable to tear her eyes away from the glittering river of colours sliding through the seamstresses' hands.

She pointed to the array of tailor's dummies. 'What's those?'

The girl smiled. 'When a lady comes here for the first time, we get her to take off all her clothes and put on a special tight cotton dress. That way we can see what shape she is.' She turned one of the dummies round on its metal stand so that Alix could see it better. 'Then we fill the dress with horsehair padding until it looks just like the lady, see, from her neck to her hips. Later, when we want to make her dresses, we can use the dummy to make sure they fit.'

Alix looked puzzled. 'Why are all these so much fatter than those ones over there?'

The PR girl laughed. 'Those thin ones are the ones we use for our models. Even the dummy of a beautiful lady looks overstuffed and fat compared to those, because the models are so slim. That's why we don't usually let any of our customers see their own dummy, in case it upsets them.'

'Does Mama have one?'

'Of course she does, *cara*. Her own, special one. Your mama has lots of dresses made here.'

Joanna frowned and gave the child a little push in the small of her back. 'Fascinating. But we really don't have time for a tour of the entire building.'

The PR girl looked chastened. 'I'm so sorry, Signora Cerreni.' She hurried quickly down the corridor, then turned and smiled down at Alix's tumble of auburn curls as they reached the main salon. 'But then your daughter is so charming, so pretty.'

Joanna's stare was cool.

Alix quietly followed her mother through the ornate double doors into the main salon, a long, well-proportioned room tastefully furnished with antiques and *objets d'art*, its walls covered with century-old rose silk and decorated with lesser-known but original paintings by Monet, Matisse and Picasso. Its ambience was one of ordered wealth and privilege; it was a room designed to make the couture customer feel they were in familiar surroundings where the spending of thousands of dollars on an outfit that would be worn perhaps three times was not an extravagance. Near to the double doors, two rows of gilt chairs had been set out; directly opposite them was a low catwalk covered with rose silk that exactly matched the walls.

Alix climbed awkwardly on to one of the gilt chairs and stared at the catwalk, her thumb straying towards her mouth. Her mother slapped her hand away.

'Don't do that, Alexandra. It's unladylike.' She glanced at Alix's patent leather Mary-Janes, hanging far above the faded Aubusson rug that covered the floor. 'And don't swing your feet.'

Alix froze guiltily and ducked her head, trying to stem the flood of instant tears. Sometimes it was so hard to remember all Mama's rules.

Suddenly she felt a warm arm around her shoulders and glanced up at the smiling woman on her right.

78

'It's terribly exciting, isn't it? Sort of like the theatre before the curtain comes up.'

Alix nodded, unsure what a theatre was but hoping that this kind lady might explain it to her. 'In a minute, lots of beautiful girls are going to come out wearing pretty dresses, and your mama and I will choose the ones we like and then have them made for us.'

Alix frowned thoughtfully, her tears forgotten. 'But why can't you just go shopping?'

The woman laughed. 'This is shopping. A special shopping. If we don't like a collar, or we want a dress in a different colour, then we can have it. Whatever we want.'

'Why doesn't everybody come here then?'

'If they did, it wouldn't be special any more, would it?'

'Sort of like a birthday?' Alix said, wrinkling her forehead as she struggled to understand. 'It's your special day. No one else shares it with you or it wouldn't be yours, would it?'

The woman laughed again. 'Something like that.'

The lights suddenly lowered and the woman kissed the top of Alix's head, then turned to the slender young boy standing awkwardly by the wall of the atelier. 'You don't need to stay if you don't want to, Matt. Why don't you meet me back here in forty-five minutes? I should be almost through by then.'

The boy nodded in relief and disappeared. Caroline Logan picked up her handbag and extracted a leather-bound notebook which she opened and balanced on her knee. On Alix's left, her mother did the same. As a soft swirl of Vivaldi filled the darkened salon, Alix gazed enchanted at the rose-silk catwalk. A tall, dark-haired English girl announced the first outfit, and she heard the muted scribble of pencil on paper as the women around her started to jot down their notes.

From the moment the first model emerged on to the catwalk, Alix was transfixed. She watched the girls twirl gracefully under the lights, their skirts and dresses swishing against their long legs as they moved along, slipping off jackets, displaying the clothes in all their glory. She stared, unable to believe that such beauty, such magic, could really exist. When the lights came up half an hour later, she was still gazing at the empty catwalk.

The woman on her right smiled as she shut her notebook. 'Well, *cara*, which did you like the best, or don't you have a favourite?'

Alix turned to her, considering. 'They were all beautiful. But I liked the green one most.'

The woman returned her serious gaze. 'And why was that?'

'Because it was beautiful, but the lady was beautifuller,' Alix said, smiling shyly. 'The dress made her look so pretty. I forget all the other ladies. Their dresses were too nice.'

The woman stared at her for a long moment, then flipped open her notebook and scribbled something down before bending and giving Alix another kiss. 'Yes, *cara*. I know exactly what you mean.'

'That daughter of yours has an impeccable eye,' Caroline told Joanna as the two women sat sipping espresso in the main salon, waiting for the fitter to come over to them. 'She was absolutely right, they were all exquisite, but the green one – number seventeen – didn't distract attention from the model in the same way. How extraordinary that she should be able to see that at her age. I guess she must take after her mother.'

Joanna smiled noncommittally. 'Perhaps.'

'More than my son does, I'm sorry to say.' Caroline gazed tolerantly as Matt re-entered the atelier and stood uncomfortably by the door. 'He's here under protest – we're on our way to meet my husband in Sicily for the summer, and part of the bargain was a brief stop in Rome along the way. I'm afraid Christopher – my husband – doesn't really approve of my wardrobe. But then I don't approve of his, of course. He's worn the same Barbour for fifteen years, it's practically falling apart on his back.' She laughed. 'And judging from the bored expression on his face, I rather think my son takes after him.'

Joanna followed Caroline's glance and couldn't help her sudden intake of breath. The boy was young, very young, no more than fifteen or sixteen, but she could almost feel the waves of latent sexual promise emanating from him. Startled by the force of her reaction, she studied him carefully. Soft, rich-brown hair flopped untidily across his forehead and his eyes glowed a brilliant green above strong cheekbones; the planes of his face were already firm and challenging despite his youth. His body was strangely graceful, his long legs encased in faded Levi's which emphasised his firm thighs and slim hips, his shoulders already broadening beneath his simple white T-shirt. Then she knew what it was that had caught her attention. The boy reminded her of Roberto. They both had the same animal grace, the same sexual magnetism. Only this boy hadn't yet learned how to use it. For a brief moment, she felt a pang of envy at the thought of the unknown woman who would one day awaken it.

She was distracted as Janet hurried over to them, her expression one of apology. Joanna wondered irrelevantly how old the woman was. Her skin was smooth and unlined, but the hair scraped into a tight chignon at the nape of her neck was steel-grey. Joanna guessed she was in her fifties, but she could have been a decade either way.

'Signora Cerreni, Signora Logan, I'm so sorry to have kept you waiting.'

Alix watched with astonishment as her mother changed out of her pale blue silk suit and stood naked but for her slip. She was three and a half, and she had never seen her mother undressed until this moment. Without her beautiful clothes and pretty jewellery, her mother suddenly seemed almost ordinary. Alix had never realised before that underneath the exquisite dresses which she was never allowed to touch, there was a real woman no different from her nannies.

She frowned, puzzled. She'd always believed that her mother was somehow different from everybody else. But if Mama was real, just like everybody else, it must be her that was different.

Maybe that was why her mother didn't love her.

Nine

Rio de Janeiro, Brazil
Saturday 27 July 1974
6.00 p.m.

Elizabetta hugged the wall behind the greengrocer's, trying to make herself invisible against the bricks as she waited for him to go back inside. Her camouflage was better than she could have hoped: her grubby face and filthy dress were almost exactly the same shade of grey as the wall itself. Only her large, turquoise-blue eyes betrayed her.

The greengrocer heaved a wooden crate of oranges into his arms and staggered back inside the shop. Elizabetta counted three to give him time to reach his back room and darted from the shadows, scooping half a dozen apples into the torn skirt of her dress and disappearing down the street before the greengrocer had seen her. She kept on running, taking random turns along the interconnecting maze of alleyways until she was certain she was safe. She had no illusions about what would happen to her if they ever caught her. In this city, they didn't just punish street children they found thieving.

They exterminated them.

Elizabetta sat down on a low stone wall near a huge heap of refuse and excrement, knowing from past experience that it was the most effective deterrent against unwanted attention.

She picked up one of the apples and sank her teeth gratefully into it, so hungry that she had to remind herself to chew before swallowing. Sometimes she was so ravenous that she didn't care, and ended up paying for it with knifing stomach pains six hours later.

She ate round the apple with quick, eager bites, leaving nothing, not even the pips and core. It was the first thing she'd had to eat since the half-chewed hot-dog she'd found yesterday in a waste-paper bin on the Avenida Rio Branco. She glanced at the five remaining apples in her lap, weighing her current hunger against the length of time she knew might elapse before her next meal. The logistics of carrying the apples around the city finally decided her. She would need to keep back two each for the boys; the fifth she would eat now.

When she and her two brothers had first been forced on to the streets, they'd tried to stay together all the time, but it had proved impossible. They simply attracted too much attention; tourists were wary of clusters of street children who frequently used the youngest, most appealing member to distract them while the older ones picked their pockets, and would give nothing when they begged; and there was no way the three of them could sneak a few apples from the stalls without being noticed. Instead, they'd worked out a system, separating during the day and meeting up by the subway air vents at nightfall. So far, in the six months they'd been on the streets, this system had worked.

Elizabetta finished her second apple and crammed the others into her pockets. She felt a brief flicker of irritation at the near-certainty that neither of the boys would have anything to show for their day's scavenging. Gabriel could perhaps be excused; he was still not yet six. But Miguel was nine, a year older than she was. He should be able to help look after them, but somehow he'd never truly recovered from their mother's death. He remained locked in his own world, silent, numb, completely cut off from what was happening around him. Elizabetta didn't even know if he understood who she was.

She sighed as she emerged on to the Avenido Rio Branco and glanced warily around to make sure there were no police anywhere nearby. It had been more than three years since their mother's death, but to Elizabetta it was still vivid.

She didn't know what had happened to the baby. Her sister, Carmel, had done her best to keep the rest of the family together, even though she'd only been eleven years old herself. She'd taken over her mother's regular customers and managed to earn enough to feed, if not clothe, the four of them. Slowly Carmel had built up her own clientele, composed mainly of Western men in their sixties who appreciated her youth and beauty, unmarred by childbearing, and had talked themselves into believing that at her tender age she was more likely to be free of disease. Carmel had followed her mother's example religiously: she always appeared grateful, and had found herself pregnant before she'd even had her first period.

The prospective father had been a childless Brazilian widower of sixty-seven, delighted by this unexpected proof of his virility and determined to make the most of his final flirtation with youth. He'd been in the unusual position of knowing for certain that Carmel's child was his, having reserved her exclusive services for an entire month after the satisfaction he'd gained from her on their first encounter. In a romantic blush of excitement, he'd married the twelve-year-old mother-to-be, his foresight doubly rewarded when, one week later, Carmel gave birth to two healthy boys. He'd been feverishly delighted with his new family, taking advantage of every opportunity to display his sons to anyone who cared to see them.

With his bride's existing family, he'd been less pleased.

When the twins were six weeks old, Carmel had taken Elizabetta to one side and tearfully told her that her new husband insisted that she and the boys leave. Pressing the last of her earnings into Elizabetta's hand, she'd exhorted her to take good care of the boys and do her best to keep them all together. The sisters had parted knowing they would almost certainly never see each other again. Few children survived on the streets for very long.

Rio de Janeiro was a city without rules, without morals. Anything was permitted if you had the money to finance it. And for those who didn't, the city did not care.

Elizabetta emerged into a wide square, scanning it carefully. At this time of day there would probably be no police; the street children were too wary and too fast, there were too many exits from the square to cover. At night, it was a different story. The portals of the church on the far side offered a degree of shelter; the air vent from the subway provided warmth and with it some illusion of home. It was a favourite place for the street children to bed down, and the police raided it frequently, taking advantage of the cover of darkness and the children's confusion. They slept in groups of ten or more, curled around each other, and took it in turns to keep watch, but it was hard not to fall asleep, lulled by the warmth and the reassuring rumble of the trains beneath them. The police only ever killed one or two, quietly, from the outside of the group. The first the others knew about it was when they awoke the next morning.

Elizabetta ran across the square and perched on the raised platform of the air vent, pulling her knees up to her chest and curling her skinny arms around them. They all knew the risks they took on the streets. At night, in the darkness, they whispered the terrible stories they had heard to one another, as if constant repetition would make the danger seem less real.

'Ellie, you're here already. We didn't expect you for ages.'

Elizabetta turned and smiled at her younger brother. 'I was lucky.' She reached inside her pockets and pulled out two of the apples. 'I kept these for you. Eat them slowly, you don't want to end up ill.'

Gabriel took the apples and handed one to Miguel, pushing it into his hands. Elizabetta felt her heart twist inside her as her elder brother stared at the apple as if unsure what to do with it. Gabriel took a large bite and stared at his brother. 'Go on, eat it.' He lifted Miguel's hand towards his mouth. 'Eat it, Miguel.'

Slowly, Miguel focused on the apple and bent his nose to it, sniffing its skin as if he were a dog. His eyes moved to meet his sister's, then returned to the fruit. Elizabetta turned away, unable to bear it any longer. She watched a blonde woman tourist walking slowly across the square, deliberately letting her mind drift so that she didn't have to think about Miguel. Deep inside her, she knew it was already too late for him. It was only the fierce desire for life that kept you going, day after day. Miguel had given up long ago.

It was several moments before she realised that the blonde woman was heading towards them. Elizabetta tensed, gripping Gabriel by the shoulder, poised to run.

The woman recognised her fear and stopped walking. When she spoke, she used Portuguese rather than English. 'Please, don't be afraid. I only want to talk to you.'

Elizabetta didn't move. The woman reached inside her bag and pulled out several cruzado notes. 'I thought we could buy some food first. Then talk. Maybe some bread, cheese? Whatever you want.'

'Why?'

'Because I don't like talking on an empty stomach, even if you do.' The woman smiled. 'My name is Lucy. Please, I don't mean you any harm.'

Gabriel looked up at Elizabetta, his eyes filled with longing. 'She said she wanted to buy us food. She seems nice.'

Elizabetta was torn. Instinctively she trusted this woman, but she was wary of drawing attention to themselves. The secret of staying alive on the streets was not to be noticed, to become part of the shadows. She glanced around the square, wondering if anyone had seen the exchange. With relief, she saw Raoul, the leader of their group, slipping quietly into the square, several of the other boys following him. Raoul could decide. He was twelve and a half, and had been on the streets for more than four years. She turned to the woman and nodded in his direction.

'Ask Raoul. He's in charge.'

The woman waited until Raoul had reached them and held out the notes again. 'Your friend here seems to think you'll know what food we should buy. Perhaps you'd like to take this and choose?'

Elizabetta stiffened at the implied intimacy the woman had suggested and glanced at Raoul. 'She wants to talk. She said she'd buy us some food if we talk to her.'

'Who are you?' Raoul asked, his dark eyes wary.

'I work with my brother, David, for a charity called *Children First*. A couple of years ago, we opened a shelter here in Rio for street children like you, but sometimes to know how we can help you best, we need to talk to you.' The woman sat down on the edge of the air-vent platform. 'I just wanted to chat to you and your friends for a little while.'

'What about?'

The woman shrugged, understanding his suspicion without resenting it. 'About how life is for you. How you eat, how you sleep. What happens at night. I don't want to interfere, and I won't tell any policemen anything you say. We just want to know how to help.'

'That's all?'

'That's all.'

Raoul stared at her for a long moment, trying to make up his mind. Suddenly he grabbed the notes from her hand and nodded at two of his friends. They disappeared across the square and the woman made herself comfortable on the air vent next to Elizabetta and the two boys. Around them, the other children in Raoul's group were gathering for the evening, their expressions curious.

The woman turned to them. 'Who's the oldest of you here?'

'Raoul,' one of the girls said. 'He's nearly thirteen. He wants to get a job soon, but no one will give him one.'

'I'm the youngest,' Gabriel interrupted proudly. 'I'm five and three-quarters. My birthday's on October the twenty-first.'

The woman smiled. 'I'll try to remember that.'

Raoul appeared at their elbows clutching three loaves of bread and a paper bag filled with slices of ham. The two other boys carried cans of Coke and hunks of cheese. With military precision, Raoul organised sandwiches for the twelve children who made up their group, ensuring that everyone had an equal share, even the youngest. When he'd finished, he collected the leftover food and ran across the square towards the church.

'Where's he going?' the woman asked, surprised.

'He'll give it to the children over there,' Elizabetta answered. 'We don't need any more. They're hungry too.'

The woman watched as Raoul distributed the food amongst the children on the other side of the plaza. These children had nothing, and yet what little they were given, they shared automatically. She found the gesture humbling.

Raoul returned and took up his place in the centre of the group. 'Right. You can ask your questions. But no names.'

'No names for you,' she agreed. 'OK. But please, call me

Lucy. Why don't we start by you telling me how long you've been on the streets?'

Immediately she received a dozen answers from all directions. Laughing, she held up her hand. 'How about you tell me, Raoul? If someone wants to add something, perhaps they should tell you first.'

Raoul nodded, glancing round at his team. 'I've been here the longest, four years. Claudio, over there, only came last week. His mother died and there was no one to look after him. The others in between.'

'How do you eat?'

Raoul shrugged. 'We find food. Or we steal. We don't want to, but it's better than starving to death. Sometimes people give us money, but not often. They're too scared.' He smiled bitterly. 'They believe what they say about us in the papers. That it's our fault we're on the streets, that we're just thieves and prostitutes, vermin. They think we damage their tourist industry.'

A few of the children laughed derisively. Lucy glanced around at the tired, grubby faces, shocked by the cynicism in their young eyes. 'You said earlier that some of you have died. Can you tell me how?'

There was a moment of silence, then a sudden clamour of voices.

'Pedro, he was ten. The security guards caught him begging for food in the supermarket. They took him and sprayed him with cold water from the hose. Then they shut him into a deep freeze –'

'One of my friends was sleeping here, on this air vent. It was his turn to be on the outside of the group. When we woke up, we found his throat had been slit, so deep his head was almost sliced off. He was twelve –'

'The police raped Maria right by the church. We saw them do it, but there were four of them, we couldn't stop them. She was only nine. Then they shoved a broken beer-bottle up inside her, again and again. She bled to death right there in the street –'

'Xavier was shot, right through his eye, you could see the other one looking at you –'

'She was only seven but they still did it to her –'

The stories came one after the other, the children chipping in with tales of horror they had witnessed, their voices relentless.

Lucy stared around at them. 'Can't you tell the police? Won't they help you?'

The children laughed scornfully. 'It's the police who do it.'

'The police? But that's murder –'

'They don't think of it as murder,' Elizabetta said suddenly. 'They think of us as rats that they have to exterminate to clean the streets. The shopkeepers don't want street children sleeping in their doorways at night, or scaring away the tourists. So they pay the police to get rid of us.'

'Are all the police like that?'

Raoul smiled bitterly. 'Oh, not all. Some would rather make us work for them. They get us to steal things – watches, cameras. We have to give what we take to them. If it isn't enough –' he shrugged eloquently – 'they shoot us.'

One of the children tugged his shirt suddenly. 'Raoul …'

He turned and stood up, scanning the square. 'We have to go. It's too dangerous to talk any longer.'

'I'll be back,' Lucy promised quickly as the children started to melt back into the shadows. 'We do want to help, you know.'

Raoul smiled, this time without rancour. 'I know. But you can't do anything. There are too many of us.' He shook his head. 'Too many of us for anyone to help.'

Elizabetta woke stiffly and lay where she was, unwilling to

move and disturb the children sleeping on either side of her. It was her turn to be at the centre of the group, the warmest position, and the safest. She stared upwards at the church front, watching the dawn pink the grey stones. Vaguely she remembered her mother's reverence for Father Lucio, the crosses, the incense, the chanting. The priests had talked a great deal about sin, and evil, and wickedness. As far as she could see, they hadn't done much about it. They seemed to think stopping a baby was the worst thing a person could do. Why did they let people have so many babies and then do nothing to help the children when they were born? Didn't they matter once they'd safely been baptised for Jesus? It was too many babies that had killed her mother. Carmel said she'd had twelve children in eleven years. She'd only been twenty-five when she'd died having the last one.

The boy next to Elizabetta mumbled in his sleep and turned round. As if on cue, the whole group moved into more comfortable positions, wriggling around each other like a litter of newborn kittens. The warm air from the vent eddied around them as a train passed through the tunnel below, sending up a dry, gritty smell. Elizabetta sat up, careful not to disturb the others. It must be nearly six o'clock; she wouldn't get back to sleep again now.

Her stomach rumbled, and she remembered the two apples still in her pockets. After the woman – Lucy – had given them the bread and cheese, she'd forgotten about the fruit. Perhaps she could share them with the boys for breakfast. Stepping carefully, she worked her way over the sleeping bodies to the edge of the air vent. Behind her, the others moved to fill the gap she had left.

On the edge of the group, to her left, she saw Miguel, a rare smile on his pinched face as he lay sleeping, his eyes tightly shut. She moved round the others towards him and stood looking down, reluctant to wake him. He seemed so peaceful.

She sighed. If only he could be like that when he was awake. She reached out to touch his bare shoulder.

His skin was like ice.

Elizabetta touched his cheek. It was cold, colder than anything she had ever felt before. Suddenly she realised how still he was. She backed away, her fist in her mouth.

'Gabriel. Gabriel!'

Tears blurring her vision, she scanned the group of sleeping children, trying to locate her younger brother. On the far side, she recognised his small, dark head and the filthy jumper that had once been blue. Her sobs coming faster as her panic grew, she ran towards him, grabbed his shoulder, turned him towards her.

His eyes stared glassily up at her, his mouth a perfect 'O' of surprise. Beneath his chin was a wide red smile of blood.

One of the other children stirred and sat up. Automatically his eyes followed Elizabetta's anguished gaze, and he screamed as he saw Gabriel. His terrified cry woke the others and they leaped to their feet, scattering away from the air vent as if it had suddenly become alive.

Four of the sleeping bodies did not move.

Raoul quickly examined each of them, then returned to Elizabetta, his expression grim. 'Four of us. They took four of us in one night.' He shook his head. 'I should never have let that woman talk to us. Never. It attracted too much attention. I should have known.'

Elizabetta clung to him. 'Why did they have to kill them both? Miguel didn't want to live.' Her sobs grew harder. 'But Gabriel – little Gabriel – why him as well? Why did they have to die?'

She reached out towards the bodies, but Raoul pulled her back. Her body twisting with sobs, she allowed him to lead her away, the shock deadening the anger she knew would come later. For the rest of her life, she would remember the moment she woke to find her brothers, murdered, beside her.

It was only later she realised it was her eighth birthday.

Ten

Hotel d'Inghilterra, Rome, Italy
Friday 30 August 1974
4.15 p.m.

Matt raised his hand to knock on the door, then let it fall again.
He glanced up and down the corridor. No one had seen him.
He could just walk away now and no one would ever know.
He started to turn away, then stopped, irresolute. She would
know. She'd think he was a coward, a kid, too afraid to go
through with what he'd started. After all, he'd been the one
who'd called her. No one had forced him to pick up the phone.

Quickly he rapped on the door, a hard, determined sound
that gave him no choice but to stay, or risk her seeing his back
as he fled.

The door opened. Matt instantly dropped his gaze and
studied his feet as if discovering them for the first time. The
brief surge of courage that had brought him this far suddenly
deserted him, and it took every ounce of his willpower not to
back away and race down the hall.

Joanna studied the top of his head and smiled. 'Hello,
Matt.'

'Um. Hi.'

She opened the door a little wider and stood to one side.
'I'm so glad you decided to call. Why don't you come in?'

Matt sidled past her and shot straight over towards the

window, staring down into Via Bocca di Leone as if completely absorbed by the flow of sophisticated women into and out of Valentino's salon below. He still couldn't quite believe he was here. If his best friend, Luke, hadn't talked him into it, he probably wouldn't be. Even with Luke's encouragement, it had taken him four weeks of wet dreams and unbearable sexual excitement in Sicily to summon the courage to call the telephone number she had discreetly slipped into his pocket as he had left Pavesi's with his mother. He had spent the whole holiday unable to look at the long brown limbs and damp swimsuits of the nubile young girls around him without getting an erection. But it had been Joanna who had filled his fantasies. Now that he was actually here, he had no idea what he was supposed to do next.

Joanna watched his evident indecision with amusement. He was even more attractive than she'd remembered. The weeks in Sicily had given his skin a golden tan, and he seemed to have taken another step closer to manhood even in the short time since she'd seen him. She felt a surge of moisture between her legs just looking at him and had to remind herself to take it slowly. She had to draw him out, let him discover how much he wanted her for himself. She had the feeling he'd be a very fast learner.

She moved towards him and touched his bare arm lightly. He jumped as if she'd burned him and swung round to face her.

'Matt, would you like a drink?'

Matt looked uncertain. 'I don't really drink that much –'

She laughed. 'I don't know about you, but I'm pretty thirsty. It's been a hot day. Coke, soda water, orange juice?'

Matt looked sheepish. 'Yeah, that'd be good. Coke, please.'

Deliberately casual, Joanna kicked off her high cream pumps and walked on stockinged feet towards the minibar.

She tossed him a can of Coke. 'You can sit down, if you like. Sorry there are no chairs – this hotel doesn't really seem to go in for them. It's the bed or the floor, I'm afraid.'

Matt glanced around the room as if verifying her statement, then perched reluctantly on the edge of the bed, sipping his Coke and studying the room with the intensity of an interior decorator summoned to pass judgement on it. Joanna watched as his eyes flickered from the window across the heavy wood panelling, lingering briefly on a mediocre but original watercolour of St Peter's Square, then around the rest of the room until his gaze finally came to rest on the cream and crimson rug beneath his feet.

'Oh, dear, am I that terrifying?'

For the first time, Matt looked directly towards her. 'I'm sorry?'

Joanna laughed and took another casual sip of her mineral water. 'You look like you've just been called into the headmaster's study.'

Matt grinned suddenly. 'Yeah, well, if you'd ever been summoned by him, you'd be terrified.'

They both laughed and Matt felt some of the tension drain away from him. She really was very pretty, and much younger than he'd remembered her. Last time he'd seen her, at that designer's, she'd been all dressed up in some expensive blue silk suit, her hair on top of her head, her make-up and jewellery perfect. She'd looked just like one of the models in the magazines his mother read, beautiful and unapproachable and utterly unreal. If he hadn't had her card to prove that she wasn't just another mannequin, he'd hardly have believed she was even human. Now, she looked more like one of his friends' older sisters. She was wearing a sleeveless white cotton dress that buttoned down the front, her waist-length ash-blonde hair tumbling loosely around her shoulders, framing her face and making him want to reach out and touch it. She wore no jewellery or make-up, her expression relaxed as she smiled at him. Suddenly he wanted to be close to her. She seemed so fresh and pretty. A tremor passed through him and he looked away, concentrating furiously on his drink.

Joanna saw the expression in his eyes and felt a sudden surge of pleasure. It had been so long since any man had looked at her like that. Her relationship with Roberto had deteriorated to a series of dutiful, perfunctory embraces that held little affection and even less desire. It had been over a year since he had even touched her. Suddenly it felt good to be wanted again. She was still only twenty-six: she needed to feel beautiful. This would be the first time she had ever betrayed her husband; she had been faithful to him for seven long years as she had watched her marriage slowly wither and die. She knew Roberto no longer loved her – if indeed he ever had – just as she knew she would never be able to stop loving him. But at least she could banish the loneliness for a few brief hours in the arms of a man who did want her.

'I'm so glad you called me,' Joanna said softly. 'When I didn't hear from you last month, I thought perhaps I'd been wrong about you. Then when you rang yesterday –'

Matt looked up, startled. 'Wrong about me?'

'You seemed to be – ready. I could see it, in your eyes.' She shrugged easily. 'And then you didn't call. I guessed you must have been too young, after all.'

'I did call,' Matt said, stung. 'As soon as I could. We had to go to Sicily the day after that show, so I couldn't call before. We only got back to Rome yesterday – we wouldn't have come back here at all, but my mother wanted to collect some clothes from that designer's where we met you. She's there now. She thinks I'm at the Vatican, doing Michelangelo and all that.' He grinned boyishly. 'I bought the guidebook on the way here, just in case she asks me about it.'

'You could always go and see the real thing. You don't have to stay here.'

Matt shook his head, blushing. 'No. I want to be here.'

Joanna smiled and put down her drink. She crossed the room and sat down next to him on the bed, lifting his Coke out of his hands and setting it down on the floor.

'How old are you, Matt?'

'Sixteen. Well, almost. In November.'

He could smell the heady scent of her perfume as she turned her head towards him and stared directly into his eyes.

'Have you ever made love to a woman before, Matt?'

Matt's voice was low. 'No.'

'Do you want to?'

Matt was unable to meet her eyes. He nodded.

'With me?'

'Yes.'

Suddenly, Joanna reached up and undid the top few buttons of her cotton dress, revealing firm, high breasts, the nipples a soft, dusky pink. Matt felt a tug in his groin as his cock hardened, and couldn't suppress a low moan deep in the back of his throat. Joanna took his right hand in hers and placed it over her left breast, feeling the tremor that ran through him as he cupped its weight in his palm. His eyes flickered up to meet hers, then he reached for her other breast, cradling them both in his hands.

'Have you ever held a woman's breasts before?' Joanna murmured, her voice husky.

Matt shook his head.

'Kiss them, Matt,' Joanna instructed gently. 'Taste them, feel them.'

The ache in his groin grew stronger as he bent his head and took her right nipple in his mouth. Tentatively he sucked it and felt it harden in response to his touch. He ran his tongue experimentally over the surface of the stiff bud and heard her

99

sigh, her back arching so that her breast rose to meet him. Without pulling away, she took his left hand and brought it to her mouth, moistening his thumb and forefinger, then guided it back down to her free breast. Intuitively Matt rolled the hard pink tip between his dampened fingers, still sucking on her other breast.

Her hand reached out to stroke him and he tensed, her touch burning through the heavy material of his jeans and suddenly driving every other sensation from his mind. He groaned and moved against her as she gently unzipped him and his cock sprang free. He felt her take him in her hand and stroke his length, her fingers centring every thought and feeling in his body on the few pulsating inches of flesh. His hand tightened unconsciously on her breast as he surrendered to the unbelievable sensations she had aroused in him. He felt the heat building within him and knew he was going to come at any moment.

Abruptly she pulled away from him and stood up. He stared at her, his face flushed, wondering what he'd done wrong. Joanna gently stroked her fingers across her naked breasts, down her stomach, over her thighs before returning to caress her nipples.

'Take off your clothes, Matt.'

Matt stared at her uncomprehendingly.

'This isn't just for you,' Joanna said softly. 'I want to enjoy it too. I want to see you naked. Now, take off your clothes.'

He watched her stroking her breasts, making soft sounds of satisfaction and, suddenly annoyed by her apparent lack of need for him, he stood up and pulled his T-shirt over his head, shucking off his jeans and underpants and kicking off his trainers in one easy, fluid movement. He stood naked and unselfconscious in front of the window, waiting for her to come to him, his tanned body gleaming gold in the afternoon sunshine, his dark hair burnished to a rich coppery red by the mellow light. Meeting her eyes, he saw the same glitter of appreciation he had seen in the eyes of his friends' sisters, and knew Joanna wanted him as much as he wanted her.

'I want to see you come,' Joanna said softly. 'I want to watch you do it.'

Matt was suddenly confused again. 'You want me to do it? You mean by myself, with you watching?'

Joanna smiled and sat down on the bed. 'Now. With me watching.'

'I – I can't. Not just like that.'

'Why not?' She laughed. 'Don't tell me you've never done that before either?'

Matt coloured. 'Of course I have. It's just – not with anyone else watching. I can't see why you want me to. Can't we –'

Joanna shook her head and slowly started to undo the rest of her buttons. Matt felt his cock stiffen even harder as she revealed her taut stomach, the skin the colour of honey, then lower, the white triangle of flesh between her thighs, the blonde thatch of hair tufting its centre, just visible beneath the filmy gauze of her panties.

'The first time a man comes with a woman is always too quick, Matt. For her, at least. You'll learn to control that, with a little practice.' Joanna's smile was cool, amused. 'I want to watch you come just by watching me. Then I'll let you touch me. I'll teach you how to give me pleasure, the way I know you can. Once you've earned it.'

Matt felt a surge of anger. He had come here to meet her as an equal, not to act like a performing animal for her pleasure. He knew she was playing with him. But instead of cooling his desire, somehow his anger and indignation only increased it. She might be ten years older than he was, experienced, skilled in the game she was teaching him. But when he finally plunged his cock into her, he'd be the one who was in control, she would be the one who needed him. He would fuck the arrogance out of her.

He watched as she stood up and let her dress fall to the floor, leaving her naked but for her sheer cream silk stockings and panties. His eyes never left hers as she unclipped her suspender belt and slowly rolled her stockings down her legs. Instinctively his hand moved to his cock as she hooked her fingers in the sides of her panties and pulled them down, standing naked before him. His movements grew faster as she lay back down on the bed, propping herself against the pillows and parting her thighs so that he could see the moist shell-pink softness of her cunt. With one hand she cupped her own breast, her other moving down to stroke the hard pink bud. He couldn't tear his eyes away from her as he grasped his cock and pumped it, his frustration and anger intensifying his excitement to such a degree that he thought he would explode. He'd never experienced anything like this before.

And they hadn't even started yet.

With a groan of release, Matt came, the warm sticky dampness spurting across his fingers. He collapsed across the bed, suddenly unable to think or even breathe, his body overcome with the inertia of fulfilment. Joanna twisted sideways and bent her head, and Matt felt a jolt of surprise as she took his spent cock in her mouth. Too sated to question her, he lay back and let the warm feelings gently ripple through his body as she worked her tongue around him, probing, teasing, pulsing against him. To his amazement he felt his cock stiffen again almost immediately.

Joanna laughed. 'You really do learn fast.'

She continued to suck him gently until he was hard, the feelings stirring within him not as fierce as before, but somehow deeper, more intense. He reached out for her, but she slid away from him.

'I think it's your turn now,' she said.

Matt watched as she wriggled back against the pillows and opened her thighs to him. Slowly he moved towards her, curious and at the same time afraid. What would she taste like? What if he didn't like it? How on earth would he tell her?

Tentatively he reached out his hand, his fingers sliding easily down the cleft between her labia until they reached her opening. A flame of desire forged its way through the questions in his mind and he realised that he wanted her, wanted to taste her on his tongue, wanted to arouse the same sensations in her that she had in him. He bent his head and inhaled the musky sweetness, then tasted her on his lips as he moved his mouth over her. She groaned and guided his head upwards until his tongue found the stiff pink bud and teased it with swift, instinctive feather strokes.

'Gently, Matt, gently,' Joanna whispered. 'Just the tip of your tongue across the top … yes … yes … oh, yes, that's it, just like that.'

Matt raised his head, his glance travelling across the flat surface of her stomach until his eyes met hers, and he saw the need and desire for him written there. He reached upwards to caress her nipples and felt her shudder as his tongue and fingers worked in unison. He felt his cock harden in response and drove his tongue more fiercely against her.

Suddenly she grasped his shoulders and pulled him upwards towards her, kissing his lips and tasting her own juices on his mouth.

'Now, Matt. I want you inside me, now.'

Matt propped himself on his elbows and stared into her eyes. With sudden insight he knew that she'd been just as uncertain of his response as he himself had been of her. He knew little about the etiquette of sex, but enough to realise that the man was supposed to make all the running, leaving the woman free to abdicate responsibility for success or failure. In choosing him, Joanna had taken it all upon herself; if their encounter failed – if *he* failed – it would be down to her. She wouldn't have been human if she hadn't wanted some support. Suddenly he saw her not as the means of his satisfaction, but as a person in her own right, with fears and doubts of her own, and saw that of all the things she had taught him today, perhaps this was the most important.

With a sudden thrust, Matt plunged into her, feeling her warmth envelop him as he moved against her, the sudden clenching of her muscles as she drew his cock inside her.

Next time, he would be the one teaching her.

Eleven

West 34th Street, New York, USA
Thursday 5 September 1974
10.00 a.m.

Stephi Kay tucked the purple telephone between her shoulder
and her chin and searched through the mountain of glossy PR
folders on her desk. 'OK, Jojo, I've got the Saint Laurent
invitation here in front of me. It definitely says two places,
sweetheart, not three. Yes, I'm absolutely certain.' Her
fingers drummed an impatient tattoo on the desk. 'OK,
darling, I'll wait.'

The telephone still jammed beneath her chin, Stephi caught
her shoulder-length hair in her hands and twisted it on top of
her head, spearing it into place with a pencil. She glanced up
as Ceci placed the coffee in front of her, careful not to mark
any of the folders ranged across the desk. 'Oh, thank God,
Ceci, I've been dying for that all morning. I just wish you
could pump it into me intravenously. It would save so much
time.'

'Just add it to the coke, darling. I'm sure it'll make a novel
mix.'

Stephi turned her attention back to the PR girl on the other
end of the telephone. 'Jojo. Yes, I thought there had been a
little mistake somewhere along the line. Three would be

perfect, darling, I definitely owe you one. Give my love to Yves, I'm sure the collection will be an absolute sensation. You too, sweetheart.'

She slammed down the telephone and threw the Saint Laurent folder across her desk, just missing her coffee. 'Idiots. *Elan* has had three places at Yves' collections since his first show for Dior in 1958. Why on earth should I have requested two this season? No one ever asks for *less* than they've been given, for heaven's sake.'

Ceci scanned the array of messages propped between the rows of her typewriter keys so that she couldn't miss them. 'Jojo's probably trying to keep back a few spare seats. Maybe she wants to have a couple of favours in hand.'

'Well, she should bloody well know by now that keeping me happy is the biggest favour she can do herself,' Stephi said. 'As if I haven't got enough to do without fixing the damn seating plan for every collection we're covering this season.'

Ceci ducked her head to hide her smile. She knew Stephi wouldn't have it any other way.

At twenty-six, Stephi Kay was fast becoming one of the most respected and influential journalists in the fashion industry, renowned for her ability to be not just abreast but one step ahead of every trend and rumour that swept through a business that thrived on them. She managed this by knowing the right people, being at the right places at the right time, and most of all, by maintaining an iron grip on every part of her empire within *Elan* magazine. As fashion editor, there was nothing Stephi did not oversee and control, from the layout of the pages to the colour of the paper clips used in the typing pool. She arrived at the office before the cleaners and left it long after the overnight editor had gone home. If she had a private life, no one had ever been able to discover when she led it. Her reputation was built on scathing but accurate critiques of the collections she viewed; unlike most of those

106

who worked in the fashion industry, Stephi was not afraid to say the Emperor was wearing no clothes if she could see his cock metaphorically staring her in the face.

Ceci leafed through Stephi's diary, amending appointments where necessary and making a brief note of the rare few Stephi had to keep, and those – the majority – which could safely go by the board. 'Tom Devlin called twice this morning; he wants to talk to you about the Quant layout for the December issue. He asked me to get you to ring him back after eleven. I don't think he's very happy with what Sash has been doing.'

'I'm not very happy with Sash Gessner myself.' Stephi drained her coffee and scrunched the plastic cup in her hand. 'I spend more time correcting his copy than I would if I wrote it myself. I'm supposed to be the bloody fashion editor of this limp rag of a magazine, not some two-bit copywriter. What I need is a decent writer who knows the difference between toile and terrycloth, not some miserable runt of a failed designer who wants to play *Vogue*.'

Ceci sighed sympathetically. Sash Gessner was an unlikeable, untrustworthy, talentless fashion school dropout blessed with acne, halitosis and a paedophiliac fondness for young boys. His only redeeming feature was the fact that his father owned 51 per cent of Gessner/Devlin Publications, part of which included the *Elan* Magazine Group. Stephi, and the President of EMG itself, Tom Devlin, were stuck with Sash until he either grew bored or Tom could afford to buy out Gessner Senior, neither of which looked likely to happen in the near future.

Stephi scanned the dummy pages for the next issue of the magazine, which would not be on the news-stands until mid-December. Despite the fact that publication was still more than three months away, most of its pages were already committed, the advertisements long since sold and all but two of the features shot.

Abruptly Stephi slapped the dummies with the flat of her hand. 'I can't go with this. He's talking about Quant as if she's the latest bright young thing to have appeared on the scene. This is 1974, for God's sake. He's got to go. I don't care if Daddy has a pink fit and closes the whole bloody magazine down, I'm not printing this.'

'If you spike Sash's piece, what on earth are we going to replace it with?' Ceci asked reasonably. 'We're not exactly swamped with brilliant young writers just waiting to set the pages alight with new ideas.'

Stephi groaned. 'Shit, I know. Oh God, thirty-six hours before deadline and I've got eight empty pages with $12,000 worth of advertising riding on them, and no writers, let alone a story. I don't deserve this, even if you include all the excesses of my previous lives.'

'Think about it, Stephi. If you dump Sash, and even supposing we don't get thrown out on to the street, who will you bring in instead?' Ceci argued. 'It'll have to be someone bloody good to justify firing Gessner Junior to his daddy.'

'I'll cross that bridge when I come to it.' Stephi slung the offending dummies into the bin. Spiking her unconventional chignon with another pencil, she eyed a thin, blonde girl in flowered bell-bottoms who was skittering nervously towards her. 'Yes? What do you want?'

'Can we talk about Paris?' the girl asked desperately. 'I need to know when to book a flight for the Valentino, and what about Givenchy?'

'What about Givenchy?' Stephi said.

'Well, we want to be there, of course, but Pavesi's showing the next day, in Rome, so –'

'Oh, for God's sake,' Stephi groaned. The telephone on her desk jangled, and before Ceci could intercept the call, Stephi had snatched up the receiver. 'Tom, yes, yes, Sash Gessner, I know. We need to talk about him. Look, hang on a moment –' she turned to the girl still standing by her desk – 'Do I look like a flight guide? Go and work it out and come back to me when you've mastered the twenty-four-hour clock. OK, Tom – look, I'm going to have to get back to you. I'm supposed to be on a six o'clock flight to Rome, and I'm never going to make it at this rate. I'll come to your office and brief you before I go.'

She replaced the receiver and stared at the dummy magazine pages in front of her. 'Oh, God, Ceci. Eight bloody pages. Roberto Cerreni had better give me an interview this time, that's all I can say.'

Twelve

Via Appia Antica, Rome, Italy
Friday 6 September 1974
8.15 p.m.

In his private study, Roberto Cerreni sat motionless in his armchair in front of the fireplace, his gaze on Stephi as she bent her head studiously over her notebook and scanned his replies to see if there was anything else she wanted to ask. He was well used to giving interviews – as number two at the Italian Foreign Ministry, he frequently found himself explaining the rapid changes of his government's foreign policies to a confused international press corps. But he had never granted such a personal interview as this, and he found it disconcerting. He realised he had grown used to hiding behind the protective façade of his job. Since his return to Rome, his work had become the centre of his life. He had willingly assumed more responsibility as his reputation in the government had grown, driven as much by his desire to escape the oppressive atmosphere of his home as by his fierce ambition. These days he spent three-quarters of his life abroad, promoting Italian industry and foreign policy as he discreetly built up the contacts he knew he would need when he finally made a bid for the Italian Premiership itself.

His one regret was that while his work abroad gave him freedom from Joanna, it also took him away from his four-year-old daughter for weeks at a time. If his career was the focus of his life, Alix was its essence. All the love he was unable to give his wife he now lavished on his little girl. Over the years, he had disciplined himself to believe that she was enough to fill the emptiness at the heart of his marriage. He hadn't been lying to Joanna when he had told her that he hadn't looked at another woman since they had met. He'd been faithful to his wife ever since they'd been married, less because he'd been determined to keep his vows than because he hadn't met any woman who'd particularly captured his interest. He was no longer sure if his fidelity was reciprocated, nor did he really care. If Joanna had been able to find some pleasure outside their sham of a marriage, he didn't begrudge it as long as she was discreet. He had been the one who'd failed her. If he had loved her more, perhaps their marriage might have stood a chance. Instead, they were both trapped in a *mésalliance* from which he could see no way out.

In the first year after their return to Italy from Rio, his unhappiness had been such that he had even contemplated divorce, but deep down he had always known that Joanna would never let him go. In any case his freedom would have cost him both his career and his daughter, the two things that mattered most to him.

But the girl now sitting in front of him was different. She demanded his attention simply by the fact of her existence.

He'd wanted her from the moment she'd walked confidently into the room, her mulberry velvet cape swirling about her ankles as she fired her first question at him before she'd even sat down. Something about her had stirred a feeling inside him which he'd thought buried for ever. It wasn't that she was beautiful; she was far too individual-looking ever to be called that. Everything about her proclaimed her defiance to the world, right down to her white, patent leather knee-high boots. She was tall, almost as tall as he was, and she moved with a

111

confident, loping awkwardness that reminded him of a colt not yet used to the length of its legs. She did not fit the current ideal of beauty in any sense, yet Roberto found her unfashionable curves and glowing American complexion far more alluring than the pale, flat-chested women currently in vogue. Stephi Kay was also indelibly American. Everything she wore, from the crocheted tam o'shanter perched crazily on top of her head to the myriad necklaces of pop beads in shades of green and pink, clashed wildly; yet, somehow, it worked. After Joanna's discreet elegance, Robert found Stephi's careless exuberance incredibly refreshing and exciting. She was no clinging, fragile flower pleading for reassurance and love.

'Signor Cerreni –'

He jumped as Stephi's voice broke into his thoughts. 'I'm sorry. You were saying …?'

'Signor Cerreni, does the name Gruppo Italia mean anything to you?'

Roberto frowned. 'No, I can't say that it does.'

'The Magnoli Group?'

'No, I'm sorry.'

Her expression was carefully neutral as she phrased her next question. 'What about Giulio Pavesi?'

Roberto felt a chill. He guessed her question was not born of idle curiosity. He leant back in his armchair and forced himself to sound relaxed. 'The designer? Of course. My wife spends half my salary at his couture house.'

'I understood you knew him yourself. Personally.'

'My wife has invited him to a number of our parties, but I'm afraid our connection is no closer than that,' Roberto said.

'The Magnoli Group owns a collection of factories in southern Italy which manufacture clothing, mainly for the House of Pavesi,' Stephi said briskly. 'They've produced Giulio Pavesi's ready-to-wear lines since he first started designing, and have just invested a great deal of money in a

112

new plant and machinery. Gruppo Italia are also a clothing manufacturer, but they're a great deal bigger than Magnoli. It's my understanding that Signor Pavesi is about to break his contract with Magnoli and switch to Gruppo Italia, who're presumably undercutting their costs sufficiently to make any penalty Pavesi has to pay worth while.'

Roberto sighed. 'All very interesting, but I really don't see how this concerns me. I work in the Foreign Office. This sort of business rivalry has nothing to do with me –'

'Forgive me, Signor Cerreni, but my sources tell me that you've had quite a bit to do with Signor Pavesi in the past.'

Roberto wondered how much she knew. Not enough, clearly, or she wouldn't be fishing like this. He watched her carefully, his eyes drawn to the nape of her neck as she bent her head over her notebook, and felt a sudden stab of arousal. He knew he was going to make love to her. The only question was when.

Almost as if she had read his mind, Stephi glanced up and met his eyes, and he read the unmistakable flicker of desire written in their depths. Neither of them said anything. They were too conscious of the electricity between them to risk breaking the spell with words. Without stopping to think, he was at her side, pulling her into his arms. No woman had ever stirred such a powerful reaction in him so quickly. As he kissed her he sensed the fire in her and was possessed by the overwhelming need to have her, to plunge unthinkingly into her. He kissed her again, harder still, his fingers already seeking her breasts.

Abruptly Stephi pulled back from him. Interpreting her withdrawal as fear of discovery, Roberto paused. 'Don't worry. This is my private study, the only room in this house I can really call my own. No one would dare to come in without knocking first.'

'What makes you think that's what I was thinking? Don't you have a party to go to this evening?'

Roberto shook his head. 'Tell me the truth.'

'OK.' Stephi paused. 'I just want to know: do you do this all the time?'

'I could ask you the same question. You're the journalist, after all. For all I know, this is just part of your research.'

Stephi laughed. 'I asked first.'

'Then you tell me. Do you care?'

Stephi tried to consider her honest response to his question. Did she really care? She was hardly a virgin herself: a true teenager of the Sixties, she'd done her fair share of experimenting, from impulsive one-night stands to the occasional threesome, none of which she'd regretted, although so far she'd always drawn the line at knowingly sleeping with a married man. But then at this moment she felt she'd never wanted a man as much as she wanted this one. For over an hour she'd sat demurely by the fire asking him questions about his political ambitions and family background, all the while burning with erotic images of what it would be like to have him inside her, his weight crushing her as he took her.

Suddenly she realised that she didn't care if Roberto Cerreni fucked a different woman every night of his life, as long as tonight he was fucking her.

'No,' she said, standing up and unbuttoning her clothes. 'I don't give a damn.'

Roberto moved towards her as she slid the top of her pants suit down to her waist, cupping her exposed breast in his hand and bending his head to take the hard, rosy nipple in his mouth, sucked insistently at her breast. He sank to his knees on the Persian carpet in front of the fire, and she moved with him, her fingers struggling to undo the belt of his trousers as he expertly unzipped her boots and slid her pants suit over her feet. Catching hold of her panties with the crook of his little fingers, he eased them down over her thighs, rocking back on his heels to stare at her nakedness as she knelt in front of him.

The dim light from the lamps flickered over her body, illuminating the voluptuous swell of her breasts and stomach, the soft hollow at the base of her throat, the tangle of hair between her thighs.

He crouched over her for a moment so that she saw his cock rising urgently from the dark nest of hair at the top of his legs. Reaching upwards as he threw off his shirt, she cupped his balls in her hand. Then she took him in her mouth, her teeth gently grazing his length as she moved her mouth up and down against him. His hands slipped down to cradle her soft, heavy breasts, his thumbs and forefingers rolling her taut nipples between them, in time with her skilled manipulation of his cock. She felt as if invisible silver threads were connecting her breasts directly to her cunt, every wave of pleasure from his fingers magnified a hundred times.

Roberto parted her legs and slid his fingers between the damp lips of her cunt, exploring her wetness before bending his head to her. She groaned as his tongue found her engorged clitoris.

'Oh, God, Roberto, if you do that I'm going to come.'

He flicked his tongue across her, once and then again, just enough to keep her on the edge of orgasm without allowing her to plunge over into the abyss. Half out of her mind with desire, Stephi reached for his cock and began to tease him, until the two of them ceased to exist but for the pulsing, throbbing centre of their bodies.

With a supreme effort of will, Roberto raised himself up and stared down at her, his cock poised between her thighs. 'Ready?'

'Jesus, yes, oh yes, now,' Stephi gasped. 'Please, Roberto, now, now, now!'

With a thrust Roberto was in her, and Stephi was overtaken with shudders of pleasure so intense they were almost indistinguishable from pain, obliterating everything except this exquisite, unendurable glory.

'I'm coming, I'm coming! Oh God, Roberto, oh God, oh God, oh God!'

Roberto felt her orgasm as it swept through her body, and gripping her breasts so hard his fingernails drew blood, he allowed his own orgasm to break free, groaning her name again and again as he spurted hotly into her. Suddenly exhausted, he slumped across her, burying his face in her neck and covering her with kisses as she held him dazedly against her.

'Oh Jesus, that was unbelievable,' Roberto breathed after a long moment.

Stephi smiled lazily. 'I know. And I know something else, too.'

'Mmm?'

'In a few moments, you're going to do it all over again.'

Roberto laughed. He licked her throat, tasting the saltiness of her sweat as she eased her hand along the damp surface of his stomach towards his spent cock.

Neither of them noticed Joanna standing frozen in the doorway.

Joanna backed away from Roberto's study, the image of her husband bent over the girl's pale body burned indelibly into her mind. She half ran, half fell towards the stairs, Roberto's newly-pressed tuxedo clutched forgotten in her hands. The pain was like a vice around her heart. She'd tortured herself a thousand times with images of his betrayal in her mind, but coming face to face with the reality was far worse than she could ever have imagined. She'd only turned to Matt because Roberto had left her with little choice. She'd never stopped loving her husband.

But he had never wanted her. He'd wanted that girl instead.

She sat down on the bed, remembering the way they'd slept

the night before – he on one side of the bed, his back towards her, she on the other, facing the wall, a great gulf of emptiness between them. With sudden clarity, she realised that she was closer to losing him now than she'd ever been. Whatever her suspicions and accusations in the past, she had no idea if he'd been unfaithful to her before. But this time it was undeniably real. There was a flesh-and-blood woman downstairs, a woman who might fight for Roberto every bit as hard as his wife. Somehow she had to stand back from her own pain and anger and humiliation and think what to do. She'd learned enough from watching her own mother handle her father's endless affairs to know that a showdown now was the worst thing she could orchestrate. Perhaps this girl was just a passing fancy, a brief liaison that meant nothing. If she could manage to ignore it, sooner or later he would tire of his mistress. He had to.

She had waited long enough for Roberto to love her. She could wait a little longer.

Her eyes fell on the photograph of Roberto and Alix propped up on her dresser and she stared at their laughing faces. It had all started to go wrong, she thought, about the time Alix was born. Nothing had been the same since then. She'd tried so hard to recapture his affection by being the perfect wife, dressing immaculately, exercising daily, hosting parties for a thousand people without a word of complaint. But she'd failed. Roberto had shown more affection for their daughter than he ever had for her. How could he love his daughter so much and yet find nothing left over for her mother? He gave his daughter everything. His own wife he gave nothing – not even his fidelity.

Slowly Joanna turned the picture over again and gazed at the child, her finger tracing the outline of her small face. She had always been indifferent to her daughter.

Now for the first time, she realised she actually hated her.

Thirteen
Piazza di Spagna, Rome, Italy
Monday 9 September 1974
4.45 p.m.

Stephi climbed out of the taxi and paid the driver, telling him to keep the change and ignoring his disgruntled expression as he glanced from the meter to the notes in his hand. Picking up her Louis Vuitton tote bag – one of her few concessions to the impeccably accessorised Italians – she headed across the cobbled piazza towards the Spanish Steps on the other side of the square. Already the worn stone stairs were crowded with Roman teenagers chatting and smoking as they glanced each new arrival up and down. Despite the Vuitton bag, Stephi suddenly felt brash and very American in her loose Biba pants suit and long, flowing mulberry velvet cape. Italian teenagers did not follow the latest fashion trends but opted for conservative, expensive classics; Stephi guessed most of them had never heard of Carnaby Street or Mary Quant, but every one possessed at least one pair of Gucci shoes and a Hermès scarf.

She shaded her gaze from the glare of the sinking afternoon sun and gazed out across the piazza. Directly opposite her, the House of Pavesi occupied an entire block of the most exclusive real estate in Rome, sandwiched between Via Condotti and Via Borgognona.

Swiftly, Stephi ran through everything she knew about

Giulio Pavesi. He had achieved an incredible degree of success since he'd founded the House of Pavesi with his lover, Edouard Chambrun. He'd literally appeared from nowhere; when he'd launched his first collection in 1965, it had taken the entire fashion industry by surprise. *Vogue* had hailed it as the most exciting show in decades; and where the prestigious magazine had led, the rest had followed. Pavesi had instantly been catapulted by the fashion press to the level of first-ranking Italian designers such as Valentino and Armani.

Stephi edged along the step to make way for two entwined teenagers and lit a cigarette as she peered across at the curtained windows of the designer's atelier. She was not so sure about Giulio Pavesi. In her opinion, his first collection had been promising, rather than brilliant; it had presaged great things to come and hinted at an exciting future. Yet somehow, since then, he hadn't managed to deliver.

For several seasons, Stephi had reserved judgement on him, waiting to see if his apparent lack of direction was simply the inexperience of a designer still not yet twenty-nine. But in the last couple of years his ideas had failed to develop and deteriorated into repetition. His collection in July, though commercially successful, had been unremarkable, and Stephi had dared to say so publicly in the revered and feared magazine *Elan*. She knew the piece would have come as one hell of a shock to the cosseted, pampered designer.

After her scathing attack, she'd fully expected relegation to a back seat at his next show, or perhaps even exclusion from it altogether; instead, she had been granted a rare interview with him, a privilege few had ever been granted. Roberto Cerreni's word must carry weight indeed.

She wondered for the hundredth time what the connection between Cerreni and Pavesi actually was. One of her sources had suggested that they'd been very close when Cerreni was Ambassador to Brazil, and given the way Italian politics worked, perhaps Cerreni was taking some sort of cut for putting work Pavesi's way. For the first time in her life, she hoped her sources had got it wrong. Suddenly it had become very important to her that Roberto wasn't involved in anything corrupt. If she had to choose between her principles as a journalist and the man she hadn't been able to get out of her mind since she met him, she wasn't sure she'd have the strength to do what was right.

Stephi crossed the piazza and entered the softly lit reception area – designed with Pavesi's sensitive forty-something clients in mind – and gave her name to the immaculate receptionist.

In his office Giulio Pavesi reread the offending article that Stephi Kay had written in *Elan* and placed the magazine face down in front of him, carefully aligning its edges so that they were exactly parallel with the sides of his antique desk. He was not used to criticism, and he rolled the unfamiliar taste of it around his mouth. *Dull. Repetitive. Displaying unfulfilled potential.* He refused even to consider that she might possibly be right.

'Maestro? Miss Kay is here.'

He nodded and leant back in his Louis XIV chair, his hands clasped together across his slight paunch. 'You may send her in.'

His secretary opened the door a little wider, careful to keep her feet a respectful distance outside the cream carpeting of the Maestro's office.

Stephi glanced around Pavesi's office with curiosity, well aware that, as an American, such vulgar interest was not only expected but almost required. On one wall, black-and-white photographs of Pavesi as he stood with such luminaries as Jackie Onassis, Sandie Shaw and Margot Fonteyn jostled for space with faded, yellowing preliminary sketches for what were now universally hailed as design classics. Crammed in between them were framed newspaper cuttings of celebrities in Pavesi creations at Oscar ceremonies, film premières and royal weddings. The room itself was a strange mixture of opulence and economy that puzzled Stephi, until she suddenly realised that it reflected the tastes of both Pavesi and his alter ego, the elusive Edouard Chambrun.

She extended her hand. 'Signor Pavesi. It's a pleasure to meet you at last.'

Pavesi half-rose from his chair and brought her hand to his lips in a gesture that would have seemed faintly ridiculous coming from anyone else. 'Miss Kay.' He gestured for her to sit opposite him. 'Would you like some coffee?'

Stephi slid her notebook and pencil out of her tote bag and placed it neatly beneath her chair. 'That'd be perfect.'

'Cappuccino? Espresso? American?'

'Espresso, please.'

She caught his flicker of surprise at her request, and chalked one up to herself. In Italy, only tourists drank cappuccino after eleven o'clock in the morning.

Stephi studied the designer. He was shorter than she'd expected, perhaps five foot six, and already thickening a little at the waist despite his general air of energy and youth. To Stephi his appearance seemed quintessentially Italian: long, blue-black hair slicked back into a ponytail of baby curls, dark eyes fringed with silky lashes longer than her own, and a soft, voluptuous mouth that gave his handsome face a strangely feminine edge.

But what she had failed to anticipate was the raw animal sensuality he exuded. To her surprise, she felt an unmistakable frisson. He was gay, for God's sake, and even if he hadn't been, he was hardly her type.

Pavesi was apparently oblivious to the brief but powerful effect he had had on her. 'So, Miss Kay. I am glad that I finally meet you. I have always thought of you as a very nice person. But Edouard, he thinks you are a little cruel. Me, I know that today's gossip, it wraps the fish the next day. A journalist doesn't have a good day at the collections – perhaps you are seated behind a lady with a large hat, no? – and suddenly, Giulio Pavesi, he is dull, *passé*, *démodé*. I know how it is. Tomorrow it is different, yes? It is best not to pay too much attention to these things.' He sighed. 'But Edouard, he takes this sort of criticism seriously. He says the unappreciative should not be permitted to criticise what they do not understand. But I talk with him, I make him relent. And so we are all friends again, yes?'

Stephi tried to hide a smile. She knew the enigmatic Edouard Chambrun to be many things, but over-sensitive wasn't one of them. If he had been disturbed by her article, it was more because it could damage sales than because it had offended his sensibilities.

Pavesi seemed to take her silence for assent and smiled expansively. 'You see, Miss Kay, it is so easy to be misunderstood. I am the creator, yes, but you are the interpreter. The rest of the world listens to you. So, I want to make things better for you.' He sat back in his chair. 'Ask me. Ask me anything you wish and I will give you my answer.'

Stephi met his challenge head on. 'Signor Pavesi, does it worry you that no one around you dares to criticise what you do?'

'You did,' Pavesi said reasonably. 'Have I made a fuss? Did I ban you from my collection, say no, this woman, she did not like what I did last season, so she cannot come again?'

'No, but here we are, sitting in your atelier, while you give me your first interview in over three years,' Stephi pointed out. 'You wouldn't have done that if I'd praised your collections to the skies, would you? Did you agree to meet me for my novelty value alone, or are you just terrified of criticism?'

Pavesi laughed. 'It is always a pleasure to meet someone with views as refreshing as yours. But no, I am not afraid of being criticised. Only of not being understood.'

'Then tell me, what exactly is there to understand?' Stephi asked, leaning forward. 'After all, we're not talking modern art or Einstein's theory of relativity here. A chic suit doesn't really need interpretation, particularly if it's scarcely any different from last year.' She paused. 'I realise your clothes are not exactly practical, but neither are they very complicated or avant-garde. What have I missed that you think needs understanding?'

'My ladies do not need to be practical,' Pavesi said airily, ignoring the thrust of her question. 'They employ servants to be practical for them. They need only to be beautiful, decorative. In the clothes I create, that is what they are able to do.'

'This is 1974, Signor Pavesi. These days women work, lead busy, active lives –'

'Not my ladies.'

In those three words, Stephi suddenly saw ranked behind the designer a bastion of Italian misogyny that she'd never be able to penetrate in one interview; nor would there be much point. She'd learned everything she needed to know about Pavesi's fashion philosophy from that one remark. She changed tack.

'Tell me, is there any truth in the rumour that you want to pull out of your contract with the Magnoli Group at the end of this season?'

The question had been intended to wrongfoot him, but Pavesi's expression did not change. For a moment, Stephi wondered if her source was accurate.

'Another rumour? Who was it this time? Valentino?

123

Gucci? Those people in France whose names I cannot possibly remember? I can't tell the difference between one of them and another. Tell me, Miss Kay, is it on purpose that everything they make looks the same or what?'

Stephi smiled, recognising the evasion behind Pavesi's legendary denigration of French designers. But she wasn't going to let him off the hook. 'So, do I have your word that you have no plans to pull out?'

'Miss Kay. I promise you, I have no plans to pull out of Magnoli.'

Stephi was satisfied with his answer. She knew he wouldn't lie; *Elan* was too important for him to risk alienating her permanently. The Magnoli Group rumour had been a reason for trying to see him, but she had plenty of material now to make a fascinating feature on the quixotic designer without it. She sipped her espresso and turned the page of her notebook, firing off half a dozen questions about his upcoming collection and those of his rivals. She scribbled down Pavesi's answers, again surprised by the energy and humour in the designer which somehow failed to translate itself into his work, and glanced surreptitiously at her watch. It was already ten past six. If she hurried, she would just be able to make it to Roberto's office by seven, as they'd arranged.

As she was about to wind up the interview, the door to Pavesi's office flew open and a striking woman strode confidently into the room. She was immaculately groomed, her long dark hair drawn into a neat chignon at the nape of her neck, her make-up discreet and expertly applied. Stephi recognised her instantly as Angela Lindsay, Pavesi's long-time confidante, the woman who was reputed to be the inspiration for many of his designs. The English model halted her stride as she saw Stephi, then continued towards Pavesi, ignoring her magnificently.

'Giulio, darling. We need you downstairs. There is a slight

124

problem with one of the outfits for Signora Cerreni. Sebastian is not happy with the toile.' She spoke in the clipped, assured tones of a woman used to getting her own way. 'As it is la Signora's first order and Sebastian is keen to get the preliminary garment right before he cuts the silk, I told him that you would be with him as soon as your work allowed.'

Pavesi rose apologetically. 'Miss Kay –'

'No, no, I understand,' Stephi said, swiftly recovering from the shock of hearing Roberto's wife's name. 'I've another meeting this evening, and I'm already late. But I must thank you for giving me so much of your time.'

Again Pavesi bowed over her hand. 'The pleasure is all mine. Angela, *cara*, perhaps you could show Miss Kay out? I have an urgent telephone call to attend to, and then I will be down.'

Stephi picked up her bag and followed the model out, trying to comfort herself as she watched Angela's shapely rear with the thought that the girl probably spent her life ravenously hungry in order to keep that figure.

Behind them, Pavesi's expression remained one of genial good humour until he heard the door shut. As soon as he was certain he couldn't be overheard, he reached for the ancient telephone desk and punched out the numbers.

Right now, returning Fernando Moreno's call took priority over everything.

Fourteen

Via Appia Antica, Rome, Italy
Friday 24 September 1976
7.00 a.m.

Alix tried to lie absolutely still beneath the bedclothes. At nearly six years old, it was difficult, because she was trembling with excitement, but she didn't want the covers to move and give her away. She was supposed to be fast asleep. That was all part of the game.

She heard her bedroom door creak open and stifled a giggle. Suddenly the covers were ripped away from her body and she squealed as the cool air from the open window hit her.

'Daddy! Daddy! I was asleep!'

Roberto swung her up in his arms. 'Asleep? At this time of day? It's nearly lunchtime!'

'Put me down, Daddy!'

Roberto leant over the bed and upended her, so that her long pink cotton nightgown fell down over her face.

'The other way!' Alix cried, her voice muffled by her giggles and the nightgown. 'Put me down the other way!'

'Oh, the other way? In that case, I think you mean put me up.'

Alix's bare legs flailed in the air. 'Put me up! Put me up!'

Roberto laid her gently down on the bed, and Alix emerged

from the folds of her nightgown, her face flushed with excitement. 'Now, Princess. Time to get dressed.'

Roberto walked towards the door, his step lighter than it had been for many months. He felt a delicious tingle of anticipation, like a child on Christmas Eve. Stephi would be here in a few hours, and for the first time in many months they had the whole weekend to look forward to.

It was always so difficult for them to spend any real time together. Even when he was away on business, Joanna never seemed to relax her guard, telephoning him in the middle of the night to check that he was in his hotel room, sifting through his credit card statements for unexplained purchases, inventing excuses to call his office and verify the day he was due back so that it was almost impossible for him to steal an extra day with Stephi at the end of a business trip. On one occasion she had even turned up unannounced at his hotel in New York with Alix. He had been forced to fly back to Rome with her for the sake of their daughter, posing for the press photographers she had alerted to their arrival at Fiumicino airport as if they were in truth the perfect, golden family Joanna wanted the world to see.

In the early days of his affair with Stephi, the intrigue and secrecy had added a piquancy to their relationship. But as the months had passed and the affair had deepened, Roberto had found the situation increasingly frustrating. They could never go to the theatre or cinema for fear of being recognised, never dine out with friends, never take a weekend together for granted. Their love-making was frequently interrupted by telephone calls from Joanna about some problem at home, almost as if she knew they were together. It always left both of them feeling angry and guilty.

It was only on those rare occasions when Joanna visited her family in England that Stephi was able to slip into Rome to stay at the villa. For the few brief hours that she was there, both Alix and he knew real happiness. Stephi adored his daughter almost as much as he did. It was no wonder they both looked forward to Stephi's arrival with such anticipation.

Roberto felt his heart clench. His daughter had every material benefit he could provide, yet there was a quiet sadness inside her that he could never quite dispel, no matter how much he tried to show her he loved her. He glanced around the luxurious bedroom, at the brass-and-lace four-poster bed that was every little girl's dream, the immense wardrobe of clothes whose designer labels Alix couldn't even pronounce, the playroom next door filled with extravagant toys from a huge English rocking-horse to a doll's house twice as tall as she was; all of it chosen and given to her by him.

But it was the Raggedy Andy doll that her mother had given her on her third birthday that Alix cuddled at night. Whenever he tried to tell himself that Alix couldn't possibly realise the extent of her mother's rejection, since she'd never known anything different, it was the way she cherished the Raggedy Andy that told him the truth. Alix was an intelligent child.

Alix watched as her father left the room, then scrambled off the bed, pulling the rumpled covers quickly across the mattress before abandoning it half-made. The maid could do it properly later.

She loved days like today – days when her mother was away – all the restricting rules that governed her life were dispensed with. She could wear what she liked to school, and afterwards, Daddy and his special friend, Stephi, would meet her at the gates. Daddy was different when Stephi was there: he laughed more and made lots of jokes, and didn't worry if she hung on to him and got his suit creased.

Alix thought that if only her mother went away more often, life would be wonderful. Just her and Daddy – and Stephi.

The days when she had her father to herself were the most

special days of all. She adored the rare mornings when he burst into her bedroom and pulled off her covers, teasing and tickling her until she screamed through her laughter for him to stop. Sometimes he waited for her to have her shower and cuddled her afterwards, filling her with a glow that lasted the whole day. Those were the days when she felt the most loved, when even her mother's indifference didn't matter.

She'd often tried to remember that special feeling when she was alone, but somehow it wasn't the same.

She'd long ago accepted that the love she shared with her father had to be kept hidden from her mother. Sometimes she felt as if she was two people, a quiet, subdued little girl in her sombre clothes and sensible shoes, her unruly auburn hair pulled back into a tight pleat, for her mother; and in her father's presence, a carefree princess dressed in beautiful clothes, loved and beloved. It was difficult to know which one was the real her.

Fifteen

Rio de Janeiro, Brazil
Monday 20 September 1976
6.00 p.m.

David Conto stared out of the grimy window of the taxi as the
expensive shopping arcades of Rio gave way to the less
developed suburbs whose poverty was only too evident. In the
twenty minutes since he had left the shelter he ran for
Children First in the centre of town, the city had gradually
petered out into clusters of warehouses and tenements linked
by uneven concrete pavements that finally became no more
than patches of dusty bare earth. Strings of washing looped
across the front of battered apartment buildings, many of their
windows barred, others patched with cardboard and scraps of
packing cases, their grey walls crumbling and peeling. The
road grew steeper, the tarmac degenerating with every
kilometre until they were racketing across potholes and cracks
more substantial than the road itself. At last the taxi came to a
halt.

The driver gestured towards the street and shifted a wad of
tobacco from one cheek to the other. 'You get out now.'

'Are we there?' David asked doubtfully. 'Are you sure?'

'*Dez minutos*. No drive.'

David climbed out of the car and stared around at the blank
grey streets. This suburb was not as poor as some of the shanty

towns he had visited up in the hills – certainly not as deprived as *favellas* like the one that had been swept away in the mudslide six years ago – but it was still a grim place. He felt very conspicuous despite his worn jeans and cheap white cotton shirt.

The driver hawked and spat into the street. 'Eh. Twenty dollar.'

David didn't even glance at him. 'Wait here. I'll pay you when I come back.'

He ignored the man's angry protests and walked away from the car. The driver might abandon him anyway, but at least there was an even chance he'd stay if he thought that was the only way he'd get his fare.

David pulled a grubby scrap of paper from his back pocket and stared at it, then headed up the hill, taking care to step around the rubbish and excrement.

His footsteps sounded loudly in the empty streets; several times, rats darted across his path as he disturbed their scavenging. After about fifteen minutes of steady walking a clammy rain began to fall and David began to wonder if he should give up and go back.

Just as he was about to turn round he heard the faint hum of machinery. The sound seemed to be coming from his right. Crossing the dirt street, he saw a narrow alleyway he had almost overlooked leading directly between two weathered wooden warehouses. He hesitated for a moment, then plunged into the dark alley, and he climbed the rickety staircase at the end. A locked door greeted him at the top, with a shiny new entry phone to its right. David pressed the buzzer and shouted his name. After a few moments he heard the sound of bolts being drawn and the door swung open.

Inside, the room was filled with the stench of human bodies crowded too close together for too long. As his eyes grew used to the half-light from the two filthy windows set high on either side of the room, he was able to make out a dozen or so wooden workbenches, each bearing a number of ancient Singer sewing machines. The women hunched over them stared fixedly at the flickering needles, machines clattering. If the workers noticed his entrance, they gave no sign. Half a dozen children, some as young as five or six, flitted between the benches, gathering heaps of partially finished materials and carrying them from one bench to the next. He guessed that each row of women was responsible for a different part of the final garments – sleeves, collars, buttons – which were scooped off the last workbench at the rate of around one every five minutes.

David turned as a fat, bearded man in a filthy shirt emerged from the gloom and wiped his hand on his crumpled trousers before extending it to his visitor. Swallowing his instinctive repulsion, David shook his hand.

'Mr Grimaldi?'

David remembered that was the name he'd given over the telephone and nodded.

'It's a pleasure to meet you, Mr Grimaldi. I'm Jesse Owens, the overseer of this place. If you'd like to come into my office, sir –'

David made no move, nodding instead towards the work-benches. 'These are all your workers?'

'Yes, indeed. They all work an eighty-hour week, some-times more.'

He leant towards David, a note of pride entering his voice. 'Worst paid in the city. We give them less than two-thirds of what anyone else pays. It's up to them if they want to take it.' He laughed. 'After all, they can always starve.'

David realised that he was supposed to find this informa-tion amusing and forced a smile. They walked past the rows of women towards the overseer's office, Owens pausing now and then to display a sample of their work.

'Best workers in the business,' he said complacently. 'These girls can do anything; you want Armani shoulders, Lacroix beading, they can do it.'

They reached his office and Owens scrambled to clear the single wooden seat on the other side of his cluttered desk before inviting David to sit down. 'So, Mr Grimaldi. What sort of order did you have in mind?'

David shrugged. 'That depends on what you can deliver. What's your current output?'

'Most of our work is subcontracted from Gruppo Italia. Naturally the labour here is cheaper for them than Europe. We're currently workng on an order for 3,000 Giulio Pavesi day suits – ready-to-wear, you understand – and another 2,000 Kehaar jackets. All genuine, not rip-offs.'

He eyed David for a moment, then leant forward, obviously deciding to risk a confidence. 'Although of course, if there's something you want, a specific name, that can be arranged without the – ah – formality of paperwork.'

'The order I'm thinking of might be quite substantial,' David said. 'Naturally, we'll be looking for the best possible price. Of course, if you use children, we wouldn't expect to pay the same sort of fee as for skilled adults –'

'I quite understand. My workers are very good, but still … training. Apprenticed, shall we say. Apart from the supervisors, not one of them over fourteen. Of course, at their age they can't expect to get a full wage. But they're skilled.'

Despite the suspicions that had brought him here in the first place, David was shocked. The workers in the next room looked like old women, not girls barely into their teens. David's own mother was Brazilian. If she hadn't met an American sailor and emigrated to the States, it might have been his sister, Lucy, shut up in there. Perhaps it was the same thought that had led Lucy to join him in Rio in 1971, the moment she'd finished her college course at Vassar, to help

133

set up the shelter for *Children First* in the wake of the 1970 disaster at Nova Esperancia. They both felt a shared sense of guilt that their American passports had allowed them to escape a heritage that had trapped so many others.

He stood up. He'd heard enough. It probably wouldn't get this miserable bastard convicted, but the tape recorder in his pocket would at least get the place closed down. Too bad for Pavesi and Kehaar and all the other Western designers who, knowingly or unknowingly, allowed their manufacturers to make use of the child sweatshops in Latin America and Asia to bring down their labour costs.

He forced a neutral expression on to his face. 'If I could just look around ...?'

He followed Owens back into the workroom. There was something slightly off-key about the place, and it took him several minutes to work out that there was none of the buzz of conversation he would have expected on a factory floor. He wondered how many of the pampered women who would buy these garments from boutiques and department stores in London, Paris and New York had any idea of the appalling conditions in which they had been made. They would be a great deal less willing to part with $1,000 for what they believed was an expertly crafted designer garment if they knew it had really been churned off a wooden bench in Rio de Janeiro by a fourteen-year-old slum dweller at a cost of perhaps $40 – and that included wages and materials.

'I'll leave you to look around, then,' Owens said genially, rubbing his hand across the doughy rolls of his face. 'I've just got to get some paperwork together and I'll be right back.'

David waited until the overseer had left the workroom, wondering where to start. His eyes met the contemptuous glare of a young girl gathering scraps of material from the floor. To her he was just another fat-cat garment manufacturer, after big margins and easy profits. At least her anger was better than the dead hopelessness in the faces of the girls around her.

He bent down to help the girl pick up the wisps of pale pink linen. She was extraordinarily beautiful beneath the grime. Brilliant blue eyes stared defiantly out at him from beneath a cloud of dark hair. Their expression held him mesmerised.

She made to leave, but David reached out his hand. 'What's your name?'

She shook her arm free and glared at him, remaining silent.

David quickly glanced along the length of the workroom, then pressed his card into her hand. 'Look, I want to help children like you, to stop you from having to work in these places.' He realised how unlikely his promises sounded, even to himself. 'If you come to me, I can find you somewhere to live, organise school, maybe get you a job at the end of it.'

The girl stared at the card.

David gazed at her helplessly. What could he tell her that she could possibly understand? That he was part of an international organisation dedicated to stamping out this kind of exploitation and child labour? That it was his way of expiating his guilt at having been born into a better life simply by an accident of genealogy? That he had quite literally taken his life in his hands just by coming here?

'I think what's happening here is wrong,' he said simply. 'And I want to stop it.'

The girl turned the card over in her hands. Watching her, David was struck by a nagging feeling that he'd seen her somewhere before. For a brief moment, he felt a flicker of hope. He couldn't hope to save all the children, but if he could just help her, perhaps his efforts would have been worth while.

The girl handed back the card abruptly. 'I don't want this. I can't read.'

'My name is David Conto,' he said clearly, straightening

up as he heard footsteps. 'Just remember *Children First*. If you ever need me, you'll find me there.'

Elizabetta watched as the dark-haired young man who spoke Portuguese with an American accent walked back towards Owens' office. She felt a terrible bitterness. He didn't have to tell her to remember the name of his organisation. It was already engraved indelibly on her brain. They'd offered her help once before. The next day she'd awakened to find Miguel smothered, little Gabriel's throat slit.

She knew it wasn't their fault. These people meant to help, but they just brought more destruction in their wake.

It hadn't taken her long after her brother's deaths to realise that if she wanted to reach her ninth birthday, she had to find a protector, someone better equipped than Raoul to keep her alive. Even then she'd known that there was only one way. She'd seen the way men looked at her. She'd been aware that she looked older than her eight years, her body even then beginning to develop womanly curves. She knew that if she didn't exploit her looks herself, it was only a matter of time before someone else did it for her.

She'd chosen the man only after a great deal of careful consideration. Her greatest danger had always potentially come from the corrupt police round-ups; the only way to protect herself against them was to lodge herself firmly on their side. For the few weeks following her brothers' murders, Elizabetta studied the policemen on her beat, weighing them up against each other. In the end, she'd chosen Garcia Costelo, a married man in his early thirties with daughters of his own, only a little older than herself. She guessed that he thought of them when he looked at her and treated her a little more tenderly because of that.

The first time he'd entered her she'd thought she was going to die, and had almost welcomed the idea. Two years later, she didn't think twice about it, servicing him every night he was on duty, blanking out his actions with a skill born of long practice. Six months after that agonising first time, Garcia had salved his conscience by finding her the job in the garment warehouse. Fortunately the overseer, Owens, preferred young boys, so she had been safe from his attentions. Together with the money Garcia occasionally gave her, it had been enough to survive. At least she didn't have to worry about an assassin's knife when she curled up in some doorway. Garcia always told her the areas that were safe on any given night, and for that at least she was grateful.

A whistle blew, signalling the end of the shift, and Elizabetta abandoned her basket of scraps gratefully. She had spent the last fourteen hours cooped up inside the dusty warehouse, crawling around the floor. Outside, the warm air was still humid, but at least it was fresh.

She ran down the wooden steps and along the alleyway to the main road, keeping an eye out for the ramshackle bus that usually passed at this time of night. As soon as it stopped to disgorge its passengers, Elizabetta leaped up on the rear bumper and joined two boys clinging to the rail beneath the back window. Despite the danger and discomfort, she enjoyed this ride back into town, the wind cooling her, the journey a brief respite between her work at the warehouse and Garcia's demands.

Forty minutes later, she jumped off the bus as it turned the corner into the main square just off Avenido Rio Branco where she was supposed to be meeting her protector, Garcia. She headed for the doorway of a shuttered pharmacy and crouched down in the corner. She hoped Garcia wouldn't want to share her with his friends tonight. In the last few months, he'd grown increasingly fond of watching her with other men, stroking himself to orgasm as the others took it in turns to fuck her in alleys and doorways in any way they

137

chose. It occurred to her that perhaps she was getting too old for Garcia to be tempted by her charms alone. At ten, she'd outgrown her childish gawkiness. Perhaps she should start looking around for another protector, one more interested in her curves than her innocence.

In the distance she heard the clock strike 9.30. Garcia was forty-five minutes late. She couldn't risk hanging around here any longer; already she'd attracted too much attention from men loitering around the square.

She headed towards the beach. Garcia often met her on the beaches of Ipanema or Copacabana, finding some strange satisfaction in taking her on the sand where, a few hours before, the city's wealthiest citizens had sunbathed and played volleyball with their children. After dark, the beaches became part of another world, sinister and violent.

As she ran down the steps on to the beach she saw him almost immediately, kneeling upright near the water's edge. She would have recognised his bare buttocks anywhere, the red slash across his left cheek where a bullet had grazed him one night, several years ago.

He was not alone. In front of him a small child was standing, perhaps seven or eight years old, clinging to his waist for balance as Garcia forced her to take him in her mouth. Several feet away, a woman who might have been the child's mother sat quietly, helpless as her daughter was brutally violated.

Elizabetta felt a violent anger as she watched, an anger that reached beyond her anguish for the child and embraced all the indignities and humiliations she'd endured. She'd allowed this man to use her any way he chose. It had been a pact with the devil, but she'd entered it by her own choice. But what he was doing to this child went beyond any deal, any agreement.

Garcia half-turned as Elizabetta sank the blade of the knife she always carried beneath her skirt for her own protection into the soft pale flesh of his throat. She twisted it sharply through his neck and pulled the child to her as Garcia's fat body fell forwards on to the sand, his hands groping at his throat. She watched as he choked and gurgled in front of her, waiting to be certain he was dead, before she kicked his body towards the surf until she was sure the undertow would catch him and suck him out to sea. Less than two minutes had passed since she'd arrived at the beach.

Then she thrust the little girl into the woman's shocked arms and walked as quickly as she dared towards the beach promenade. She didn't waste a moment in grief or regret. Garcia's children were better off without him. The man she'd killed was a sadist and a paedophile. But he was also a policeman; his death would not go unnoticed. Too many people knew about her – the friends of his she'd gratified in the past, for a start. She'd be the first person they came looking for when the sea finally disgorged her protector's body.

She headed back into the city, knowing exactly where she was going. *Children First* had twice offered her help, and twice she'd refused.

Now she had no choice but to accept.

Sixteen

West 34th Street, New York, USA
Monday 11 October 1976
10.00 a.m.

Stephi staggered into the meeting room, a heavy bundle of magazines clutched in her arms. With a sigh of relief she deposited them on the glass-and-chrome table in the centre of the room and eased a misshapen canvas tote bag off her shoulder. 'Whoever said the pen is mightier than the sword got it slightly wrong. Heavier is the word he was looking for.'

Elan's managing editor, Kitty St John, nodded at the magazines. 'Don't tell me. This is your answer to Jane Fonda's latest workout.'

Stephi eased herself into one of the uncomfortable black leather bucket seats. 'Seemed like a good idea at the time,' she said ruefully. 'So much for inspiration.'

A pale, cadaverous young man leant across the desk and picked up several of the magazines, propping them behind his back and settling against them. 'At last, a use for the drivel on which I waste my talent,' he said conversationally. 'I loathe these fucking chairs.'

'Mark, you're breaking my heart,' Kitty said. 'I hate to be the one to remind you, but no one's forcing you to take $70,000 a year for the occasional – and I do mean occasional – article you actually get around to writing.'

Mark sighed. 'I can't help it. I haven't got time to write. I spend all my time in court with one or other of my ex-wives. Bankrupting me seems to be the only thing they've ever agreed on.'

Stephi grinned. 'Ah. Alimony. The curse of the writing classes.'

'If only they'd got on this well with each other when I was married to them,' Mark said. 'They wouldn't even speak to each other then. Now they're practically setting up a self-help group together.'

Sash Gessner coughed loudly. 'Fascinating as this is, would someone like to explain the purpose of all these?' He waved at the slew of *Elan* back copies spread across the table. 'I was under the impression this was an editorial meeting, not some kind of therapeutic discussion group.'

'Have you read them recently?' Stephi asked. 'I picked one up the other day when I was waiting for a friend at the dentist's. I was halfway through it before I realised it was the October 1972 issue.'

Sash frowned. 'So? You've got a lousy memory.'

'Maybe, but that's not the point. The magazine was four years old, Sash, and I didn't even notice.'

'Yeah, well, shows how ahead of our time we were –'

'Or how behind we are now.'

There was a brief silence. Sash leant forward. 'Look. Our readership has gone up over half a million in three years. If it ain't broke, don't fix it.'

Stephi prayed for patience. She'd known Sash would object to anything she said on principle, but it was Kitty St John she really had to convince. 'I'm not suggesting there's anything particularly wrong with what we're doing.' She spoke carefully. 'I just thought perhaps we should all take a second look at the women we're doing it for.'

'You've obviously got some sort of remedy in mind, Stephi. What is it?' Kitty asked.

'Look, this is 1976, we've all taken our Pill and read our Germaine Greer. But anyone would think our readers were still debs sifting through *Fortune 500* for a likely husband. We tell them how to be the perfect hostess, discuss the etiquette of *décolletage*, how to deal with their mothers-in-law at Christmas.' She paused for a moment, glancing around the table to make sure she had everyone's attention. 'But when was the last time we mentioned sex, abortion, divorce? We need to bring our features into the Seventies. Affairs, lesbians, single motherhood. Real life, not happy-ever-after. If we can offer our readers that, as well as the news and fashion we've got now, we'll be giving them more than any other publication on the market.'

Stephi sat back and waited. She'd made her pitch; it was up to Kitty now.

'How many pages do you have in your column now?' Kitty asked thoughtfully.

'Four. Always have had, you know that.'

'Make that six,' Kitty said briskly. 'I want a new feature from you every month. Short, witty, anything you think is relevant to our readers' lives. I'll give you six months. If it works, the pages are yours for good.'

Mark shook his head. 'I'm not sure I'm ready for all this. I've only just got used to my wives wearing shoes in the kitchen.'

'That explains the alimony,' Stephi laughed.

'I swear, I'm not getting married again. Next time, I'm just going to find a woman I don't like and give her a house.'

'Excuse me, Kitty, but if you give Stephi two extra pages, where do you think it's going to come from?' Sash said. 'We can't cut the space for advertising, you know that. And it's got to come from somewhere.'

'Then cut your editorial. We don't need it anyway.' Kitty ignored Sash's splutter of outrage and turned back to the table. 'So, anything else?'

'I think you should know that Pavesi's opted for FMs for the next three issues,' Mark said, grinning maliciously at Stephi. 'Now you'll have to say something nice.'

Stephi groaned. Usually Pavesi only paid for run-of-paper ads in *Elan*: the cheapest option open to a designer, an ROP guaranteed an ad but not where it would be placed in the magazine. The Rolls–Royce of advertisements were the OBCs, the outside back covers, whose limited availability effectively doubled their price. The cost of an FM – facing matter – ad fell somewhere between the two, the designer paying for an advertisement opposite a fashion editorial that featured his work. It went without saying that the article would be complimentary. Stephi disliked the feeling of being bought, but she'd learned from experience that there was nothing she could do. No magazine editor was prepared to bite the advertising hand that fed them all.

The meeting broke up and Stephi headed slowly back towards her office, mentally reviewing topics for the new pages Kitty had just given her. Thanks to Roberto, she wasn't short of inspiration. A passionate affair with a married man whose career depended on keeping the relationship secret – a man who also lived on the other side of the Atlantic – should provide her with enough copy for at least the next six issues.

She stared moodily out of her office window, down at the grey streets of Manhattan. She should be feeling elated after winning her point with Kitty, but somehow the thought of Roberto had taken the edge off her happiness. She'd been seeing him for more than two years now, and in a few weeks' time she would be twenty-nine. All her friends were starting to settle down; scarcely a week passed without an invitation to a wedding or christening. It wasn't that she wanted to get married herself, but it would be nice to have had the option.

Who was she trying to kid? She'd give anything to marry Roberto, but he was never going to leave his wife. He'd made that quite clear from the beginning. He'd worked too hard to get where he was to give it all up now. And of course, there was Alix to consider. Roberto would never risk losing her.

How had she managed to get herself into this situation? She'd been so certain she could handle it. A light affair with a successful, intelligent older man – no strings – had seemed the perfect attachment. Regular sex, fun, and no emotional commitment.

Only it hadn't quite worked out like that. She'd made the cardinal error of falling in love. Suddenly a small piece of Roberto wasn't enough. She wanted him all.

Stephi glanced up as her secretary, Ceci, placed a plastic cup of coffee in front of her and handed her a sheaf of yellow telephone messages. She forced herself to forget Roberto. 'Anything urgent?' Swiftly she scanned the half-dozen messages. 'What's this one? *Sheraton, Tel Aviv, 13?*'

Ceci shrugged. 'He didn't leave his name. He just gave the message and said you'd understand.'

Stephi stared at the message as Ceci left the room, suddenly dizzy with anticipation. It could only be from Roberto. He'd mentioned something about a business trip to Israel when she'd been in Rome a couple of weeks ago, but she hadn't taken any notice. She'd grown too used to his plans falling apart at the last minute to get excited until they were actually standing in the same room together. But perhaps this time he'd pulled it off.

She pulled her flight guide towards her and skimmed through the pages until she found the New York–Tel Aviv listings. The message had said 13. Today was the eleventh.

Her article for the magazine would just have to wait.

'You're damn lucky Ceci's such a good secretary. If she'd written down the wrong day, I could still be sitting at Ben Gurion airport now.'

Roberto laughed. 'Lucky for me you're not.'

Stephi gazed out across the glittering blue sea. 'I can't believe I'm really here. New York was in the depths of winter when I left. I had no idea Tel Aviv would be so warm at this time of year. To be honest, I had no idea it was even on the coast. Geography was never really my strong point.'

'Nor history, it would seem.'

'I'd love to go to Jerusalem and Bethlehem,' Stephi said wistfully. 'Just to see the Church of the Holy Sepulchre and walk along the Way of the Cross. Can we actually go up on to the Mount of Olives?'

'We could, though it's not nearly as romantic as you probably think it is. It's very much geared up to the tourist trade these days.'

'I know, but just to see all these biblical places for real –'

'I felt the same the first time I went to New York. I'd seen all these movies about Manhattan – the first time I actually saw a signpost for the Bronx and Queens I felt like I'd driven on to a film set.'

'That's hardly the same,' Stephi said. 'You're Catholic. Doesn't all this religious history mean anything to you?'

'I don't really think about God any more,' Roberto said. 'My mother was very strict with me when I was younger. We had to go to church every evening, fast on Fridays, the whole thing. In those days it was all very remote – Mass was said in Latin by some old priest far away at the end of the church with his back to you. It didn't really mean much to me. As soon as I was old enough to make a decision, I rebelled against it. I don't think of myself as Catholic now. I've drifted too far away.'

'Because of us?'

145

'Partly.'

Stephi sensed a reserve behind his words that for some reason disturbed her. 'I still don't know how you managed to steal four days here,' she said lightly. 'What did you do, bribe the whole Cabinet?'

'Something like that.'

She laughed. 'It could only happen in Italy.'

'I have to work tomorrow,' Roberto warned. 'I only managed to get away at all on the pretext of seeing the Israeli Foreign Minister. But I'll be free on Friday and Saturday – it's *Shabbat*, the Jewish weekend, no one will be working.'

'You have to go back to Rome on Sunday?'

'Yes.'

Stephi was silent. She wasn't sure how much longer she could stand sending him back to his wife. And yet if she had to choose between living like this and losing him for ever, she wasn't sure she was strong enough to let him go.

She caught his hand as he stroked her neck and brought his fingertips to her mouth, then stopped as she felt the cold metal of his wedding band against her lips.

'Do you have to wear this when we're together? It makes me feel so – I don't know – sordid, ashamed.'

'I can't just pretend I'm not married,' Roberto said quietly.

'I know. I'd – I'd just rather not be reminded of it all the time, that's all.'

'If I take it off, the sun will tan my finger. Joanna would see the white band had gone and realise I'd taken my ring off. It wouldn't take much to guess why.'

'Surely she'd never even notice –'

'She would.'

In a sudden burst of anger, Stephi gripped his hand in hers and yanked the gold band from his finger, hurling it away from her.

146

'Stephi –' Roberto stood up and ran towards the wedding ring. 'Are you crazy?'

'I think I must be.'

'Did you have to do that?'

Stephi turned away, suddenly ashamed. When had she become the dependent, tearful mistress begging her lover to stay? She bit her lip. She was becoming a person she no longer recognised and didn't much like.

Yet she could not stop the weeks and months of frustration from welling up inside her. 'I'm tired of eating in darkened restaurants that nobody knows in case you get recognised. I'm tired of leaving the airport in separate taxis. I'm tired of never being able to telephone you, of spending birthdays and holidays alone. I hardly ever see you any more.'

'I'm trying to make it work,' Roberto said wearily. 'You have no idea what I had to do to get these few days alone –'

'I know. But in the end, you always have to go back.'

They walked back across the sand towards their hotel, close but not touching. Neither of them spoke as they showered and changed for dinner. She didn't refer to their discussion on the beach, and he didn't press it. They left the hotel and headed towards a restaurant overlooking the shore, where they ate a quiet meal of salad and salmon bagels, their conversation drifting around safely neutral subjects – anything to stop them mentioning what was on both their minds.

Finally Roberto paid the bill and followed Stephi out of the restaurant, standing silently beside her as she stared out across the darkened beach.

'You know it's over, don't you?' Stephi said eventually.

'Yes.'

Stephi kicked off her heels and bent to pick up her shoes as she walked on to the sand. The water rippled across her bare feet as she reached the sea and started heading along the beach towards their hotel. Roberto stood watching her for several minutes, then ran to catch up with her.

'Will you swim with me?'

Stephi stopped. 'Now?'

'Why not?'

'I don't have anything to wear –'

'No one will see us. Please?'

She glanced around the deserted beach. No one was watching. What did it matter anyway? She would be gone the next morning. Now that she'd made up her mind to end it with Roberto, she couldn't stay. She hesitated a moment longer, then unbuttoned her white silk shift dress, and with a final look round, slipped her panties off and ran into the surf.

They could see the bright lights of the shoreline strung out in front of them, the warm water caressing their bodies as they stood in the waves. Roberto smoothed Stephi's damp hair away from her face; his heart lurched at the thought of his life without her. He had never believed he could love anyone – apart from his daughter – as much as he loved Stephi. He couldn't lose her. If it cost him his career, he had to have her.

'Stephi?' Suddenly the decision was easy. 'I'm going to ask Joanna for a divorce.'

Seventeen

Avenida Rio Branco, Rio de Janeiro, Brazil
Thursday 14 October 1976
11.30 a.m.

Fernando Moreno shifted his gaze from the window and glanced back at the letter in his hand. He hadn't moved for the last half-an-hour. As soon as he'd opened it and read it through once he'd told his secretary to hold all his calls. He needed to make a decision on this now, before he had to destroy the document. There was no way he could risk keeping it.

He studied the familiar letterhead again. He'd done business with the Speretti Institute many times before over the years. They were one of his most regular customers; in the days when Roberto Cerreni had still been at the Italian Embassy and had rubber-stamped the necessary documents, there'd been a steady flow of illicit goods towards the Paraguayan border with Brazil, where the Institute was located. Even now, despite the irksome incorruptibility of the present Italian Ambassador, Fernando's dealings with the Speretti Institute had remained constant, if a little more circumspect – particularly given the drop-off in the number of clients Giulio Pavesi had been able to supply. Either Pavesi had exhausted his range of contacts, or he was simply getting cold feet. Either way, he wasn't going to be much use now.

This new proposal went far beyond the scope of any transaction that he, Roberto or Pavesi had ever entered into in the past.

The ethics of the situation didn't concern Fernando: it was simply a question of security. Until now, all his dealings with the Speretti Institute had been conducted under cover of a number of legitimate operations whose activities were incontrovertibly humanitarian; Father Lucio's Welfare Centre near Salvador actually received official government aid to carry out its work. Even if Fernando's own connection to the Institute could be traced, which he doubted, he could be accused of little more than misguided philanthropy.

But if he accepted the deal that the head of the Institute, Pedro Rochas, carefully suggested in his letter, there could be no such defence if he were ever caught. It would all be over. On the other hand, the financial rewards were they successful might be staggering. He'd be a dollar millionaire several times over within a few years. He didn't even have to do anything more than he was already doing now; all the mechanics were already in place.

The letter had been carefully phrased, but Fernando knew exactly what lay behind its subtle words.

Murder.

He reached for his Caligri cigarette lighter and held the letter over the metal wastepaper bin at the side of his desk, watching the flame reduce it to ashes. Dropping the corner he'd been holding into the bin, he pulled a blank piece of paper towards him and picked up his fountain pen, scribbling the date and Rochas' name across the top.

> *'Many thanks for your helpful comments regarding the marketing of our goods; in particular, your suggestion that a far greater profit may be realised by disassembling the goods on arrival at your end and selling their component parts separately. Perhaps you*

could give me details of the enquiries you've already received regarding future orders. Given the complexity of reducing the complete goods to their components, the price of each part will be substantially greater than the original product. I trust this will not be a problem. Naturally, there will be some wastage which is regrettable, but in the circumstances, unavoidable ...'

Fernando paused, glancing up at the clock as he searched for the right words. Almost one o'clock. That would make it nearly six in the evening in Rome.

He wondered if Roberto had received his message yet.

Eighteen

Via Appia Antica, Rome, Italy
Tuesday 26 October 1976
3.30 p.m.

Joanna wound back the tape and leant forward in her chair, waiting for it to reach the beginning. She knew Stephi Kay had been here again in her absence. This tape would give her all the details Roberto thought hidden from her: the words they murmured to each other when they thought they were safe, the secret trysts they made that they thought she would never discover.

The machine clicked on and began to replay every telephone conversation Roberto had made or received during the past fortnight. The pleasure of her secret knowledge had become so enmeshed with the pain of betrayal that Joanna was no longer able to separate them. She only knew she had to hear every word, no matter how much it hurt.

After two years, she knew everything they'd say to one another even before they said it. There was nothing about her husband's affair she didn't know, from the places they made love to the perfume that Stephi used. It was a pyrrhic victory.

In the last couple of years she'd taken plenty of lovers herself, young, eager boys who reminded her of Roberto. Every time she slept with another man she felt a brief sense of power and triumph that was all too quickly replaced by an ache that nothing seemed to fill. She never slept with the same man twice. It wasn't sex – or even companionship – she craved, but the simple knowledge that she was still attractive, could still arouse a man's desire even though her husband hadn't touched her for nearly six years. The feeling had become a drug, the high from each hit growing shorter and shorter, until she'd finally taken to haunting hotel bars she knew none of her circle frequented, picking up men whose names she never even bothered to ask and screwing them in their rooms upstairs before coming back down and searching for another fix. Even though she knew she was slowly destroying herself, it was the only way she could survive the interminable waiting for Roberto to tire of his mistress and come back to her bed.

She clung to that thought like a lifeline. He would come back to her. *He would.*

She leant forward suddenly as she heard Stephi breath-lessly answer the phone, guessing from the background noise that Roberto had called her at her office in New York. And then she heard Roberto's own voice, cool, determined, a thread of excitement running through it that she'd never heard before.

She didn't need to listen to Stephi's reply as he told her he'd taken the first step towards securing a divorce and asked her to marry him. She already knew what it would be.

She stared stonily at the tape recorder as it spooled on. So, it had finally come. She'd been half expecting it for two years, but somehow she'd never really thought it would happen until, without warning, just when she'd been beginning to think she was safe, it had. After all, if married men were going to leave their wives, they did it straight away, in the first few months, didn't they? They didn't wait for two years and then make up their minds, even if that's what they told their mistresses to keep them happy.

Joanna twisted the engagement ring on her left hand, her fingers trembling slightly. Ever since she'd witnessed her husband screwing that bitch on the floor of his office, her whole life had been geared to making sure he had no reason to leave her. She'd never confronted Roberto, never questioned him. It had taken every ounce of her willpower and self-control not to hurl herself hysterically at him every time he came home from a business trip reeking of his mistress – but somehow she'd done it.

And now Stephi Kay wanted to take even that small part of him she still had left.

But Joanna hadn't fought for him for two years to lose him now. He'd promised to love and honour her until death parted them.

She reached out to stop the tape and her hand froze above the buttons as Roberto's voice answered another call. She knew the other man's voice.

Fernando Moreno. Why would he be calling Roberto now, after all this time? It had been six years since they'd left Brazil, and as far as she knew he hadn't spoken to Roberto since.

She sat on the edge of her chair as she listened to Roberto tersely inform Fernando that he'd got his message. Joanna was frightened. What message? Roberto hadn't mentioned anything to her.

'I need your help,' Fernando's voice said, 'with the Speretti Institute.'

There was a long silence before Roberto replied. Joanna wondered what the hell the Speretti Institute was.

'I've finished with all that,' Roberto's voice said eventually. 'We agreed. No more deals.'

'I think you'll find this is an opportunity too good to miss. This is something altogether different –'

'I'm not interested, Fernando. You'll have to find someone else.'

'I don't need you to turn a blind eye to a few illegal goods trundling across the Brazil border into Paraguay.' Fernando's voice was oily smooth. 'I'm talking about imports this time. Into Italy. And I'm afraid no one else will do, Roberto. You're the Senior Foreign Minister. You'll have to arrange the necessary documentation.'

'I said no –'

'Roberto, I'm not asking you. I'm telling you.'

There was a long silence. 'Do I have a choice?'

Fernando laughed. 'Well. I could make a few telephone calls – I'm sure the paparazzi would be fascinated to learn what you rubber-stamped for me in Rio. Not to mention the truth about your daughter. Of course, she may forgive you, eventually –'

'What is it you want me to do?' Roberto sounded weary, defeated.

'I've already told you. I'll need some paperwork to be sorted out at your end –'

'What exactly are these imports you want me to get through for you?'

Joanna couldn't believe what she heard next. Her hands shaking, she stopped the tape and rewound it. She knew her husband had been involved with the High Court judge in some deals that she suspected were outside the law during his time in Brazil. And of course, there was Alix. But this made those risks pale into insignificance.

And all to protect his daughter.

Joanna ejected the tape and stood up. Roberto had just handed her the one weapon she needed to make sure he would never leave her. He might hate her for it, but he'd be tied to her for ever.

She would enjoy hearing him tell Stephi.

Nineteen

Upper West Side, New York, USA
Friday 29 October 1976
11.00 p.m.

Stephi had imagined the end of the affair many times before now, but never believed it could happen like this. That she would hear Roberto telling her over the telephone that he'd made a mistake, it was all over, he never wanted to see her again. She'd known at once that there was no point in arguing. She'd never heard Roberto sound so distant. He'd been lost to her before she'd even answered the call.

She wasn't a fool. She'd known the risks of having an affair with a married man – particularly such a prominent one – right from the beginning. Married men aren't fair game. The only rules are: there ain't no rules.

Now she knew how it must feel to be the betrayed wife.

She told herself that the misery would pass. She had her work, her friends, she would get over him and find someone else.

In the meantime, she was alone with her pain.

Book Two

1981–1987

One

Basra, Iraq
Sunday 3 May 1981
2.20 p.m.

Matt lay on the filthy floor of the coach as another hail of bullets sang against its side. In the brief pause that followed, he reached for his camera bag and slithered along the glass-littered aisle towards the front of the vehicle, peering through a six-inch hole that had been gouged out of the metal by flak from an artillery shell.

'Great time for a school reunion,' he said to the journalist lying on the floor next to him.

David Cameron shifted slightly along the length of the aisle so that Matt had a clearer view. 'Shame the other guys couldn't make it. They don't know what they're missing.'

Somehow they had walked right into the middle of the front-line battle currently being fought between Iran and Iraq around the Iraqi seaport of Basra. Even as he watched, bombs and artillery shells thumped into the marshy desert, sending showers of dirt and sand swirling into the air, plumes of water rising like geysers whenever one of the missiles chanced to land in the marsh lakes themselves. Burnt-out armoured personnel carriers and jeeps, mangled date palms and the debris of war – guns, helmets, rocket launchers – dotted the bloodstained sand. The ripe stench of bodies left to rot in the sun mingled with the acrid smell of gunsmoke and the pungent scent of human fear.

Matt had grown used to the smell of death. He had been working as a freelance news photographer for four years now. In that time he had seen more horror and cruelty than he had ever imagined could exist.

In the school years that had followed his rescue of the Brazilian girl in Nova Esperancia, Matt's interest in his father's work had deepened into a commitment as strong as that of Christopher's. Despite his mother's objections, he insisted upon joining his father wherever he happened to be for his work with *Children First* at least twice a year. He had seen at first hand the indifference and inhumanity his father battled against, the appeals which were so often ignored, the warnings that were never heeded until it was too late.

He had also witnessed the immense power of the media. Twice when travelling with his father, Matt had met David Cameron, the former school prefect who'd done his best to protect Matt from bullying by his head of house, Simon Derby–Lewis. David had become a freelance television journalist the year after he'd left St Francis'. Matt had seen for himself how a single three-minute report on the fledgling news service, INN, and a photograph on the cover of *Newsweek*, had achieved more than weeks and months of campaigning by his father for *Children First*.

When Matt left school at eighteen it had been Caroline Logan who had forced him to take his place at Oxford. It was the one issue on which she had remained adamant: Matt would follow her father and his own brother, Hugh, to Oxford. After that, he could do what he wanted. Matt had grudgingly agreed, persuaded by his mother's argument that the world would still be there when he'd finished his degree.

He'd barely completed two terms of Politics, Philosophy and Economics when he had realised that he had made a mistake. He'd been unable to sit still and study the philoso-phies of long-dead statesmen when there was so much he wanted to do to change the attitudes of those who were living. Christopher had supported his decision to drop out at the end of his first year, and had done what he could to moderate his wife's fury. He'd even financed the first two difficult years when Matt had tried to make his mark amongst experienced and jaded photo editors.

He'd been forced to cover the most difficult and dangerous stories, delivering on to the desk of photo editors at Reuters, AP and the *New York Times* the first pictures of mass graves heaped with skulls in Cambodia, dismembered remains of missionaries in Rhodesia, the guerrilla wars and their inno-cent victims in El Salvador and Nicaragua. His deep sense of outrage at the horrors he witnessed infiltrated his pictures and more than made up for his inexperience. Within two years, his byline was appearing on the front covers of *Time* and *Newsweek*. Now, four years later, at the tender age of twenty three, he was one of the most sought-after young news photographers in the business.

There had been many women since Joanna; none of them had held his interest for long. He had never found a woman able to understand the time and space he needed when he returned from an assignment having photographed horrors that no one should ever have to witness. His girlfriends sympathised for as long as it took him to unpack his rucksack, then dragged him out to a dinner party or a cocktail reception and subjected him to endless inane questions from City analysts and advertising executives about what it was really like to be shot at, or how many dead people it took to make a massacre. Matt had given up trying to form a lasting relationship with anything but his camera.

He studied the battlefield now for a moment. 'We're sitting

ducks here. Somehow we have to shift this death-trap of a vehicle over the dunes behind us and out of the line of fire.'

David glanced briefly at the Iraqi driver slumped over the wheel, his brains splattered across the dashboard. 'I'm not sure I fancy explaining this to his friends on the other side when we appear out of nowhere driving his coach.'

Matt had to shout above the renewed rattle of gunfire. 'It'll be easier arguing with them than with those guys out there.'

'I thought this area was supposed to be Iraqi-held territory?' David yelled back. 'So much for a display of Saddam's glorious 7th Corps in the midst of victory.'

'The best-laid plans –'

'Did someone mention getting laid?'

David grinned and turned to see his cameraman, Sebastian Kelly, easing his way along the aisle on his stomach to join them. 'If you've got any suggestions, Seb, we'd be happy to hear them.'

Seb nodded towards the dead driver. 'I think it's time someone gave that guy a break.'

'You volunteering?'

Seb shook his head. 'Someone has to take the pictures, right?

Matt brandished his Pentax. 'Guess you got the short straw, David.'

David groaned. 'Just make sure you get them in focus this time, OK?'

Apart from David and Sebastian, who worked together as television freelancers and sold their material to the highest bidder, four other journalists – from Reuters, the *New York Times*, *Newsweek* and the *Daily Chronicle* – had joined the Iraqi photo facility to Basra to witness what had been described, with stunning inaccuracy, as 'a decisive victory for Baghdad over the defunct and demoralised Iranian army'. Matt was the only stills photographer on the trip, for reasons which became only too apparent the moment he had seen the coach that was to take them on the five-hour journey to Basra. All of its windows had been deliberately covered with thick mud so that he could neither see out nor take the photographs which were the whole purpose of his journey. When he had protested to the Iraqis, he had been curtly informed that the mud was intended to prevent the windows from glinting in the sun and attracting enemy aircraft fire. So far, it didn't seem to have made a great deal of difference one way or the other.

As David and Seb heaved the driver's corpse out of his bloodied seat on to the floor, Matt used the base of his portable tripod to knock out the lower portion of the window set into the coach door. Immediately the Iraqi minion skulking in the back of the coach let out a yell of protest.

'You can't do that! No pictures!'

Matt pointed to the row of shattered windows along the side of the coach. 'I won't tell them how it happened if you don't.'

Another barrage of gunfire thumped into the ground around them, drowning out the Iraqi's protests. 'You can't drive this coach! This is an Iraqi coach! Only an Iraqi is permitted to drive it!'

David settled into the driver's seat. 'I'd be happy to change places.'

'No! It's not permitted! *Mahmnou!* Forbidden! This is a hijack! There will be serious trouble! You could all be shot!'

David wiggled the gearstick experimentally and peered through the shattered windscreen at the blank desert in front of him. 'Do they drive on the right or the left here?'

Matt braced himself with his wrists as an explosion threw him against the side of the coach. 'Just forward would be nice.'

Slowly the coach lurched away from the front line, David wrenching hard on the wheel to keep the vehicle from drifting into the minefield on their left. As soon as the coach had shifted from the centre of the battlefield, the Iranian guns seemed to lose interest in it as a target. Within fifteen minutes, they had reached the main Iraqi bunker tucked behind the front line.

As the coach halted, several Iraqis emerged from the bunker screeching for the journalists to get out. Matt heard the bizarre sound of distorted Persian music as he stepped out into the blinding sun and the Iraqis hustled them into the underground shelter.

'Did you get what you need?' he asked David.

David shook his head. 'The Beeb will want more than this if I'm going to make it into a headline story. Same with ABC or CBS in the States.'

'Ditto. I'll never make the cover of *Newsweek* with a blurred shot of a few wrecks scattered around a couple of dented palms. Take away the sand and you've got more action off the Falls Road on a Saturday night.'

'What do you want to do about it?'

'Go back.'

Their eyes met. Both men were only too well aware of the risk they would be taking if they tried to head back towards the Iraqi front line. But they would be marginally safer if they attempted the trip together. An extra pair of eyes watching your back never hurt.

Matt had worked with David a number of times. Both men had preferred to choose the stories they considered important and worry about selling their material afterwards. There were few men Matt would rather be with than David when he was really up against it.

Now they lolled against the back wall of the airless underground bunker, waiting for the sweating Iraqi official to finish listing the many glories of Saddam Hussein. Then the group of journalists were led back out into the searing sun. The Iraqis gathered in a huddle, evidently debating how to get

164

the journalists back to Baghdad now that the vehicle was unusable. David winked at Matt, then wandered casually towards a bland sand dune behind the bunker. Seb followed, balancing his camera on his shoulder as David hooked up his sound mike and clipped it to his lapel. He turned to face the camera, angling his body slightly to the left. 'Claims by the Iraqi Army's 7th Corps of a decisive victory in the battle for the southern marshes seem to be exaggerated. We have no pictures of the Iranian bodies or their prisoners, so we must assume that Baghdad is distorting the truth in a propaganda war which Saddam Hussein is losing. David Cameron, Basra, Iraq.'

Matt watched as the cluster of Iraqis raced across the dunes towards David, almost choking on the date stalks they had been munching. Karim, the Iraqi minder who'd been with them on the coach, pulled a handgun from the waistband of his khaki trousers and furiously fired several shots into the sand around David's feet, screaming abuse.

'Liars! Liars! You are all infidels and liars! I will be executed if you say that! You must tell the truth.'

David shrugged. 'I can only say what I see. If you show me something else –'

'What? What else do you need to see?'

'Take us back and let us see the dead,' Matt said. 'If we can record the truth, we will make sure the whole world knows it.'

The Iraqi turned on his heel. Moments later he returned driving a jeep plastered with the green, red, white and black flag of Iraq. 'I will take you.'

The three men clambered into the jeep.

'Wait! I'm coming with you.'

David turned as one of the four print journalists ran towards them.

'What makes you think you're coming with us?'

The girl gripped the side of the jeep with both hands and

swung herself up next to Matt, her blue eyes challenging. 'What makes you think I don't need to?'

'I didn't notice you battling with the Iraqis to let you go back,' Matt said coolly.

'Want me to go over and get them to sign permission in triplicate?'

David sighed. 'Never mind. Just keep your head down, OK? And stop acting as if you've got something to prove. We've got enough to deal with as it is.'

The girl smiled. Matt was startled to see how pretty she was beneath the grime and attitude. 'Jane Cavendish.'

Any response was drowned out by the crump of a shell hitting the sand less than fifty yards away from the jeep. Karim swerved wildly and the four journalists crouched low in their seats as sand and grit rained down on them. None of them spoke for the remainder of the twenty minutes it took to get back to the front line.

'Impossible to go any further,' Karim said, slamming the jeep into neutral and slewing it to the side of an abandoned armoured personnel carrier. 'You take your pictures from here.'

Matt and David moved swiftly along a trench gouged out of the sand, coughing and covering their faces as they smelled the corpses littering the battlefield.

'Jesus, these boys can't be more than fourteen or fifteen!' Jane exclaimed. 'They're just children!'

Matt took a roll of pictures, then wound back his completed film and pocketed it. He'd already started to follow Jane when he heard the high-pitched whistle of a shell and threw himself to the ground, covering his head with his hands. When he looked up, the children's corpses had vanished, a smoking crater in their place. Grit and sand tumbled around him as he fought to stand up.

'Jane! Jane, are you OK?'

'Can you see her?' David's voice came from a few yards behind Matt.

Matt rubbed his eyes, trying to see through the smoke and tumbling sand. 'No, I can't. She went too far ahead. I'll have to try to find her. She may have got caught when the trench collapsed.'

His eyes streaming, he scanned the corpses littering the trench as he moved forward, desperately hoping Jane wasn't among them. Turning a corner he found a wall of fire blocking his way. On either side of the trench, bullets sang into the sand.

'Jane! Can you hear me?'

Her voice was faint but strong. 'Over here!'

'Are you hurt?'

'No, but I'm trapped beneath the side of the trench.' Fear laced her voice. 'It's collapsed on to my legs. I can't move.'

Matt stared at the flames, then at the ground above him. Fear twisted in him. He knew his chances of bringing them both back alive were next to nothing, but he couldn't just leave her there.

'I'm going to try to get to you. Just hang on.'

Covering his nose and mouth with his handkerchief, he launched himself out of the trench, praying that smoke from the fire would give him just enough cover to get through to Jane unnoticed. He expected a hail of bullets to slice through his flesh at any second. The few moments it took him to reach Jane seemed longer than the rest of his life put together.

Jane struggled to sit up, scrabbling at the sand and shrapnel that trapped her legs as she saw Matt emerge through the smoke.

'Don't move,' he yelled. 'You could bring the rest of the trench down on us.'

Carefully and quickly, he worked at the sand and rubble holding her prisoner, silently praying she hadn't injured

167

herself more than she realised. If he had to carry her, they wouldn't stand a chance. After a few minutes she let out a cry and pulled her legs free.

Matt gripped her hand and helped her to stand. The less time they had to think about their chances, the better. Unsuccessfully he tried to block out the sound of bullets slamming into the sand they had to cross, then suddenly, on impulse, swung back and caught her in his arms, kissing her on the lips. After a long moment, he released her and smiled into her startled eyes.

'OK. Now let's go.'

Two

Via Appia Antica, Rome, Italy
Monday 4 May 1981
10.30 p.m.

Alix listened in the dark as the door creaked open and her
father crept into the room.

'Princess? Are you awake?'

She felt the bed sink as Roberto sat down. Gently he
reached for her hand and laid it against his trousers. 'See how
much Daddy loves you.'

Alix took hold of his erection and tried to move her small
hand the way he'd taught her the last time he'd come to her
bedroom. That had been more than six months ago, the day
after her tenth birthday. She was surprised he had waited so
long. Usually he came much more often.

She couldn't really remember when he'd first started to
visit her in the middle of the night. It didn't stand out in her
mind because her father had always had to play secretly with
her so that her mother wouldn't get angry. She thought she
must have been about six or seven years old the first time he'd
climbed into her bed, because it had been just after Stephi had
suddenly stopped coming to see them. Alix still didn't know
why Stephi had gone. Her father had stopped smiling and
joking and when he'd dropped her off at school he hadn't
seemed bigger and brighter and more exciting than all her

friends' fathers, the way he had before. He didn't even bother to argue with her mother any more, he just gave in.

Once, when she was about seven, Alix had asked her father when Stephi was coming to visit them again. It was the only time in her life she could remember him getting angry with her. He'd told her curtly that he didn't want to talk about it and had walked out of the room. He hadn't spoken to her for two days and she hadn't dared to ask again.

When he'd first started visiting her at night, her father had just cuddled her and stroked her hair, the way he always had. But somehow it had been more exciting in the dark, part of the special secret they shared which excluded her mother. Gradually his cuddles had got more special, making her feel all warm and loved. The last time he'd come, when he'd taught her how to hold him down there, she'd sensed a change in him, as if there was something he wanted to say or do that he wasn't quite sure about. Perhaps that was why it had taken him so long to come back.

She sensed her father smile in the darkness as his hands slipped beneath the covers and moved up her legs. He was her father. He knew what was best, not her. If this was what he wanted, there was nothing to be scared of.

By the time Alix came down to breakfast the next morning, her father had already left for the office where he was scheduled to escort the British Prime Minister, Margaret Thatcher, to lunch. Roberto was rarely at home these days; as the senior Italian Foreign Minister, he spent most of his time fighting his country's corner in Europe and elsewhere.

Alix slid into her seat, barely able to meet her mother's eyes, conscious of her own guilt without really knowing what it was she had done wrong. Hannah, their English house-keeper, sensed the tension between them and placed Alix's proper English breakfast of bacon and eggs in front of her before scuttling from the room. Alix stared at her plate, watching the fat from the bacon mingle with the tomato juice and solidify, forming congealing white islands in a red sea.

'I'm not hungry.'

Joanna looked up from her half-grapefruit. 'Don't be ridiculous, Alexandra. You won't have anything else to eat until lunchtime. You need your food.'

'But I'm not hungry.'

Joanna's voice was cold. 'Just eat it, please. No more arguments.'

Alix picked up her knife and fork. Her stomach rumbled with hunger, but somehow the thought of actual food in her mouth filled her with nausea. She glanced away from the plate, looking for distraction. Her mother was sipping a cup of steaming black coffee, idly flicking through a magazine.

'Who's the lady on the cover of your magazine? She's very beautiful.'

Joanna turned the magazine flat on the linen tablecloth and studied the cover. 'Her name is Angela Lindsay, not that that will mean anything to you.'

'Is she a model?'

'She was. An extremely famous model, in fact. She's just left the House of Pavesi to start her own modelling agency. *Body Image*, I think it's called.'

'Why?'

Joanna shrugged without interest and picked up the magazine again. 'How should I know? Perhaps she wanted to get out before people decided she was too old. She must be at least thirty. Now stop playing with your food and eat your breakfast.'

Alix raised a forkful of mushrooms to her mouth, then put it down again. Her eyes drifted back to the woman on the cover of the magazine, taking in her tiny waist, the endlessly long legs, her flawless face. She flicked her own heavy chestnut plaits over her shoulders contemptuously. She hated them, and the powdering of freckles on her cheeks and nose. She would have given anything for her mother's exquisitely fragile looks, to have inherited her platinum blonde hair, pale skin and brilliant blue eyes. Alix knew her fairytales. The princesses in her stories always looked just like her mother. None of them ever had freckles or unromantic, ruddy good health. And they certainly didn't wear the ugly metal braces that were twisted around her own teeth, making her too embarrassed to even smile.

Her mother threw her magazine down in exasperation. 'Are you going to eat that breakfast or shall I call Hannah to take it away?'

Alix jumped. 'She can take it away.'

'Oh, all right. But don't blame me if you change your mind three minutes after walking into school.'

Alix felt a shiver of triumph at her mother's irritation. It was rare that she dared to disobey Joanna; usually she was more concerned with removing herself from her mother's presence as quickly as possible than with rebellion. She rather liked the feeling of power her act of defiance had given her. It was worth the hunger pangs that were already twisting her stomach.

She stood up and tucked her chair neatly back beneath the breakfast-room table, leaving the room on a small but definite wave of triumph.

Three

David Conto stared at the neatly typed pages in front of him, trying to make some sense of the endless list of names, the tables of figures. Every one of them represented a living human being, yet the letters and numbers danced across the page, as meaningless as hieroglyphic script. There were just too many to take in. He read them again, more slowly this time. Over 500 street children aged between six and twelve had been murdered in the Brazilian cities of Rio, São Paulo and Recife this year alone. Another 2,500 were 'reported missing'. In the nine years that he and his sister, Lucy, had run the shelter on behalf of *Children First*, they'd seen the numbers spiralling almost out of control, doubling once and then tripling. No matter how hard they fought against the tide, the sheer scale of the task defeated them before they'd even started. The thirty or so youngsters they had rescued and brought to the huge house at Duque de Caxias seemed pitiful by comparison with the number they had failed to save.

David saw now that his mother had been right. Nothing was as simple as it had seemed when he'd decided to stay here in Rio and open a shelter for street children in the wake of the tragedy in Nova Esperancia ten years ago. He'd faced opposition from numerous groups – the police, the tourist industry – who saw the children as vermin to be cleared from the streets, not rescued and supported. Most of the abuse had taken the form of anonymous telephone calls and letters; but the flat he and Lucy shared had been burgled twice, and he was certain that he'd been followed several times in recent weeks.

His mother had fiercely objected to him joining *Children First* right from the beginning. Daniella Conto had wanted a career for her son, a profession – law, medicine – something he wouldn't have had if she'd stayed in Brazil where she'd been born. She never tired of telling them how she'd married their father, a US Marine called Joe, so that she could escape to the States and give her children all the opportunities she'd never had. She and Joe had met when he'd been on leave in Rio de Janeiro at the end of the war, and had married in Kansas just one week later. It had been an unhappy match that had ended when Joe Conto was killed in Korea in 1950, leaving Daniella alone with a five-year-old son and a two-month-old baby daughter. She'd supplemented her late husband's meagre army pension by taking in sewing and washing, scrimping and saving to put the children through school. All her dreams had come true when she'd seen first David, and then Lucy, win scholarships to Yale and Vassar.

David knew his mother still hadn't forgiven him for – as she saw it – throwing everything away, but he'd needed to feel he was giving something back. Lucy had joined him in Rio the moment she'd graduated a year later. Neither of them had ever married. They had their work, and each other. Until now it had been enough.

The door to David's office opened and Lucy appeared, a cup of *maté*, the herbal leaf tea popular in South America, in each hand.

'Hard day?'

174

'Aren't they all?'

Lucy sighed. 'I know. Have you seen today's *O Povo*?'

David shook his head.

'It's even worse than usual.'

David took the newspaper. He stared at the front page for a moment, sickened. *O Povo* specialised in covering the gruesome, violent deaths that occurred in the city, but this time it had outdone itself. He threw the paper down as a skinny Latino of perhaps twenty-two knocked, then came hesitantly into the room, blinking hard at David. 'Senhor Conto?'

'Yes?'

The young man pushed his wire-rimmed glasses further up his nose and glanced nervously at Lucy, obviously reluctant to speak. David smiled. 'This is my sister, Lucy. She works with me here –'

'It's all right, David, I was just leaving anyway. I'll see you later.'

David kissed his sister on the cheek, then waved his unexpected visitor towards a patched fake-leather sofa opposite his desk. When it became clear the young man needed further prompting, David picked up his cup of cooling *maté* and busied himself stirring the leaves. 'Did you just want to look round the shelter?'

'No, no, it's nothing like that.' The young man glanced nervously around the office. 'I'm sorry. I don't quite know where to begin –'

'How about if we start by you telling me your name?'

'Paulo Estoban.'

'OK, Paulo. Where are you from?'

'I live in a town called Pedro Juan Caballero. It is in Paraguay, on the border with Brazil.' Paulo smiled for the first time. 'I miss it very much. I have a beautiful girl there, we're

175

hoping to get married soon.' He scrabbled around in his pocket and pulled out a dog-eared photograph. 'Maria.'

David took the photograph and studied it. 'She is very beautiful.' He handed the picture back. 'It's a long way to come to Rio. Was it just to see me?'

The young man's eyes were watchful. 'I thought someone here should know. Everything I have to tell you starts here, in Rio. When I discovered it, I had to do something. Maria's parents lent me the train fare. I told them I was looking for work – there's nothing in Caballero except the Institute. But I couldn't work there.'

David leant forward. 'Paulo, you're talking in riddles. I promise you, anything you say won't go further than this room unless you want it to.'

'Perhaps you won't even believe me. You must be the judge. I can only tell you what I have seen. I thought – running this shelter you must care – you would be the one person who might –'

'Please, Paulo, start at the beginning.'

'Have you ever heard of the Speretti Institute?' Paulo asked.

David was taken aback. 'No, I can't say that I have.'

The young man looked at David fully for the first time. 'After what I have to tell you, it's a name you will never be able to forget.'

David sat in his office for a long time after Paulo had gone. He had no doubt that the young man was telling the truth. His terrible account had crystallised the half-formed fears that had been surfacing in David's own mind over the past few months. Too many things suddenly made sense.

He didn't even see Elizabetta enter the room; then she was standing beside him, a willowy form half hidden by the evening shadows.

'David? Is everything OK?'

David jumped. 'Oh, Ellie. You startled me. Yes, everything's fine. I'm just tired.'

'You work too hard. You should take some time off once in a while. This place wouldn't fall apart without you – at least, not straight away.'

'Thanks for the vote of confidence,' David laughed. 'It's nice to know I'm needed.'

Elizabetta blushed. 'That's not what I meant. I just don't like to see you like this –'

'I know what you meant,' David said.

He felt the blood pounding in his ears as he stared at the girl in front of him and tried to remind himself that she was a mere child, not yet fifteen, it was just a crush; she was simply grateful to him and substituting him for the father she had never had. But her eyes told him otherwise. She was in love with him, in the way a woman loved a man.

And – God help him – he loved her back.

In the years since he had first seen her working in the sweatshop and given her his card, he had seen her blossom from a scrawny child into a breathtakingly beautiful young woman. He'd taught her to read and write her own language, and to speak passable English, albeit with an American accent; he'd found clothes for her that, if not new, were clean and neat and, on her, looked almost as good as Parisian couture. In recent months she had shot upwards and now stood almost as tall as he did at five foot eleven; she was still whippet-slender, but her hips were rounded and womanly, her firm, high breasts tantalised him. It was as much as he could do not to reach out and take her now, here on the floor.

It was Elizabetta who broke their gaze. Abruptly she moved around behind him, her small hands resting lightly on his shoulders. 'Come on, David. The others will be waiting for you in the common room. Leave all this now.'

'I'll be down later. There are some things I still have to do –'

She leaned against his desk, her warm, bare legs just millimetres from his own. 'You haven't had supper with us for ages.'

'I know, and I'm sorry, Ellie. I've been so tied up. Look, you go ahead. I promise I'll be down later.'

Elizabetta edged along the desk so that her beautiful legs were between his own as he sat facing her. 'Do you have to treat me as if I'm still a child? Look at me.'

David sighed. 'You're right, you're not a child. You're old enough to understand that things can't be the same between us any more.'

'Why can't they?'

'You know why. Ellie, I'm thirty-six, more than old enough to be your father. It wouldn't be right to pretend things haven't changed.'

'You still care about me, don't you?'

'Of course I do.' David took her hands in his and held them between his own. 'But I can't treat you the way all the other men in your life have treated you, Ellie. You're still very young, and you need your childhood. I've done my best to give you one, and I'm not going to destroy it now.'

Elizabetta lowered her eyes. 'But I love you, David.'

'In a few years, you'll find someone who can love you decently, someone your own age. You'll thank me then.'

'I don't believe you!' Elizabetta snatched her hands away. 'You love me, too, I know you do. You just won't admit it because you're scared.'

David was stunned by the passion in her voice. He knew if he touched her once, he'd be done for.

Elizabetta stood up and walked unsteadily towards the door. Tearful and angry, she didn't even see the coffee table until she walked straight into it. With a sharp cry, she fell across it, trying unsuccessfully to keep her balance.

'Ellie! Are you all right?' David was already beside her. 'Here, let me see.'

Elizabetta leant back on her elbows as David examined the swelling already beginning to darken beneath her skin of her calf. 'No, nothing broken. You'll live.'

He glanced up at her just as she smiled, and in that moment, he was lost. Without even realising what he was doing, he had pulled her towards him, the months of denial welling up inside him and filling his kiss with more passion than he had known he had in him. Elizabetta threw herself into the embrace, pressing herself against him. She was so slight, she weighed so little. David groaned, fumbling with the buttons of her blouse. He lifted her skirt and pulled down her panties, fastening his mouth on one small nipple as she pushed herself towards him. She freed his stiffened cock from his trousers, guiding him towards her with a need so strong she could hardly bear it. For all her experience, she had never felt desire like this.

And then suddenly he was gone.

She screamed as he was ripped out of her arms and thrown back against the wall. She struggled to sit up, but two men she had never seen before had caught her arms and pinned her down.

'David! David!'

Wrenching her head round, Elizabetta bit down hard on the wrist of the man nearest to her then screamed again as two more men punched David twice in the stomach. The man whose wrist she had bitten slapped her across the face.

'You'll pay for that, bitch. You should have shut up and kept quiet. It's your boyfriend we've come to see.'

David looked up, his face bloody and bruised, as the man walked over to him until he stood inches away, his strange eyes glowing with an emotion David recognised, with terror, as pleasure. 'You've been causing quite a stir with your questions and your shelter and your sympathy for these gutter-rats, Mr Conto. We didn't like it, but we tolerated it – you simply weren't important enough to bother with. But then you had to take it one step further.'

'I don't know what you mean.' David's mouth was full of blood.

The man smiled without humour. 'You haven't been very careful choosing your friends, have you? We've been aware of Paulo Estoban for quite some time, although we didn't think he would be stupid enough to go to you.' He shrugged. 'It hardly matters now. He's dead.'

They wouldn't be telling him this, David thought, if they hadn't already decided that he was going to die too. 'Please, whatever you want to do with me, let her go. She knows nothing. She's just a child. Let her go.'

'How touching.' The man turned to Elizabetta, rubbing his wrist. 'But I'm afraid the young lady has already made this personal. Rodriguez, Juan, she's all yours.'

Elizabetta screamed.

'You're going to watch every moment of this,' the ringleader hissed at David. 'I want you to enjoy it. It will be the last thing you see before you die.'

David watched, dry-eyed, as one of the men knelt between Elizabetta's legs. She caught David's gaze and held on to it like a lifeline as the man yanked open his trousers and thrust his cock inside her. Her face reflected nothing but her love for David as the man plunged into her. After a few minutes, the man climaxed and pulled out of her, zipping up his trousers and switching places with the man holding her down. The second man quickly forced himself into her, already so aroused by watching his companion's assault that he came almost immediately.

180

The ringleader's eyes were glittering. 'It's all right, she isn't going to die. But she's going to watch you die. Slowly. Painfully. Now.'

Four

Rio de Janeiro, Brazil
Tuesday 28 June 1983
6.20 p.m.

Eason Cassidy held the tiny velvet box out to the beautiful girl sitting opposite him. 'Ellie, I'm asking you to marry me. Surely that can't be so unexpected?' He frowned as she continued to stare silently into her glass. 'Honey, can't you give me some sort of reply? Don't you at least owe me that?'

Elizabetta glanced up and saw the hurt in his brown eyes, usually so shrewd, now unexpectedly vulnerable. Eason wasn't used to asking for things. He mostly just got what he wanted. He might be old enough to be her grandfather, but his proposal had dignity. She took the velvet box he was thrusting into her hand. Despite herself, she gasped as she opened it and saw the immense sapphire and diamond ring nestling on the pale blue cushion. 'Oh, Eason, it's absolutely beautiful. I don't know what to say –'

'Just say yes,' Eason urged. He took the box from her shaking hands and slipped the huge ring on to her engagement finger before she could protest. 'Please, Ellie. Just tell me you'll be my wife.'

'It isn't anything to do with you,' Ellie said. 'I promise, if I was thinking of marriage, I couldn't hope for anyone more special than you. But it isn't that simple.'

'What's so difficult about it?' Eason said. 'Is there someone else?'

'No one else.'

'Well, what is it then? Is it my divorce? Honey, *she* left *me*, remember. For my golf coach. I didn't treat her bad or throw her on to the streets.' His voice softened as he took her hand. 'Anything you want, it'll be yours. I'll take care of you. And you'll be well looked after when I go, I promise you that. You won't be left high and dry. Is it my age? I know sixty-seven must seem old to you, but I haven't disappointed you in bed, have I?' He laughed shakily. 'I may take a little longer, but I get there in the end.'

Ellie glanced up at him, stricken. 'Honestly, you're wonderful in bed. Kind, considerate, loving – and no, it's not your age or your divorce, or your children, or your money.' She sighed. 'It's me. You don't know what you're asking –'

'In hell I don't!' Hurt and confusion made Eason angry. 'I'm no green wet-behind-the-ears kid, Ellie. I've been running my company single-handed for years. I've been widowed and divorced and I've raised three grown-up children on my own. I know exactly what I'm asking. There's nothing a slip of a girl like you can teach me about marriage, or anything else for that matter.'

'So why do you want to marry me?' Ellie said quietly.

Eason's anger faded as quickly as it had come. His voice was thick with emotion. 'Honey, I'm crazy about you, that's why. I don't need any other reason.'

Ellie nervously twisted the stem of her glass between her fingers. In one stroke, Eason was offering her the chance to escape from the nightmare she'd been living for the past two years. She'd be crazy to turn him down; yet something held her back. She would become his property. Her life since David's murder had been very tough, but at least she'd lived it according to her own choice. It seemed a betrayal of all she'd

183

fought for to give up now and hand herself over to a man she didn't love for the sake of financial security. There was more than one type of prostitution.

She'd met Eason Cassidy in the same bar in which they were now sitting, just over three months ago. One of her regular customers had stood her up – his wife had just discovered how he spent his Thursday evenings when she thought he'd been having Portuguese lessons – and Eason had offered to buy her a drink. His quiet charm had touched her. She'd seen the discreet Philippe Patek watch on his wrist, the absence of either a wedding ring or a telltale white band on his left hand, and decided to accept. He'd treated her with old-world courtesy, pulling out her chair for her, never once allowing his hand to brush her arm or his eyes to stray towards her legs. He'd listened attentively to her conversation and escorted her back to the apartment she now shared with two other girls without asking himself in for coffee. Instead, he'd politely requested a second date, and the following week they'd had dinner at a small French restaurant.

Eason Cassidy had explained that he owned an oil company in Texas, was here in Rio for three months to work out the details on an important deal, and had been divorced long enough for it not to matter to him any more. They hadn't slept together until their fifth date, and he had been a gentle and thoughtful lover, if a little less active than she was used to. After that first night, he'd given her a pair of tiny gold hoop earrings, the first present she'd ever received. A turquoise and silver bracelet had followed, then a simple gold necklace and a Victorian locket. He'd wooed her as if she were a normal, decent woman any man might want to marry, not a hooker who sold herself to the highest bidder. She'd never told him the truth about what she did for a living, and he'd never asked.

But she couldn't let him marry her. She cared for him too much to do that to him.

184

'Eason, I'm sorry. I can't marry you. I wish I could, but I can't. You don't really know anything about me, about my life. If you did, you wouldn't be sitting there right now.'

Eason's eyes were filled with compassion. 'Oh, Ellie. Did you think I didn't know? I'm not a fool. Beautiful young girls of nearly seventeen don't allow themselves to be picked up in bars by old men like me just out of sympathy.' He took her hand in his. 'I'm in love with you, Ellie. I don't care what you've done, or who you've been. I'm offering you the chance to start again. I don't expect you to love me; at least, not right away. I think you care for me a little – and that's all I ask.'

'I do care for you, you know I do. Very much,' Ellie said, her eyes filling with tears.

'Please, Ellie. At least promise me you'll think about it?'

Ellie pulled the ring off her finger and handed it to Eason, knowing she never intended to take it back. 'Yes, I promise I'll think about it. But you must keep this. It wouldn't be right for me to have it yet.'

Reluctantly Eason pocketed the ring.

Half an hour later Ellie unlocked the door to her fourth-floor apartment, and threw her raincoat over the arm of the battered orange sofa in the living room. She glanced around, wondering if she was crazy to even think twice before accepting Eason's offer. What had her independence earned her that she was so reluctant to give up? This cramped apartment crawling with cockroaches and spiders, a fifth-hand bed riddled with bugs and fleas, a filthy toilet that flushed once in seven days? The same pair of shoes she'd been wearing for two years, rotten food from the piles of spoiled and overripe produce rejected by more discerning shoppers? A lifetime of opening her legs to bullies and perverts little better than the bastards who'd raped her and murdered David?

But no matter how far she ran or what she did, it always came down to the same thing. She only had one asset, her body. And it was for sale to the highest bidder. Even Eason, kind and gentle as he was, would exact a price for his protection. She didn't doubt that he loved her, but he wouldn't have been so ready to forget her past if she hadn't been young and beautiful and very skilled in bed. David had been the only man she'd ever met who'd demanded nothing from her.

The familiar pain tugged at her heart. There wasn't a single day that passed that she didn't think of him, didn't wish she'd died beside him that night. She'd left the shelter, wandering the streets for two days without food or sleep, unable to think what to do next. Eventually her hunger and exhaustion had penetrated her stupor, and she'd allowed one of the men who'd propositioned her on the beach to fuck her in exchange for enough money to buy a meal.

Somehow she'd slipped into a routine of trawling the beaches every day for clients, disappearing into an alley or the back of a car for as long as it took to earn enough for the next meal, sleeping rough in doorways whenever she could walk no more. Her age and her arresting beauty had guaranteed her safety, although she no longer cared what happened to her. Instead of clearing her off the streets, any policeman she encountered invariably became her next customer. After six months on her own, she'd thrown in her lot with two other girls. Working the beaches, they'd been able to earn enough to keep themselves off the streets, renting this filthy apartment and occasionally joining forces professionally for favoured customers willing to pay extra. Apart from the payoffs to the police, most of her customers now were wealthy tourists; they paid better, and were less inclined towards violence.

Eason was offering her the first chance she'd had to escape and she was going to turn him down. Despite everything, a part of her still believed in marrying for love. She whored because she had no other choice if she was to survive; to her, the sex she sold was as far removed from love and marriage as the soft tomatoes she bought half-price.

She heard footsteps on the stairs and quickly crossed the hall to check the main bedroom she, Annie and Rosa used exclusively for clients. Opening the top drawer of the bedside table she took out a tiny mirror and packet of white powder. She tipped the cocaine on to the mirror and used a piece of card to divide it into four white lines. It cost her almost everything she earned, cheap as it was in Rio, but it was worth it. Without it she didn't think she'd survive.

She was back in the other room just as Annie led their client through the front door. She hadn't seen him before, although she knew he was one of Annie's regulars. He'd requested a threesome this evening, and since Rosa was out of town, she'd agreed with Annie to accommodate him.

She plastered a smile on her face. 'Can I get you a drink, Senhor Colhor? Whisky, beer?

The client's eyes travelled up and down Ellie's body. 'Whisky. Neat, no ice.'

He threw back his drink as soon as it was handed to him. 'I'm paying you two $200 an hour. I expect more than a whisky and a few smiles. Where's the bedroom?' His pale mouth was compressed into a thin line. Ellie hoped Annie knew what she was doing with this one. To her, he looked like trouble. This man was clearly wealthy, and she had a vague suspicion that she'd seen him somewhere before – perhaps on television or in a newspaper. Whoever he was, he could clearly afford whores far more expensive than they were. But then maybe it wasn't that easy to find women – even whores – willing to give him what he wanted.

Annie sashayed across the room and made as if to undo Colhor's shirt buttons. He slapped her wrist and pushed her back on to the bed. 'I'll do that myself. You, take your clothes off.' His glance took in Ellie, still standing by the doorway. 'And you.'

Annie unzipped her loose cotton dress. Beneath it she wore only the scantiest black panties, which she eased gracefully down her legs and left on the floor. She stood unselfconsciously in front of Colhor as he took in the full breasts with their large pink nipples, the slender waist, the russet tangle between her thighs. His glance moved across to Ellie. 'Now you.'

Ellie fought back her reluctance and lifted her blouse over her head, unbuttoning her skirt and tossing them both into a corner of the room. She hesitated for a moment as she reached to unhook her bra, then unsnapped it in one quick, determined motion. In the past two years she'd had more men than she could count. She could hardly start being squeamish now. She sensed Colhor's eyes on her as she bent to wriggle out of her panties, and to her surprise felt an answering pulse of excitement and fear between her legs. Something about this man had breached her normal professional detachment and drawn a personal response from her, however unwilling. She perched on the edge of the bed and crossed her legs, trying to quell the almost overwhelming desire to turn and run from the room.

Colhor nodded at Annie. 'Fuck her.'

Ellie lay back on the bed to accommodate the other girl. She'd done this hundreds of times before. The cocaine made her body throb with desire even as her mind went numb. She barely registered Annie as the girl stroked her breasts and manoeuvred her own body so as not to obstruct their client's view.

'I said, fuck her,' Colhor said coolly. 'Not play with her. Fuck her.'

Annie bent over Ellie and sucked her breast gently, rubbing a dildo she had by the bed across Ellie's cunt in an attempt to arouse her sufficiently to take the object inside her without it hurting.

Suddenly Colhor stood up and snatched the dildo away from Annie. 'Forget it, you stupid bitch. Just suck my cock and I'll do it.'

Colhor shoved the dildo roughly into Ellie, his thrusts synchronised with Annie's mouth as she worked his cock with her tongue. Ellie blocked out the pain and concentrated on Annie's breasts as they rose and fell with the effort of her work, deliberately conjuring up erotic images of the two of them entwined together so that her arousal smoothed the path of the object.

The fury of his actions seemed to soothe Colhor and abruptly he threw the dildo over the side of the bed, pushed Annie's head away from him and lay back next to Ellie. 'Why don't you show me why I'm paying you so much money?' he said. 'I want to taste just what you're made of.'

Ellie knelt up on the pillows on either side of Colhor's head, her back against the headboard, and lowered herself on to him so that he could just taste her musky sweetness without quite being able to reach her.

Annie regarded their client truculently from the end of the bed. 'Just how adventurous are you?'

Colhor's tongue flickered impotently in the direction of Ellie's cunt and he reached up and gripped her buttocks, pulling her towards him. 'More than you can handle, sweetheart.'

The two girls grinned at each other over his head, as Ellie caught his left hand and snapped the handcuff attached to the brass bedpost and concealed beneath the pillows around his wrist. As she moved to fasten his right, Annie grabbed his ankles and manacled them to the bed so that he was spreadeagled in front of them.

Colhor's face was expressionless. 'I hope this is a game you two know how to win.'

Annie kissed Ellie on the mouth, her hands gently pulling at the other girl's nipples as she hooked one leg around Ellie's waist and pressed her mound against her. Ellie's small firm breasts jutting forward, the two girls moved to a familiar rhythm, both of them clearly aroused. Colhor squirmed on the bed, resenting their pleasure yet unbearably excited by the unfamiliar feeling of not being in control. He was forced to wait until they pulled apart and turned to him, almost as if they'd forgotten he was there.

'Are you ready for us now?' Annie stared pointedly at his erect cock. 'I think that's a yes.'

Ellie kissed Annie again and climbed back on to the bed, manoeuvring herself back into position behind Colhor's head so that the inside of her thighs caressed his cheeks. She bent over him so that he could take her small dark nipple into his mouth and suck, the curtain of her hair blocking his view of the room so that he didn't see Annie unhook the leather trapeze seat that was suspended over the centre of the bed. He groaned as Ellie straightened up out of his reach, then gasped as he saw Annie sitting on the trapeze, her legs raised in a wide 'V' almost to the level of her shoulders, her cunt glistening just a few inches above his groin. Ellie gripped the two chains holding the seat and twisted them round and round. He could feel the draught across his naked body as the girl turned again and again, each twist knotting the chains tighter.

Ellie pulled the other girl into position over Colhor's cock and Annie lowered herself on to him, the muscles in her cunt working him as if she had a dozen tiny hands inside her. He shuddered and thrust himself upwards to meet her, his wrists and ankles straining against the handcuffs holding him to the bed. Suddenly Ellie let go of the twisted chains above Annie's head and she began to spin round as the links untwined, Colhor's cock still inside her.

'What the hell –'

Faster and faster Annie turned as the untwisting chains gathered momentum, gripping her ankles tightly with both hands as she spun around. Colhor sank back on the bed and surrendered to the incredible sensation, unable to think or breathe as he was quite literally screwed into the mattress. Ellie watched his narrow face suffuse with colour, his chest rising and falling rapidly as he was driven to the edge of orgasm. She knew he'd be back for more; no man who'd tried this once was ever satisfied with anything less again. One of their more descriptive clients had once described the experience as 'like fucking a virgin and receiving fellatio from a top-class whore at the same time'.

Colhor came, his entire body twitching as he poured himself into Annie. As his eyes flickered open, Ellie leant over to unfasten the handcuffs around his wrists, then moved to help Annie lift the trapeze out of the way. Colhor smiled lazily at Ellie as she bent to unshackle his ankles.

'I hope you can match that, darling. It's some performance to live up to.'

Ellie met his sardonic gaze. Suddenly she felt as if a river of ice had flooded her body. She gripped the bedpost with both hands as she stared at him. She couldn't believe she hadn't recognised him earlier, but then in the past two years she'd done her best to forget everything about him. It was something in the way he'd smiled that had given him away, that terrible mixture of cruelty and satisfaction that she'd only ever seen once in her life, and had hoped never to see again.

Five

Rua Joaquim Nabuco, Rio de Janeiro, Brazil
Wednesday 29 June 1983
8.00 p.m.

Fernando Moreno stood in the centre of the shabby apartment
and scanned the room. His angry gaze missed nothing.

He was too late.

The room looked as if it had been ransacked. Pale squares
stood out against the grimy wallpaper where pictures had been
hastily removed, drawers still gaped where they had been
yanked open and emptied. The filthy orange sofa cushions
stood up at odd angles as if they had been pulled apart in the
search for something lost, or perhaps concealed, behind them.
He took a few steps across the room and glanced through the
doorway of the main bedroom where he'd had the orgasm of a
lifetime less than twenty-four hours ago. It too had been
stripped of everything portable; the wide double bed was bare,
its soiled mattress half-wrenched on to the floor. The wooden
chest at its foot had been emptied, but the two gilt chains of the
trapeze still hung in their place over the centre of the bed,
swaying slightly in the draught from the shuttered window.

He was certain he'd only missed them by minutes, but it
might as well have been days. They would have disappeared
by now, vanishing back into the slime of the streets, and he

might spend weeks – months – searching for them without success.

He had thought her dead. After Conto's murder, he'd been certain she'd returned to the streets and gone the way most of the street children did within a few months. But he'd obviously underestimated her. She had kept her head and managed to outmanoeuvre him. Another woman might have hoped he hadn't recognised her. This girl had clearly decided not to leave it to chance.

She'd been wise to flee. If he ever found her again, he'd have to kill her. It had been a serious error of judgement that he'd allowed her live at all; he just hoped it wasn't a mistake that would come back to haunt him. Her existence put him in danger; now it could only be a matter of time before she discovered exactly who he was. He knew instinctively she had not fled her apartment out of fear, but because she was not yet ready for him. He had no doubt that one day, she would be.

But when she came for him, he would be waiting.

Six

East Lambrook Manor, West Sussex, UK
Sunday 23 October 1983
4.30 p.m.

Matt peered through the taxi windscreen, eager for the first familiar glimpse of his family's home. The thick row of conifers on the left suddenly thinned, and the driver swung into the driveway, stopping in front of the five-barred gate that blocked their way. He reached to unbuckle his seatbelt, but Matt was already out of the car, his feet crunching across the gravel as he ran towards the gate.

Jane smiled as she watched him unbolt it and leap boyishly on to the bottom rung, leaning forward and using his weight to carry it open. She had a sudden image of him as a boy of eight doing exactly the same thing.

Matt caught her smile as he scrambled back into the car. 'Was it something I said?'

'I was just wondering where you keep your conkers and collection of dead spiders.'

He grinned. 'My father used to go mad when I was younger, said I'd break the hinges and wreck the gate.' He glanced through the back window. 'Still seems to be standing, though.'

'That's parents for you.'

'Yeah. Why is it anything fun is always bad for you?'

Jane slid her hand along his thigh towards his crotch. 'Not everything.'

A breeze blew through the half-open window, ruffling Jane's dark hair and carrying with it the rich autumn scent of damp leaves, bonfires and apples. Matt was reminded of a dozen Octobers, spent eagerly collecting shiny brown conkers from beneath the horse-chestnut trees on the far side of the lawn. Every season here had its own particular smell, one he could recall immediately no matter where he was in the world.

'Matt, how long is it since you've been back here?'

Matt thought for a moment. 'God, it must be three years. I hadn't realised how much I've missed it until now. When I'm in England I want to spend my time with you. Grabbing a few days in London at the flat is difficult enough, without trying to get down to East Lambrook as well.' He stared out of the window. 'I'm just making excuses, I know. I could have brought you ages ago. Maybe I would have done if my parents didn't always make it so difficult.'

'Don't they like you coming down?'

'God, no, it's nothing like that. And it's fine as long as I see them separately. I usually meet Mother in town, go shopping, take her to the theatre, though I haven't even done that, much, since you and I have been together. Dad's easy, we just go to his club.' Matt's voice was flat. 'On their own, they're great. It's when they get together the trouble starts.'

'But if they argue that much, why are they still together after all this time?'

Matt shrugged. 'Don't ask me to explain. They're like bookends. As long as there's plenty of distance between them, they're fine, and if you took one of them away, the other would collapse. But put them together, and they're totally useless.'

They rounded the final curve of the drive and the Manor

came into view. 'It's lucky you have such a huge house. Sounds like they need it,' Jane said.

Matt gazed at the mellow stone of the house as the taxi pulled up in front of it; he knew each room that lay behind the sash windows as if he lived there still. The house was more than three centuries old and gave an overwhelming impression of genteel *déshabillé*. It had been Matt's home all his life, and he had never felt truly safe anywhere else.

The front door swung open and Matt saw his parents. They managed to stand barely inches apart and yet convey the impression that they were complete strangers. If he was seeing them for the first time, as Jane was doing, he would have assumed that they'd never even been introduced.

In the past, Caroline Logan had always made a point of disliking Matt's girlfriends on principle; had she ever known that he had lost his virginity at the age of fifteen to Joanna Cerreni she would have been appalled. The cards were already stacked against Jane: not only had she ensnared Caroline's adored younger son, but she dared to believe she could have her man and an independent career as well. At twenty-six, a year older than Matt – another black mark against her – Jane Cavendish was one of the *Daily Chronicle*'s most respected international correspondents, travelling as much, if not more, than Matt himself in the course of her work. She'd already won a major award for her coverage of the battle around Basra which she and Matt had so narrowly survived.

'I've put you in your old room,' Caroline said over her shoulder as they entered the house. 'Jane, you'll be in the blue room; Matt will show you the way. You should find towels and so on there already.'

'That's very kind of you –'

'Mother,' Matt interrupted. 'You know perfectly well that

Jane and I have been living together in London for the past eighteen months. Do you really want me dashing naked down the corridor as the clock chimes midnight?'

'What you get up to in your own home is your business, but when you're under my roof, I expect you to follow my rules.'

'I think putting them in separate wings is a little extreme, dear,' Christopher murmured. 'They're not children any more.'

'Look, really, it's no problem,' Jane said. 'This is the most beautiful house, you know. You must be terribly proud of it.'

Caroline's expression softened slightly. 'It's been in my family since it was built. Three hundred and twenty-four years. Do you know this part of the world at all?'

'A little. We have some relatives who live not far from here –'

'Really? Not the Daire-Cavendishes in Cuckfield?'

Jane shook her head. 'I don't think so. At least, not that I know of, anyway.'

Caroline paused to straighten a picture as they walked through the hall. 'Tell me, what did you say your father does?'

'He's a marketing director for a brewery in Kent, or rather he was. He's retired now.'

'A brewer's. I see. And your mother?'

'She's a sculptor. I'm afraid I haven't inherited any of her talent. I'm utterly useless with my hands; if it wasn't for my word processor, I doubt I'd even have made it as a journalist.'

'Private patrons, or does she exhibit at all?'

'Oh, no, nothing like that,' Jane smiled. 'Most of her work is still dotted around the garden, although she's done a few pieces for friends, and the odd commission. She's very good, though we've never been able to persuade her to take it seriously.'

'How interesting,' Caroline's voice was cool. 'You must

have had a very unusual childhood. Where was it you said you went to school?'

'For heaven's sake, Caroline,' Christopher exclaimed. 'Would you like the poor girl to submit a résumé before she comes down to dinner?'

'Perhaps Matt could show me the way upstairs?' Jane said quickly. 'It is getting rather late –'

'Of course. Dinner is at eight.' Caroline turned to her and smiled graciously, taking in Jane's faded jeans and crumpled linen jacket. 'I'm sure you'll want to wash and change after your journey, so we'll leave you to it. Come along, Christopher.'

Jane and Matt fled thankfully up the stairs, trying to stifle their giggles.

'I'm sorry about my mother,' said Matt. 'I think she's never really forgiven herself for what she sees as "marrying down" when she met my father.'

'I don't think she likes me,' Jane said mournfully.

'It's nothing personal,' Matt sighed. 'She's never liked any of the girls I've brought home. She particularly won't like you; she disapproves of women having a career. She thinks if a husband and children aren't enough to occupy you, you should just join a few more charity committees or become a pillar of the WI.'

Jane giggled. 'Oh God. I think I'm a lost cause.'

'I certainly hope so.'

Leaving Jane to shower in peace, Matt headed downstairs. As he passed his father's study, Christopher emerged and beckoned him, shutting the door quickly behind them.

'Your mother not around? Good.' Christopher walked towards the bookcase that stood against the far wall and pulled out Volume IV of Butler's *Lives of the Saints*. Winking at Matt he extracted a three-quarters-full bottle of Glennfiddich.

'Your mother'd kill me if she knew I keep this here. Never before the sun's over the yardarm, that's her rule. Want one?'

Matt nodded. 'Please. I think I'm going to need one.'

'Oh, don't take your mother to heart,' Christopher said, easing himself into a chair opposite Matt. 'She just can't bear to let you go, that's all.'

'Yes, I know. She wanted me to follow in Hugh's footsteps, get my degree, join all the right clubs, marry the right girl. I must be a great disappointment to her.'

'It's not you she's angry with, it's me, Matt. She's always hated me working for *Children First*. She never saw it as a real job, even when I was President. Not the sort of thing she could boast about over bridge with the other company wives, I suppose. And of course she blames me for filling your head with idealistic notions.'

Matt felt a sudden surge of love for his father. Christopher had always been there for him. It was hard to remember that he would be seventy this year. It had been his father who'd broken the news to his mother that Matt had dropped out of Oxford, and it had been his cheques that had seen Matt through the early lean times, when he was still trying to make his name as a war photographer. Matt still recalled his father's face that terrible day of the Nova Esperancia mudslide. His father had known the danger, but still he'd let him go. No matter how it had hurt or what it had cost him, Christopher had always tried to allow Matt to find his own way.

The two men sat in companionable silence, sipping their Scotch and enjoying the peace and warmth of the fire. It was Christopher who finally broke it. 'You're serious about Jane, aren't you?'

'You don't miss much, do you, Dad?'

'It's not difficult. It's written all over your face.' He stared into the fire. 'Have you asked her to marry you yet?'

Matt shook his head. 'It's not that easy. Living together is one thing, but marriage? We've been together for more than two years, but we're hardly ever home at the same time, and even when we happen to be on an assignment together we're both up to our necks in muck and bullets. Is that any basis for a lifelong commitment? What happens when the excitement and the danger stops and we're just left with each other?'

'Do you love her?'

'I love *being* with her, I love her spirit. I love the way she looks when she's just come in from a story covered in mud, I love the way she sulks when she loses at Monopoly and throws the board across the room. But is that enough?'

'How do you know which pictures you take are the ones that are going to make the front page?' Christopher asked.

Matt looked puzzled. 'I don't know. I just do. They grab me here, in the pit of my stomach. I always know which is the right one.'

'Then do the same with Jane. Trust your instinct.'

'Did anybody ever tell you how much sense you talk sometimes, Dad?'

Caroline came into the room. She kissed the top of her son's head. 'I might have known you'd be in here. We're about to eat.'

Matt followed his mother into the hall just as Jane came down the stairs, her long dark hair caught into a loose topknot. Caroline smiled distantly and swept past on a cloud of Chanel No. 5.

'I'm so glad you didn't bother to make an effort for dinner,' she said as she glanced at Jane's best blue velvet jacket.

'Sometimes I could kill my mother,' Matt said as he unpinned Jane's hair four hours later and let it tumble slowly around her shoulders.

Jane slid her hands around his back. 'At least they didn't

200

murder each other over dinner. When your father started talking about the Falklands, I thought she was going to have a fit.'

'It's a sore point. They didn't speak to each other for six months over that war; my mother thought my father was a lily-livered pacifist, and he accused her of imperialism and war-mongering.'

Jane caressed him suggestively. 'I'd rather discuss another sort of point …'

Matt's cock stiffened beneath her touch. 'God, Janey. You're enough to drive any man wild.'

'I don't want any man. Just you.'

Matt slipped her velvet jacket from her shoulders and saw the outline of her tanned breasts revealed through the fine silk of the cream camisole she was wearing beneath. He kissed her throat, savouring the sweet fresh smell of her skin as his fingers unfastened the tiny buttons of her black trousers as she relaxed into his embrace. Gently he batted her hands away as she reached to undress him, the hardness of his cock thrusting against the delicate silk of her panties.

'I want to see you,' he murmured thickly. 'Just for a moment, just as you are.'

Jane stepped away from him, easing the straps of her camisole down around her shoulders and stepping out of her panties. She lay down on the bed, her honey-coloured skin glowing against the white counterpane. Matt gazed at her. He couldn't name the exact moment in that terrifying journey from the trenches in Iraq back to the safety of the jeep that he had fallen in love with her. It could have been the way she'd smiled in relief when he'd pulled the wreckage from her legs; or the moment when he had first kissed her, determined that if he had to die, it would be with the taste of a woman on his lips. He only knew that by the time they'd tumbled into the back of the battered vehicle and David Cameron had driven desperately away from the shellfire, he had decided he couldn't let this difficult, infuriating, demanding woman go.

They had had endless fights in the intervening two years, and a furious and continual jostling for power in a relationship that was made up of two determined, dominant partners. Their frequent separations gave their reunions an energy and heat that invariably found its expression in bed. Matt couldn't imagine a world without her.

He knelt by the bed, suddenly absolutely certain of what he wanted.

'Janey, my darling. Please, will you marry me?'

Seven

Santa Susanna School, Rome, Italy
Thursday 7 June 1984
1.00 p.m.

'Is that really all you're going to have?'

Alix put down her half-empty container of strawberry yoghurt and made a face, as if she really couldn't bear to eat any more. 'Yes, I'm stuffed.'

Sarah Martini gaped. 'I don't know how you do it. I simply don't have the willpower.'

'Don't you feel well?' Kay Jordan asked.

'Oh, I'm fine,' Alix said. 'I'm just on a diet, that's all.'

'A diet?' Kay repeated. 'Which one?'

Alix thought for a moment. In the beginning, when she'd decided to take her dieting seriously, she'd read armfuls of books from the library to make sure she got it right. *The Hip and Thigh Diet. The Fibre Plan. Becoming a Vegan: the Right and the Wrong Way.* The books had given her ammunition against her mother's scepticism; but they'd also contradicted each other on almost every nutritional point. To be on the safe side, Alix had decided to follow every rule in all of them, which hadn't left her with a great deal she could eat.

'Well, not any diet in particular,' she improvised. 'I just sort of made one up, on my own.'

Sarah stared guiltily at the chocolate icing crusting the cake in her hand. 'What *can* you eat on it?'

'Not that, for a start,' Kay said.

'Well, I just have black coffee for breakfast,' Alix said. She knew it sounded the height of sophistication. She didn't tell her friends how much she hated it and the tiny saccharin tablets she put in it in an attempt to make it more palatable – the sweetener left a synthetic aftertaste that was almost as bad as the coffee itself. But it was all her mother usually had for breakfast, and if Joanna could do it, so could she.

'No cereal?'

'Have you seen what they put into cereal?' Alix said disapprovingly. 'All those chemicals! Not to mention the vegetable oil and salt. And the sugar! Over a hundred calories an ounce!'

'How do you keep track of the calories?' Kay pulled the tab on a can of Coke. 'All those numbers, it sounds worse than maths.'

'It's easy when you get used to it.' Just for practice, Alix quickly added up the calories in the packed lunch that Hannah, their English housekeeper, had given her that morning. Peanut butter sandwich, 300 calories; an apple, 65 calories; salt-and-vinegar crisps, 150 calories – not to mention the horror of the salt itself, all that water-retaining sodium; and a bottle of fizzy orange, 125 calories. Over 600 calories altogether! She'd dumped the lot in the rubbish bin outside the school building as soon as the driver was out of sight, with the exception of the crisps. Those she'd kept for Hannah to find at the bottom of her satchel; she knew the housekeeper would become suspicious if her charge claimed she'd eaten everything she had been given. Discreet as she was, Alix's obsession with her food hadn't gone entirely unnoticed.

'I bet you eat masses when you get home,' Sarah said,

licking her fingers. 'You can't possibly live on what you say you eat.'

Alix looked indignant. 'I do not eat masses! I just have an apple or yoghurt for lunch, then some boiled vegetables for dinner. I wouldn't even eat those, but my mother makes me.'

'Vegetables are fattening.' Sarah was keen to regain the upper hand after the weak will she'd displayed in eating the chocolate cake.

'No, they're not, not if you don't smother them with sauce,' Kay answered, eyeing Sarah's ample frame with disapproval. 'Boiled, they're fine.'

'They're still fattening,' Sarah insisted. 'Potatoes, cauli-flower, rice, they've all got starch in. I read it in a magazine.'

'Since when has rice been a vegetable?' Kay scoffed.

Alix felt a flicker of fear. Suppose she'd got it wrong? Suppose the broccoli spears and diced carrots she insisted on every evening were in fact just as fattening as the meat and gravy she refused to eat? She'd been certain vegetables were all right – it was one of the few points on which all the books agreed. Her mother ate vegetables and she could still fit perfectly into her wedding dress; she made a point of wearing it every year on their wedding anniversary to annoy her husband – Alix had seen her. She made a mental note not to eat any more vegetables until she'd checked.

'If rice isn't a vegetable, what is it?' Sarah scented victory.

But Kay was bored with the conversation. Alix stood up and threw her half-empty yoghurt pot into the wastepaper basket on the edge of the school lawn, trying to still a pang of longing as the discarded yoghurt spilled out of its container. She slid her hand surreptitiously inside the waistband of her pleated school skirt, as she did at least twenty times a day, feeling a surge of triumph at how loose it was. She could even see the faint outline of the bones in her wrist if she held it up to the light. If she kept this up, she'd be transformed; not quite one of those beautiful models in the magazines, but not so far away, either. No wonder her mother kept trying to stop her dieting – she must be jealous.

Kay brandished a magazine in front of Alix, and pointed to the picture of Simon Le Bon spread across the two centre pages, naked from the waist up. 'God, isn't he gorgeous. He's one sort of biology homework I wouldn't mind taking home.'

Sarah giggled. 'Kay, you're terrible. What on earth would your mother say if she heard you?'

'She'd have a fit, what do you think? My dear, sweet mother still buys me Barbie dolls for Christmas. I just hope she never finds out what I'm really up to.'

Sarah stared. 'You don't mean –'

'I most certainly do.'

'You haven't!'

'Well, not quite,' Kay revelled in the sudden attention. 'But almost.'

'Who with?'

Kay blushed and fiddled with her shoelaces. 'Alfredo.'

'Not your tennis coach? But he must be twenty, at least!'

'Twenty-two.'

'You've never kissed him?' Alix was shocked.

'Of course I have. I'm not a baby, you know.'

Sarah leant forward eagerly. 'Did you let him touch you? You know, *there*?'

'Well, not at first. We just held hands and kissed the first time, then I let him put his tongue in my mouth –'

'Sounds disgusting,' Sarah said.

'Well, that shows how much you know,' Kay retorted. 'It was fantastic, actually. He's given me his identity bracelet.'

'And then what?'

'I could hardly keep saying no after that, could I? I mean, he must be quite serious to give me his bracelet, so I let him undo my bra and touch my breasts.' She sighed. 'I can't tell you how difficult it was to stop him after that, especially when he started kissing me and touching me, you know, down there. I don't know what I'm going to do on Tuesday when I have my next lesson.'

'But you like it, don't you?' Alix asked.

'Of course I do, but that's not the point. If I let him go all the way too quickly, he'll think I'm easy.'

Alix frowned. 'I still don't understand. If you like him, and he likes you, why don't you just say yes?'

'Don't you know anything?' Kay said scornfully. 'Your virginity is your biggest bargaining tool. You don't just give it to anyone.'

'I knew this girl once,' Sarah said, rolling on to her back and staring up at the sky. 'She was in the same ballet class as my sister. She was fifteen and her parents had arranged for her to marry her cousin or something, he was incredibly rich and handsome, and everyone thought how lucky she was. It was all fixed, everyone had been invited – she even brought a picture of her wedding dress to class to show us – and then suddenly it was all cancelled.'

'What happened?' Alix asked. She had a feeling she didn't want to know.

'She got pregnant.'

Kay shook her head. 'I wouldn't let that happen to me. You can do something about it these days.'

'But couldn't he just marry her anyway?' Alix said.

'It wasn't that simple. You see, he wasn't the father of the baby. It turned out that the father –' Sarah paused for dramatic effect – 'was her own brother!'

Kay gasped. 'But that's disgusting!'

'Well, it's true. They took her away to this special clinic to fix it and tried to keep it secret, but it was too late, her reputation was ruined. No one wanted her after that. I'm not surprised, either.'

Alix's head was spinning. Making love, sex, whatever you wanted to call it – it was the same thing, surely, no matter who you did it with? Just a special way of showing someone how much you loved them, that was all. If you loved someone, what did it matter who they were?

A sudden chill settled over her heart. What would Kay and Sarah say if they knew about her father?

'I still can't believe anyone could do that kind of thing.' Kay stood up, brushing a few blades of grass from her skirt. 'Her own brother! I mean, that's incest, isn't it? It's illegal, she could have gone to jail. People like that shouldn't be allowed to mix with normal people.'

In the distance, a bell clanged to signal the end of the lunch break, and clusters of girls began to drift reluctantly across the lawn towards the school building. Kay picked up her lunchbox and glanced at Alix, still sitting silent and motionless on the grass. 'Are you coming?'

Alix stared stupidly up at her. She tried to speak, but her tongue suddenly seemed too big for her mouth. The words died in her throat. Slowly she got to her feet, her limbs moving as if they belonged to a different person.

She managed to get through the rest of the day on autopilot, as she sat through French, geography and maths. She felt as if she were surrounded by an unbreakable glass wall through which she could see but not touch. The nameless foreboding she'd felt ever since her father had come to her room that night three years ago had finally crystallised in her mind.

Now she had a name for what had happened many times since then.

Somehow she kept going until the final bell rang, then fled the classroom before anyone could speak to her, thankful that her father's driver was already waiting for her outside so that she didn't have to stay and chat to her friends. As soon as the driver had dropped her off outside the villa, she ran round to the kitchen door and up the back stairs before Hannah could see her.

She had no idea how long she lay on the floor of her room. Eventually the fading light reminded her that she still had to go downstairs and face her father across the dining table. She stared at her reflection in the mirror. The blank face that gazed back didn't seem to be her. Impatiently she pushed her waist-length auburn hair back from her face, suddenly hating its luxuriant abundance. Her father had always loved her hair, saying it was one of her best features; he would spend hours twisting it around his fingers, burying his face in it as he kissed her and told her how much he loved her.

Abruptly she wrenched open the medicine cabinet above the mirror and pulled out the scissors on the top shelf, running the cool blades along the inside of her wrist, then seized a handful of the hair her father loved so much. Within minutes she stood in the centre of a heap of red-gold hair, staring at her shorn head in the mirror. Without its halo of colour, her face seemed small, lost and vulnerable. Tears stung her eyes as she threw hanks of hair into the wastepaper basket. Perhaps if she'd done this three years ago he would never have wanted to do what he'd done to her and everything between them would still be all right. Now it was spoiled for ever.

Eight

Teklima, Texas, USA
Friday 29 November 1985
3.30 p.m.

'Almighty God, our Father, we firmly believe that your Son died and rose to life. We pray for our brother who has died in Christ. Raise him at the last day to share the glory of the risen Christ, who lives and reigns…'

A hand prodded Ellie in the back and she half turned. Her stepdaughter nodded towards the open grave, barely bothering to conceal her contempt beneath her black veil. Ellie straightened her back and walked carefully towards the heap of cold red earth discreetly covered by a sheet of tarpaulin. Her new black court shoes pinched and she was conscious that her skirt was too tight and too short. She'd bought it eighteen months ago for a party. It was unsuitable for a funeral, of course, but this had all happened so quickly she hadn't had time to buy another one –

'May eternal light shine on him, O Lord, with all your saints for ever, for you are rich in mercy …'

Ellie reached the graveside and stared into the deep, narrow trench. She didn't know what she was supposed to do next. She glanced round at the mourners behind her for an expression of sympathy, a fleeting smile of support, but saw only averted faces and cold stares. She turned helplessly back towards the priest, shaking with fear. She was only nineteen years old. If Eason was here, he would know what was expected of her. He would tell her what to do.

But Eason was gone.

The realisation hit her and she gave a broken sob, the first tears she'd been able to shed in six days.

'We now commit his body to the ground in the sure and certain hope of the resurrection…'

She would never see him again, never feel his arm around her shoulder, never hear his calm, wise words of advice as she struggled to cope with the family and the world that had become hers by her marriage.

She threw the fistful of soil on to the coffin as the gravediggers slowly lowered it into the ground, then turned away, stumbling over the rough grass.

'You can't leave now,' her stepdaughter Debra's hard, over-made-up face blocked her way. 'You've got to wait until the end. The least you can do is *pretend* you care.'

Ellie watched as her stepdaughter joined Eason's two sons at the graveside and ostentatiously wiped a tear from her eye as she bent to throw her own handful of dirt. A fresh tide of misery swept over Ellie as she recalled that the only buffer between her and her stepchildren's malevolence had gone. She would have to cope with them on her own.

Debra Cassidy had made her feelings towards her father's teenage Brazilian bride quite clear from the moment they'd met at Dallas Fort Worth airport. Everything had happened so quickly that Eason hadn't had a chance to warn his daughter that he was bringing home a new wife along with his Carnival souvenirs.

Ellie would never forget the look of horror and dismay on Debra's face as Eason had introduced them. If Fernando Moreno's sudden reappearance in her life hadn't meant that

211

she would never dare return to Brazil, she would have caught the next flight back to Rio there and then.

In retrospect, Ellie couldn't really blame Debra for being shocked. She'd been exactly half her new stepdaughter's age, a foreigner in a town where a New Yorker was considered an alien, and Debra had grown used to being the only woman in her father's life. Ellie had been shrewd enough to see that, to Debra, a new stepmother – and the possibility of a new half-brother or sister – threatened her inheritance. What she hadn't known then was just how much was at stake.

Ellie had realised the first day she'd met Eason that he was rich, but so were most Americans on holiday in Rio. Rich to her meant being able to eat without having to fuck a stranger first. Her first idea of Eason's real wealth had come when they'd flown, first class, to America. Even now she could feel the hot wave of embarrassment that had swept over her when Eason had caught her shoving the airline's complimentary toiletries and soap into her knickers. He'd gently told her to put them back, promising she'd have more than she knew what to do with when they reached home. Reluctantly she'd replaced them, though she'd kept the stainless steel knife and fork from her airline meal that she'd already slipped into her new calfskin boots.

Nothing had prepared her for the vast Cassidy ranch that dominated the tiny Texan town of Teklima. She'd imagined a house perhaps a little bigger than the *Children First* shelter in Rio, with maybe its own bit of garden. But even in her wildest dreams she'd never come close to the reality. The entire village of Nova Esperancia would have fitted into the red-paved courtyard at the centre of the ranch. Under Eason's benevolent eye, she'd walked through the house in a daze, opening door after door to bedrooms, bathrooms, rooms whose purpose she could only guess at: a billiard room equipped with two full-size snooker tables, a card room, a sauna, a pine-floored gym complete with its own weights and equipment, a jacuzzi, an Olympic heated swimming pool and a cold plunge pool – the ranch went on and on, a maze so endless she'd imagined she could get lost in it for a week.

Debra had followed behind them, her thin mouth compressed into a tight red line, her face pale with fury. As they'd reached the art room which housed Eason's private collection and Ellie had gazed in awe at the spotlit paintings, Debra had turned on her father, unable to contain her rage any longer. She hadn't even bothered to lower her voice.

'What the hell do you think you're doing?'

Ellie's back had stiffened as she listened.

'Debra, she's my wife.'

'Oh, for God's sake, Daddy. She's a cheap little gold-digger who doesn't even speak proper English. Screw her if you must, but don't make a complete fool of yourself. Whatever farce of a marriage she dragged you through in Rio can soon be undone. No one's going to believe her word against yours –'

I'm not having my wife's position questioned, by you or anyone else,' Eason interrupted. 'I'll marry her again if necessary, in front of everyone.'

'Daddy, be serious! She's young enough to be your granddaughter! What will people say?'

'People will say whatever I tell them to in this town.'

Debra had stalked towards the door. 'When you come to your senses, I'll be back. Until then, you're on your own.'

Ellie knew that if it hadn't been for Eason's money and position, she would have met the same overt hostility from his friends and associates as she did from Debra. Instead, he had organised a wedding in Teklima even more lavish than that of the Prince of Wales and Lady Diana Spencer. Not one of the 2,000 guests he'd invited declined; they all accepted either out of fear or plain curiosity. She and Eason had repeated the wedding vows they'd made on the beach at Copacabana, only this time in front of Texas' oldest and most prestigious families on the sun-dried lawns of the Cassidy ranch. Afterwards she'd stood next to her husband in her $50,000 Pavesi cream lace wedding dress, a fixed smile plastered on her face, as Eason had greeted each of the guests entering the vast pink silk marquee he'd had erected over the courtyard. Her head had ached unbearably in the hot sun, her cheeks burned with humiliation as she'd listened to the snide, crude comments she was meant to overhear the moment Eason's back was turned.

She'd hoped she could win his children round by making it clear she didn't intend to steal their inheritance or replace them in their father's affections. But Debra Cassidy had refused point-blank even to visit the ranch while she was there. Her brothers had followed suit, although Ellie suspected it was more to avoid their wives' nagging than out of any real animosity towards herself. She knew from the hot glances both men gave her that they could see exactly why their father had married her.

Eason had done his best to help her fit in: he'd doubled his contributions to the charity committees around which the social life of Teklima revolved, thrown lavish parties, and exerted silent pressure on his business partners to persuade their wives to include Ellie in their social calendars. His efforts had at least ensured she had avoided the indignity of being publicly snubbed. She'd taken care never to upstage women twice and three times her age by wearing any of the magnificent jewellery or expensive couture clothes Eason had given her. But she'd never felt that the invitations to the coffee mornings and tennis foursomes had been genuinely issued, and she had even fewer friends now than she'd had on the streets of Rio. However hard she'd tried, she hadn't fitted in.

214

She'd seen the sneers when she'd used the wrong knife to butter her bread, or ordered red wine when she was eating fish. These women spoke a coded language of wealth and privilege that she hadn't understood. Time and again she'd found herself sitting alone while the other women discussed schools, politics or indulged in other local gossip. The loneliness had been almost unbearable. Even her old ally, cocaine, hadn't really helped.

Eason had always known she'd taken the drug, although he'd never once confronted her with it. She guessed he'd assumed that once she'd left Rio, she'd given it up. He'd had no idea how unhappy she'd been, that she retreated to her bedroom and the comforting white powder almost every evening. It was all too easy to find a supplier. Much of his time he was at his office working, and when he'd been home, she hadn't liked to bother him with her problems. It had seemed so churlish when he had already given her so much. After all, without him she'd still have been on the streets, or probably dead if Fernando Moreno had managed to find her.

Rescue had come from an unexpected source. Eason's older sister, May, had seen how much her brother loved his young bride, and, unlike his children, she appreciated how happy Ellie made him. May Cassidy was seventy-four, a spirited, forthright woman who didn't give a fig for public opinion and had never found a man she'd considered worth marrying. She'd seen Ellie's plight and taken her under her wing, as much to spite her niece and nephews, whom she'd always disliked, as anything else. But May had also recognised that beneath Ellie's confusion and bewilderment was an intelligent, aspiring girl eager to learn. The glimpse of another world that the years with David Conto had given her had made Ellie fiercely ambitious, determined not to end up like her mother, dying in squalor before she was thirty. Wanting to escape from poverty she'd pestered David to teach her

English, and after he'd died she'd kept practising with Annie, the English girl she'd whored with in Rio.

By the time she'd met Eason, Ellie had been able to speak passable English, and if she hadn't yet been able to afford to dress like a lady, she was able to recognise those who could. The transformation from slum child to poised, accomplished woman, which had started with David Conto, was completed under May's tuition and with Eason's money. The older woman had corrected Ellie's grammar and execrable accent, patiently teaching her to read and write. She'd filled in some of the other gaps in Ellie's education, providing her with a rudimentary grasp of American politics and world history, showing her how to use an atlas, a dictionary and an encyclopedia. Once a week she'd invite Ellie over to her wing of the huge ranch for lessons in etiquette, teaching her how to use a knife and fork correctly, how to swallow an oyster or deal with lobster, to break her bread rather than cut it, and to eat asparagus with her fingers.

Ellie had absorbed everything, knowing she wouldn't get a second chance. Sooner or later she knew she would be on her own again, and when that moment came, she wanted to be ready. She'd watched the way May and Eason had treated the servants, and imitated their quiet authority. She made it her business to read up on Eason's art collection until she could identify and price a Monet or Picasso as accurately as he could. She learned to drive the soft-top Mercedes Eason had given her for their second wedding anniversary, and arranged tennis, piano and skiing lessons. She still had few friends in Teklima, but two years after she'd married Eason, she could hold her own with the best of them. She'd even managed to cut down the cocaine to once or twice a week.

The only thing no one had never had to teach her was how to dress. Ellie read every magazine and colour supplement the moment it came out, memorising the words and pictures as if

216

they would make up for seventeen years of deprivation. Instinctively she knew what was right for her. She could never have enough beautiful clothes; after a lifetime of wearing the same rags until they were so filthy she couldn't even remember their original colour, clothes were her one real indulgence.

But for every designer outfit she bought, she sent the same amount by anonymous cheque to *Children First*. However beautiful the clothes she wore, she never forgot who really made them.

Loneliness swamped her now as she climbed into the limousine and sank back against the leather seats. Despite their many differences, she and May had become close friends. When the old woman had died suddenly in her sleep almost a year ago, Ellie had mourned her loss almost as deeply as Eason himself. Now there was no one left to share her grief.

She yanked the black silk of her Chanel suit over her knees and tapped on the glass partition that separated her from the driver.

'Home, Mrs Cassidy?'

'No. Dallas Fort Worth.'

The driver twisted round to stare at her. 'The airport?'

He shrugged and slowly eased the car forward between the cemetery gates. Ellie saw Debra Cassidy turn to glare at the limousine with unconcealed hatred. She eased the stiff black hat from her head and unpinned her waist-length dark hair. What Debra Cassidy thought of her no longer mattered. She wouldn't be seeing her again.

She picked up her vanity case and flipped open the catch, scanning the array of jewellery. Sapphires, rubies, emeralds and diamonds winked up at her from bracelets, earrings, necklaces and rings. Every one of them represented a piece of her life – the simple sapphire and diamond ring Eason had given her when he'd asked her to marry him, the intricate gold butterfly set with pearls and rubies she'd received on her eighteenth birthday, the aquamarine earrings that had marked their first anniversary. But they were more to her than just her memories; they were her future.

By leaving Teklima without a word of warning or a backward glance, Ellie knew she was giving up land and property worth millions of dollars, perhaps billions if she included all the stocks and shares Eason had left to her. But she didn't regret it for a moment. Even if she won the bitter court battle that would inevitably ensue once her stepchildren found out what he'd done, it would almost certainly take many years, years she didn't want to waste. Apart from her clothes, she would keep only the jewellery Eason had given her and the one thing she valued above everything else: her American passport. The rest they could have.

At the airport terminal, Ellie shielded her eyes from the wintry afternoon sunshine as she gazed out towards the glittering high rise city of Dallas and the country that had briefly been her home. She had no idea where she would go after she reached London, or what she would do with her life. For the first time, she had no obligations, and the freedom and money to do what she wanted. She walked towards the Delta desk without looking back, oblivious to the stares her exotic appearance was generating, opened her handbag and pulled out her ticket and passport, smiling sadly as she read her name. Elizabeth Cassidy. Eason had given her so much; best of all he'd given her a new identity. No one looking at her now would have any idea that she'd once had to pick through dustbins. She glanced at her reflection as she passed a column covered with tiny mirrored tiles. She had had beauty and allure before she'd met Eason, but his money and May's influence had given her polish and elegance. In her expensive black suit and handmade shoes, her glossy hair carefully styled, her fingers manicured and her figure still trim but now toned from hours at a private gym, she looked exactly what she was: a rich, young, exceptionally beautiful widow. Only her eyes hadn't changed. They still held the hunger of a slum child.

She handed over her passport and ticket at the desk. 'First class to London, please.'

The girl behind the desk smiled. 'Return?'

Ellie said firmly, 'Just one way.'

She opened her handbag to search for money to pay the porter and realised that she had nothing smaller than a $100 bill.

'Excuse me, did you want some change?'

Ellie turned at the words of the elegant woman standing behind her. 'Oh, that would be wonderful, thank you. As soon as I've finished here I'll get some small notes – '

'Don't worry about it. It's only ten dollars.'

'Thank you so much. That's really very kind of you.'

'You shouldn't thank me until you know what I really want in exchange,' the woman laughed.

Ellie looked puzzled. 'I'm sorry?'

'Don't be.' The woman held out her hand. 'Angela Lindsay. I know we've only just met and you know absolutely nothing about me, but tell me – have you ever done any modelling?'

Nine

Thokoza Township, South Africa
Tuesday 24 December 1985
11.30 a.m.

Jane Cavendish ducked low to avoid the helicopter's rotor blades and ran across the tarmac apron, clutching her canvas satchel to her chest.

'Room for one more?'

The co-pilot shook his head, mouthing something that Jane couldn't catch over the noise of the whirling blades.

'Are you sure?'

Matt leant forward from within the helicopter and put his mouth next to her ear: 'We're overloaded as it is. You sure you need to come out? I thought you'd already filed for tomorrow's edition?'

Jane's dark hair whipped across her face. 'I have, but Eddie's suddenly decided he wants a Christmas special – you know, The Season of Goodwill in a Township at War and other clichés we've come to know and love.'

'If only he'd let us know earlier, we might have been able to do something about it,' Matt yelled.

The co-pilot turned round again and scowled at Matt. 'Look, do you want to go up or not?'

One of the other journalists crammed into the back of the Puma unbuckled his seatbelt and stood up. 'Hey, Jane! You can take my seat, I was only along for the ride. To be honest, you're welcome to it. I hate helicopters.' He turned to the co-pilot with exaggerated politeness. 'That OK with you?'

Jane stuck her head through the open door of the helicopter. 'Doug, are you sure? I don't want you getting it in the neck on my account.'

The Reuters journalist shook his head. 'Don't worry about it. Ken's already on board to cover the violence for us. I was just after a bit of colour for a holding piece I'm working on. It'll wait.'

'Doug, I think I love you.'

Matt grinned as the two exchanged places. 'And I thought it was me you couldn't live without.'

'Darling, you know I never mix business with pleasure.'

The pilot muttered something in Afrikaans to his companion, who swung round and frowned at the half-dozen journalists. 'Is everybody ready? Good. You may take pictures as we fly over the township but please, nobody is to stand up or move around the helicopter until we're back on the ground. Is that clear?'

'I guess we should be grateful there's no mud on the windows,' Matt said.

As the helicopter chuntered across the arid landscape towards Thokoza, Matt focused the Pentax through its Perspex window, trying to work out the best position from which to get an overview of the township when they reached it. Clearly the front of the Puma was the best place to be, but there was no way the pair of clowns running this show were going to go for that. Press facilities such as this were usually something he avoided; it was almost impossible to get anywhere near the real action, and even if you did, an exclusive was out of the question. But that was the way the South African authorities insisted they played the game, particularly in the five months since President P. W. Botha

221

had declared a state of emergency. If he wanted to get any pictures at all, he had no choice but to go along with it.

'Hey, guys, directly ahead,' Jane interrupted. 'Just past twelve o'clock. Isn't that a roadblock?'

'I can see smoke.' One of the journalists pointed to Matt's left. 'I think things are hotting up.'

Matt cursed as the helicopter suddenly swung upwards. 'What's going on? I need to go in lower, I'll never get anything at this height.'

'It's too dangerous,' the co-pilot snapped.

'Don't be ridiculous.' Jane shuffled forward until she was crouching down between the pilots. 'We're paying you to overfly the township, not take us on a package holiday. How do you think we're going to get what we want when we're so far away we can hardly see the ground?'

'That's your problem. I told you, it's too dangerous.'

Jane pulled a wedge of $100 bills out of her shirt pocket. 'You sure about that?'

The pilot glanced at his companion. 'It's possible we could go round again –'

The co-pilot nodded.

'I hope you got a receipt,' Matt muttered as Jane made her way back towards him. 'How much did you give him?'

'Don't worry, the *Chronicle* can afford it. Serves Eddie right if I blow his budget. This is hardly my ideal way to spend Christmas Eve.'

'Never mind. Next year we'll be lazing on some sun-drenched beach in the Caribbean –'

'Yeah. Next year.'

Jane leaned across him. 'Matt, that looks like hand-to-hand fighting down there. Vigilantes?'

Matt crouched over his Pentax as she edged forward again to speak to the pilots. On the ground, he could see a group of about a dozen black youths darting between the tin shacks of the township, throwing home-made petrol bombs and stones into the street near the impromptu roadblock before disappearing back into the alleys. Several streets away, hidden from the township residents manning the blockade, three yellow armoured police Caspars were blocking the main road into the area, their occupants standing in circles around the parked vehicles, fingers resting on the triggers of their guns as they faced the few residents who had ventured out of their homes nearby. Clearly the police had decided to let the violence between the rival gangs take its course without intervening. Matt rattled off several pictures of them, then turned to reload his camera.

Before he had a chance to unload the film he had already shot, there was a sudden crackle of rifle fire and the helicopter lurched to the right, throwing him against its side.

Matt cursed. 'What the fuck –'

'We're hit!' the co-pilot cried. 'We're going down!'

Jane struggled to keep her balance as the Puma spun wildly from side to side, rapidly losing height. 'Where? Where did we take the hit?'

'Not the petrol tanks, thank God,' Matt said. 'We wouldn't be here talking about it if they'd been hit.'

'We were lucky.' Sweat was running into the pilot's eyes as he scanned the instruments in front of him. 'The bullet must have clipped the rotor blade, but it hasn't pierced the skin. I think we should be able to land.'

Jane kissed Matt on the mouth before turning to buckle her seatbelt. 'That's the last time I insist on coming with you. Next time, I'm staying at home with the mince pies and brandy.'

The helicopter rocked crazily as the pilot was forced to hover, the damaged rotor blades hiccuping against the spindle as they spun round. Matt could smell the tension and fear as the journalists waited silently for the Puma to land. None of them dared move for fear of upsetting the precarious balance he had somehow managed to achieve. For a moment the helicopter hovered above the waste ground, then lurched downwards. Matt felt Jane brace herself beside him. A thousand images of the moments he'd shared with her ran through his mind – the way she smiled when he woke her in the morning, the way she cried every time she heard the theme music to *Chariots of Fire*, the way she gazed at him with such passion when he made love to her. Whatever happened now, at least they were together. When she squeezed his hand he knew she was thinking the same.

There was a breathtaking thump as the helicopter touched down and rocked forward on the uneven ground. Matt prayed that the rotor blades wouldn't clip the earth and send them spinning out of control. Through the window he saw the blades arc towards the ground, inches away from the surface.

The Puma lurched in the opposite direction and the rotors swung clear of the earth as the helicopter settled on the waste ground. The pilot cut the engines and the rotors slowed, spinning safely overhead.

Before they had a chance to unbuckle their seatbelts, rifle fire erupted around them. There was a crack as a bullet shattered the Perspex windscreen and embedded itself in the co-pilot's shoulder. Matt yanked open the door to his left and jumped to the ground, pulling Jane with him and propelling her towards the shelter of a low brick wall on the edge of the waste ground as the pilot fled in fear from his own side of the cockpit. As they crouched against the wall, the rest of the journalists joined them.

A high-pitched scream rent the air and Matt pushed Jane down below the top of the wall. 'What the hell was that?'

The journalists watched as a group of four men emerged from a small corrugated iron and cardboard shanty on the other side of the dirt street. The men were dragging a scrawny black girl of around seventeen between them, her bare legs scraping across the ground as she screamed and struggled. In the middle of the street they stopped, and one man grabbed the girl's cornrows and brutally yanked her head backwards as the others forced her on to her knees. Two of the youths quickly lifted a tyre over her head and rammed it down, pinning her arms against her sides. The ringleader let go of her hair and seized a can of petrol, pouring it over her as she coughed and choked.

Before Matt could stop her, Jane had broken free and climbed over the wall. As she reached the dirt street, the ringleader threw a match into the terrified black girl's hair. Jane shouted and ran towards the burning girl. For a split second Matt saw panic in the man's eyes as he spotted the moving figure. Even as Matt tried to run forward, the man raised his gun and a hail of bullets rang out.

Ten

Via Appia Antica, Rome, Italy
Saturday 13 September 1986
9.30 a.m.

Alix stepped on to the bathroom scales, her fists clenched by her sides as she steeled herself to look at the dial. She stared at the wavering needle between her feet. Eight stone nine! She'd put on almost a pound since yesterday!

Frantically she listed everything she'd eaten in the past twenty-four hours. Nothing that could have caused such a horrific weight gain, she was sure of it.

At sixteen years old, Alix was a veteran dieter. She knew the calorific value of everything, from half a peanut to a four-course meal at one of Rome's top restaurants. She'd long since passed the stage where she substituted saccharin for sugar, skimmed milk for whole, black coffee for cappuccino. She knew every helpful slimming hint listed at the end of her diet book by heart; they'd become unbreakable rules which she would recite daily as she pored over pictures of the models in her magazines, using their perfection to force herself onwards to even greater sacrifice.

Eat in only one room of the house.
Use smaller plates so your portion looks like more.
Remeasure, reweigh. Try harder.
Keep in mind that weight leaves the body in two main ways:

226

*bowel movements and urination. The longer you spend on
the toilet, the better.*

Her father went on and on at her – there was nothing left of
her, she was skin and bone – but she knew he was only telling
her that to get her to do what he wanted. She could see in the
mirror what was really there. A thick, solid, disgusting layer
of fat. She squeezed her stomach in fear. This had to go. And
this. She pinched her small breasts and watched the flesh
quiver. It had to go.

She turned away from the mirror and picked up her white
towelling robe from the floor. Even now, after all this time, it
wasn't easy. People assumed that if you were on a diet long
enough, you didn't want to eat. But you did, all the time. Food
was all you could think about, every waking minute of the
day. Every night she dreamed of shopping counters and
shelves stacked with raspberries and strawberries, sweet, tiny
tomatoes and succulent peaches. There wasn't a moment
when she didn't long to cram her mouth with everything she
could see even while the very thought of doing so repulsed her
so much she felt sick.

She knew she'd never have stuck to her diet if it hadn't been
for her magazines. Every time she lapsed she withdrew to her
room and studied them. If top models could do it, so could she.
All it took was willpower.

Lunchtime wasn't too bad, because she had an audience at
school, a reputation to uphold. Gradually her half-pot of
yoghurt had dwindled to a third, consumed excruciatingly
slowly with frequent references to how full she was. It had
become a daily ritual among her friends: how little she could
eat. Kay and Sarah had both tried to join her several times in
the two years since she'd first begun her diet, but neither of
them had ever lasted more than a few days, a week at most.
Breakfast was easy too; she refused to give in to temptation in
front of her mother, pacing her sip for sip as she drank her

227

black coffee, gaining a strange and painful pleasure from her mother's ill-concealed impatience. She knew Joanna didn't give a damn about her health. Her mother just didn't like the idea that her daughter had a mind and will of her own.

Dinner had been the problem. It had been impossible to refuse to eat with her parents, so she'd learned countless ways of controlling her food without drawing attention to what she was doing. Peas were easy, since she could eat them one by one, spearing them individually on her fork. Brussel sprouts could be unwrapped leaf by leaf, corn could be nibbled, prolonging the meal so long that her parents didn't notice she wasn't actually eating. She'd taken to wearing baggy jumpers and unflattering leggings even in midsummer so that they wouldn't see how much weight she'd lost, but she'd known it was only a matter of time before they realised what she was doing. She'd managed to diet down to a size eight, but then she'd reached a plateau and the weight had stopped coming off. She'd had to find a way to avoid dinner altogether. Since her father refused to allow her to go out on dates until she was eighteen, the only way out had been to enrol herself in as many classes after school as she could, and then claim she'd already eaten by the time she returned home.

Tennis, hockey and squash had all been out. She couldn't risk revealing her body in the skimpy clothes. She'd already had to start inventing excuses to miss games after her gym mistress had rung her parents one day to voice her concerns about Alix's weight loss. Fortunately her father had been away on business and her mother had taken the call. Joanna had listened in silence, then hung up the telephone and summoned Alix into the drawing room. Alix would never forget the cool contempt in her mother's eyes as she'd studied her daughter and noted the lank hair, dull complexion, her painful thinness that even her thick sweater couldn't hide.

'You won't keep it up, you know,' Joanna had said. 'You

don't have the willpower. You'll starve yourself now, then binge and put it all back on later. I was a size eight when I married your father, and I can still get into my wedding dress. *That's* willpower, Alexandra.'

After that, Alix hadn't needed to look at pictures of skinny models to find the determination to stick to her diet. She'd signed up for two classes after school in art and design, neither of which interested her but which clashed nicely with her parents' schedules. To her intense surprise, she had discovered not only that she enjoyed them, but that she had a hidden talent she'd never even suspected. Her mind had been swamped with images and ideas her clumsy fingers had been unable to capture on paper. She'd worked every spare moment she had to acquire the basic drawing skills, discovering that her talent with pencil and cloth had a natural outlet in designing and creating costumes for the plays put on by her school at the end of term. In her spare time, she spent hours experimenting with different fabrics. Designing different outfits had become her secret refuge, the one part of her life where she could forget the darker side of her privileged world: her mother's dislike, her father's abuse, her own obsession with her body. While she held a pencil in her hand, she could forget everything else.

Alix pushed the scales back into place beneath the basin. Quarter to eleven. In two hours senior Italian politicians and diplomats were expected at the villa for lunch, and her father had told her she must attend. Bending over the bath, she turned on the taps and added a couple of capfuls of Badedas, watching the bubbles form on the surface of the water and trying to banish the tempting image of cappuccino from her mind.

Suddenly she felt a pain knife her belly, a stab so sharp she doubled over, clutching her abdomen with one hand as she gripped the side of the bath. She felt a hot wetness between her legs and glanced down. Several bright red drops of blood had already stained the carpet. Horrified, she reached between her thighs and brought her hand up to her face. This was no period. There was too much blood.

Suddenly everything slotted into place. The sickness she'd felt every morning for the past few weeks. The tenderness in her breasts. The weight she'd gained, the slight swelling of her abdomen.

'Alix? Are you in there?'

Alix sat on the edge of the bath, ignoring her father's voice. She should have thought of this possibility before. Her father came to her almost every week. It was only a matter of time before he'd get her pregnant …

The door-handle rattled again. 'Alix? Alix, is everything all right?'

She felt a sudden flash of anger and reached for the heavy glass jar of bath salts next to the basin and threw it at the door with all her strength. The glass shattered and sent a spray of sweet-smelling pink chips across the bathroom, the wooden panels of the door almost splintering under the impact. This was all *his* fault. He knew she couldn't stop him, knew it was wrong, and yet he'd kept on coming. She picked up a bottle of bubble bath and threw that too, then followed it with a jar of face cream, shampoo, anything she could reach.

She grimaced as the pain hit her again. At least she wouldn't have to worry what to do about the baby. Nature was taking care of that. But she couldn't live at home any more. She had to get away from her father. She had a few thousand dollars in her savings account, her birthday and Christmas money. She'd manage, she'd find a job somewhere. It had to be better than staying here.

Eleven

Little Italy, New York, USA
Saturday 6 December 1986
2.30 p.m.

'You wanna 'nother cappuccino?'

Matt looked up at the waitress and nodded. She disappeared between the tables, her plump bottom wiggling beneath the tight pink dress that stopped a good ten inches above her knees. He picked up his empty coffee cup and idly turned it in his hands, his gaze drifting to the grey street outside. Through the rain-smeared window of the café he could see a few figures hurrying past with the determined, unbreakable stride that characterised New Yorkers. He had never encountered a people anywhere in the world so permanently eager to be somewhere else as soon as possible. They negotiated puddles, beggars, fire hydrants, tourists – anything or anyone blocking their path – with the speed and expertise of soldier ants, brooking neither obstacle nor interruption.

The waitress dumped his cappuccino in front of him, slopping a third of it over the edge of the saucer and on to the Formica top. Matt quickly picked up the portfolio he'd left on the table before the spilt coffee could seep into the photographs, his gaze still on the street outside. New York was the most exhilarating, exciting, dynamic city in the world if you were part of it. But if you were on the outside looking in, there was no place on earth more lonely.

He sifted through his photographs, trying to look at them with a less jaundiced eye. In the six months he'd been looking for work in Manhattan, Matt had learned the hard way not to include any of his war photography in his portfolio, award-winning or not. The fashion industry traded on dreams and illusions, not poverty and war. After half a dozen rejections, Matt had been forced to edit his portfolio to include only the soft feature pieces and the few portrait sittings he had steeled himself to do in the year since Jane's death. He loathed most of the pictures, knowing they were far from being his best work, but they were the closest he had to the kind of fashion photography work he was looking for now.

But however much he'd hated having to do it, editing his portfolio didn't seem to have made any difference. After visiting every advertising agency in New York and placing hundreds of calls to fashion magazines, he was still no closer to receiving his first commission than he had been when he'd started. He might as well give it up as a lost cause.

Matt threw the folder back down on the table, staring at the glossy pictures as they spilled across the Formica. It was no wonder no one wanted to give him a break. The photographs were technically perfect; the lighting was right, the models were skilfully posed, the composition was clever and original. But they possessed no soul, no fire, none of the passion and anger of his news photography. His heart simply wasn't in them, and it showed.

The familiar pain twisted inside him and he closed his eyes, willing it to pass. Whatever passion he'd once felt for his work had died twelve months ago, along with the woman he loved. Even now the loss of her was as sharp as ever. He'd taken many women to his bed since then to try to help him forget, but they only made the pain more acute. He'd begun to doubt that it would ever fade.

It had taken him six months after Jane's death even to pick up a camera again, and when he had, he'd found he couldn't go back and carry on where he'd left off. His pain and anger were too deep for him to take on the anguish and misery of the world around him. He found himself unable to care about it any more. The work he'd once loved more than life itself had taken from him the only thing that had ever mattered more. He couldn't forgive it, and he couldn't forgive himself.

'The coffee really that bad, or are you just feeling sorry for yourself?'

'Luke! What the hell are you doing here?'

Luke Tambo's black face split into a broad grin as he slid into the chair opposite Matt's. 'I kinda figured you'd come here after the Robert & Powers go-see, and thought you might like a shoulder to cry on. Their ad agency isn't far from my office. No joy from them either, I take it?'

Matt frowned and stared at his coffee. 'How'd you guess?'

'One look at your face is enough.' Luke's expression became serious. 'But I would've known even if you'd been dancing a jig on the Formica. Things aren't quite as straightforward as they seem.'

'Do you know something that I don't?'

'You could say that.' Luke twisted round in his chair and raised his arm to attract the attention of Matt's sulky waitress. 'I don't know about you, but I'm starving. Mind if I order before we get down to business?'

The waitress slouched over to their table.

'Carpaccio for me, and a spaghetti carbonara,' Matt said without looking up. 'Oh, and a Bud. Cold, if you can manage it.'

'Make that two,' Luke smiled.

The girl disappeared. Luke picked up Matt's folder. 'Mind if I have a look?'

Matt shrugged. 'Be my guest.'

Luke's face was expressionless as he laid the photos one by one on the table. He paused for a long moment over the last picture in the folder. 'She was very beautiful, Matt. You must miss her terribly.'

'We didn't even have time to get married. We kept telling ourselves there'd be time after the next story, the next assignment, but the moment never seemed to happen. Work always came first.'

Luke reached out and gripped Matt's hand. 'Jane isn't coming back, Matt. You have to accept that, and get on with your life. It's what she would have wanted. I told you once, any time you need a friend, I'm here. I meant it then, and I mean it now.'

'I don't know what I'd have done without you,' Matt said. 'No man could have asked for a better friend.'

Luke looked away, embarrassed. 'That's what we're all here for. To help each other when times are bad. You stood up for me when you didn't have to, and I'm not about to forget that now.'

Matt smiled. He and Luke had remained good friends since their schooldays, although they'd followed very different paths since then. Luke was ambitious, but not driven the way Matt was. He'd always seemed much more settled, more sure of what he wanted out of life.

At twenty-nine, Luke Tambo was just under a year older than his friend. His parents had been Rwandan, members of the educated, aristocratic ruling class; Luke, their only child, had come to England with them at the age of eleven when his father had been appointed as an attaché to Rwanda's Ambassador to the UK. His parents had made the decision to send him to St Francis' to board when they'd been recalled to

Rwanda two years later, in 1971. Apart from school holidays, Luke had never returned to live in Rwanda. When both of his parents died in a cholera epidemic the year he'd left school, even those brief visits home had ceased. Luke wasn't ashamed of his African heritage, but he'd known that his future lay in the West.

He'd completed his three-year course in business studies at Bristol at the same time Matt had dropped out of Oxford to become a news photographer. He'd met his wife there, a tiny blonde American called Kip, who'd been studying textiles and design in the year below Luke. They'd married soon after graduating and had set up their own business together, importing exotic African jewellery from Luke's home town in Rwanda and selling it on a stall at the Walcot Street flea market in Bath. Matt always thought they complemented each other well; Luke provided the business acumen whilst Kip used her contacts in the fashion world to ensure that their jewellery received plenty of high-profile, free advertising by supplying it for magazine shoots. Within two years they'd given up the market stall and opened their first shop in Bristol, and two others had quickly followed in London and Salisbury. They'd had to expand their range of products, taking on a full-time costume jewellery designer to keep one step ahead of the trends. Now, seven years later, Luke owned six shops and employed nearly thirty people. He also supplied jewellery to prestigious department stores, including Harvey Nichols in London and Saks and Bloomingdales in New York.

When Luke and Kip had moved to Manhattan two summers before, to be near Kip's family after her father had had a stroke, Kip used the opportunity to launch her own career as a fashion stylist. Already she was one of the most sought-after in the business. Luke had appointed managers to run his UK shops and transferred the centre of the jewellery business to a tiny fourth-floor apartment in Manhattan's Lower East Side.

It was a standing joke that, one day, Luke would have a corner office overlooking Central Park. Matt didn't doubt he'd make it.

Kip and Jane had taken to each the other the moment they'd met. The four of them had gone skiing together in Vail on several occasions, and had even spent a few weekends down at East Lambrook Manor in Sussex with Matt's parents. It was Jane who'd dropped an important assignment to be with Kip when she'd had the first of her miscarriages, and Kip had invited Jane to stay with her and Luke one Christmas when Matt had been stuck in Beirut working.

Matt knew they'd mourned Jane's loss almost as much as he had. In the past year, he'd come to rely on Luke more than his own family. It was Luke who'd been there for him in the days and weeks after Jane's funeral, when everyone but his father had tiptoed around him, throwing up a tactful wall of silence that had only made Matt feel more alone. It had been Luke who had refused to allow him to sit at home and brood, hauling him out to countless parties around London and finally dragging Matt back to New York with him when he'd decided he couldn't cope with the memories at home. It had been Luke who'd suggested that he try his hand at fashion photography when Matt had been prepared to throw his cameras away for ever. Matt knew that if it hadn't been for Luke, he would have given up after six weeks and returned home, drowning his sorrows in Scotch and self-pity.

'Carpaccio, carbonara, two Buds. OK?'

The waitress tapped her foot impatiently while they cleared the photographs away, then slammed down their order and flounced back to the kitchen. Luke pulled his plate of carpaccio towards him. 'Not bad. It may look like a dump, but this place serves the best carpaccio in Little Italy.'

Matt waited until Luke had half-cleared his plate. 'OK. Enough of the tea and sympathy. Why don't you tell me why

I'm getting nowhere with my pictures, since you're obviously in a position to know?'

'I don't think you're going to like it –'

'I didn't suppose I would.'

'It seems your past – and mine – is catching up with you at last. You remember our old enemy, Simon Derby-Lewis?'

Matt stared at him. 'Damn right I do. He's hardly someone either of us is going to forget.'

'Well. It seems Derby-Lewis has gone on to bigger and better things since those halcyon days at St Francis. A contact of mine told me a few weeks ago that thanks to his father, he's now the senior director at Pierce Leason & Isaacs –'

'The advertising agency?'

'The most influential advertising agency in New York,' Luke corrected. 'They've got three-quarters of the most prestigious cosmetics accounts in the country, and the other quarter are practically beating their doors down trying to get in.'

Matt frowned. 'But I haven't even tried for a job at Pierce.'

'You don't need to. Once I'd found out that Derby-Lewis was in the frame, I started to do a bit of asking around. The consensus seems to be that one word from our dear Simon and no magazine is going to touch you.'

'Are you serious?'

'Why else do you think you're getting the cold shoulder all over town?' He smiled as Matt glanced automatically at the folder of photographs. 'Matt, those pictures may not be ready for the front cover of *Vogue*, but even if they don't quite do your work justice, they're still better than anything 95 per cent of the guys out there can produce. It's not your fault you haven't been getting the commissions. If Derby-Lewis tells a client that your name spells trouble, they aren't going to risk using you. And if they won't, the magazines they sponsor certainly won't. They only need three or four advertisers to pull out and they're in deep financial water.'

Matt smiled ruefully. 'I can hardly believe this same guy is fucking up my life for the second time.'

Luke sighed. 'I won't kid you, Matt. If he's put the block on you, there's precious little chance of you getting out from under. At least, not through the usual channels …'

'That sounds like you have something else in mind.'

Luke grinned. 'I might just have a little something up my sleeve.'

Matt laughed. 'So let's hear it. I don't see anyone else beating my door down with good ideas.'

'Probably because they can't make it up six flights to your damn apartment,' his friend said.

'I happen to like it. It's huge, it's cheap, and it's just around the corner from Vanni's Delicatessen. What more could I ask for?'

'Don't forget the fish,' Luke said.

'I love the fish –'

'Yeah. So I see.'

'Hey, I thought you had some idea that's going to save my career, or did I just imagine that?'

Luke nodded. 'Derby-Lewis can influence most of the magazines in this town, but not all of them. Thanks to Kip, I happen to know that the editor of *Elan*, Stephi Kay, isn't exactly his greatest fan; she doesn't like the closed shop he operates, or the pressure he puts on some of the smaller magazines to run pieces favourable to his clients. Stephi also likes to back the underdog, which in this case is you. If you can get one decent assignment, I'm fairly certain she'll run it. And if it's good enough, the other magazines will take it, Derby-Lewis or not.'

Matt regarded Luke sceptically. 'Yes, but who's going to risk using me? I'm *persona non grata*, remember?'

'Not to me.'

Matt looked surprised. 'You?'

'Why not? My UK branches are well established, and we're not doing too badly here in New York, given that we're selling our jewellery through the big department stores rather than from a boutique of our own. But our biggest problem in the US is profile. We simply don't have the customer recognition. There's only one way to change that.'

'You want me to shoot an advertising campaign for you?' Matt frowned. 'Luke, I really appreciate your faith in me, but I just don't have the experience for something like that. You've seen what I've done: a few portraits and some magazine features, but nothing like what you're suggesting. If I get it wrong, it'll be a very expensive mistake on your part.'

'You let me worry about that,' Luke answered. 'I'm putting my money on the fact that if you're doing it for me, you'll give it everything you've got. I think it'll be more than enough.' He sat back and picked up his beer. 'I'm not just doing this out of charity, Matt. If you're the hit I think you'll be, I'll have got you cheap.'

'It's not just you, though, is it?' Matt said. 'What about a model? The big agencies like Elite and Ford aren't going to touch me if it means upsetting their relationship with Pierce.'

'I don't want to use one of the big names. Apart from the fact that I probably couldn't afford it anyway, we want to create as much of a stir as possible. The simplest way to do that is to discover someone new, someone who'll set the world alight and put us right in the centre of the map.'

'You've found her already, haven't you?'

Luke grinned. 'She's with Angela Lindsay's agency in London. She's been in the business several months and done a few low-key assignments, but nothing like this. I saw some prints of her last week. She's absolutely perfect, Matt. She has the most unique face I've ever seen – beautiful by every traditional standard, but with something more. I don't quite know what it is about her. She's very accessible, easy to identify with, and yet at the same time there's a part of her that seems utterly unreachable.'

Matt laughed. 'And I thought you were a happily married man. You sound more than half in love with her already.'

'You wait till you see her,' Luke said. 'I think that's part of her secret: it's impossible to look at her face and not want to know everything about her. It's not just me, either – every person I've spoken to has had the same reaction, women as well as men. Matt, she's going to be more famous than any other model in the world in a very short space of time. I'd like it to be you and me who take her there.'

Matt's interest was sparked for the first time in many months. 'So tell me. What's her name?'

'Ellie Cassidy.'

Twelve

Greenwich Village, New York, USA
Monday 19 January 1987
10.00 a.m.

'Another satisfied customer?'

Matt buckled his jeans and moved towards the iron rail
which ran around the edge of his overhead loft. He peered
down into the vast studio below and grinned as he saw Romi,
his photographic assistant, struggle awkwardly through the
heavy studio door, her arms laden with unwieldy camera
equipment. 'I don't know what you mean.'

Romi kicked the studio door shut with one Niked foot and
dumped the equipment on Matt's work table. 'Sure you don't.
I mean that beautiful creature I just passed on the stairs. I
swear they get younger every day. She can't have been more
than fifteen.'

'Seventeen, actually.' Matt pulled a faded grey denim shirt
over his head as he descended the wrought-iron spiral
staircase. 'I guess her agency figured the best route to my
studio was via my bed. They sent her round with strict
instructions not to leave until I'd taken her picture, with or
without her clothes on.'

'And?'

Matt shrugged. 'She's a pretty girl, moves well –'

'But?'

'Yeah. But.'

'I hope you told her that before you swept her off her feet and between your sheets,' Romi said.

Matt looked indignant. 'What do you think I am?'

Romi held up her hand placatingly. 'I know, I know, you never mix business with pleasure. You don't need to bribe girls into your bed, they just keep on coming, right?'

'Can I help it if I'm just too damned attractive for my own good?'

Romi knew Matt was teasing, but she knew he was also right. In the four months she'd been working for him, she had witnessed the girls queuing at his studio door.

Matt sighed theatrically. 'Anyway, it's your fault, you know that, don't you?'

He was only half-joking. If Romi hadn't been such a talented assistant that he daren't risk losing her, he'd have moved heaven and earth to get her into bed. She was far from beautiful, but she had the most arresting face he had ever seen; half-Cherokee, half-Irish, she'd inherited both the jet-black hair and narrow dark eyes of her mother's Indian people, and the milky-soft complexion of her father's Galway ancestors. Matt longed to see that proud face stripped naked of its self-control in the abandon of his love-making. Just once.

Romi read his mind. 'You stick to your cute seventeen-year-olds, kid,' she said amiably, counting the rolls of film she'd laid out on the work table. 'They'll be less hassle in the long run, believe me. OK, let's get this thing organised. Sami and Andrew will be here in half an hour, and we've still got to clear away this junk to make some space for them.'

Matt's loft, deep in the heart of New York's Greenwich Village, measured just over 5,000 square feet, most of which was taken up by his photographic studio. At the far end, opposite the doors, was Matt's darkroom, and next to it, the bathroom. On the right, the spiral staircase led up to a narrow gallery that ran the width of the studio, which Matt used as his living space. The gallery was empty but for his bed, a heap of cushions, and teetering piles of books scattered along the polished wooden floor like stepping-stones to nowhere.

The remaining area of the lower studio, between the darkroom and a Chinese ebony coffee table, Matt used for his fashion shoots. Backdrops, polyboards, flats and lighting equipment filled the space, leaving little room for the models to change or the make-up artists and hair stylists to do their work. The loft was flooded with natural light even on the cloudiest of New York days, one of the main reasons Matt had rented it. As well as the huge windows running along the length of the studio, three-quarters of the ceiling was made up of heavy glass cobbles which formed the bottom of a shallow pool on the roof of the building, and for whose existence Matt could find no reason. In the early morning and late evening, they cast strange, dappled shadows into the studio which he sometimes incorporated into his pictures; during the rest of the day, strong sunshine bleached the light clear. At night, Matt often lay in bed watching the shadows of fish swimming over his head.

He looked up as the studio door opened and Luke's wife, Kip, darted in, a bunch of carrier bags in each hand. 'Hey, Romi, do you have ten dollars? The guy downstairs can't break a hundred.'

Romi rummaged in her jeans pockets and handed Kip three five-dollar bills. 'Give him this and maybe he'll carry the gear upstairs for you.'

'Cheers. I'm going to need a hand with this stuff. Sometimes I could kill Luke.'

Kip threw the carrier bags on to the Chinese coffee table and ran back down the stairs, her boots clattering on the bare boards.

'What the hell did you tell her to get?' Romi asked. 'I

thought this was a shoot for designer costume jewellery, not the latest in DIY for beginners.'

Matt laughed. 'Ask Luke, he's the art director on this one. It's all his idea.'

'What's all my idea?' Luke arrived in the doorway and shrugged off his coat.

'For some reason, Romi blames me for the fact that my fashion stylist is carrying a pair of medieval stocks up six flights of stairs to my studio.'

Luke looked pleased. 'Yeah, great idea, huh? I saw Kip and some taxi guy with them as I came in. They look good to me.'

Romi handed Kip a cup of coffee as she returned and sank into a chair. She pulled an extravagant black velvet beret from her head and shook her Marilyn Monroe blonde curls free. 'God, Romi, do I need this. You have no idea how long it took me to find those damn' things. I even called the Tower of London in England, for Chrissakes.'

'Luke seems pretty happy with them, wherever they came from.'

'Yeah, well he didn't have to carry them,' Kip said with feeling.

As Romi moved around checking that all the electronic flash units, modelling lights and power packs were in working order, the double doors opened again and Sami and Andrew spilled into the room, a tall, elegant, willowy girl with skin the colour of milky coffee trailing behind them.

Matt stared at her as Luke introduced them, his cool momentarily deserting him. His friend had been right. This girl was going to take the modelling world by storm. It wasn't just that she had the most perfect face he'd ever seen. He knew at once that she'd photograph well. It was more than that. Her beauty was compelling. He wanted to look at her for hours. If he could only capture that on film ...

Luke smiled as he watched Matt's reaction. 'Well?'

'She's dynamite.'

'I know.'

'You said she's been in this business nearly a year?' Matt asked, his eyes following Ellie as she crossed the room to talk to Sami. 'How on earth has Angela managed to keep her under wraps this long?'

'Angela's no fool. She's been letting Ellie cut her teeth on some low-key stuff, a few beach shots and swimwear ads while she learns the business. A high-profile campaign like this is just what Angela's been waiting for. If we get it right, these ads will make Ellie a star overnight.'

'Who is she? Where's she from?'

Luke shrugged. 'History doesn't relate. I don't even think Angela knows herself. Ellie doesn't give much away.'

Kip came over and put her arm around her husband's waist and Luke bent to kiss the top of her blonde head. Matt turned to ask Ellie if there was anything she wanted to discuss before they started the shoot, and stopped short as he saw the expression on her face. She was staring at Luke with such a look of such hunger and longing he felt almost embarrassed at having witnessed it. He watched his friend laugh and ruffle his wife's hair. Obviously Luke had no idea how Ellie felt. Luke and Kip had been happily married for seven years, but his friend wouldn't have been human if he wasn't tempted by someone as beautiful as Ellie. He hoped the model had the sense to keep her feelings to herself, particularly while Kip was around. He didn't want anything disrupting this shoot.

Sami interrupted his thoughts as she cast about for somewhere to unload her silver make-up boxes. 'Jesus, Matt, don't you ever give me any room to work? What do you want, I should hang out of the window?'

'Hey, Sami. There's always the bathroom.'

'Plugs, darling, plugs,' Andrew scolded, stamping his feet to warm them. 'You want me to blow her hair dry myself?'

245

'Just keep talking and you should have no problem.'

Ellie smiled. 'Don't you listen to them, darling. I think you make me look fabulous.'

'Ellie, with you, that's easy,' Andrew said.

Ellie threw herself into one of the metal chairs at the coffee table. She could sense the undercurrent of excitement in the studio. Luke had inspired everyone with a conspiratorial feeling that they were part of a fantastic secret about to be revealed to the world. He'd not only managed to talk Kip into being their fashion stylist – much to the annoyance of *Vogue*, who'd wanted her for a shoot in the West Indies that week – but had also persuaded Sami and Andrew to turn down the same shoot so that they could work with an unknown photographer and inexperienced model for next to nothing. As Ellie watched Andrew unroll a length of black canvas and begin to sort through the combs and pins slotted neatly into its folds, she felt a buzz of excitement that had nothing to do with the cocaine she'd taken before she'd come to the studio. This glamorous, crazy world was her world now. In all her twenty years, she'd never felt as much at home as she did in front of the camera.

When Angela Lindsay had first approached her as she'd waited to catch the Delta flight from Dallas to London Heathrow just over a year ago, Ellie had dismissed the idea of modelling out of hand. She'd had enough of trading on her looks, of using her body to survive. She'd left Teklima with enough money in her checking account to keep her more than comfortably solvent for several months, and after that, she'd still had all the jewellry Eason had given her. She'd had no clear idea of what she was going to do once she'd reached England, but for the first time in her life she'd had to answer to no one but herself.

For the next three months she'd shuttled between suites at the Dorchester in London and the Hotel George V in Paris until she'd been shopped out. She'd bought so many clothes she hadn't even got around to taking the six-figure price-tags off half of them. She'd deliberately avoided any kind of romantic entanglement, holing herself up in her room with Thomas Hardy and D.H. Lawrence every evening rather than going out, politely refusing any overtures of friendship that came her way. She'd toured museums and art galleries, pottered around Camden Market and down the King's Road, and wandered through the streets of Montmartre with the freedom of a woman who had no agenda but pleasing herself.

Five months after Eason had died, she'd walked back into her hotel bedroom laden with yet more discreet plastic bags from Harrods and Harvey Nichols, and suddenly realised that she'd had enough.

She'd contacted Angela Lindsay more in the hope of diversion than with any serious intention of modelling. She hadn't really needed the money, although the funds in her bank account had diminished far faster than she'd anticipated. For a slum child, she had expensive tastes. La Perla underwear at $300 a throw, cashmere stockings from Fogal costing $200 a pair. There had still been Eason's jewellery, of course, but somehow she hadn't wanted to part with any of that. It represented too much of her life for her to want to trade it for cash.

When she'd seen the expression on Angela's face the day her test shots had come back, she knew that, for the first time in her life, she could use her body on her own terms. Her work gave her a kind of power. The camera – and the money it earned her – insulated her from the world. She was able to give herself to the lens as she had never been able to do with another human being. It had never hurt her, never betrayed her. It had only ever loved her.

Sami opened her heavy make-up box and began to lay out the brushes and cosmetics on a small side table near one of the

247

windows. She'd heard rumours that Sami and Matt had been an item for a few months a while back; but then, according to Angela, Matt's name had been linked with almost every woman he had ever worked with, the only notable exception being Romi.

She eyed Matt covertly as he made a few last-minute adjustments to the set. No wonder Sami still carried a torch for him. It was impossible not to notice the breadth of his shoulders underneath the soft, loose cloth of his overshirt, the faded black Levis that hugged his thighs. His bare feet and forearms were tanned, his soft, dark, poker straight hair flopping over his forehead no matter how many times he pushed it back. But it was the vulnerability beneath that confident, charming smile that was so irresistible. It made you want to reach out and soothe away the pain in the depths of his eyes even while you knew you were the one who'd end up with a broken heart.

Matt was one of the most attractive men she'd ever met. Three months ago, she might have been tempted. Three months ago, she hadn't met Luke.

Late on Christmas Eve, Angela Lindsay had called her into her London office for a meeting with an important client. Ellie remembered being surprised; in the eight months she'd been working for Body Image, Angela had never once bothered to introduce her to a client before a shoot. But she'd had nothing else planned, apart from an evening curled up on the sofa with a copy of Oscar Wilde. Even after a year, she'd made virtually no friends in London. Christmas was just another chance to spend some time alone. She'd changed quickly into a pair of faded jeans she'd known made her legs look endless, and braved the crush of frantic last-minute Christmas shoppers to walk from the immaculately furnished, impersonal flat she'd rented when she'd joined Body Image, in Dilke Street just off the Chelsea Embankment, to Angela's office halfway down the King's Road. She'd enjoyed the raw feeling of the freezing air on her skin, and arrived warm and glowing.

The moment she saw Luke leaning against Angela's desk she wished she'd got a taxi, or at least bothered to put on some make-up. He wasn't especially good-looking; his ebony face was too jumbled, his body too solid, for that. But something in him had reminded her irresistibly of David Conto, something in the way he'd moved, the way he'd smiled. His eyes were alive with warmth and humour, and his enthusiasm for the project he'd outlined to Angela was catching. And he was so in control, so masculine. Ellie had jumped at the chance to take the assignment, knowing it might be just what she needed to launch her career, but also hoping it would give her the opportunity to get to know Luke better. Even after he'd left and Angela had told her he was married, she hadn't been deterred. She'd never yet met a married man who hadn't tried to get her into bed. Until Luke.

In the fourteen months since she'd been widowed, there'd been no one who'd even tempted her from her self-imposed celibacy. She found it hard to make even the most casual friends, let alone take a lover. But she knew Luke was already very important to her. He'd got under her skin.

'You wanted something dark for her eyes, yes?' Sami asked Kip over her shoulder.

'I think so,' Kip said. 'She'll be wearing a deep blue velvet to set off the jewellery, so I think she needs a pretty strong colour around her eyes to balance it.'

Sami rifled through her make-up box. 'MAC sent me a stunning midnight blue shadow last week which'd be perfect. It's so dark it's almost black, but it's got fabulous depth when it's photographed. It should keep its colour without bleaching, if I can only find it. I must clear out this chaos some time. I just get so much stuff these days, I don't even know what's in here.'

Matt peered into the lens of his Hasselblad camera at Ellie as she walked on to the plexiglass. She really was spectacular. If she hadn't been so obviously gone on Luke …

After an hour, he straightened up from the Hasselblad and pushed his hair out his eyes. 'How many's that, Romi?'

Romi looked up from the roll of film she was numbering. 'Seven so far; this will be the eighth.'

'OK, let's take a break. Ten minutes.'

Matt watched Ellie as Kip handed her a tall glass of Evian water and a straw so that the model would not smudge her make-up as she drank. He caught Luke's eye and the two of them moved towards the far end of the studio.

'This is all too controlled, too restrained. This jewellery is very sophisticated and elegant, and so is the dress Ellie's wearing. I think we need to risk losing some of the control, and she's the key. Mind if I try?'

Luke shrugged. 'You're the photographer.'

Matt waited until the set had cleared before moving next to Ellie. She could feel the heat of his body as he leant towards her. 'I want you to make love to that camera,' he breathed softly. 'I want to look into your eyes and see the same expression I'd see if I was going to fuck you. I want to see your nipples rock hard beneath that dress, and I want you liquid by the time I take a photograph. Fuck me through that lens, Ellie. I want you to make me so hard I can barely focus that camera.'

Ellie stared at Matt, aroused despite herself. Luke walked back on to the set. She wanted him so much. As Matt began to take pictures, she was vibrating with an excitement and energy she'd never felt before as she stared into the lens. Matt shot roll after roll of film without pause, refusing to allow the usual tinkering with hair and make-up. As Romi adjusted the lighting and logged each spent roll, she too found herself responding to the sexual charge in the studio, her breasts

250

tingling as waves of desire swept over her. With a few words, Matt had changed the whole atmosphere; he hoped the pictures he was shooting now would possess exactly the untamed, sensual power he wanted.

The telephone in the corner of the studio rang, breaking the spell, and Romi answered it with mingled relief and disappointment. 'Matt. It's Stephi Kay for you.'

'OK, I'll be right with you.'

Matt picked up the telephone. From the electric buzz in the studio he knew he'd got the pictures he wanted. The rest was up to Stephi.

Thirteen

Via Condotti, Rome, Italy
Tuesday 17 February 1987
4.40 p.m.

Alix tried to tug the skirt of her severe black Chanel suit over
her knees as she sat down on the grey sofa the receptionist had
indicated. She was acutely conscious that the skirt was too
short and badly in need of cleaning, but she hadn't got
anything else even remotely suitable for an interview at the
House of Pavesi. When she'd left her parents' home she'd
simply grabbed the first things that had come to hand and fled.
She'd only taken the Chanel at the last minute. She'd never
really liked it: it made her look pale and washed-out, but it was
versatile and she knew it made her appear older than she was.
Apart from a few pairs of Versace jeans and a couple of shirts,
she'd left the rest of her clothes behind. Most of them had
been bought for her by her father, and she hadn't wanted any
reminders of him. It had never occurred to her then that she
might actually *need* her clothes. Until she left home she'd
never needed anything in her life.

'Signora Evans will see you now.'

Alix jumped up, nervously shifting the strap of her bag over
her shoulder. The receptionist gave her a cold stare, then
pointed a gilded fingernail towards a small door on the left of
the reception area. 'Through there.'

252

Alix found herself in a narrow, windowless corridor very different from the one she remembered being escorted through on her rare visits to the House of Pavesi with her mother. There was no thick grey carpeting here, only worn lino that felt sticky underfoot. The grubby cream walls were scuffed and badly in need of a coat of paint, and it felt dark and cramped and smelt of sweat and stale cigarettes. This was a side to the House of Pavesi the couture clients never got to see.

She stopped in front of the first door she reached, wondering if this was where she was supposed to be. As she raised her hand to knock, the door opened and a short, scrawny woman dressed in a worn grey smock stuck her head out.

'You the one who's come for the job?'

Alix's heart sank as she saw the nicotine stains on the woman's fingers and the cluttered, airless office behind her.

'You'd better come in, then. Mind how you tread, there's pins everywhere.'

Alix followed the woman into the room, carefully picking her way through the bolts of fabric and dozens of cardboard boxes that littered the floor. The room was so small that if she'd reached out her arms she could have touched both walls. She stood uncertainly in the centre as the woman squeezed between the wall and the edge of her crowded desk to sit down, a cloud of papers fluttering to the floor as she did so.

'There's a chair somewhere behind you,' the woman said, bending to pick up the papers.

Alix moved two open boxes of pink ribbons from the seat of a battered wooden chair and sat down. The woman ignored her as she briskly sorted through her papers, putting them in order. Alix could see they were drawings of some kind, tiny swatches of material pinned to the corners with notations scribbled underneath them.

Finally the woman looked up. 'So. You're the girl Stephi Kay recommended?'

Using Stephi's name had been the only way Alix had been able to think of to get an interview. She tried to look convincing as she opened her bag and pulled out some designs her teacher at school had given straight As. 'She thought you might want to see some of these –'

The woman took the drawings and studied them. Alix watched her, wondering how old she was. From the look of her, she could have been anywhere between forty and seventy. Her skin was waxy-looking and her iron-grey hair scraped into a neat bun at the nape of her neck, her button-dark eyes quick and shrewd as she scanned the designs. She had a no-nonsense air about her that reminded Alix of her English teacher at school. All at once she knew that the woman wasn't taken in by her story for a moment.

The woman handed back the drawings. 'They're too complicated and overdrawn, but you've got some good ideas. You need to work at your drawings, get used to how they'll translate from paper to fabric. In a few years –'

'But I need a job now!'

The words were out before she could stop them. The woman stared at her in surprise, then her expression softened. 'My dear, there's no way you're suitable for a position as an assistant designer. You have talent and a great deal of promise, and I have no doubt that you could go far. But not yet.'

Alix tried hard to hold back the tears. This job had been her last hope.

She'd had exactly $2,700 in her overseas savings account when she'd left home. She'd withdrawn it immediately, before her father could contact the bank to freeze her access to the money in an attempt to force her to return. It had translated into just over four million lire, which had seemed a fortune at the time. She'd checked into the Hotel d'Inghilterra, telling the clerk to charge her bill to her father's account, and set out to look for an apartment, confident that she'd be able to find a decent place to rent and have enough money left over to keep her going until she found a job.

The hotel clerk had recommended an upmarket estate agent in Via del Babuino, and she'd walked straight there and explained what she'd wanted. The realtor had taken one look at her expensive MaxMara coat and Louis Vuitton handbag and scented an easy commission. She'd handed Alix a sheaf of details for one-bedroomed flats in the centre of Rome, and Alix had visited several apartments before she'd decided on a spacious, airy flat overlooking the Piazza del Popolo.

The realtor had smiled as she'd filled in the paperwork. 'Is this your first apartment?'

Alix had nodded.

'I think you've made a good choice. The flat's only been available for two days – we don't get many in that area. When were you thinking of moving in?'

'Tomorrow?'

'I think that should be possible, provided I can contact the owner this afternoon. Of course, you will be required to pay a month's rent in advance, plus a month's deposit. That isn't a problem, is it?'

Alix had opened her handbag. 'No, of course not. Could you tell me how much that is?'

'Let me see – the rent is two million four hundred thousand lire a month, so that's four million eight hundred thousand – plus our commission – let's call it five and a half million, as you're here now.'

'Five and a half million!'

The realtor had looked up, a flicker of suspicion crossing her face for the first time. 'I thought it wouldn't be a problem?'

'I never expected it to be so much –'

The realtor had bridled. 'It *is* one of the most sought-after addresses in Rome, signorina. I think you'll find it's very reasonable.'

'I'm sure it is. I just didn't think the rent would be quite so high –'

'I see. Perhaps one of the other less exclusive apartments would be more suitable?'

Alix had flushed. She'd never had to think how much things cost before, much less be unable to afford them. 'Which – which is the cheapest?'

'The apartment near the Colosseum is perhaps the least prestigious address on our books. Two million a month, and that includes access to the gardens –' She'd frowned at the expression on Alix's face. 'Tell me, signorina, how much did you have in mind?'

'I thought – perhaps half a million lire – three-quarters at the most –'

The realtor had laughed and closed her books. 'Signorina, I suggest you return home to your parents and make up your differences, whatever they are. The only property you'll find for that sort of money you wouldn't want to rent for your dog.'

'I – I can't go back. I have to find somewhere. Please, don't you have anything?'

The woman had seen the desperation in the young, thin girl's face and suddenly taken pity on her. It hadn't been that long since she'd been scraping together the deposit for her first apartment herself.

'Wait here. I'll see what I can do.'

She'd disappeared through a door at the back of the office, returning a few moments later with an address scribbled on a dog-eared scrap of paper. 'Here, it's in Trastevere, near the river. Six hundred and fifty thousand a month, and you can forget the commission.' She'd held up her hand as Alix started to thank her. 'I warn you, it won't be what you're used to. For that kind of money, things tend to be rather – basic. I strongly advise you to go home to your parents, signorina.'

Less than an hour later, Alix stared round the dingy, foul-smelling apartment and wondered if the woman had been right. Perhaps she should just give up and go back home. Basic wasn't the word. There was no carpet, the ancient furniture was alive with bugs and lice, the toilet bowl was stained brown, and she had to share a bathroom with four other tenants in the apartment block. Then she'd thought of the contempt in her mother's face and her father's secret visits in the middle of the night, and she'd swallowed her pride. It was only a start, after all. She wouldn't be here for long. Once she had a job, she could afford something better.

Next day, she'd started looking for work, after a sleepless night listening to mice scuttling beneath her bed and cockroaches skittering across the bare floorboards. Armed with her portfolio and brightest smile, she'd spent four weeks trailing from one designer to another, only to be told there was nothing available for someone with no training and no experience. Most of the time she hadn't even got past the receptionist. As her funds had dwindled, she'd left the portfolio behind and looked for work as a shop assistant or waitress, but prospective employers had taken one look at her pinched, starved face and expensive clothes and turned her down.

It hadn't taken her father long to track her down; she guessed he'd found out from the hotel clerk which estate agents she'd used, and the realtor had told him the rest. He'd written to her first, and she could tell from the weight of the envelopes that he'd sent her money. She'd returned them all unopened.

He'd been waiting for her outside the apartment block six weeks after she'd left home. The moment he'd seen her emerge, he'd leaped out of the car and run towards her. Tempted to go back inside, Alix had known he'd just sit there waiting for her until she did come out. She took a deep breath and walked briskly past him as if she hadn't seen him, but he followed her down the street, calling her name. Finally she stopped and faced him.

'What do you want?'

Her father spread his hands in supplication. 'Alix, darling, please. Come home. I'm sorry. It won't happen again –'

'Leave me alone. I don't need you now.'

'Alix, I can see that isn't true. Look at you. You look terrible. Have you seen yourself lately? Look at where you're living. When did you last have a hot bath or a change of clothes? Is this really what you want?'

Alix had caught a glimpse of her reflection in the window of a parked car, and suddenly she saw herself through her father's eyes. She'd done her best to wash herself and her clothes in the filthy bathroom, but there were limits to what she could do with a flannel and water that never got beyond tepid. She hadn't been able to bring herself to get in the bath itself. She'd tried to clean it, but the effort was futile. After too many generations of careless tenants it was beyond redemption. Her auburn hair had dulled to a muddy brown and hung, limp and greasy, around her pallid face. Huge circles were under her eyes, and she had two cold sores on her lips. Her fingernails were grimy, her clothes soiled and creased.

'Alix, please. Come home.'

Two children had run past them, waving pieces of tinsel like miniature lassos. It would be Christmas in just over six weeks. She'd thought of the previous year, the hundreds of presents beneath the Christmas tree, the fire blazing in the hearth, the warmth of her own clean bed, the soft, fluffy towels as big as sheets in her bathroom. Then she'd thought of the disgusting bedsit she was living in now, the toilet that didn't flush, the bedclothes that were alive with lice.

But when her father reached out his hand to touch her arm, she'd leaped back as if she'd just been burned. 'Get out of my life, Daddy. Get out, or I'll tell everyone exactly what you did to me.'

He'd left her alone after that, but it had been a pyrrhic victory. She'd sat on the floor of her lonely room on Christmas Day and stared out of the window, wishing it could all have been different. She'd lost everything she'd ever known: her family, her home, even her friends. She could hardly bring them home to her flat, and even if she had, they'd have nothing to talk about. They still lived in a world where double maths and pop stars were all-important. They didn't have to struggle to find a job in order to eat.

When she'd left home, how she would pay for food had been the last problem on Alix's mind. She'd certainly never expected to feel hungry. She'd spent the previous three years trying to avoid eating, yet the moment she was away from her mother, the impetus pushing her to diet had dwindled away. The anger that had driven her for so long faded, and now that she had control of her own life, controlling what she ate suddenly seemed less important. She hadn't been able to afford the expensive diet products she'd insisted on eating anyway – the low-fat yoghurts and spreads, the exotic fruits, even the black coffee and Evian water. At the end of a long day spent searching for work or tramping the streets just to escape from her damp, freezing apartment, she'd been too tired to think about counting calories. In her desperation to find a job, food had simply become the fuel that enabled her to get out of bed the next morning. But old habits died hard. Even when she felt hungry, she still found it difficult to eat more than the absolute minimum. She'd spend her carefully hoarded lire to buy a piece of pizza that made her mouth water, only to find she could barely choke a quarter of it down.

By the beginning of February she knew she'd only be able to last another couple of weeks on her savings. Her father had written to her again, and this time she hadn't returned the bulky envelope. But she hadn't opened it. She'd only take his money if there was no alternative. She'd sat looking at the envelope propped up on her windowsill, and suddenly decided to give the job-hunting one more try. After that, she'd have to admit defeat.

Alix had headed towards her favourite café in the Piazza di Spagna and sat nursing a cappuccino for an hour while she made a list of all the places she hadn't tried. There was still the American Bar in the north of the city, although she wasn't too sure about the clientele. They tended to be a bit rough and over-familiar, from what she'd heard. If she could swallow her pride and run the risk of meeting one of her mother's friends, she could always try skivvying –

She'd clutched the table as two girls had pushed past her and sat down, the coloured threads clinging to their grey smocks identifying them as seamstresses. About to return to her list, she'd heard one of them mention Giulio Pavesi's name. Automatically she'd tuned in to the conversation. The House of Pavesi had been the one place she hadn't looked for a job, because Giulio Pavesi had always been her mother's favourite designer. But now she was desperate.

'– and sacked him there and then,' one of the girls was saying. 'Of course, Signor Chambrun was furious. Pavesi needs his assistants. He can't afford to lose any of them, especially with the collection in two weeks' time.'

'What will he do?'

'Find someone else, I suppose. Though how he'll get anyone at such short notice –'

And here she was now.

She stared at the woman across the desk, knowing her desperation showed in her face. She had exactly 62,000 lire in her handbag. Less than $50. She was already behind with this month's rent, and she hadn't eaten for two days. Her stomach rumbled and she thought desperately of the food she'd turned her nose up at when she'd been living at home. She'd give almost anything for just one decent meal. The irony wasn't lost on her.

The woman interrupted her thoughts. 'Tell me, signorina, how old are you?'

'Nineteen,' Alix lied.

'The truth, if you please.'

Alix stared at her hands. 'Seventeen. Well, nearly.'

Janet Evans concealed her surprise. She'd guessed from the tears that the girl in front of her must be quite young, but she looked older than sixteen. She was painfully thin, of course, which always added years, and the severe black suit didn't help. But it was a Chanel, if a couple of years old, and her shoes were clearly expensive and hand-made. Her accent was educated, her movements graceful and somewhat imperious despite her plight. She had had money once, even if she didn't have it now. Her designs were clever and original despite the lack of technical skill. Janet wondered what her story was.

In the thirty-five years she'd been in the fashion industry, first as a seamstress and now, finally, as head fitter, Janet had lost the ability to be surprised by anything. She'd started at Hartnell back in the Fifties when she'd been the same age as this girl was now, a young Welsh innocent from the valleys, and in the intervening years at Dior, St Laurent and now Pavesi's, she'd learned far more than how to run a fashion house. Most of the dramas she'd witnessed had involved a man in some way, and she guessed it was the same with this girl now. She thanked God, as she did at least once a day, that she'd never married. Men were only good for two things, and the DIY she could do herself.

'I'm sorry, Alexandra – it *is* Alexandra, isn't it? If you were just a little older –'

'And a little more experienced, yes, I know. I'd just like to know how I'm supposed to get this experience when no one will give me a job.' She stood up and extended her hand. 'Thank you for seeing me, signora.'

Janet watched her pick her way towards the door. She hadn't missed the girl's anger and frustration. Another child her age would have resorted to sobs and pleading to get her way. This girl had pulled herself together remarkably quickly and come back fighting. And her drawings *had* been good, perhaps exceptionally good given her youth. With an instinct born of of nearly four decades in the business, Janet made a quick decision.

'Alexandra, I can't offer you the job you'd like – at least not yet. But perhaps I can find you something else …'

The girl froze in the doorway.

'I need a seamstress in one of the ateliers. It will be hard, dull work, long days and the pay is not good. But the job's yours, if you want it.'

For the first time since the girl had entered the room, Janet saw her smile.

There were times in the next six months when Alix regretted ever having walked into the House of Pavesi. Janet hadn't been exaggerating. Alix would crawl home after each gruelling, eighteen-hour day too exhausted to do anything but collapse into her narrow bed and sleep, her dreams filled with an endless parade of dancing scissors. Her hands were red and covered in blisters, her back ached from bending over the sewing table, her eyes were red-rimmed and itched from all the close work. But she carried on even when she was so tired

262

she wanted to cry, knowing that she was getting a better training here than she could ever hope to find on a design school course. She began just by putting up hems, adjusting seams. But soon she graduated to more complicated work.

Under Janet's critical eye, she quickly mastered the art of handling even the most difficult and delicate fabrics used in the *atelier frou*. Impressed, Janet took a special interest in her new employee and quietly encouraged her to experiment with colour and texture, teaching her how to cut and work the different materials, showing her what worked and what the customer would never accept, no matter how avant-garde or creative. Alix was humbled by how much she had to learn. She could see now how naive her precious A-grade designs had been. Gradually she learned to adapt the talent she knew she possessed to the new skills she was learning, and began to translate her ideas for designs on to the pages of her notebook. Janet studied them carefully, offering advice and pointing out weaknesses. On rare occasions, she'd just nod. Those were the only designs Alix didn't throw away.

But she learned far more than technicalities of design. Over the months Janet gave her the information that would enable her to survive in an industry built on who you were and what you knew. She taught Alix who was important and who only thought they were, whose name would open doors and whose would shut them, who was feuding with whom. It was a syllabus she could never have learned at school, but Alix knew it was at least as important as her ability to sew chiffon or sketch an outfit so that a cutter could interpret it correctly.

She rarely saw either Giulio Pavesi or Edouard Chambrun, although she knew both of them by reputation, of course. Most of the workers at the couturiers were terrified of Pavesi's legendary tantrums, especially the women, to whom he was particularly unforgiving. Chambrun was a more shadowy figure, remote, detached from the day-to-day running of the design house. From the gossip she overheard, Alix discovered that although the two men were still lovers, Pavesi had never been faithful. They looked so different – Pavesi at forty was still voluptuously handsome despite his weight, his long hair black and curly, his chubby, boyish face unlined. Chambrun had not aged so well. At fifty-two, his features had become pinched, and he looked old before his time.

Alix soon found that Janet had a great deal of respect for Edouard Chambrun. He'd started the House of Pavesi twenty-two years ago to keep his lover happy, knowing next to nothing about fashion, and devoured books on the fashion industry, working eighteen or twenty hours a day to complete his self-imposed workload. It hadn't made him popular, but it had made Pavesi's one of the most successful couture houses in Italy. Apart from the prestigious couture collections on which Giulio worked alone, Alix learned that the House of Pavesi also produced ready-to-wear lines for men, women and children, each line designed and managed by one of the assistant designers Giulio so despised. The Pavesi Group had also recently acquired two established cognacs, a leather goods company, and a small but exclusive range of retail outlets across the world, in addition to the only family interest – an ancient and distinguished champagne label – from which Chambrun's furious parents had not been able to disinherit him when he'd eloped with Giulio. Janet was less impressed with the man whose name the design house bore. In her view, Giulio Pavesi might have had the design talent – once – but Chambrun alone had built the House of Pavesi into a multimillion-dollar empire.

Alix made few friends amongst the other seamstresses. Her accent, her background, her class set her apart. She belonged neither to their world, nor to that into which she'd been born. Her only real friend was Janet herself. The older woman had taken her under her wing from the beginning and had gradually come to mean more to Alix than any woman in her life since Stephi. It was Janet who'd finally helped her to get her obsession with food under control by sitting down with her and making her eat breakfast, lunch and dinner, chatting to her to take her mind off the food, giving her the confidence to relinquish her rigid control. Alix knew she would never be curvaceous, but at least dieting had ceased to be the focal point of her life.

It was during those first exhausting, gruelling, isolating months that Alix realised there was only one thing she wanted to do with her life. Every night when she fell into bed, she dreamed that the name on the labels she sewed into each $10,000 dress was her own.

Fourteen

Via Condotti, Rome, Italy
Wednesday 18 November 1987
5.30 p.m.

Giulio Pavesi faced Edouard Chambrun across the width of
his desk, his face a mask of fury and frustration. Twenty
minutes of bitter argument had failed to resolve the differences that divided them and threatened to split them apart. The
silence between them stretched into minutes, neither of them
willing to give an inch.

When Chambrun finally spoke, his voice was weary but
uncompromising. 'Giulio, we *must* diversify if we want to
stay ahead. Now more than ever.'

'No!'

'I just don't see what your problem is!' Chambrun shouted.
'I'm not saying we should become less exclusive, far from it,
but we must expand into new areas if we want to survive. I just
don't understand why you're being so unreasonable.'

'No, you don't understand. You never do!'

Chambrun's narrow lips were a gash in his pale face. 'And
just what is that supposed to mean?'

'What do you think I am, another Cardin? A man who will
sell his name to anyone, if the price is high enough? In Tokyo,
even the steaks in the supermarket have Pierre Cardin
stamped into them! Is that what you want?'

'I'm not asking you to start selling Pavesi hamburgers,' Chambrun said. 'But it wouldn't do you any harm to remember that Pierre Cardin is probably the richest designer in the world. His turnover is more than 2,500 million dollars a year. That's a lot of steaks.'

'Is that all the business means to you? Money?'

Chambrun ignored him. 'Giulio, you know as well as I do the advantages of granting licences to a few reliable, established manufacturers. Look how much we make from the ones we have already – the sunglasses alone outperform even our best ready-to-wear lines. We've almost reached the stage where we hardly need the couture, except for the prestige it gives the name we put on everything else.'

Pavesi scowled. 'I'm not going to sell my name to the highest bidder like some whore. Tell me, Edouard. Who will pay me $50,000 for a dress which has taken hundreds of hours to sew by hand, when they see shop girls wearing $40 outfits that also carry my name – outfits I haven't even seen, much less approved? What will the name of Pavesi mean when you can buy it on a bar of soap or a photograph frame for a few lire?'

Chambrun sighed. Both men knew that the line between free promotion and over-exposure was very narrow; Chambrun hadn't even bothered to reply to the manufacturers who had requested a licence for Pavesi dental floss. But at the same time, the many customers who couldn't afford a Pavesi suit or evening dress would spend millions between them buying into the designer dream with a pair of gold 'P' earrings, or a tissue-thin Pavesi silk scarf. Chambrun knew there was money to be made, and he intended to be on the receiving end.

'This is 1987, Giulio. Why do you think Chanel and Vuitton put their logos on the *outside* of their handbags? People don't care if any of us actually make the damn things

267

we put our names to, or even if they're any good.' Chambrun's temper suddenly dissipated as he looked at his lover across his desk. 'Giulio, *you* are all that matters to me. But this is a business. It has to be run like one.'

'*Your* business,' Pavesi muttered bitterly. '*Your* creation, *your* toy. Not mine. It's never been mine.'

Chambrun gazed at the cluster of framed photographs on the surface of the desk as if searching for inspiration. He didn't know why he was so surprised by Giulio's behaviour. Ever since he'd fallen for him the designer had acted like a spoilt child, unable to take even the mildest criticism and given to throwing violent tantrums if he didn't get his own way in everything. Once he'd sulked for three weeks, not speaking to anyone, when Chambrun had dared to alter the colour of the House of Pavesi stationery from white to cream without consulting him. Usually he was easily placated once the source of his upset had been identified. But lately he'd been impossible, objecting to every proposal Chambrun made, insulting and abusing the assistant designers on whom he depended – although he'd never admit that – and frequently reducing the seamstresses and house models to tears.

Edouard picked up a picture of Giulio standing with Angela Lindsay. She'd been the only person in the world who could handle Giulio when he was in one of his moods, but she was no longer here. She'd left the House of Pavesi to start her own model agency, Body Image. Edouard could hardly blame her, but her absence had made his own life that much more difficult. He'd never really been able to control Giulio, even in the beginning. Now, after more than two decades as lovers and partners, his word carried less weight than ever. The irony of the situation was not lost on Chambrun: as his influence had grown within the fashion industry, it had waned with the one man for whom he had done it all.

He turned and faced Giulio, trying to ignore the sulky expression on the younger man's face as he lolled in his chair and fiddled idly with the heavy gold identity bracelet on his left wrist.

'Giulio, just tell me. What is it you want?'

'You know what I want. Ellie Cassidy.'

'Oh, Giulio, we've been through this before –'

'Yes, but have you once stopped to listen to what I've been saying?' Giulio cried. 'I want a woman who will be the face of Pavesi, like Chanel, like Saint Laurent. This girl is the hottest model since Twiggy – ever since she did that jewellery campaign everyone has been trying to get her. I know if we brought her here, arranged some photo-opportunities around Rome – Bulgari, the Trevi Fountain, the Spanish Steps – we'd be front-page news. Think of the publicity! If we could persuade her to sign an exclusive contract …'

Chambrun sighed. 'It's too risky to invest everything in one girl. What if it went wrong? Giulio, do you have any idea how much she would cost? Millions of dollars, and with no guarantee of success at the end of it.'

'How do you know?' Pavesi shouted, for all the world like an eight-year-old having a tantrum. 'When did you ever let me have the chance to do anything by myself? When did I ever have the freedom to discover if I could succeed without you holding my hand every step of the way?'

Chambrun stared at him, stunned by the bitterness of the attack. 'What can I say, Giulio?' he said finally. 'Except that I did it all for you.'

Pavesi was unable to meet Edouard's eyes. He knew only too well the debt he owed him, but instead of softening his anger it merely served to intensify his guilt and resentment. After so long at the top, he was no more than a figurehead, a cipher for the business Edouard Chambrun had created. He stared out of the window across the Piazza di Spagna, suddenly remembering the first time he'd seen this view. He'd walked into the room that was to become his office, his first collection no more than a sheaf of half-finished drawings, and had been filled with an overwhelming sense of excitement at the future opening out before him.

And Edouard had given it all to him. He hadn't had to fight for anything. Edouard had found the backers, leased the building, negotiated with the fabric manufacturers, employed the seamstresses, courted the fashion journalists and wooed the celebrity customers. When Giulio had been overwhelmed at the unexpected success of his first collection, it had been Edouard who'd brought in assistant designers to help him overcome his fear of producing second-rate work that failed to live up to his début. In return, Chambrun had asked only for his love, and at first Giulio had thought he could give it to him. He hadn't realised then how easy it was to confuse love with gratitude.

Stephi Kay had been right all those years ago when she'd said that his collection showed unfulfilled promise. He'd taken the easy way out, relied on the talents of others when he doubted his own. He'd never had a chance to grow and develop because Edouard had left him with nothing to achieve.

He glanced briefly at the row of yellow telephone messages stuck to his desk. Fernando Moreno had called three times, presumably to discover if Giulio had found any new clients for his Brazilian merchandise. Pavesi knew he was already in too deep with Moreno; but was it any wonder that he wanted to take risks, to have just one part of his life that Edouard couldn't control, didn't even know about? Edouard wouldn't even let him choose the model he wanted. At least with Moreno he could take his own chances, live by his own wits. The danger was like a drug. It terrified him, but it had become something he couldn't live without. Even that was Edouard's fault, he thought to himself.

Chambrun left the room, his mind churning. Perhaps Giulio was right about this model he wanted – he seemed to have a golden touch when it came to generating publicity. If only his designs were as inspired.

For a long time he had known that Giulio was not a genius like couturiers such as Yves Saint Laurent or Giorgio Armani. Giulio's talent was only ever going to be mediocre. If it hadn't been for his own brilliant business mind and Giulio's undoubted ability to exploit his celebrity status and play the role of Maestro, the House of Pavesi would never have become so successful. But it couldn't last for ever. The assistant designers he'd already brought in had managed to keep things going this far, but although all six of them were talented, none had the creative genius Chambrun knew was needed now to shore up Pavesi's weakening hold on his market. He needed someone new. God knows where he was going to find anyone that talented who was desperate enough to design to be prepared to put up with Giulio's moods.

He walked into his office and immediately noticed the papers on his desk. Unlike Giulio, he kept the polished glass surface clear but for his diary and telephone.

He picked up the papers and stared at the drawings. Suddenly he knew he'd found his answer.

Book Three

1992 – 1994

One

Via Condotti, Rome, Italy
Tuesday 5 May 1992
6.15 p.m.

Roberto glanced at his wristwatch. He'd already been sitting here for over an hour, long enough to begin to attract unwelcome attention. He didn't dare wait much longer. There were simply too many people watching him these days.

He sighed. The loss of his privacy was one of the lesser penalties he paid for having survived at the centre of Italian politics for more than three decades.

Roberto shifted his large frame uncomfortably in his chair, shaking free the pages of the financial paper he was pretending to read, and folding it precisely along the centre crease. His head was angled so that he appeared to be absorbed by the recent vagaries of the Italian currency, but his dark eyes were focused on the street outside. He had chosen this table so that he could see through the open doorway into the Via Condotti. Several times he'd thought he'd seen the woman he was waiting for, only for his excitement to turn to disappointment. He couldn't bear it if she didn't come today. It had already been so long that his craving for her was like a physical pain in his side.

A few early summer tourists dressed in jeans and high-tech trainers mingled with the serious shoppers clad in Armani and

Valentino, their handbags swinging from their shoulders as they headed briskly along the most expensive street in Rome. In this part of the city even the schoolchildren wore Versace and Moschino, gold bangles jangling at the wrists of both sexes. The Café El Greco didn't balk at charging $10 for a coffee in a street where even the cheapest handbag cost over $500.

Roberto sensed someone staring at him from behind, and stiffened. Even though his visits to the café were outwardly innocent, he'd still made every effort to avoid being followed. He had no wish for any one to start digging too deeply into his private affairs. There was too much for them to find.

Forcing himself to relax, he lowered his paper just enough to allow him to glance in the mirror hanging above the bar. His eyes locked with those of the girl staring at him, then quickly looked away. When his gaze returned a moment later, she was still watching him.

Disconcerted, Roberto buried his head in the paper and willed himself not to turn round. The brazen sexual invitation in the girl's eyes hadn't fooled him; despite her air of sophistication, she couldn't have been more than fifteen. He didn't even dare to smile at her in case someone was watching. The Italian public might not care about the sexual indiscretions which had been faithfully reported by the paparazzi following his doomed affair with Stephi Kay – he thanked God he wasn't an English politician – but a teenage girl young enough to be his daughter … no, younger than his daughter. This girl was probably no older than Alix herself had been when she'd walked out of the house and out of his life almost six years before. Sometimes it was hard to imagine her as she must be today, a young woman of nearly twenty-two. To him, she was still his baby, his little girl. He wondered if he would ever get over losing her.

He'd gone through the motions of living: his career had

steadily continued to climb, although he knew he was never going to achieve the Premiership he'd once wanted so badly. He no longer had the hunger to reach for it. His ambition had died the day his daughter had left him. His marriage had long been a sham; he and Joanna led completely separate lives, appearing in public together just often enough to stem the gossip. He only stayed with her because there was nowhere else to go. There was only one thing he wanted now: reconciliation with his daughter, and he knew it was never going to happen. She'd returned all his letters unopened, until eventually he'd stopped sending them. He'd never approached her again; not because he was afraid she would carry out her threat to expose him, but because he couldn't help hoping that one day, if he gave her enough time, she'd forgive him.

He paid the cashier and walked out into the street. He was fifty-nine years old, one of the most prominent politicians in the country, rich, aristocratic, handsome, successful – and utterly alone.

He turned into the Via Condotti and headed away from the Piazza di Spagna, suddenly cold despite the mild evening. He might live for another twenty years and never find again the brief love he'd shared with Stephi. Yet he'd had no other choice but to give her up once Joanna had played him the recording of his conversation with Fernando Moreno. It had been the only way he could see to keep his daughter.

And he'd lost her anyway.

He thought of all the misery and anguish he and Joanna had inflicted upon one another in the quarter-century they had been married. He had to live with the bitter knowledge that the mistake had been his; when they'd met, Joanna had been an innocent child of nineteen, he an experienced man of the world fifteen years her senior. He should have known better. He should have recognised his infatuation for what it had been, and not mistaken it for love. He should have seen the warning signs in Joanna's behaviour – the sudden rages, the unreasoning jealousy, the obsessive hatred for any woman who came near him from his mother to his infant daughter. If he'd learned to handle her earlier, perhaps she would never have become the person she was now. With another man, in another time, she might have been a different, happier woman, but with him she'd turned into a hard, brittle, damaged woman who had sought refuge in money and status, who even now loved him to the point of hatred.

Roberto's steps slowed as he neared the end of the Via Condotti. If his marriage had been different, would things with Alix still have turned out the way they had? Or would they even now be sitting down together at the Café El Greco, sharing the day's news over a couple of espressos, like so many of the fathers and daughters he saw there?

And then he saw her.

His heart pounded as he shrank bank into a shop doorway and watched Alix emerge from the side door of Pavesi's, a large folder clutched under her arm. She smiled and waved to someone standing behind her, then glanced upwards at the sky as if assessing the weather before turning left and walking briskly down the street in his direction.

Roberto stared fixedly into the shop window next to him, drinking in every detail reflected in the glass as she walked along the cobbled pavement. She was still thin, but no longer dangerously so. Her hair was short, cut into an elegant bob that just skimmed the top of her shoulders, and gave her an air of quiet composure that made her seem older. Her clothes were understated and well cut, reinforcing the impression of self-control she projected.

But it was more than the polish and sophistication he might have expected from a girl who'd spent the last six years working at the centre of one of the world's most prominent

278

fashion houses. As he watched her, Roberto realised that the image his daughter presented now was attractive and well groomed, but completely untouchable, as if she had erected a wall between herself and the outside world.

She'd never made any real attempt to hide the fact that she was still living in Rome and working at Pavesi's, but Roberto had no idea how she would react if he suddenly reappeared in her life now. She might disappear again, this time for good. He had no doubt that if she wanted to make herself impossible to find, she would be able to do so. She was a grown woman now with a career, not the terrified child she'd been when she'd run away.

He followed her at a safe distance as she made her way along the street and turned left into the Via del Corso, guessing that she was heading back to the apartment in Piazza Capranica she'd moved to just over two years ago. Roberto had made it his business to find out everything he could about her life. He'd known the moment she'd got her first job as seamstress at Pavesi's when she was sixteen, coolly using Stephi Kay's name to get her foot through the door; but it had been her talent, not her connections, that had taken her from the sewing atelier to the design studio as Guilio Pavesi's youngest assistant designer a year later. Roberto also knew she'd dropped his name when she'd started at Pavesi's, adopting his mother's maiden name, D'Alfonsi, instead.

He watched as she entered her apartment block and shut the door behind her. She'd been no more than a few metres from him, but it might as well have been a thousand miles. As he turned, lost in his thoughts, he walked straight into someone. He looked up to apologise, and found himself staring directly into the dark eyes of the girl from the café.

He knew at once that she'd followed him. Her expression held no surprise at seeing him, only invitation. Automatically he ran his eyes over her body with the expertise of a

279

connoisseur valuing a work of art. Her small breasts were firm and high beneath her polo-neck silk jumper, her long, young legs shown to advantage by a pair of clinging black leather jeans. His original estimate of her age had probably been right: she was fifteen, sixteen at the most. Under age. He should walk away from her now, before anyone knew he'd seen her. If she'd found him so easily, who knew what other eyes might be watching? She could even be bait, set out to tempt him; a man as powerful as he, had plenty of enemies.

He thought of Fernando Moreno. He knew the Brazilian had enough problems of his own now that his country's democracy, in the form of President Collor de Mello, had turned sour. Roberto doubted he had time to worry about what his old partner and foe was doing at the moment. Even so, he'd no intention of taking Fernando's indifference for granted. The moment he thought he was safe from the Brazilian for ever and relaxed his guard was the moment Moreno would strike. He hadn't been biding his time for twenty years to let Roberto off the hook now.

Roberto thought how ironic it was that Alix should choose to work for Giulio Pavesi. Apart from Joanna and Fernando, Pavesi was the one person who had the power to end Roberto's career at a stroke, albeit at the price of his own. And Alix was now one of Pavesi's closest colleagues.

Seeing his daughter had made Roberto ache for distraction; perhaps the girl in front of him could provide it. Abruptly he decided it was worth the risk.

Roberto turned and threaded his way through the crowded streets towards Via Bocca di Leone and the Hotel d'Inghilterra. The girl followed, as he'd known she would. Roberto ignored her until he reached the corner of Via Bocca di Leone and Via Borgognona, then stopped beside an old man selling hot chestnuts from a brazier. His eyes scanned the street around him as the old man parcelled the chestnuts into a paper funnel. He visited the hotel often enough for his presence to go unremarked, but he didn't want anyone to see the girl follow him in.

Certain he hadn't been followed, Roberto handed the old man a 10,000 lire note and crossed the cobbled courtyard towards the hotel. A clerk appeared from a small office at the far end of the marble entrance hall and smiled in recognition as Roberto approached the reception desk. 'Signor Cerreni, how good to see you again. Another conference?'

'*Buon giorno*, Alberto. Yes, another conference.'

'Of course. Your usual room?'

Roberto accepted the leather key fob. If the receptionist doubted his explanation, he gave no sign. The Hotel d'Inghilterra was renowned for its discretion.

He didn't wait for the lift. He climbed the stairs two at a time and walked across the corridor to his room. He left the door slightly ajar and waited.

Moments later the girl slipped into the room and shut the door behind her, leaning against it, her hands still on the handle behind her back. Her gaze came to rest on the ancient four-poster bed which took up most of the room. She moved towards it and sat on the edge, testing the mattress, then stood up again, opening and closing the minibar with the aimless curiosity of a child.

'Do you want something to drink?'

The girl shrugged. 'If I did, I'd have helped myself by now.'

Roberto smiled. 'I'm sure you would.'

'Don't treat me like a child.' The girl stuffed a chocolate from a bowl next to the bed into her mouth.

'Do you think they know? About us, I mean?'

'I hope not. I'd have to find some way of silencing them. And you, of course.'

The girl glanced at him to check that he was joking.

Roberto's neutral expression told her nothing. Nervously, she turned away and began fiddling with the arrangement of dried flowers on the chest of drawers. 'I'm Francesca.'

'Roberto.'

'I know.'

'Yes, I thought you might,' Roberto said. 'But that's no reason why we shouldn't be properly introduced.'

He held out his hand and Francesca moved to take it, returning his sudden smile. Somehow his handshake became an embrace. 'My friends call me Chesca. Or Chess.'

'Do I count as one of your friends?'

Francesca pulled his head towards her. Her mouth tasted soft and sweet as he allowed her to dictate the strength of their kiss, his cock hardening as he pulled her groin towards his so that she could feel his excitement. 'Is this what you want, Chesca?'

She reached for him through the thick cloth of his trousers, her touch sure and knowing. Roberto moved towards the bed and fell on to it with her. His left hand found the gap between her silk jumper and leather jeans and moved to cup her small bare breast. She murmured his name in a whisper of encouragement. For the first time he realised how small she was as his body covered hers, almost crushing it beneath his weight. He heard her grunt in discomfort and slid to the side so that his hip just overlapped hers without pressing down on her.

'We aren't here to play games, Chesca,' he said softly. 'Take off your clothes.'

'No, I want you to do it.'

'Do I look like a lady's maid?'

'Do it for me. I like it better that way.'

'And you always get what you want, I suppose?'

She grinned. 'I got you, didn't I?'

'I just hope you're sure you haven't got more than you

bargained for.' His hands were already unfastening the buttons of her leather jeans and pulling them down over her thighs. 'This isn't the nursery now.'

She lay still as he slipped her jumper over her head and pulled her arms free. He studied her for a moment, then bent down to kiss her breasts, his lips trailing downwards across her baby-soft skin towards the black satin and lace of her panties.

'Does your mother know you wear this sort of thing?' he mumbled.

He kissed her between her thighs, before standing and removing the rest of his clothes. He stood naked between her legs, unashamed of his body despite the disparity in their ages. His skin was lightly tanned except for the white bar across his groin, his shoulders still muscular, his stomach taut. His legs were firm from forty years of tennis and squash, his buttocks full, the hair covering his body still thick and only touched with grey. His cock reared proudly from a bramble of dark curls. Chesca watched him as she trailed her fingers across her naked breasts with deliberate sensuality.

'I think it's about time we took these off, don't you?'

'Rip them.'

'Rip them?'

'Hard. Go on. I want you to rip them off hard.'

If she was trying to shock him, she'd come to the wrong place. But her gaze was unfaltering as she returned his look, the expression in her eyes not one of defiance but desire. Whatever game she was playing, he knew she was not just trying to impress him. She wanted him to force her, and she knew he would enjoy doing it.

With one swift movement, Roberto ripped the fragile lace away from her body. She did not flinch. He slapped her face, not violently, but hard enough to leave an imprint of his palm on her cheek. She gasped at the suddenness of his action, but was neither surprised nor afraid. Instead, she smiled.

'I knew you wanted to do that,' she said. 'I knew the moment I saw you what kind of man you are.'

'Oh?' Roberto knelt over her, forcing her legs apart with his knee. 'So tell me, Francesca. What kind of girl wants a man like me?'

'The kind you like. The kind you want to hurt. So go on. Do it.'

'Don't tempt me, little girl.'

Chesca reached for his cock, but he pushed her hands away, stretching over the bed to pull his jacket towards him from the chair where he had thrown it. He groped in the pockets for a moment and found what he was looking for.

'Close your eyes.'

'Make me.'

Roberto suddenly tired of her teenage truculence. He picked up his tie from the floor and bound it swiftly around her eyes, tight enough to bite into her flesh, although she said nothing. His hands forced her thighs further apart and he bent his head to her cunt, tasting her arousal on his tongue.

'You really like this, don't you?' he muttered. 'How much do you like it?'

Before she had a chance to answer, he forced into her cunt two of the hot chestnuts he had taken from his jacket. Chesca gasped in pain and surprise. 'Jesus, what the fuck are you doing? Those are bloody hot!'

Roberto shoved three more into her. 'They should be. Amazing how well they keep their heat, isn't it?'

'Take them out! Fuck you, Roberto, take them out!'

Chesca groped for her blindfold, but Roberto was too quick for her. He moved over her, pinning her legs to the mattress with the weight of him, holding her arms above her head. He bent his head to kiss her as she twisted in his grasp. 'Oh come on. Don't tell me you're backing out already.'

Chesca stopped wriggling. 'I didn't say that. But you could've given me some warning.'

'And ruin the surprise? I expected more of you.'

She giggled suddenly. 'Want to know what I can do with your chestnuts?'

'Tell me.'

'Why don't you take a look? Don't worry, I won't run away if you get off me.'

Roberto released her hands and moved down the bed. He laughed as he slid the chestnuts from her cunt one by one and saw that she had cracked them open with her inner muscles. 'Francesca, has anybody ever told you that you've missed your calling?'

Roberto covered her body with his own, his cock searching blindly for her entrance. He lunged into her, burying himself in her so swiftly that she gasped. His hands covered her small breasts easily as he thrust harder into her body, his thumbs rubbing her nipples so that they stiffened. She lifted her hips with precocious desire, drawing his cock deeper as her arms encircled his waist. He felt her fingers dig into his back, but she had no nails to mark him with. He remembered that she'd bitten them away.

She started to wriggle beneath him, hard, energetic movements that almost dislodged him. It was as if she were pushing him away even while another part of her urged him on. Annoyed, he stopped supporting himself on his elbows and fell on to her, his weight crushing her against the mattress. She struggled, unable to shift him, unable to see him through the blindfold which still covered her eyes. Her movements became more frantic as he forced the breath out of her lungs and she gasped for air, her hands clawing helplessly against his back.

'Please … no … get off … me! Please!'

Roberto was aroused by her struggles. His hand was at her throat, forcing her to keep her head still. 'Tell me this is what you want,' he hissed, making no move to lift his weight from her. 'I'm waiting!'

'Yes … you know … you know it is! Now please … get … off me!'

'Tell me again.'

She was panicking now, her body twisting beneath him. 'I want … you! I want you!'

Roberto had not stopped thrusting inside her even as she had been half-suffocating. He pushed himself up on his arms and watched her gasp desperately for air, coughing and choking as she filled her lungs. Her cunt spasmed around his cock; her panic had made her dry. Now he drove into her harder, knowing that it really hurt.

He saw the pain flicker across her face, this time untempered by pleasure. 'Whoever taught you this, they didn't teach it well enough,' Roberto murmured. 'Time to learn, Chesca.'

His next thrust was savage. She screamed, and he slapped her face so hard that her head whipped sideways against the pillow. He grasped her long hair and pulled her head towards him, his next blow catching her across her cheekbone. He ground into her, her cunt suddenly tight and small around him. For the first time, she seemed the child she was.

Roberto tweaked her nipples between his thumb and forefingers. She jerked upwards from the mattress, crying out in pain, her tears seeping out from below the makeshift blindfold. All trace of the Lolita had vanished. He saw her for what she was: a frightened little girl. He rocked into her, his excitement intensified by her terror. He had not dared to let himself go like this, not for a long time, but could not stop himself now. She'd asked for it. It was her fault. She wanted it. *She wanted it.*

As his climax built within him he slapped her again and again, heedless now of the harm he was doing to her. Her scream was the sound of a terrified child in the grip of a nightmare.

'Stop! Please, please, stop!'

Roberto came into her in one blind, furious spurt. Beneath him she lay limp and silent.

After a long moment he opened his eyes and looked at her. His conscience stirred as he saw the bruises and cuts he had inflicted. He told himself that she'd wanted them. She'd asked him to hurt her. He'd only been doing what she wanted. That was all. Only what she wanted.

Chesca pushed the blindfold from her eyes but didn't open them. Roberto stared at her in horror as he realised what he had done. She was just a child, barely sixteen.

But this girl wasn't Alix. Hurting her hadn't brought his daughter back.

He stood up abruptly and went into the bathroom, sat down on the edge of the bath and put his head in his hands. He'd always known that what he'd done to Alix had been terribly wrong, but at least he'd done it out of love. With this girl he couldn't even offer that excuse.

He heard the door slam as Francesca fled the room. He wasn't afraid of what she might say. Somehow it didn't seem to matter. The only thing he had left to be afraid of now was himself.

He was a lost soul, and he knew it.

Two

Avenida Presidente Vargas, Rio de Janeiro, Brazil
Wednesday 27 May 1992
11.30 a.m.

Fernando Moreno studied the magazine cover carefully. It was the same girl. He'd know that face anywhere.

He'd always guessed that Elizabetta Ferreira was still out there somewhere. Instinct had told him that she wasn't dead. It was nearly ten years since she'd bolted from her apartment – his men had searched for her for weeks without success – but he'd always known she'd come back into his life one day. He'd just never expected it to be in this way.

He didn't need any distractions right now. Already he was struggling to extricate himself from the scandal which had blown up around the Brazilian President. Fernando had backed Collor de Mello in the presidential elections three years ago in return for the position of chief Finance Minister in his Cabinet. It had seemed a good choice then; Fernando had been sixty-one, tiring of the High Court circuit, determined to break into politics before it was too late. Collor de Mello had appeared ideal: young, personable and electable. He'd won the Presidency by promising hope to a nation struggling to outrun a monthly inflation rate of over 80 per cent. But almost immediately his administration had run into trouble, its ambitious economic austerity plan collapsing

288

under its own weight. Allegations of corruption and misman-agement of federal funds had not been far behind. Two weeks ago, Collor de Mello's estranged younger brother had made a series of disclosures which appeared to implicate the President in a number of corrupt practices. Only yesterday the National Congress had approved the creation of a special inquiry to investigate the allegations.

Fernando knew it was only a matter of time before Collor de Mello fell, and as the President's closest financial adviser, he was in an extremely precarious position. His only hope now was to show himself absolutely beyond reproach. If this girl started making accusations – even if she couldn't prove them – he was doomed.

He flipped open the magazine and scanned the inside cover, looking for her name. Ellie Cassidy. He stared in surprise. Even he had heard of Ellie Cassidy; she was one of the top supermodels, mentioned in the same breath as Cindy Craw-ford or Naomi Campbell. He'd never seen her picture before, so he'd failed to make the connection with the girl he'd been hunting. This was hardly surprising: last time he'd seen her, she'd been a two-bit street whore. He looked at the cover again. It looked as if little Elizabetta Ferreira had come a long way in the last ten years.

The chances were she wouldn't come after him now. She had almost as much to lose as he if her past was revealed. Those lucrative modelling contracts would go out of the window if the world were ever to discover she'd once earned her living as a Brazilian hooker.

But he'd made the mistake of underestimating her before. Now she'd finally surfaced he wasn't about to do it again.

Three

Via Condotti, Rome, Italy
Thursday 25 June 1992
2.30 p.m.

'If I can't fuck in this dress, I'm not buying it.'

Alix swallowed a smile as Lola Bryan studied her image in the mirror. 'Look, darling, this is hopeless. How am I ever going to get anywhere in this skirt without taking the whole thing off?'

Alix took a couple of pins from the small cushion strapped to her wrist and carefully began to repin the muslin toile around Lola's hips. At least this customer had voiced her objections while they were still in the preliminary stages of making up the dress; had Lola waited until they'd actually cut the $800-a-metre fabric they'd be using for the final garment, it would have been a great deal harder to accommodate her.

'Is that more the feel you had in mind?'

Lola wriggled her hips experimentally. 'That's much better. Only do make sure you don't go and sentence me to a lifetime of virtue when you make up the real thing, won't you?'

Alix waited until Lola had slipped out of the dress and picked up the toile, careful not to dislodge the pins. 'If that's all –?'

Lola nodded. 'I think so. We decided against the trouser suit in the end, didn't we?'

Alix quickly consulted her notes. 'You chose the silk and chiffon halter dress instead.'

'Perfect.' Lola watched as Alix carefully picked up the bolts of fabric she had selected, then crossed the room and caught Alix's arm. 'You will make sure that no one else has the dress, won't you? Only I'm planning to wear it to the Academy Awards …'

'Don't worry,' Alix smiled politely. 'There's only been one other order for this dress, and that was to one of the Saudi Arabian princesses. Now that you've commissioned it, it will be unavailable to our other clients.'

Alix left the salon, her back and head aching. A fitting with Lola Bryan was always entertaining, but like most of Pavesi's clients, she was also extremely demanding. In just under an hour, she'd spent in excess of $150,000, and Alix felt she'd earned every cent personally. In her early days as a seamstress at Pavesi's, she'd assumed the fitters and designers looked exhausted when they emerged from a session with a client because they'd spent so much time kneeling on the floor or carrying heavy bolts of material backwards and forwards through the warren of passageways that connected the workrooms with the main salon. Now she knew it was not the work that had exhausted them but the customers themselves.

Alix had changed in the five years she'd been working at the House of Pavesi. She'd gradually managed to overcome her eating problem, and although she still found it difficult to put on weight, she was no longer painfully thin. Her unruly chestnut curls had settled into an elegant, glossy bob. She'd grown taller, and at nearly twenty-two she had finally grown into the haughty little face that, at sixteen, had seemed too severe. The terrified teenager had vanished, replaced by a poised, outwardly confident young woman. Only Alix knew that behind the tortoiseshell glasses she now wore for reading and close work, she was the same frightened, insecure child she had always been. She had a luxurious new apartment, she designed for some of the most beautiful and famous women in the world, but she rarely left it except to go to work. She was at her desk by seven in the morning, and still there until ten or eleven at night, six days a week. On Sundays she strolled around the city by herself, looking for new ideas, or stayed in her apartment sketching. She had few close friends, and she'd never taken a lover. Her work was her life.

'Problems?'

Alix jumped as Janet came out of the models' *cabine*. 'That depends on your point of view.'

'So, did Lola decide on the gold or the bronze for the evening dress?'

Alix laughed. 'As if you didn't know. The bronze, of course, just as you said she would.' They reached the door of the *atelier frou*, where all the evening garments were made, and Alix nudged it open with her hip. 'She agreed to keep the skirt of the dress as it is, though.'

She scanned the workroom for the seamstress responsible for Lola's order as she manoeuvred awkwardly through the narrow doorway. A skinny black woman in her late forties detached herself from a group by the window who were discussing the discrepancy in shade of two bolts of green silk which should have been identical. 'I think we can go ahead on the silk and chiffon evening gown, Elisa,' Alix said, handing the fabrics and muslin toile to the seamstress. 'I'll be down later to go through the other garments with you. Most of the changes are quite straightforward.'

'That bronze evening dress for Lola – it's your design, isn't it?' Janet asked.

Alix stared at the fitter in surprise. 'You don't miss anything, do you? How did you know that?'

292

'You think I don't know what Giulio Pavesi is capable of designing? That dress is out of his league, Alix.'

Alix smiled. Janet was not so much a fixture at Pavesi's as an institution. Somehow she maintained order in the models' *cabine*, soothed spoiled and capricious customers, orchestrated the in-house shows and still found time to pick up every rumour and piece of gossip, from the battles that continued to rage between Pavesi and Chambrun to the squabbles amongst the models. Alix had grown extremely fond of the woman who'd become her guardian and mentor. She'd never told Janet her real name or why she'd had to leave home, and the older woman had never asked. Sometimes she teased Alix about her lack of boyfriends, but she never pried. Even though Alix now worked directly under Giulio Pavesi in the design studio, she still relied on Janet for advice.

'You can't allow Pavesi to hijack your work time after time,' Janet said. 'He'll end up ruining you.'

Alix looked startled. 'That's not quite fair, Janet –'

'Isn't it?' Janet turned to face Alix. 'Well, what is *fair* about Pavesi forcing you to sketch your designs on to his own templates so that even your drawings look as if they're his? And then he has the audacity to sign them, for heaven's sake.'

Alix sighed. 'I know. But that's the way it works. I'd prefer it if they had my name on the bottom, of course I would. But I'm his assistant. It's my job to contribute designs for use in his collections. How many couturiers – even the best – can come up with completely original ideas for ninety garments four times a year by themselves? Pavesi's the one who determines the whole direction of the season; all I do is expand his ideas. It's what I'm paid to do. Every designer does the same. Some of the other assistants have been working for him on that basis for more than fifteen years, and they've never complained.'

'It's too late for the others,' Janet said. 'They'll never do anything else now. None of them have what it takes. But you're too good to spend your life and talent propping up someone else.'

'What do you expect me to do?' Alix said wearily. 'I'm not yet twenty-two. I've only been working in the design studio for five years, I have no money, no influence, and precious little experience. This is 1992, we're in the middle of a recession. So, Pavesi takes my ideas and scribbles his name at the bottom. At least my work ends up on the catwalk, not in the bin. What choice do I have?'

But Alix knew Janet was right. She'd been aware of Pavesi's resentment from the moment she'd become his assistant. Until now she'd assumed it was because of her sex: Pavesi saw women as necessary accessories to his talent, created to show off his clothes, buy them, even write about them – but certainly never to design them. She was still the only female assistant in the design studio, and she knew how hard Edouard Chambrun had had to battle to get her admitted. She guessed that part of Pavesi's animosity stemmed from Chambrun's obvious regard for her. In the past few years, Alix had come to greatly respect the reticent, private man who toiled quietly behind the scenes to keep the House of Pavesi successful and solvent. If it hadn't been for Chambrun, she doubted any of Pavesi's assistants would have put up with his foul moods and plagiarism for so long, herself included.

Alix stared moodily over the top of her design easel, her concentration disrupted. She glanced at the half-finished drawing on the sketchpad in front of her. Janet had been the one who'd got her the job as an assistant designer, she was sure of it; it was not by accident that her designs had found their way on to Edouard Chambrun's desk. And yet Janet was now encouraging her to risk everything she'd achieved for the sake of seeing her own name on the sketches she drew.

294

'Alix, have you got a moment?'

Alix turned as Nicole, one of the house models, stuck her sleek head round the studio door. 'Is there a problem?'

Nicole pulled a face. 'It's February. She's throwing a tantrum because the Maestro is using Ellie Cassidy for the collection. February's refusing to wear anything unless Ellie's dropped from the show.'

Alix groaned. 'There's only five days to go. Why on earth hasn't this come up before?'

'Ellie wasn't available before. Apparently her booker rang up this morning and said she was scheduled to be in Rome now after all, and if the Maestro still wanted her, she could do the show. He was hardly going to refuse that, was he?'

Alix shook her head. Whatever she might think about Giulio Pavesi's ability as a designer, his talent for publicity was unequalled. He'd been the first designer to pick up on the phenomenon that Ellie Cassidy was to become after the jewellery shoot that had appeared in *Elan*. As far back as the autumn of 1987, Pavesi had paid a fortune to bring Ellie to Rome to model his clothes at locations around the city for a forthcoming advertising campaign. It had been about a month after Alix had been made an assistant designer, and it was the first time she'd been involved in anything quite like it. The visit had supposedly been shrouded in secrecy, but details of each location had mysteriously been leaked to the paparazzi the day before Ellie arrived. Together with Pavesi and half the world's press, Alix had accompanied the model everywhere to make sure her clothes were immaculate for each photograph. Three thousand fans had turned up at the square by the Trevi Fountain, and Ellie had been in danger of being mobbed. When Pavesi panicked, Alix rescued the model and safely managed to spirit her through the back kitchen of the nearby El Moro Ristorante and into a taxi. Ellie's picture – and Pavesi's clothes – had knocked every other fashion designer off the front pages the day Italian Fashion Week opened in Milan.

Ellie Cassidy's appearance on the catwalk now would guarantee headlines around the globe no matter how lacklustre the clothes she was wearing. Even though she hadn't wanted to become the public face of Pavesi's collections, he'd courted her assiduously every year and been rewarded by a far greater share of publicity than his clothes deserved. Much to his fury and despair she'd turned down his request for the first time this year; he was hardly going to risk driving her away now, even if it meant putting his favourite house model's exquisite nose out of joint.

February – who refused to admit to any other name – had been Giulio Pavesi's inspiration for almost a decade, filling the vacuum that had been left when Angela Lindsay defected to start her own agency; the same agency which, by an ironic twist of fate, now represented Ellie Cassidy. Unfortunately, whilst February possessed the beauty and ego to more than match her predecessor, she lacked Angela's intelligence and her invaluable ability to handle Pavesi's tantrums. Nine times out of ten February actually caused them, stirring up trouble amongst the other house models with her imperious demands and sudden rages, then watching complacently as Pavesi was forced to intervene on her behalf. This latest outburst had been designed to ensure that Ellie was dropped from the show, but for once Pavesi wasn't going to give her what she wanted. Alix knew that if she didn't defuse the situation, all their lives would be made utterly miserable for the next week.

February stalked across the room towards her, an expression of defiant outrage on her chalk-white face. 'Alexandra! *C'est impossible*!' She plucked at the delicate chiffon of the dress she was wearing with furious disregard for the fragile material. 'I cannot wear zis! Giulio would never want me to wear somezing zat makes me look like zis!'

'Perhaps you're right. It is a little young –'

'What do you mean, young?' February's accent was slipping and revealing a broad hint of Manchester patois.

Alix nodded. 'Yes, definitely. You're absolutely right to refuse to wear it. I'll give it to one of the other girls –'

'I'm not sure zat will be necessary,' February quickly recovered both her composure and her accent. She swirled around so that the chiffon clung to the shapely curve of her leg, her eyes on her reflection in the mirror opposite. 'Perhaps with ze right make-up…'

'Perhaps wiz a little less,' Nicole muttered.

February's make-up, though flawless, was oppressive and typically Italian. Her wide brown eyes were all but obscured by the heavy turquoise pencil around them, her generous mouth and long fingernails coated with a deep and garish shade of crimson at least five years out of date. Her dark hair was pulled back into a chignon far too severe for her over-powdered face, giving her a predatory look at odds with her girlish manner. Alix knew that naked, her face scrubbed clean of cosmetics, February was an extremely beautiful woman. Yet she wouldn't come within a five-mile radius of a camera without enough make-up to put a call-girl to shame.

February wisely decided to ignore Nicole's comment and concentrate on winning Alix's sympathies. 'But Aleex, are you sure zis dress doesn't make me look too fat?'

Alix gritted her teeth. 'February, darling, how could it? It was made with you in mind. It's absolutely perfect.'

'But what about ze others?'

'What others?'

February gestured sulkily towards the rail of clothes at the side of the *cabine*. 'All ze best ones 'ave been given to zat American cow. She even 'as ze wedding dress; I always 'ave ze wedding dress, you know zat!'

'I think the problem is that Giulio had designed rather a

sophisticated collection this season,' Alix murmured diplomatically. 'I think perhaps your look is a little too *ingénue* for some of the outfits –'

Nicole gave a strangled cough and disappeared behind a row of unfinished dresses. February turned and confronted her image in the mirror, clearly also having difficulty in accommodating this new idea of herself. 'You may be right,' she said. 'Let me try zem all again. Zen we will see.'

Alix breathed a sigh of relief as February left the room; clearly there was nothing she wouldn't believe if she wanted to hard enough.

'Shall I go away and come back again tomorrow?'

Alix swung round. 'Ellie! I didn't expect you today –'

Ellie laughed. 'Once I heard how popular I was likely to be over here, I couldn't resist arriving early.'

Alix threw her notes on to a side-table and gave Ellie a quick hug. She was shocked to discover how fragile the model felt. Ellie had always been slender, but now she seemed like a bag of bones. She was thinner than Alix herself. Alix scanned her friend's face anxiously, noting the dark circles beneath her eyes, the tiny pupils at the centre of the blue irises that betrayed her. 'Ellie? Is something wrong?'

'No – it's nothing…'

'Don't lie to me, Ellie,' Alix said sharply. 'I thought we had a deal?'

Ellie couldn't meet her eyes. 'I will stop, I promise.'

'That's what you said last time.'

'I know, but –' Ellie broke off. She'd promised Alix so many times. She couldn't bear to disappoint her again.

Ellie had been taking cocaine for so long now she couldn't imagine life without it. Garcia, the policeman in Rio, had started her on it when she'd been all of eight years old. It had helped her blot out the horror when he'd fucked her, so she'd kept on taking it until the day she'd killed him on the beach

298

and had had to take refuge with David Conto. She had gone straight back on the drug the day David had died. It had been the only way she'd been able to cope. She'd managed to cut down during her marriage to Eason, but even then she'd needed the confidence and buzz the coke gave her to get through the lonely days. Then she'd started modelling, and she'd always been meaning to give it up, but somehow the moment had never quite arrived. She was so busy, racing from one location to another, criss-crossing the Atlantic every week. She didn't need to eat or sleep if she took a hit. It kept her weight down. It helped her forget.

Alix felt a surge of pity as she watched Ellie chewing nervously on her thumbnail. She was four years younger than Ellie, yet she'd always felt protective, as if Ellie was the one who needed looking after. She'd often wondered about the demons that haunted her friend. By an unspoken agreement, they'd never discussed the past: their conversations were always about the people they knew, the work they did. Alix knew how Ellie felt about Luke, and she'd confided her own dreams of becoming a designer to Ellie, but she suddenly realised she knew next to nothing about her friend. All Ellie had ever told her – all she'd ever told anyone – was that she'd been born in Brazil and moved to America when she'd been a small child. The best efforts of the world's press to uncover some scandal in her past had so far proved fruitless. It was as if Ellie Cassidy had been born aged twenty the day she'd done the photo shoot for Luke. Alix guessed her mystery was part of the allure that had made her one of the world's highest-paid supermodels.

'You were doing so well,' Alix said. 'Three months –'

'Something happened. I know it's silly, but –' she fiddled with her bracelet – 'I got burgled last week. Someone broke into my apartment in Chelsea.'

'Did they take much?'

'No. Nothing. That's what's so weird. All my jewellery from Eason – I know I was going to put it in a safety deposit box, but somehow I've never got round to it, and anyway, it's insured – and a couple of thousand dollars tucked into my Russian dolls on the mantelpiece, silver photo frames, that little Picasso I bought at Christie's last year, you remember – they didn't take any of it.'

'Kids?' Alix asked, puzzled.

'The police said it was too professional a job. They'd jemmied open the lock really carefully, you could hardly see any marks. No fingerprints, nothing.'

'Maybe the thieves were disturbed and left before they had a chance to take anything?'

'Maybe.'

Ellie paced nervously towards the window. Alix guessed she was debating whether to confide in her and quietly waited for her to speak. After several moments, Ellie turned. 'A long time ago – before I went to the States – I saw something I shouldn't have. Something terrible. The person who did it let me go, but I met him again a few years later. I think he probably thought I was dead until then. I didn't stop to find out if he was going to let me go again when he realised I wasn't.'

'Didn't you tell the police?'

Ellie laughed shortly. 'No.'

'I don't really see what this has to do with the burglary –'

'Whoever burgled my flat was looking for information, not jewellery or money,' Ellie said. 'They went through all my files, my bank statements, documents, everything. They were very careful, I almost didn't realise that anyone had been there, but a couple of things were out of order. You know, letters in the wrong envelopes, that sort of thing.' She chewed her thumbnail. 'I know it's him.'

'You think this person you saw do something in Brazil – you think he's the person who burgled your flat?'

'Not him, no, but someone working for him.'

'Ellie, all this happened a long time ago, didn't it? You've hardly kept a low profile – it wouldn't have been difficult for him to trace you if he'd wanted to. Why should he come after you now?'

'You're right, I know. I'm just being silly. It rattled me, that's all. Knowing someone had been through my things.' She shivered. 'I haven't felt very well since.'

She certainly looked dreadfully pale, Alix thought to herself. 'It's a natural reaction. No one likes being burgled. I just think you're jumping to conclusions, that's all. Now, I don't suppose we could do your fittings before February returns and has another tantrum? Given that it's all your fault, of course.'

Ellie shrugged off her long, cream silk raincoat and threw it across one of the clothes rails. She spread her arms dramatically and closed her eyes. 'I'm all yours. Just tell me where you want me.'

'I bet you say that to all the boys.'

Ellie unbuttoned her simple shift dress, and slipped into the pale beige, cashmere *paletot* that Alix handed to her.

'Perfect.' Ellie glanced in the mirror. 'I knew I was going to regret saying yes to this assignment. I'm going to want to buy every single outfit you've designed, I can tell.'

'They're not mine –'

Ellie laughed. 'Of course not, Alix. The Maestro slaved over every single one himself, just to please me.'

'If he'd known you were coming, he probably would've done,' Alix said. 'He'd even sew the buttons on himself if he thought it'd get you on to his catwalk.'

Ellie sighed longingly as Alix carefully pinned the hem. 'Alix, this really is heavenly,' she said as the cashmere swirled gracefully around her ankles.

'I thought you'd like it,' Alix mumbled through a mouthful of pins. 'You look stunning.'

Alix looked up at the beautiful Brazilian girl without a trace of envy or rancour in her eyes. Ellie smiled at her. 'It's the coat, not me. You'd look sensational if you were wearing it, believe me.'

Alix brushed a loose strand of hair from her eyes. 'I don't think so. But thanks anyway.'

Ellie watched the designer thoughtfully as she moved back towards her worktable and began to read through the list of accessories that had been selected for the coat. Alix was almost as tall as Ellie herself. Beneath the loose, casual cream silk T-shirt and simple black Versace jeans Alix was wearing, Ellie could see that despite the weight she had gradually put on over the past couple of years, she was still almost too thin and she moved around the *cabine* with the grace of a racehorse. For a moment, Ellie wondered what Alix would look like if she ever allowed her hair free from the neat chignon at the nape of her neck and took off the tortoiseshell glasses. In all the years she'd known Alix, Ellie had never once seen her dressed any other way.

She measured the planes of Alix's face with the expertise of nearly seven years in front of the camera and felt a flicker of surprise. The cool, professional, almost severe image Alix presented to the world was so convincing that even she had not troubled to look further until now. She was beginning to realise that somewhere beneath that self-effacing reserve was a woman she'd never even noticed.

She wondered again what had caused Alix to take refuge in her work. She knew so little about her. Alix had never discussed her family or ever once mentioned a boyfriend. Ellie guessed Alix too had secrets she didn't want to discuss: it was almost as if she had taken a conscious decision to downplay her appearance so as to deflect any attention she might attract from the world. Ellie smiled. Alix could not have chosen a more perfect medium than the fashion industry. It was filled with people only too happy to look at her and see nothing but their own reflection.

'I'll be glad when this collection is over and done with,' Alix said. 'Thank you for coming in today. Tomorrow's bound to be absolute chaos.'

'It's not me you should be thanking,' Ellie said, her voice muffled as she pulled her Anna Sui over her head. 'Even without the burglary, I would have had to come over early anyway. Stephi Kay had some sort of a crisis at *Elan* and asked me to fill the breach with a piece on Rome.'

'Stephi Kay?'

'Yes, you must know her. The editor of *Elan*? Striking woman, has the most amazing eyes. Can't think why she never married, though rumour has it there's a Significant Other somewhere in her life. Maybe she's gay.'

'Maybe,' Alix said shortly. She changed the subject. 'Anyway, how did the photo shoot for Luke's new campaign go on Monday?'

Ellie perched cross-legged on Alix's work table. 'It's agony. I can't decide whether it's worse to see him and pine unrequitedly, or not to see him at all.'

'Is he still married?'

Ellie's voice wobbled. 'Very. And happily. It's so unfair. Of all the people I could choose to fall in love with, why did it have to be him?'

Alix glanced across at her friend and felt a pang of sympathy. She didn't know why Ellie was so obsessed with a man she scarcely knew, except on a professional level – Ellie had admitted she didn't really know, herself – but Alix didn't doubt the depth of her feelings. Ellie had never revealed how she felt to anyone but Alix; certainly never to Luke himself. Instead, she'd taken up almost permanent residence in the gossip columns as her name was linked first to one man and then another, none of the claims substantiated and all petering out after a few months. After five years without a single definitive romance, the more cynical commentators were openly questioning her sexual orientation. Ellie laughed it all off, but deep down Alix knew she suffered.

The door opened to admit one of the seamstresses holding a polystyrene cup of cappuccino in each hand. Alix took hers and lifted the plastic lid. 'So, who's your photographer on this shoot for Stephi?'

'Matt Logan, thank God. At least he's fun to work with.'

'What's he like?' Alix asked.

'You mean you've never met him?' Ellie laughed. 'No, of course not. You'd remember if you had.'

'Is he really that attractive?'

'It's not the way he looks, exactly, although he *is* gorgeous. It's more the way he is. It's hard to put into words.'

'Have you ever –?'

Ellie grinned. 'No, although I'm probably the only woman in London, Paris or New York who hasn't. I guess that's part of his charm – every woman wants to be the one to hold him. I might have been tempted once, before I met Luke, but Matt and I have known each other too long now. It'd be rather like bonking your brother.'

'What would?'

The object of their recent discussion strolled into the room. 'You must be Alix. Ellie tells me you're the only designer whose clothes she'd get out of bed for, even without the $10,000 she's paid to wear them.'

Alix was covered in confusion. Matt shook her hand and she felt her face flush as he held it a fraction longer than was necessary. 'Ellie's told me a lot about you, but she didn't say how beautiful you were.'

Alix withdrew her hand.

'He's right, but don't listen to a word he says,' Ellie warned. She glanced at her watch and stood up. 'Alix, is there a phone I could use? I promised to ring Stephi by midday Eastern time, and it's gone one already.'

'Of course. Use the one on my desk – you know where it is, don't you?'

Alix pretended not to watch Matt as he crossed the room and stared down into the piazza below. Abstractedly, she took in the length of his legs, and the breadth of his shoulders beneath the soft blue denim of his worn shirt. She knew from press reports that he was in his mid-thirties, but in some ways he seemed younger. There was a boyishness about him, a strange mixture of confidence and vulnerability. A pale white line bisected his cheek, faint but unmistakable, and she remembered that he'd been a war photographer before he'd moved into the world of fashion. She could picture him dodging bullets more easily than she could see him photographing wisps of chiffon on the catwalk. There was an air of danger about him that she found exciting. She blushed, trying to pull herself together.

Almost as if he had read her mind, Matt turned and smiled, a charming, effortless smile that caused a slow heat to start to burn between her legs.

'It's a long time since I've been to Rome,' he said casually, 'I'd forgotten what an amazing city it is.'

'It's always been my home,' Alix said. There was a pause as she cast around for something more interesting to say. 'Have you been here before?'

'Yes, many years ago –'

'Oh, yes, of course, I'm sorry. You said.'

Alix turned back to her work table in embarrassment, sifting through her notes without really seeing them. For some reason she found his presence disconcerting – even while she longed to prolong the conversation, her brain stubbornly refused to supply any coherent thoughts. 'Tell me, isn't Caroline Logan your mother? She's one of our clients.'

'A very good one, judging by Dad's reaction when he gets her Visa bill,' Matt smiled.

Alix pushed her glasses back against her nose. 'Doesn't he approve?'

'Dad used to work for a children's charity until he retired a few years ago. He still organises fund-raising events for it every year – raffles and balls and so on. He knows he could feed a whole village in Ethiopia for a month for the price of one of these dresses.'

'The fashion industry keeps hundreds of thousands of people in business,' Alix said heatedly. 'Not just those working here, in the design houses, but the people picking the cotton, making the cloth, selling the clothes. Some Third World countries couldn't survive without the income they get from the fashion industry.' She looked at him challengingly. 'And what about you? You're a fashion photographer. If you feel so strongly about helping others, why aren't you out there doing your bit for your father's charity?'

There was a brief silence.

'You don't pull your punches, do you?' Matt said.

'I'm sorry – I didn't mean – it's none of my business.'

'No, it's me who should be apologising, I started it. Anyway, you're right. You only said what I've been thinking for a while now. I just haven't voiced it before, that's all.'

Alix found herself all too aware of their closeness, the intimacy that had suddenly sprung up between them. For a brief, crazy moment she wondered what it would be like to kiss him, feel his maleness crushing her.

She could not meet his eyes, wondering if he felt the same pull of attraction or if he was like this with every woman he met. She felt acutely aware of every part of her body: the silk fabric of her T-shirt over her breasts, the tight fit of her jeans.

Matt reached out his hand and gently brushed a stray strand of hair from her eyes in a gesture of intimacy. Alix felt as if she'd stopped breathing.

She caught a glimpse of herself in the mirror. Her cheeks were flushed, her eyes unnaturally bright behind her glasses, her expression that of a child at Christmas. She felt a surge of humiliation. She looked like a virgin expecting her first kiss.

Abruptly she pulled away. Matt Logan was a dozen years older than she was, he worked with some of the most beautiful women in the world. He couldn't be interested in her. This was probably his way of getting his own back after she'd harangued him over his job. Make her drool over him, then laugh and walk away. She wasn't going to be another notch on his belt.

'I'm sorry. I have to get back to work.'

She sensed Matt was upset by her rebuff, but all he said was, 'Yes, of course.'

Alix busied herself, trying to concentrate on what she was doing. Matt strolled back towards the window and drummed his fingers on the ledge. The silence between them had lengthened, when the door opened and Alix breathed a sigh of relief as Ellie appeared.

'Matt? Stephi needs a word.'

'Sure.' He smiled politely at Alix. 'Best of luck with the collection.'

Alix nodded dumbly and watched him leave the room. Arrogant bastard. She didn't know why Ellie liked him so much. He thought he could have any woman he wanted just by smiling at her. She was glad she hadn't let him kiss her.

So why did she feel like crying?

Four

Hilton Hotel, Rome, Italy
Tuesday 30 June 1992
11.00 a.m.

Ellie opened one eye and swiftly closed it again. She rolled over and faced the wall before trying again. This time, she was able to stand the light long enough to see that the wall seemed to be swaying gently in front of her. Trying to still the wave of nausea that consciousness had brought with it, she ran her tongue experimentally around her teeth. Her mouth tasted as if she'd been drinking battery acid. What on earth had she been doing last night?

A body stirred in the bed beside her. That settled half the question. She hoped it was someone she still fancied in the cold light of day. It was funny how alcohol made hairy chests and skinny white legs seem incredibly attractive. The only other thing she'd ever known have such an aphrodisiac effect on women was a bank balance with zeros that read like an astronomy textbook.

The figure beside her mumbled and Ellie slowly eased her way from under the duvet, praying he wouldn't wake up. However good the sex had been last night – something she'd probably never know – she had no desire for a reprise this morning. Knowing her luck, she was probably better off being unable to remember anyway. She shut the bathroom door behind her and sat down on the toilet, propping her head on her hands. God, she had to stop doing this. It was going to kill her.

Slowly she started to remember. She and Matt had finished the photo shoot for *Elan* yesterday, and they'd gone out to celebrate. She'd suggested asking Alix to join them, but Matt had demurred. For some reason Matt and Alix didn't seem to like each other. Instead, she and Matt had decided to have dinner before going on to a party at Valentino's. They'd been having a drink in the bar of the Hilton, where they were staying, when Matt had been called to the telephone. It had been Luke, with the news that his wife was pregnant.

Matt knew how she felt about Luke. They'd never talked about it, but she knew he'd guessed a long time ago. He'd broken the news to her as gently as he could, but still she'd felt as if someone had stuck a knife in her heart and was slowly twisting it. She'd been aware that Kip and Luke had been trying for a child for years, but after the last of Kip's miscarriages six years ago, she'd assumed they'd given up. She'd even tried to convince herself that they didn't sleep together any more. After all, they'd been married nearly fifteen years.

Luke had told Matt it had been a total accident. They hadn't wanted to tell anyone until they were sure. But Kip had reached twenty weeks without mishap, six weeks further than she'd ever got before. The doctors were confident enough to say they could start giving their closest friends the good news.

Ellie pictured Luke holding the child he'd longed for in his arms. She could see him showing the baby off around the new offices he'd just rented – with the view of Central Park he'd always wanted – while everyone congratulated him and told him how much the baby looked like him. She knew he'd be the proudest father in the world. There wouldn't be a school sports day or parents' evening he'd miss. If only it could have been her sharing it all with him.

She rubbed her eyes angrily. Luke didn't even know she existed. In over five years, he'd never once given any indication that he thought of her as anything other than a friend.

She knew her feelings for Luke were irrational. She'd hardly known him when she'd fallen for him. He'd never given her any encouragement, they'd never shared so much as a drink alone together. They met up in New York twice a year to shoot the spring and autumn promotional campaigns for Luke's business, and apart from the occasional party, they rarely met outside Matt's studio. He seemed so capable, so much in control of his own destiny. Images of Luke and David blurred in her mind and she tried unsuccessfully to separate them. He made her feel safe and secure. No one else had ever done that. He'd always looked after her. If only he hadn't left her …

Disorientated, she blinked back tears. Her thoughts returned to the stranger in her bed. God knows where she'd picked him up.

She opened the bathroom door a chink and peered warily through the gap just as the latest occupant of her bed threw back the covers and sat up. Ellie was mildly surprised. This had to be one of her better choices – slim, young, decidedly attractive.

And female.

The phone rang and the girl in the bed answered it. She held out the receiver to Ellie without lifting her head off the pillow. 'For you. Angela Lindsay.'

Relunctantly Ellie picked up the receiver.

'You caught me at a bad time –'

'Damn right I did. What are you doing in your room?'

Ellie frowned. 'Am I supposed to be somewhere else?'

'Giulio Pavesi's. Five minutes ago. If you're not there in fifteen I'm taking you off my books. And that's a promise.'

Ellie stared at the receiver as the line went dead. Angela wouldn't dare to drop her from the agency; she brought in more money in commission than all Angela's other girls together. But she knew she'd been pushing her luck lately, and Angela's patience wasn't going to last for ever. It wouldn't do any harm to chalk up a few gold stars now, just in case. Only she couldn't go down the catwalk like this.

She pulled open the drawer beside her bed and scrabbled around for the square mirror she kept there.

'Has anyone got any *E-mergen-C*?'

Alix attempted to free one hand from the heap of dresses she was carrying, then gave up. 'Freddie, try my back pocket. I think I've got some left.'

The languid Texan model uncurled her amazing body from a stool and strolled across the atelier. 'Sweetie, you're a marvel. I'll never make it down the catwalk without this.'

A sulky-looking English brunette sniffed disapprovingly. 'I'm not surprised. I heard you didn't leave Valentino's party until three this morning. And that Ellie Cassidy. No self-control, you Americans, that's your trouble.'

Alix interrupted before full-scale war broke out. 'I don't suppose you've seen Ellie this morning?'

'Fraid not. Not since Valentino's, anyway.'

Alix scanned the room, trying and failing to spot Ellie's familiar form in the chaos of half-naked models screaming for telephones and Marlboros as dressers chased them up and down the rails of clothes, frantically consulting the working sketches as they tried to match accessories and shoes to the right girl. A tiny Bichon Frise dog raced between her ankles, its soft blue leather lead trailing a tangle of wooden beads behind it as its owner, a Czech model, rushed past on her hands and knees to rescue it before it was skewered on one of the other girls' high heels. Alix closed her eyes, wondering what else could possibly go wrong.

She didn't have to wait long to find out.

Janet grabbed her shoulder and pulled her into a corner, lifting the heap of dresses out of Alix's arms as she did so. 'You'd better give me these. We've got a problem. Well, several, actually.'

'Oh God.'

Janet smiled grimly. 'Now could be a very good time to invoke His help.'

'Ellie isn't still missing, is she?'

'Oh, no, she turned up – just in time to stage a dramatic entrance for the benefit of the INN cameras.'

'So what's the problem?'

'See for yourself.'

Alix glanced at her watch. The show was due to start in ten minutes; even allowing for the customary twenty-minute delay, they didn't have long. Already she could hear the auditorium filling up behind her as the privileged few who'd merited an invitation filed into the hall.

As soon as she reached Ellie she could see that something was very wrong. The model was sprawled across two chairs in front of her make-up table, wearing her first scheduled outfit, her long limbs seeming somehow unconnected to the rest of her. As Alix approached, Ellie stared glassily up at her, the pupils of her eyes so wide that Alix could barely see the brilliant turquoise for which she was famous.

'Darling! Fo'give me if I don' stand up. CYK, as they say.'

'CYK?'

Ellie giggled. 'Consider Yourself Kissed.'

Alix crouched down and gripped Ellie's upper arms. 'Ellie, what've you been taking?'

'Nothing.'

312

'Ellie, I'm not playing games. Never mind the show, this is your life we're talking about. What have you been taking?'

Ellie shrugged. 'I told you. Nothing special. Just something to make me a bit happier, that's all. Nothing you need to worry about.'

'She's having a bad trip, if you ask me.' Janet was beside them. 'Probably mixed too many different pills. Either that, or someone's sold her some bad coke.'

Alix glanced anxiously up at her. 'I've never seen her like this. Will she be OK?'

'I'll be fine,' Ellie interrupted.

Janet pulled Alix aside. 'I think we're going to have to risk it. Pavesi's rigged half the collection around her. There's no way any of the other girls can take on her outfits – she's just too thin. Even Naomi isn't going to get into them. We're one girl down as it is. We'll have to chance it.'

Alix's reply was drowned by the burst of music that heralded the start of the show. Freddie was sauntering out on to the catwalk dressed in the first outfit, an uninspiring belted grey silk raincoat designed to be thrust into oblivion by the more extravagant outfits that followed. No designer ever put their best work at the beginning of the collection; too many photographers were still coming in late from the previous show on the other side of town. Alix watched as Freddie sashayed back along the catwalk, pausing just fractionally to tighten her belt or shake her hair free in front of the most influential critics present – Suzy Menkes, John Fairchild, Stephi Kay. It was what Pavesi paid her, and the other supermodels like her, $10,000 an hour to do.

Janet gave Ellie a gentle shove and she swayed out on to the catwalk. Backstage she'd only just been able to walk upright; but once she emerged on to the runway in the full glare of the world's press, her spine stiffened and she slipped into a higher gear. As she completed the turn at the end of the runway, Alix breathed a sigh of relief. It was the most complicated manoeuvre a model ever had to execute on the runway without losing her balance or rhythm. Ellie smiled triumphantly as she sauntered back, winking at Stephi Kay as she passed. Despite her concern, Alix felt an unwilling surge of admiration.

As soon as Ellie reached the wings, however, she collapsed. Alix raced over and sank to her knees, shaking Ellie by the shoulders as the model murmured incoherently.

'Ellie? Ellie, for God's sake, are you OK?'

Janet bent over and placed two fingers against the pulse in Ellie's throat. 'She's way too high. She must have used everything she had. We can't send her out again, she'd never make it. She needs to come down quietly, somewhere where we can keep an eye on her.'

Ellie coughed and opened her eyes without focusing. 'Alix? I did OK, didn't I? They liked me?'

'Yes, they liked you, Ellie, but I could kill you,' Alix said, fear making her angry. 'What do you think you're playing at?'

Between them she and Janet manoeuvred Ellie out of the way, praying that Pavesi wouldn't notice his star model had just written herself out of his script. Alix beckoned one of the dressers over and quickly started scribbling an amended running order.

'You can't change the order now,' the dresser exclaimed, staring at the piece of paper in her hand. 'It's all themed. You'll ruin it – the Maestro will have a fit.'

'He'll have more than a fit if there are great big gaps while everyone twiddles their thumbs,' Alix said sharply. 'Now tell Francine, for God's sake.'

She knew the dresser was right. Pavesi had pulled out all the stops to make this show a success. Admittedly, Ellie's abrupt disappearance from the show would generate headlines, particularly after the powerful performance she'd just

314

given. But they couldn't afford the backstage chaos to spill out onto the catwalk; and, Alix knew, that was exactly what would happen if they couldn't replace Ellie.

Ellie struggled to stand, tears mingling with mascara and running down her cheek, as her legs refused to co-operate. 'Oh, God, Alix, I'm so sorry.'

Gently Janet eased Ellie back into her chair and gave her a quick hug. 'Alix, there's no way we can send her out.'

Alix glanced frantically around. 'What the hell are we going to do?'

'You do it.'

Janet and Alix turned and stared at Ellie. The model sat up, her gaze momentarily focused. 'You do it, Alix,' she repeated.

'Ellie, this isn't a game,' Alix said impatiently. 'You've been reading too many novels. I can't just walk out on to the catwalk in front of half the world's fashion press. I wouldn't know where to begin. You of all people know how much work goes into what you do. I'm not Cinderella.'

'You've watched us enough times to know how to walk. What matters is that you have the right figure,' Ellie said. 'You've hidden it all your life, Alix, but it's there, whether you like it or not. It's all you need.' She turned to Janet. 'I'm right, aren't I?'

'Yes. You are.'

Alix stared at Janet. 'Can't you see how ridiculous she's being? I can't possibly walk out there –'

'You'll have to,' Janet said simply. She started unbuttoning Alix's cashmere cardigan and beckoned to one of the other dressers. 'What's Ellie wearing next?'

The dresser stared. 'The emerald jersey dress, I think.' She ran over to the rail of clothes and pulled the dress off its padded hanger. Janet took it from her and quickly slipped it over Alix's head, turning her round and buttoning the tiny seed pearls down the back as the dresser tightened the belt at her waist and adjusted the cowl collar so that the soft folds of material fell gently around Alix's neck. It fitted her perfectly, the rich emerald folds bringing out the russet-gold of her hair and giving her pale face warmth. Smiling, she pushed Alix in the small of the back towards the catwalk. 'Just go out there and give it your best. And remember to keep your head up.'

'Janet, I haven't got any make-up on! I don't even have any shoes –'

'You look better without them. Now go.'

Francine didn't even give her a second glance as she waved at her to go out on to the catwalk, completely failing to recognise her. Alix took a deep breath and then stepped out into the lights.

A buzz ran round the room, and for a brief second the camera shutters and flashbulbs paused as everyone tried unsuccessfully to remember who she was. Then she started walking and the hurricane of camera clicking resumed. Alix was barely conscious of her progress along the carpeted runway, only realising she'd reached the end and was in danger of falling into the photographers' corral when she heard the journalists calling out to her.

'Turn this way, darling –'

'Just one more –'

'Over here, gorgeous, that's great, perfect –'

Slowly, she turned, her legs feeling like pieces of wet string knotting together beneath her dress. She was halfway there.

A voice yelled from amongst the photographers. '*Alix?* Jesus, is that you?'

Alix found herself staring straight at Matt. Suddenly she wanted to laugh when she saw his startled expression. She started back along the catwalk, her body automatically responding to the electric atmosphere she had unwittingly generated, her performance now all for Matt.

316

In the front row three feet away from her, Angela Lindsay saw the expression on Alix's face and recognised it. Barely a handful of girls in the world could generate that sort of power, and even fewer responded to it the way this unknown redhead so obviously did.

Now all she had to do was make sure Body Image got to her and signed her up first.

Five

Angela Lindsay replaced the receiver carefully and sat still for a moment. Then she picked up the heavy crystal paperweight on the edge of her desk and threw it across the room. The crystal shattered against the wall, scattering slivers of glass across the deep grey of her carpet. Damn Alexandra D'Alfonsi. That paperweight had been bloody expensive.

Slowly she counted to ten, then pressed the intercom button on her desk. Her secretary warily stuck her head round the door. 'Ms Lindsay?'

'Oh, don't pretend you didn't hear,' Angela said, waving her hand impatiently. 'Just clear it up, please. And send Ellie Cassidy's file through when you've finished, Suzy. I need to have another look at her contract.'

Suzy looked disapprovingly at the shards of crystal on the carpet, then disappeared to find a dustpan and brush. Angela moodily stared out of the rain-streaked window, watching the progression of dull, anoraked housewives trudging from Marks & Spencer's to Boots and back again. God, the King's Road hadn't been like this in her day. In the Sixties, it had been the Mecca of every fashion-conscious teenager in the world, swarming with photographers in skintight jeans and shades, and models like herself exposing unprecedented inches of thigh between miniskirt and kinky boots. She sighed. There was a hell of a lot more money in the industry now, but somehow the excitement, the fizz, had gone. Perhaps it had something to do with the disappearance of Purple Hearts and LSD. The stuff they took nowadays – crack, ecstasy, heroin – was too damned serious. You could only get away with it for so long before it started to show, and word got around. No one wanted a coke-head on an assignment, no matter how stunning. They were too bloody unreliable.

Suzy re-entered, tossed a glossy black folder on to the surface of her walnut desk and left the room, the stiff set of her shoulders showing what she thought about employers who threw crystal paperweights across the room and then expected her to clear up the mess. She'd probably have the wretched girl's resignation on her desk by the end of the week, not that it'd be a great loss. Suzy had been there over a month and still hadn't managed to memorise her own telephone extension. And she made lousy coffee.

Angela read through Ellie's contract, searching fruitlessly, as she knew, for a loophole. Two years ago she'd been so desperate to keep the model on her books that she'd signed her up for another five years. She'd known then that Ellie had a coke problem – so did many of the models on the circuit – but the Brazilian girl had always been discreet about it. She'd never been lifted at customs or caught with the stuff on location. Angela had even managed to keep the débâcle at Giulio Pavesi's eight months ago out of the papers, although that was mainly thanks to the sensation caused by the unknown redhead.

Angela permitted herself a small smile. Alix D'Alfonsi's picture had been on the front page of every tabloid the next morning, and the paparazzi had been frantic to know who she was. By the time they'd discovered that she was a genuine backroom Cinderella who'd only stepped in at the last minute, Angela had already signed her up. She hadn't bothered to tell the girl that once she became a model, she'd never be taken seriously as a designer again.

Ellie had behaved herself after the incident at Pavesi's – in public, at least – but Angela still wanted her out. Ellie refused to check into a detox clinic, insisting that the overdose had been accidental, although the incident had clearly frightened her. She swore she'd stopped taking the stuff and Angela believed her, but it hadn't affected her decision. Sooner or later Ellie would slip back. Coke-heads always did. Angela had only waited this long to dump her because she'd still had eight months to run on her three-year contract with cosmetic giant Q. And now just when it was due to expire, Alix D'Alfonsi had suddenly insisted that she would work only with only Ellie on a major new campaign for Q's biggest cosmetics rival, Après.

Alix knew damn well how much Angela Lindsay wanted this deal. When she'd signed Alix up eight months ago, she'd deliberately held back from sending her on the usual round of go-sees with fashion editors and photographers that was the lot of most new models. Instead, she'd wanted to launch Alix on the catwalk during Paris Fashion Week in October for maximum publicity, and had whisked her off to the French capital for a spot of fine-tuning. The tortoiseshell glasses had been replaced by contact lenses, the auburn hair given a fashionable gamine crop, and Alix had been taught how to walk by the fashion world's high priest of movement, Alexander Jenkins, described variously by the press as a mixture of Diana Ross, Princess Margaret and Shaka, King of the Zulus.

Even Angela had been stunned by Alix's impact when she stepped back on to the catwalk four months after her début at Pavesi's. From just one more beautiful girl with potential,

Alix D'Alfonsi had become the hottest new model to hit the circuit in a decade. She'd been inundated with offers of work, but Angela had held out for a cosmetic deal that would make Alix a millionaire overnight. Now Après wanted to use Alix to launch their new ski-wear range, and if it worked, they were offering seven figures to sign her up as the Après Girl – 20 per cent of which would go to Body Image.

Angela closed Ellie's file. If she wanted keep Alix, she was stuck with the Brazilian girl. She had to admit the two girls would look good together. But that wasn't the point. Angela didn't like being held to ransom. Alix had only been in the business five minutes and already she was using her position to gain leverage.

Angela made a mental note to deduct another 20 per cent from Alix's fee as the agency's commission on Ellie's earnings. The sooner Alix learned that nothing came free in this business, the better.

Six

Lech, Austria
Wednesday 17 March 1993
9.30 a.m.

'OK, whose bright idea was this?'

Ellie grinned without taking her eyes off the camera. 'Yours, I think.'

'Only because I didn't dare let you out of my sight,' Alix groaned. 'God, I wish they'd hurry up. I'm freezing to death out here.'

A few metres away, Matt straightened up from his camera and turned to his assistant. 'What do you think? Too much snow?'

Romi's dark eyes assessed the situation. 'Why don't you get them to move a little further up the slope? You should just be able to get the edge of the pine trees into the shot without having them in shadow. Should give you a little more contrast, at least.'

Matt nodded. 'Let's try it.'

He watched as Romi made her way across the deep snow covering the ski run they'd chosen for the Après shoot, her small feet sinking six inches into the soft powder that had fallen overnight. Behind him, the advertising agency's British representative, Nigel Trevelyn, stamped his feet and sniffled noisily. 'Is this going to take much longer? It's much colder than I thought it'd be. No one told me it would be this cold. I really do think someone could have said. Really.'

'I don't know why you're complaining,' Sami said. 'At least you can move about. Alix and Ellie have to stand still for hours. Their feet must be freezing.'

Nigel glared at the make-up artist. 'If it was only my feet, I wouldn't mind.'

Romi crunched back across the snow, slapping her sides to keep warm. 'That's about as far over as they can go. If they move any further up the slope, they'll be off-piste, and I've no idea how deep the snow is there.'

'They can't get the clothes wet,' Nigel said in sudden alarm. 'Don't let them fall in the snow. We haven't got any spares.'

Matt ignored him.

'Hey, are you going to take some damn photographs or are you waiting for the big thaw?' Ellie called across the snow.

'You're getting paid, aren't you?' Matt yelled back.

Sami looked at the two girls critically. 'Leo? I think we need a little more hairspray. The wind's getting up and we don't want their hair blowing across their faces and ruining half the shots.'

Leo pulled a face and stood up, carefully covering his canvas seat with the plaid blanket from his knees. 'Nigel, mind my seat for me, would you?'

Nigel smiled warmly, recognising a kindred spirit. 'Safe with me, old chap.'

Leo, looking slightly mollified, trudged out across the snow, a can of Alberto Mega Hold in his hand.

Romi leaped up, slamming her reflector on the ground behind her. 'Not that way, you idiot! You'll mark the snow! Go round behind me or you'll ruin the shot!'

Alix stamped her feet and waited patiently for Leo to reach them. Since she'd stepped on to Pavesi's catwalk and felt that fiirst, indescribable rush of power and excitement, she'd learned the hard way that those few moments were a rare reward for what was all too often a gruelling, demanding and frequently mind-numbingly boring job.

Her impromptu trip down the catwalk and Angela Lindsay's subsequent telephone call had caught her at a time when she'd been feeling more and more disillusioned with Pavesi, and despaired of ever having the freedom to design her own clothes. She'd worked in the fashion industry long enough to know that there was very little glamour in modelling, but she'd agreed to join Body Image because she'd thought that success as a model would open doors to her that might otherwise remain closed when – and if – she was ready to launch her own design label. It would also provide her with the finance she needed if she was ever to lure other backers into supporting her. And a part of her also acknowledged that she'd done it knowing that if she made it as a model, her father would be unable to open a newspaper without reading her name, or walk past a magazine stand without seeing her face.

After the furore she'd caused in Rome, she'd flown to Paris with Angela expecting everything to start happening immediately. For two weeks she hadn't been disappointed; she'd been chased from one hotel to another by the paparazzi, her hair had been cut, she'd had contact lenses fitted, one of the world's top movement coaches had taught her how to walk, Angela had forced her to buy some exquisite clothes more in keeping with her new status as an about-to-be supermodel, she'd been introduced to casting directors, editors and agents.

Then, abruptly, it had all stopped. Paris had emptied for the traditional August break, Angela had returned to her commitments in London, and Alix had been left to cool her heels in Rome until the Paris collections in October. She'd come close to crawling back to Pavesi's to ask for her old job back, but her pride had stopped her. Instead, she'd shut herself up in her apartment and worked on her private portfolio of designs. She'd been almost sorry when Angela had finally called at the end of September to tell her that she'd managed to persuade some of the biggest names in Paris to give her a try.

Alix had felt utterly bewildered the first time she'd walked into a couturier's changing room as a model instead of a designer. She'd thought her years at Pavesi's would have taught her what to expect, but it had all been so different when she was no longer in control. Thanks to the appalling Paris traffic she'd been late, and the PR girl at the new permanent fashion exhibition at the Louvre had been frantically pacing the room looking for her.

'Alexandra D'Alfonsi?'

Alix had nodded nervously.

'Thank God! I was beginning to wonder what had happened to you.'

'I'm so sorry. I got held up –'

'Never mind that now. You're here, that's what matters.' The PR girl had eyed her, then propelled Alix towards one of the dressers. 'Fleur, take Alix over to make-up. You'll need to do something about those shadows under her eyes. And for Christ's sake be quick, the show starts in half an hour.'

Alix had followed Fleur over to the bank of make-up desks and felt a mixture of relief and surprise as she saw the familiar face of a hair stylist she'd known from her days at Pavesi's. 'Oh, Pierre, it's good to see you.'

'Feeling lost, *chérie*?'

Alix was embarrassed. 'A little. I don't really know what I should be doing. And it was so crowded out there I thought I'd never make it through security.'

Pierre had grinned as he'd unfastened her hair from its ponytail and begun to comb it through. 'You should've been here last year, when we were still in tents on the lawn. The rain turned the whole place into a Flanders field – absolutely covered in mud, darling, no one knew where they were going, and they had far too few seats inside the bloody marquee. Everyone was so crammed together they started steaming in the heat – *darling*, it was like being in a sauna.'

Alix's nerves had dissipated slightly. 'Thank God they've built this place, then.'

'Don't I know it, sweetie,' Pierre sighed. 'Head back, there's a darling. It cost *le pauvre* French government a fortune, but at least we've got room to move.'

Alix felt completely helpless as Fleur bent and unfastened her shoes, carefully working a pair of soft silver wool stockings over her feet and ankles, while another of the dressers pressed a series of three-inch plastic silver fingernails over her own before vanishing in search of Cindy Crawford.

A harassed girl in a once-white Chanel T-shirt, now covered in foundation, powder and lipstick, stopped by Alix's chair and tilted her face towards the light. 'What've you got on?'

'Just what I was wearing this morning,' Alix said. 'Foundation, powder, a little shadow –'

The make-up girl studied her, then glanced at her watch. 'You shouldn't need too much work. I'll be able to get to you in five minutes –'

'Why don't I do my own eyes?' Alix said, her confidence beginning to return as she realised that she'd probably done a dozen times more shows than this girl, albeit as a designer rather than a model. 'I think I know what you want. No lips, right?'

'Oh, would you? You are a darling. No lips, that'd be brilliant. And a touch more gold on your lids.' The make-up girl disappeared back into the throng.

'You've just made a friend for life.' Pierre finished tweaking her hair and stood back. 'OK, *chérie*. Perfect. You do your eyes and I'll send Chantal over to approve.'

326

As Alix had stood waiting for her cue, listening to the pulse of the music overlaid with the whir of camera shutters and brief but enthusiastic scatterings of applause as each outfit emerged, she had felt far more nervous than when she'd been thrust out on to the catwalk at Pavesi's. Then it had been a crazy dream, a role she was playing for the few brief moments she'd stepped outside her own life and borrowed Ellie's. It hadn't mattered then if she'd got it wrong; she could always slip back into her own life and pretend it had never happened. But in Paris it was her career, her name and reputation on the line. In Paris it had mattered a great deal.

She'd patted the silk of her tunic over her flat stomach and nervously brushed a stray strand of hair from her eyes, the plastic silver nails catching her skin. When Helena Christensen slipped past her back into the atelier, Alix had emerged into the blinding lights, her nerves fading as the thrill took hold. She'd eddied along the runway as Angela's coach had taught her, her smoky gaze fixed somewhere in the centre of the phalanx of photographers at the end. She'd felt the familiar surge of heat between her thighs as the camera shutters hummed, and her nipples tingled with excitement. That feeling of power was far more intoxicating than anything she'd ever experienced. Those few moments made up for all the hours spent smiling to order as a throng of make-up artists, hair stylists, fashion editors and photographers pulled her apart and put her back together in their own image.

Alix would never forget her first week of collections. The day after that first show, she'd started work just after seven with the Karl Lagerfeld collection, then dashed across town to do a picture for French *Vogue* in honour of Nelson Mandela, before racing back for a Hermès fitting, picking up a much sought-after purple Hermès Kelly bag as a thank-you on the way. She'd waited for hours at Chloé when Lagerfeld had failed to turn up for the two o'clock fitting, then been late for

Valentino's at four only to discover that he, too, was running behind. Angela had called her there with an urgent request to get herself across town PDQ to Oscar de la Renta, whose show for Pierre Balmain was less than twenty-four hours away. The fitting had finished at six, giving her just enough time to try Chloé again before heading to Herve Leger across the road. Angela had tracked her down yet again to tell her that there was no time for her to fit in the rescheduled Valentino fitting the following day, so the evening she'd set aside for sleeping had to be spent standing in yet another dressing room, as still more exquisite garments were pinned around her exhausted body. By the time she'd finished and returned to her hotel, it had been past three o'clock in the morning.

By the end of the week, Alix was shattered but undeniably famous. Angela had been swamped with offers; Alix could have racked up assignments in ads and catalogues, but Angela had taken her lead from the way Claudia Schiffer's agents had handled the launch of her career and decided to stimulate demand by booking Alix sparingly. Most models were offered a contract with a big design name six or seven years into their career. Claudia Schiffer had been the youngest model ever to be given such a contract, and she'd got the deal of the century when she'd signed a thirty-day-per-year commitment to Revlon for several million dollars. Angela was determined to do the same for Alexandra D'Alfonsi. She'd wanted Alix's face associated with a top design name. Italian, German, French and English newspapers had begun fighting over Alix, America had hinted at sweet deals, but for Angela it was still too early. She'd ordered Alix back to Rome with instructions to do absolutely nothing until she called.

Again Alix was left to her own devices, but this time she'd been relieved rather than annoyed. She wanted to spend some time with Ellie. The Brazilian model had been trying to come off cocaine without checking in to a detox centre or seeing – as

328

she put it – 'a bloody shrink', but Alix knew how hard she'd been finding it. Ellie had been devastated when Luke's wife had given birth at Christmas to a beautiful boy they'd named after Matt. With nothing to do herself, Alix accompanied Ellie on all her photo shoots, determined not to let her friend slip. Ellie was pictured wearing Azzedine Alaïa in Bali, Herve Leger in Thailand, Prada in Barbados and La Perla in New Mexico, and Alix learned more about modelling from her friend in those three months than if she'd spent three years alone on the circuit.

'Do you think you could manage to ski down the slope for me?' Matt's voice broke into Alix's reverie, and she realised how cold she was getting.

She shaded her eyes. 'Are you talking to us?'

'I think these pictures are a bit static. I just need a few turns, that's all. Do you reckon you can manage it?'

'Oh shit,' Ellie muttered. 'My sense of balance is about as developed as a lemming's.'

Nigel stepped forward anxiously, his bald head gleaming in the sunlight. 'Matt, that ski suit Ellie's wearing is worth $1,000, cost price. I wouldn't want anything to happen to it –'

'Oh, what the hell.' Ellie had a well-developed sense of devilment. She brandished her ski pole at Matt. 'OK, but on your head be it.'

Alix groaned. 'I hope you know what you're doing.'

'Haven't a clue,' Ellie said cheerfully. She turned towards the mountain. 'How the fuck are we supposed to get up this thing, anyway?'

'It might help if you took off your skis,' Alix said.

Aware that Matt was watching her she quickly bent down to unfasten her bindings, sudden heat scalding her cheeks. She'd been both fearful and excited at the thought of seeing him again. They hadn't met since the débâcle of their first encounter at Pavesi's nine months ago; but even if she'd wanted to, it had been impossible to put him out of her mind. Everywhere she went his name had come up in conversation or she'd seen his picture in a newspaper, his arm draped around this bimbo or that. And she had to admit, she'd been looking for it. Ever since Angela had told her that Matt would be the photographer on this assignment, she'd been planning what to say and how she'd act when they met. She'd been determined not to let him see how much he unsettled her, to behave as if nothing had happened. After all, nothing *had* happened. She wondered if he'd make a pass at her again, terrified he would, terrified he wouldn't. If he did, she still didn't know whether she'd slap his face or fall into his arms.

But so far her fears had been groundless – they'd barely spoken two words to each other. Ever since they'd met up that morning, Matt had been treating her with careful, if somewhat distant, courtesy.

The two models started to climb the slope, kicking their boots into the crusty snow to create tiny steps, and using their poles to balance. After about five minutes they heard Matt call out: 'OK, that's high enough. You can stop now.'

Ellie turned round and gazed back down the mountain to where Matt and Romi were standing. 'Shit. It didn't look so fucking steep from down there.'

'There's only one way home now, and that's down.'

'I'm well aware of that,' Ellie muttered. 'The question is – which way up will I be? You'd better get this in one take,' she yelled to Matt. 'I'm bloody well not doing it again.'

'Ready when you are,' Matt shouted back.

She launched herself down the slope, her body slipping automatically into a natural rhythm as she moved despite her unfamiliarity with the skis. Alix waited for a single beat and then pushed herself off with her poles, following the path carved by Ellie's blades so that she would be neatly aligned behind her for Matt's shot. She heard the clatter of Matt's camera as he rapidly finished the roll of film and slipped a second into the Hasselblad.

'Where are the brakes on these things?' Ellie cried as she shot past Matt.

'Bring your knees together and pull the tips of your blades in!' he shouted.

Leo leaped up in alarm as Ellie careered towards him. Alix swerved to the left and just missed him as he abandoned his canvas chair and ran towards the trees.

'Mind my suits!' Nigel screamed. 'A thousand dollars each! Cost price!'

'I'm going to sue!' Ellie cried.

Nigel blanched and turned to Matt. 'Can she do that? Has anyone got her contract?'

'Ellie, stop, for Christ's sake,' Matt cried, doubling up with laughter. 'You're going to give Nigel a coronary.'

Ellie suddenly threw herself backwards and landed on her bottom, wiggling her legs and skis in the air like a stranded beetle, laughing too much to be able to move. Nigel wailed and ran towards her as Matt and Romi collapsed into the snow, tears streaming down their cheeks.

'I don't know if there's a single usable shot in there, but it was worth it.'

Alix finally came to a halt beneath the trees, aching with laughter, gripping a pine tree with both hands to avoid falling over. She stamped hard on the back of her bindings to release her boots from the skis, picked them up and trudged back towards the others.

'I don't know about you, but I'd say it was about time for a drink,' Ellie said.

'There's an inn at the top of this mountain,' Matt answered. 'We can go up on the chair-lift and take the cable car back down to the hotel afterwards.'

Romi quickly repacked the aluminium equipment box and

marked the rolls of film Matt had shot, as Leo and Nigel sheepishly rejoined them. 'I'd better take this lot back down to the hotel. Can you manage without me until after lunch?'

'Sure. I think we're finished for this morning.' Matt peered up the mountain. 'Looks like we've got some more snow clouds coming in anyway. I doubt we'll get much more done today.'

'I'm going with Romi,' Leo said nervously. 'Nigel?'

Nigel blossomed. 'Don't mind if I do, Leo. Good of you to ask.'

Romi hid a smile as Leo and Nigel exchanged meaningful glances. 'OK, Matt, I'll catch you later at the hotel.'

Matt picked up Ellie's skis. 'You'd better let me take these up for you. The chair-lifts can be a bit difficult until you get used to them. Coming, Sami?' He glanced politely at Alix. 'Do you think you can manage?'

Alix looked away. 'Don't worry. I'll be fine.'

They made their way towards the end of the queue for the two-seater chair-lifts up the mountain. Sami and Ellie stepped into the first one, and Matt glanced at Alix. 'Sure you know how to handle these things with your skis on?'

'I think so.'

'OK. Let's go.'

As Alix hooked her skis over the foot rest and leant back, she became aware of the cold tranquillity of the mountain, the stillness of the pines, as they stood under their blanket of snow. For the first time in many months she felt herself relax. The silence enveloped her, broken only by the gentle swish of skis on the slopes below them. The air grow colder as they climbed higher, the cloud thickening around them until they could barely see Sami and Ellie in front of them. Alix could hear the occasional thud as snow tumbled from an overladen branch, and see the tiny tracks left by birds and foxes across the snow. She was acutely aware of Matt beside her and, despite herself, glanced across at him; her stomach twisted as she saw the soft flakes of falling snow dusting his eyelashes and melting on his cheeks. She turned away quickly. He stared straight ahead, saying nothing. Why was it this man had the power to arouse feelings inside her she neither understood nor wanted? She didn't even like him – he was irresponsible, arrogant, indiscriminately charming and his looks were so *obvious*. And yet she couldn't be near him without wanting him so much it obliterated all other thoughts.

'I've always loved these mountains,' Matt said, breaking the silence. 'My father used to take me skiing every year. My mother came too, of course, but she didn't really ski. She messed around on the blue slopes with her friends, showing off the latest in designer ski-wear.' He smiled. 'It was one of the few times Dad and I had to be alone. Just us and the mountains. I've never forgotten it.'

Alix stared at him, surprised by this sudden confidence. She found herself returning his smile, despite herself. 'Are you very close to your father?'

'Yes. I love my mother, of course, but Dad –' He paused, searching for the right words. 'Ever since I can remember, I've admired him. He's so much his own person, he's always done what's right. I wish I could be like him.'

The cloud was thick now, muffling sound and blanketing them in a world of their own. Matt glanced at his watch as the wind whipped his hair across his face. 'Perhaps we should head back down once we've had a quick drink. If this wind gets any stronger, they may have to close the cable car.' He looked at Alix. 'It's a pity you don't ski. It's an amazing run down the mountain.'

'You don't have to stay with me,' Alix said, stung by his patronising words.

Matt shrugged. 'Ellie and Sami will be waiting. There'll be other days to ski.'

333

Alix felt her anger at his arrogance return. One moment he was sharing a confidence with her, and the next she was relegated to the chorus along with everybody else in his life. He just wanted an audience, it didn't matter who. She glowered as she lifted her skis off the foot-rest and helped him raise the safety bar.

'As soon as your skis touch the snow, just stand up and let the slope take you towards the inn. It's just over to your left about twenty metres down. Don't try to steer them or you'll end up falling over,' Matt instructed. He appeared not to have noticed her silence.

When Alix felt her skis brush the snow she stood up and angled them sharply to the right, bending her knees and bringing the skis together to give herself speed. She heard Matt shout in alarm behind her and smiled, tucking her poles into her sides as she reached the top of the black mogul run. Condescending bastard. Now he'd see who could ski.

She scanned the glittering snow in front of her. It looked as smooth as glass. If she mistimed just one movement, she risked spinning out of control and over the edge of the crevasse that loomed to one side of the run.

With a fierce surge of fear and exhilaration, she dug her poles deep into the snow on either side of her and flew into the first curve. As she gathered speed, she saw immediately the slope below, already enveloped in the thick cloud that would isolate her in a world containing only herself and the snow in front of her. Again and again she whipped across the whiteness, constantly scanning the path downwards.

Alix heard a shout behind her and for a split second her concentration was broken. She hit a mogul awkwardly and threw herself to the left to recover, sending her off course for the curve that followed. The gap between her skis widened as she struggled to regain control, unable to ready herself for the next mogul. She saw the looming edge of the crevasse on her left and didn't even have time to feel fear as she forced her skis together and round to the right, skimming the edge of the run only metres from the ravine. Behind her she could hear Matt's skis swishing on the snow as he raced to catch up with her, his path almost a straight line as he took the fastest route down the mountain. Her mistake had given him the time he needed to catch up with her, and she could almost feel his breath on her cheek as he matched her.

'For Christ's sake, Alix! Do I have to chase you all the way to the bottom?'

Alix ignored him, leaning into the mountain and just skimming past his left, so close that her skis were only inches away from his. How dare he treat her like a child, assume she couldn't ski just because she was on the other side of his camera! She wasn't one of his damn bimbos. It was about time someone taught him a lesson.

She gasped in surprise and swerved to the left as Matt shot past her and swung his skis back up the slope, stopping only metres in front of her in a spray of snow and forcing her off the piste.

'What the hell do you think you're playing at?' he yelled.

Alix skied gently to a halt beneath the trees. 'I thought you wanted to ski down?'

'You told me you couldn't ski!' Matt shouted angrily. 'How the hell do you think I felt when I saw you shoot off the chair-lift and down a black mogul run, thinking you hadn't a clue what you were doing?'

'I didn't tell you I couldn't ski,' Alix said calmly. 'You just never asked.'

'Stop scoring points!' Matt said furiously. 'What about the play-acting with Ellie this morning? This isn't a fucking game, Alix. You could've been killed back there – we both could have been. The cloud's too thick to ski a slope you barely know. You might have skied over the edge of the ravine without even realising what was happening until it was too late.'

'I've skied this run a dozen times with my father when I was younger.'

'Not in these conditions, not if he had any sense,' Matt snapped. 'You're acting like a stupid child.'

'Well, that's what I am, isn't it?' Alix's teeth were chattering. 'Stupid, like all the other models you photograph and then sweet-talk into bed?'

Matt stared at her. 'Is that what all this is about? Because I haven't tried to seduce you?'

Furiously, Alix pushed past him and launched herself down the mountain again, her cheeks burning with humiliation. How dare he think she'd risked both their lives out of pique, because she wanted to go to bed with him and it hadn't worked out that way! Was he so arrogant and sure of himself that he couldn't bear the thought that he'd been outmanoeuvred?

Suddenly the run opened out and Alix saw a slope as sheer and smooth as a sheet of glass loom beneath her skis. She dug her blades into the side of the mountain and felt a flicker of alarm as they refused to bite. She swung into the turn and tried again, fear concentrating her thoughts as she attempted to hold the turn and failed. The run was sheet ice. She felt the wind on her face and became aware that the new powder layering the rest of the mountain must have been swept bare on this exposed slope. If she hadn't been so angry, she'd have noticed in time to ski round it. Desperately she fought to control her descent as her skis shot forward, slipping and sliding down the mountain, out of control.

She heard the sound of skis behind her and saw Matt race past her, his head tucked into his chest as he tried to overtake. For a moment he disappeared into the cloud, and then suddenly he was there in front of her, his arms fiercely gripping her shoulders as he threw himself forward, using his weight and his own skis to guide their descent, spinning round and twisting them across the mountain and away from the ravine. They shot beneath the trees, the thick snow under the pines acting like brakes on their skis, until finally they came to a halt deep in the forest.

They stood panting for several minutes, neither of them able to speak.

Eventually Alix said shakily, 'I owe you an apology.'

'I guess you do.'

Her voice was flip. 'And a thank-you.'

Matt realised he was still holding her shoulders and released her. 'You could've been killed, Alix,' he said quietly. 'Would it really have been worth it just to prove a point?'

He watched her, his face wind-burned, the expression in his eyes unreadable, then abruptly turned away and started to pick his way carefully between the trees, not bothering to check if she were following. 'I'm not chancing the main run again. I think we'll follow the path down this time.'

Matt cradled his beer in his hands without drinking it, distracted by his thoughts. He'd been sitting in a corner of the hotel bar for over two hours, unable to think of anything but Alix. He'd been drawn to her from the moment he'd met her at Pavesi's, but he'd had no idea just how dangerous she was to him until he'd seen her plunging down that icy mountainside.

The first time he'd seen her, he'd been struck by her unusual beauty. With his experience as a photographer, he'd seen beyond the heavy tortoiseshell frames of her glasses and self-effacing manner. She carried herself with unconscious grace, her limbs as slender and supple as a dancer's. He'd found himself watching the rise and fall of her breasts beneath her T-shirt, the smooth swell of her buttocks against her snug black jeans as she leant over her table. He'd been certain she'd been equally attracted to him. She'd been giving off all the right signals. When he'd bent to kiss her, it had been an act of impulse, but one he'd thought would be welcomed. Instead, she'd frozen him out. He couldn't understand her sudden *volte face*.

Since he was fifteen, Matt had known the effect he had on women. Girls fell over themselves to go to bed with him, and it wasn't just because they thought he could turn them into the next Cindy Crawford. He was too intelligent to take his success with women seriously – most of his girlfriends were bimbos barely out of their teens – but he had become accustomed to a certain level of interest. This girl had made him think again, and her reaction had piqued him. What had started out as an idle diversion on a sunny afternoon in Rome had become more than that. After she'd gone cold on him he'd made it his business to find out what he could about her. He'd come up with surprisingly little. Five days after he'd met her he'd known her name, that she was twenty-two, lived alone and was considered one of Pavesi's most promising assistants. Precious little else.

No one could have been more astonished than he when Alix had appeared on the catwalk instead of Ellie. He'd known before that she was beautiful, but he'd realised then just how attracted he was to her. For the next week he was unable to get her out of his mind. He hadn't felt that way about any woman since he'd met Jane. But by the time he'd decided to call Alix and to hell with the consequences, she'd disappeared to Paris, and the next time he'd seen her was three months later on the catwalk at Dior. He hadn't been able to get near her during Paris Fashion Week; she'd been hounded by the paparazzi, and he'd just been one more photographer trying to sweet-talk his way past security.

After that he'd done his best to put her out of his mind, but the moment Après booked him for this assignment with her, it brought everything back. He'd felt it was his last chance. He'd deliberately played it cool, determined not to scare her off this time, and for a few moments on the chair-lift he'd really thought he was getting somewhere. Then she'd pulled that crazy stunt on the mountain, simultaneously infuriating and terrifying him. Somehow she'd got under his skin. It wasn't a feeling he liked.

'Want to talk about it?'

Matt jumped and glanced up as Sami slid into the chair next to him. 'Am I that much of an open book?'

Sami laughed. 'Only to those who know you.'

'Can I get you a drink?'

'Thanks. Dry white wine, please – French, if they've got it.'

Sami pulled off her black beret and shook her hair free, then leant back and smiled at Matt. 'Am I glad to get off that damned mountain. I thought we were going to be stuck up there in that restaurant for ever when the power for the cable car failed. Thank God there was plenty to drink.'

'Where's Ellie?'

'She went upstairs to take a bath before dinner. But more to the point, what happened to you and Alix? I didn't even see you get off the chair-lift.'

The waiter arrived and placed their order in front of them.

'We skied down the mountain.'

'You're kidding? In this weather? I thought Alix couldn't even ski?'

'Yeah, me too. Seems I was wrong.' He took a deep draught of his beer and put the glass back on the table. 'Seems I was wrong about a lot of things.'

Sami reached out and squeezed his knee, her hand lingering a fraction longer than necessary. 'Don't worry about it. At least you've had a few hours to recover while we've been stuck on the mountain all afternoon.' She replaced her glass on the table. 'Listen, I don't really feel like drinking any more down here. I've got a bottle of Moët on ice upstairs in my room …'

Matt knew Sami had carried a torch for him ever since their brief affair had ended years ago, but even though he'd have been happy to take her to bed, he liked her too much to use her for a few easy fucks when there was no future in it. He'd deliberately kept their relationship strictly professional since then, despite the subtle invitations she'd occasionally sent his way. It wasn't fair to let her think there might be a chance of anything more permanent.

He smiled gently and shook his head. 'I don't think so.'

'Don't worry, Matt, it was a no-strings invitation.' She grinned at him. 'C'mon. We're old friends now. And it'll do you good. You'll only sit here brooding if I leave you on your own.'

Over Sami's shoulder, Matt saw Alix enter the bar and perch on one of the stools nearest the door without even glancing in his direction. His heart gave an unwarranted thud.

Sami misunderstood his distraction. 'Don't worry, Matt. You'd be quite safe – I'm not going to rape you.'

Matt drained his glass, suddenly needing to escape from feelings he didn't want and couldn't understand. 'Sami, that would be a technical impossibility. I'd have to be unwilling.'

He stood up and slipped his arm around Sami's waist, feeling a mixture of satisfaction, guilt and a strange upset as he saw Alix stare at them for a second. He forced it down and kissed the top of Sami's dark head. 'What was that you were saying about room service?'

Sami clung possessively to his leather jacket as they left the bar.

Alix felt a stab of anger and acute disappointment as she watched them leave. She had been stupid to imagine there could ever be anything between herself and Matt. She might be a model now, but she still couldn't compete with someone

340

like Sami. She would never be able to bubble vivaciously, to chatter about nothing and make a man like Matt feel powerful and all-important. Both times she'd met Matt, they'd ended up arguing over nothing. She wasn't even beautiful. The waifs had proved you didn't need to be stunning to model any more, and Alix knew she just happened to have the look that was in vogue at the moment. She didn't really blame Matt for preferring Sami.

Matt didn't look back as they walked towards the lift. As they stepped inside, he opened his arms and Sami tumbled into them, her body warm and yielding against his own as he drew her head towards him. His tongue probed, searching and insistent, tasting the wine-sweetness of her mouth as he slid his hands beneath the heavy sheepskin of her jacket. She felt the hardness of his cock through the close-fitting Lycra of her ski pants, her hands slipping around his waist as she pressed herself against him.

'Matt –'

He kissed her again and felt her tremble. 'Mmm?'

Reluctantly she pushed him away. 'Not here –'

Matt laughed. 'Why not here?'

Before she could protest, he reached past her towards the brass lever set in one of the wooden panels and pulled it downwards. The lift shuddered and then stopped, the brass arrow above the door frozen between two and three. 'Matt, you wouldn't –'

'Yes I would.' Matt pushed her damp jacket over her arms so that it fell heavily to the floor and gently pressed her body against his. His kisses grew more urgent as she stroked his back and slid her hands beneath the waistband of his jeans, his lips moving across her cheek and along the curve of her throat. He stroked one stiffened nipple through the white silk of her shirt, realising that she was wearing nothing beneath it. He bent his head and sucked at it through the flimsy material, then eased her legs apart. He pushed her shirt up over her breasts and kissed them.

Sami moaned softly. 'Matt – we can't –'

She was desperate to feel him inside her as he pulled her trousers and panties down below her knees and gently inserted his fingers between the moist lips of her cunt, stroking her clitoris as she reached for his cock and pulled it towards her. 'Here, you bastard. Right here.'

Matt heard the distant sound of voices and running feet; the threat of discovery whetted his appetite.

'Give it to me now! Oh, God, now, please, now!'

Matt lifted her up in one swift movement and pulled her down on to his cock, piercing her soft moistness as she curled her legs around him and forced herself further down on to him, his hands prising her buttocks apart as he drove deeper into her. The need to bury himself inside her was so primal it drove everything from his mind, leaving only the urgency to thrust again and again until he was spent.

He felt her body stiffen in his arms as she screamed with pleasure, her orgasm spurring his own as he poured himself into her and collapsed against the wall. The sound of voices grew louder, and suddenly they heard someone thumping on the door of the lift.

'Is anybody in there? Are you all right?'

Matt yanked up his jeans and pulled the brass lever in the wall so that the lift started on its upward journey again.

Sami giggled. 'All I asked you up for was a drink.'

Sami walked towards her room, fumbling for the right key. A sudden sense of isolation swept over Matt. He felt no closer to her now than he had before: they might just as well have been playing a game of tennis. She was pretty and cute and she gave him pleasure, but there was nothing more to it than that. He felt a terrible pang of guilt and regret. He shouldn't have screwed her. Was he going to spend the rest of his life indulging his cock while his mind and heart remained forever disengaged? Was that all he had left to look forward to?

He thought of Alix, then angrily banished her from his mind, but he knew the encounter in the lift would have meant a great deal if it had been with her.

Seven

Upper West Side, New York, USA
Thursday 28 April 1994
11.30 a.m.

Stephi felt the gentle warmth of the late spring sunshine on her shoulders as she sliced an orange in half and crushed it against the plastic squeezer. Spring in New York combined her favourite season and the city she most adored. Every time she contemplated relocating to some part of the state with more trees and fewer muggers she only had to remember this particular feeling to fall in love with the city all over again.

She took two chilled glasses out of the fridge, adding a couple of slices of fresh lemon for sharpness to the orange juice as she poured it, then put the two glasses on to a tray already bearing *pain au chocolat*, plain Greek yoghurt and a small bowl of caviar-expensive, out-of-season wild strawberries, and left the kitchen.

She tiptoed into the bedroom and deposited the tray on the edge of the wide double bed.

'Oh, Steph. Twenty more minutes, please?'

Stephi pulled the covers off. 'You've been saying that for the last two hours. It's already gone 11.30. Some of us have work to do.'

Angela groped blindly for the duvet. 'And some of us have

344

jetlag. If you had any human decency at all you'd go away and leave me alone.'

'It's your own fault for treating my place as your weekend home. I'm beginning to think you must have shares in Concorde. Wouldn't it be simpler to find a place in Kent or the Cotswolds like everybody else?'

'It's bad enough living next door to everyone else during the week. I'm buggered if I'm going to do it at weekends as well,' Angela grumbled. 'Anyway, I've got no choice. Someone's got to keep an eye on Ellie.'

'Still having problems?'

'Mmm, difficult to tell. She seems clean, but her contract with Après comes up for renewal in six weeks. I don't want to take the chance of them finding out what really makes her eyes glow brighter than bright, and pulling out.'

Despite what she'd just said, Angela guessed that Ellie was telling the truth when she swore she'd stopped taking the cocaine. Alix D'Alfonsi hadn't let her friend out of her sight in the past twelve months, and Ellie seemed to have pulled herself together. Professionally, she was still as popular as ever; but to Angela's experienced eye, some of the fire had gone out of the model's work, as if she'd given up fighting a battle for which she no longer had the stomach. Angela knew it was more than just giving up the cocaine. Ellie had sold her flat in Chelsea and had refused to buy another, spending the time she wasn't away on assignment either in an hotel or at Alix's apartment in Rome. According to Alix, Ellie had got some crazy notion into her head that someone was stalking her. Angela certainly knew that for the last year, Ellie hadn't stayed in any one place more than a week. Her social life seemed to have come to a grinding halt; after the business at Pavesi's, the endless parade of boyfriends – and girlfriends – had suddenly ceased, and she'd disappeared from the gossip pages of *WWD* and *Tatler* altogether. It was as much as

Angela could do to force Ellie out to the launch parties that were part of the joint contract she and Alix had signed with Après a year ago. It was almost as if Ellie was waiting for something to happen.

Stephi dipped the tips of her fingers in one of the glasses and flicked drops of orange juice over Angela's face, breaking her reverie. 'Don't you dare go back to sleep. You've been at my apartment more than I have this month, and I've hardly even seen you. You arrive in the middle of the night and I can't get a word of sense out of you until half an hour before your flight back to London – '

'Count yourself lucky. That's half an hour more sense than you'd get if you were married,' Angela muttered, sitting up as Stephi rained another shower of juice in her direction. 'OK, OK. I'm awake. For God's sake, stop doing that. What's so urgent it couldn't wait?'

Stephi slid her hand under the duvet and gently stroked her fingers along the inside of Angela's thigh. 'I couldn't.'

'Well, why didn't you say?'

She lay back against the pillows as Stephi's fingers found their way between her thighs again, moaning softly as they slid between her moist lips and found the engorged nub of her clitoris. Stephi kissed her, tasting the sleepy sweetness of Angela's mouth. Their tongues met and danced around each other, teasing and withdrawing and arousing as their kiss deepened. After a long moment, Stephi pulled away, her eyes bright with desire as she stared down at her lover. 'God, you're so beautiful. I wish I could drink you in.'

'I see no reason why you shouldn't.'

Stephi marvelled at the youthful suppleness of a body that she knew owed nothing to the surgeon's knife. Angela would be forty-four this year – thirty-nine according to her entry in *Debrett's* – but she could safely have lopped a further five years from her age without arousing suspicion. She had inherited from her mother's aristocratic family the finely drawn features and clear skin that only grew more refined with age, the delicate tracery of lines around her cool blue eyes barely visible. But the firm tone of her body, the taut stomach and tensile strength of her arms and legs, had been achieved through a dedicated and unforgiving regime of exercise and dieting. Her tiny pink-nippled breasts were high and firm, her waist slender. Her skin glowed with the bloom of a twenty-two-year-old, thanks to decades of fanatical application of sun screen and moisturiser every time the sun dared to come out from behind a cloud. In the Seventies, her refusal to acquire the obligatory bronzed tan had lost her more than one lucrative commission as a model, but she was reaping the rewards now. It wasn't just a matter of looks; more than one ex-model she knew was currently in hospital receiving treatment for skin cancer.

Stephi blushed self-consciously as Angela reached forward and unfastened the pink silk tie of her wrap, stroking her bare shoulders gently as she eased it away from her body, even though this had happened a hundred times before. She felt the difference between them keenly. She had a vitality that belied her forty-six years, but she was acutely conscious of the lines around her eyes, the few grey hairs threading the chestnut. Angela's hair was still as thick and black as it had ever been. Stephi's own body had stayed slender and well muscled, thanks to the demands of her work, but her stomach, though flat, was soft where it had once been taut, her full, ripe breasts not as firm as they'd been when Roberto Cerreni had been her lover twenty years before. Thank God she'd never had children. No matter how hard you dieted afterwards, it was like packing a suitcase after a holiday. You might have exactly the same number of things to go in it, but somehow the lid just wouldn't shut.

She felt a strange pull at her heart as she thought of Roberto, a faint echo of the old pain that she hadn't felt for a long time. He remained as vivid in her mind as the day he'd ended their relationship without a word of explanation or apology. Stephi had thrown herself into her work in the months that followed and eventually the pain had faded, but her faith in her own feelings had never quite been restored. It had taken her two years before she'd even accepted a date with another man, and her first few attempts had been a disaster. She'd been unable to relax, ruthlessly grilling her dates about their marital status and doubting every word they said. She'd run through two dozen men in less than a year, not one of them lasting beyond a couple of dates. Her promiscuity had started to worry her; it was the early Eighties and the start of the AIDS scare, and she'd never been that conscientious about using condoms at the best of times. She'd forced herself to lower her guard sufficiently to form some sort of relationship, and there had been two that might have gone somewhere: Jonathan, a television reporter six years younger than herself, and JimBob, a computer software programmer who'd been a decade older. Both relationships had lasted just over two years; both times she'd pulled back on the brink of marriage amid a great deal of recrimination and bitterness. After she'd finished with JimBob, she'd given up dating. She hadn't wanted to cause so much unhappiness, and she'd known she'd never be able to let go of her fear enough to marry. She'd been so wrong once, she was terrified of it happening again.

Stephi started her first lesbian affair the day she read in the *International Herald Tribune* that Roberto Cerreni had finally achieved his promotion to junior Italian Foreign Minister. It had been 1987, she was thirty-eight years old, and she hadn't slept with a man in more than two years. Reading about Roberto had plunged her into a pit of self-pity, and she'd gone to drown her sorrows in a wine bar just across the road from her office in West 34th Street. In mid-afternoon the wine bar was almost empty, apart from the obligatory maudlin drunk bemoaning his alimony payments to anyone who'd listen, and a smart, well-groomed woman in her early forties sitting alone at the bar. Stephi had sat down two stools away from the woman and ordered a dry martini with a lemon twist.

'Make that two.'

Stephi looked up as the woman had opened her handbag and handed the barman a bill. 'Thanks.'

'You look like you need it.'

Stephi raised her glass. 'You can say that again.'

'Want to talk about it?'

Stephi had looked at her again, this time more closely. Her original estimate of the woman's age now seemed generous; the woman was carefully made up and quite attractive, but closer to fifty than forty. Stephi had been about to smile and brush the woman's advance away, but something made her pause. The expression in the woman's eyes, the silent sympathy and something else she couldn't quite identify, had made her pick up her drink and move along to the stool next to the woman. One martini had turned into two, and then three, and everything had spilled out – Roberto and Jonathan and JimBob and all the others – and then somehow – she still didn't really know how – she'd found herself getting into a taxi with her new friend, then stumbling upstairs to the woman's Upper East Side apartment, into her bedroom and into her arms.

Even though her middle-class self had been slightly shocked by what she'd done, Stephi had realised instantly that this was right. She'd been able to trust a woman in a way she couldn't a man. The affair with Sophie lasted several months, and after Sophie had had to go back to her home in New Jersey to look after her sick mother, Stephi found herself part of a network of professional, successful, wealthy career women, all aged roughly between thirty-five and fifty, some single, some divorced, some of them quite happily married; but all of them indulging in discreet, pleasurable liaisons with women just like herself.

She met Angela through Matt Logan in the summer of 1990. She and Matt had been good friends for several years by then, constantly in touch over work. The decade she'd had on Matt and her own reluctance to get involved with another man had protected her from Matt's lazy charm, and they had grown into the habit of pairing up for work parties to which they were both invariably invited. It had been simpler for both of them than spending the evening fighting off unwelcome advances from – in her case – leery middle-aged men or – in Matt's – starlet wannabes. She had met Angela at a launch party to celebrate Ellie Cassidy's signing with Q Cosmetics, and they'd clicked the moment they started talking. Unlike Stephi, Angela had always been lesbian. They'd been seeing each other for nearly four years now.

Angela was the closest Stephi had come to finding someone she could love since Roberto had shattered her youthful dreams of a future inhabited by golden knights on white chargers. It was quite an irony that Angela now represented Roberto's daughter, although Alix now used the name D'Alfonsi rather than Cerreni, and Stephi guessed that few people had ever made the connection. Angela certainly hadn't. If Stephi hadn't recognised Alix's picture, she'd never have guessed that Alix D'Alfonsi was the same little Alexandra she'd once known. She'd kept the secret. Angela had once told her that Alix never talked about her parents, except to say that she hadn't seen them for many years. Stephi wasn't surprised Alix had fallen out with her mother, but wished she knew what had caused the estrangement between Alix and her father. There had been no mention of any rift in the reports she'd read about Roberto. The little girl she remembered had adored her father. Stephi couldn't imagine anything powerful enough, terrible enough, to sever that bond.

She was brought back to the present as Angela took her nipple in her mouth and sucked hard as she pulled Stephi down on to the bed beside her. Any thought of Roberto Cerreni was swept away on the tide of heat that rose between her legs. She gave herself up to the sensation as Angela's tongue flicked across her skin with swift, darting movements, circling tiny whorls of pleasure along the inside of her thighs.

'You're so voluptuous,' Angela murmured. 'You have so much to offer, Stephi. You're so beautiful.'

Stephi sighed gently as Angela parted her milky thighs and buried her dark head in the crisp auburn curls of her bush, felt her tongue darting between the soft folds of her cunt and then suddenly slipping inside her. She shuddered, her whole being centring between her legs as rivers of heat spread outwards so that even her toes and fingers tingled. Greedily she reached for Angela's tiny pointed breasts, her fingertips stippling the stiffened pink nipples as Angela slid her body around her, her moist cunt open above Stephi's face even as she buried her own tongue up to its hilt inside Stephi.

Suddenly Stephi could no longer tell where she ended and Angela began. She tasted Angela's muskiness with her mouth even as she felt Angela's probing tongue in her cunt, her ripe, full breasts pressing upwards against Angela's taut stomach as she felt her lover's firm little nipples against the surface of her own abdomen. She drank thirstily, her fingers sliding into the cleft between Angela's buttocks and searching out the tiny pink pearl of her clitoris, her own body arching as Angela teased her to the brink of orgasm and then pulled away.

'I want to have you properly,' Angela breathed. 'The way you want to be loved.' She moved round again, her dark hair trailing across Stephi's belly and breasts as she brought her mouth down on Stephi's in a violent, passionate kiss that aroused Stephi as much as the gentle tonguing. She could taste her own juices on Angela's lips, feel Angela's nipples brush against her own breasts as Angela slid her knee between Stephi's thighs and pushed her legs apart.

'God, you're so hot,' Angela panted, kissing her neck and breasts as she thrust her fingers inside Stephi's cunt. 'I could fuck you for ever.'

Stephi groaned, spreading her legs and rocking her hips hungrily as she drew Angela towards her. 'Don't stop, don't ever stop.'

'Never.'

Angela forced her fingers higher inside her, pressing upwards and outwards as her thumb slid into Stephi's anus, her tongue thrusting its way between Stephi's lips so that Stephi felt as if she were being invaded and fucked in every part of her body. Fire spread outward from the rough, delicious invasion between her legs, the sweetest pain mingling with pleasure and driving out every thought in her head. Angela brought her fingers and thumb together inside her, separated only by the most fragile wall, and suddenly an almost unbearable wave of excitement gripped her so that she screamed and bucked beneath Angela's body.

Angela bit her neck and lips and throat and breasts in quick, darting little nips, one hand rolling Stephi's nipples between thumb and forefinger as the other penetrated her with fast, hard thrusts, her own mound grinding against Stephi's soft bush as she drove them on towards orgasm.

And then suddenly Stephi came, a torrent of lust and warmth and excitement and desire washing over her as she shuddered beneath her lover, her climax triggering Angela's own so that they clung together in a passionate tangle of limbs and sensation and sex.

For a long moment, neither of them spoke. Finally, Stephi opened her eyes and smiled. 'Thank God you've got jet lag.

I'm not sure I could stand the pace if you were feeling energetic.'

Angela grinned as she slid her hand between Stephi's legs and began stroking her clitoris as Stephi moaned with pleasure. 'Sweetheart, we haven't even started yet.'

Matt stared at Stephi as he walked into her office, knowing immediately what she'd been up to. Her skin glowed with satisfaction; her eyes were bright and full of fire, her hair tangled around her shoulders in a way that gave her an air of sexy dishevelment. He knew there had to be someone somewhere in Stephi's life, but she was always so bloody discreet. He'd known her eight years now and never once had he seen her with another man. He guessed there was an unhappy love affair buried somewhere in her past, probably with a married man. Nothing else would explain why a woman as vital and attractive as Stephi had stayed single for so long. Despite their long friendship, it was something he'd never asked. There were some boundaries you didn't cross.

He slung his canvas Billingham bag on the floor and threw himself into the low chair opposite Stephi's desk. 'OK, I give up. What's his name?'

Stephi bit back a smile. 'Whose name?'

'Whoever has made you look fifteen years younger and about twenty years happier,' Matt grinned. 'Not to mention making you over an hour late for our meeting.'

Stephi tried not to notice how sexy Matt was, sprawled in the low chair. She'd given up on men a long time ago, but it was impossible to be near Matt and not be slightly tempted. 'Anyway, what are you doing here? You were supposed to be in Barbados for the *Vogue* cover shoot this week. Ceci had you pencilled in for an appointment with me next Monday. What happened? Did they cancel?'

Matt frowned. 'No. I just decided to give it a miss.'

'Oh?'

There was a brief silence. Matt's gaze travelled restlessly around the room, scanning Stephi's awards for the magazine and the memo boards outlining the contents of the next issues, before settling on the array of framed magazine covers on the wall behind her chrome and glass desk. Many of them he'd taken himself: simple, dramatic images that lingered in his mind long after the magazines themselves had been consigned to dustbins and waiting rooms around the world. They were technically perfect, a skilled combination of beauty, style and something he now recognised in his more recent photographs as anger. It gave the pictures an edge. He had long been aware of his dissatisfaction with the lack of challenge in his work, but he hadn't realised how deep his restlessness ran.

'What really brings you here?' Stephi asked quietly.

'I just couldn't face it,' Matt said at last. 'Another model, another location, another shoot. Stephi, I've been doing this for eight years now. I've done covers for every magazine in the industry, I've been to every possible fashion location, I've worked with some of the most beautiful women in the world. I've won every award there is, I can pick and choose my assignments and name my own price for the ones I take on. I'm thirty-five years old, and I feel like there's nothing left for me to do.'

'There's always something new to do. But fashion photography is a frustrating discipline, Matt, you know that. Magazine editors need to flatter and reinforce women's image of themselves, to encourage the "I could look like that" feeling that guarantees sales. The magazines can't afford it if you frighten their customers away.'

'I know. That's why I've decided to pull out of American *Vogue* altogether.'

'Matt, your contract with them has to be worth three million dollars – '

'All I've been doing for the last three years is pleasing other people,' Matt was resolute. 'I'm not going to get anywhere if I don't please myself. I need my freedom. If that means less work, less money, I'll have to live with it.'

'What is it you want to do?' Stephi was trying to keep calm.

'I wish I knew.' Matt looked up at Stephi with his candid, green eyes. 'I need to put what I'm doing into some sort of context –'

'Which is where I come in.'

'Which is where you come in.' Matt paused, trying to assemble his thoughts so that they didn't tumble out in a tangle of emotion and frustration. 'Stephi, when I lost Jane I thought I'd never want to go back to news photography again. Even now, I'm still not sure that I can.'

'So what can I do to help?' Stephi asked. 'I take it you have a proposition?'

'I want you and *Elan* to take the risk I know the other magazines wouldn't. You did it once before for me when you ran Luke Tambo's campaign. I want you to do it again.'

'Matt, I have advertisers and shareholders to answer to –'

'I know that. But I believe what I want to do won't damage your circulation; if anything, it'll increase it.'

Stephi smiled. 'The floor's all yours. I can't promise anything, but at least I can listen.'

'OK. First of all, are you up to date on what's happening in Rwanda?'

Stephi was startled. 'Not really, no. I read the President got killed in a plane crash a while ago, and there'd been some sort of in-fighting –'

Matt nodded. 'There are two tribes in Rwanda. The majority of the people are Hutu, but it's the Tutsis who've always had the land and the wealth. Luke Tambo's Rwandan, and his family were Tutsi. The President who was killed was a Hutu, and his people blame the other side for his death. They

355

say the plane was shot down, and they've been taking their revenge. They've massacred half a million Tutsis so far.'

'Half a million. Jesus.'

'There's going to be a major refugee problem there any day now, Stephi. The Hutu population are terrified of what some of them have done to the Tutsis, and they're fleeing the country in thousands.' Matt paused so that Stephi could assimilate the information before carrying on. 'You know my father used to work for a charity, *Children First*?'

'I thought he'd retired?'

'Yes, he did, but he still does quite a bit of fund-raising for them. He's trying to organise a high-profile aid campaign for Rwanda now, before the problem gets any worse. That's where you come in.'

'Oh?'

'I want to shoot an ad for Dad's appeal, and have you run it in *Elan*.' Matt nodded towards the framed covers on the wall. 'Something that will reach women like your readers – wealthy, professional women who can contribute in their own right, but who can also reach out to those they know with money and power. I want to actually go to Rwanda and do a fashion shoot in the middle of one of the refugee camps.'

Stephi looked wary. 'Benetton have already done the shock ad, and it backfired. People have even been put off coming into their stores by some of the ads, especially the AIDS one.'

'I don't want to shock people. I just want to make them think.'

'A kind of "If you can afford this dress, you can afford to give something" type picture?'

Matt nodded. 'We'll run it with a phone number so that people can ring in and make pledges as soon as they see the ad.'

'I take it you'd like *Elan* to provide the financial backing as well as run the campaign?'

356

'It'll only be the flights. I'm hoping to get everyone to offer their services free –'

'Matt, you were a war photographer, you can probably cope with this kind of assignment. But where do you think you'll find models and make-up girls prepared to slum it in some Rwandan refugee camp for nothing?'

Matt knew the moment Stephi started asking questions that he'd won her over. 'Luke wants to come with me as my fixer, so Kip'll be our fashion stylist. She can also do hair and make-up, so that'll save on the cost. As for the models, I thought Ellie Cassidy –'

'She'd be perfect. I'm sure she'd waive her fee, too. Who else?'

'Alix D'Alfonsi.'

Stephi eyed him sharply and he prayed she hadn't guessed his reason for including Alix. He'd thought of her the moment his father had telephoned him last week and asked him to shoot the appeal. It was a year since he'd last seen her, on the mountainside in Lech, and he knew she must be avoiding him. He was one of the top five fashion photographers in the world: a model as successful as Alix would normally have worked with him several times a year. She hadn't used him once.

It was his own fault – he should never have gone off with Sami. He'd been afraid of his feelings for Alix and had tried to run away from them, but that was no excuse. Sami had been badly hurt when he'd made it clear that there was no chance of a relationship, and it had ruined a friendship that had lasted eight years. He'd felt sordid and cheap, and Alix had obviously thought he was some kind of playboy who was only interested in his next conquest. He'd planned to apologise and explain how he felt the next time he saw her, but she hadn't given him the chance. He hadn't been able to open a magazine without seeing her face, but the closest he'd come to her was the catwalk. He'd juggled his schedule to fit in with hers, trailing her around Paris, Milan and New York, yet he'd never even had a moment with her. He'd tried to forget her again with other women, but still without success. The more she eluded him, the more he wanted her.

He left Stephi's office knowing the *Children First* appeal was his last chance. He was counting on Alix not being able to refuse to do the shoot with him if it was for charity. If he failed this time, he would have lost her for ever.

Eight

Nairobi Airport, Kenya
Sunday 24 July 1994
9.30 a.m.

'Would Ms Kip Tambo, just arrived on flight BA 069 from London, please come to the airport information desk. Ms Kip Tambo to the airport information desk.'

Kip stopped re-lacing her shoe and glanced up at her husband. 'Shit. What do you suppose the problem is now?'

'I hope they haven't cancelled the plane to Bujumbura,' Luke said. We'll never get a flight out of Nairobi today if they have.'

'I thought your friend Ngome had fixed it –'

Luke nodded. 'He has. But this is Africa. Things don't stay fixed for long. I'd better change some dollars while you try to sort it out.'

Kip sighed, shouldered her canvas tote bag and edged her way through the crowds thronging the arrivals hall. A cluster of Arab women were crowded around the information desk, complaining and gesticulating towards the luggage carousels. Kip forced her way between them, ignoring several sharp digs in the ribs, and slammed her bag on the desk. 'Excuse me –'

A Kenyan official held up his hand, palm outwards. 'Wait.' He pulled a flexible metal microphone towards him and pressed a button at its base. 'This is the final call for Ms Kip

Tambo, just arrived on Flight BA 069 from London, to come to the airport information desk –'

Kip brandished her passport. 'I *am* Kip Tambo.'

The official yelled something to his companion, who was still trying to placate the screaming Arab women around him, then lifted the hinged flap of the desk and eased his ample belly around it. 'OK. You come with me now.'

Kip fought down her impatience and followed the Kenyan as he led the way outside on to the tarmac apron. She saw a group of shirtless baggage handlers heaving suitcases on to a conveyor belt leading into the main building, their ebony backs gleaming with sweat. The tarmac shimmered in the heat. Her throat felt parched, and her cotton shirt was already sticking to her skin. She felt the sweat begin to trickle down between her breasts and wished she'd thought to bring a bottle of water out here with her. This was the first time she'd ever been to Africa, and although Luke had warned her about the heat, she'd never expected anything like this. Even the faint breeze ruffling her hair was warm, like the air from an open oven.

She wished now that she'd stayed in New York with Matt Jnr instead of leaving him with her sister, but Luke had so much wanted her to come with him that eventually she'd given in. Ever since they'd had Matt eighteen months ago, Luke had been obsessed with returning to his roots, showing her where they came from. He said they were cheating their son of his heritage. Kip found it difficult to sympathise. Matt Jnr was American. Luke himself hadn't been home to Rwanda since his parents had died nearly twenty years ago. She couldn't see why it suddenly mattered so much.

The Kenyan official pointed to the conveyor belt. 'Can you identify these for me, please?'

Kip watched two black bin liners filled with coat hangers sail past, brightly coloured silks trailing behind them like the

360

tails of a kite. It took a few moments for the penny to drop. 'Those are my clothes! Shit, where's my fucking suitcase?'

The Kenyan stared as she raced across the tarmac.

'Stop the bloody carousel!' Kip shouted, shoving her way past the bemused baggage handlers and leaping on to the moving conveyor belt.

'Miss, mind your head –'

Kip just had time to duck as the conveyor belt trundled through a narrow gap in the wall and into the main airport building. She leaped off the carousel, angrily dragging the plastic bags after her and emptying them on to the floor in front of her husband. 'Look at this!'

Luke picked up a wisp of pale blue chiffon smeared with oil and stared at it in disbelief. 'What the hell happened?'

'That's Africa for you,' Kip said.

Her husband shoved the chiffon back in the bag. 'We'll never get replacements. I daren't even think how much this is going to cost us. Some of these garments are catwalk originals. How many of them are damaged?'

'About half, I think.'

'That many? Can we shoot round them?'

'We're going to have to.' She glanced at her watch. 'What time did you say the others are due in?'

'Matt and Ellie's flight gets in from New York in about half an hour. Alix is coming from Rome, but she shouldn't be far behind. You'd better go on to the hotel and see what you can do to clean up the outfits that aren't damaged. I'll wait for the others and catch you up.'

Kip shoved the clothes back into the plastic bag. 'OK. Catch you later.'

Luke nodded absently as he watched her go. He knew Kip wasn't happy about being here, but there were too many other thoughts crowding his head for him to pay her much attention. Rwanda was his home, even though it was so long since he'd been back. The last time there'd been a crisis like the one that was facing Rwanda now he'd been about six or seven. His parents had done their best to protect him from the horror, but the memory of the bodies lying by the roadside, the famine and deprivation that had followed the bitter civil war, had stayed with him. He could understand why Kip hadn't wanted him to come back, but he wished she could see why he felt he had to. It had been a long time since he'd been home, but he was still Rwandan.

'All alone?'

Luke jumped. 'Ellie! I didn't think your flight was due for another twenty minutes. Is Matt with you?'

'He was.' Ellie glanced behind her. 'I think he's got held up with customs, trying to get his gear through. He shouldn't be long.'

'Shit, I hope not. We've got enough problems already –' He saw her look of enquiry. 'Some of the clothes for the shoot got mangled in transit, God knows how. Kip's back at the Norfolk Hotel now trying to salvage what she can before we have to head off to Bujumbura.'

Ellie felt a sick stab of pain at the mention of Luke's wife. She'd told herself on the plane that she was over him, but just being near Luke again had instantly reopened the wound. She should never have agreed to this. She'd managed to avoid Luke for nearly two years, but when Matt had begged her to come on this assignment, she hadn't been able to refuse. *Children First* had saved her life once. This was the least she could do.

She wished Matt would hurry up and get through customs. She didn't want to be alone with Luke so she headed over to the luggage carousel that had been assigned to her New York flight, relieved to have an excuse to get away from him for a few moments so that she could pull herself together.

She'd stopped taking cocaine after the overdose that had

362

nearly killed her; not because she was afraid of dying, but because she'd finally realised that the drugs couldn't help her escape from herself. She'd refused to check into a detox clinic or go into therapy, determined to overcome her addiction on her own. She'd partly succeeded. But without the drugs, the lovers, the wild parties, she was now facing how little else she had in her life. She had no family, no roots, no home. She'd been on her own for so long that she was frightened she didn't know how to share herself with anyone else now. She'd been taught in a hard school. She'd be twenty-eight years old in a few days, she was beautiful, rich, successful, and she felt as if her life was over.

She was relieved when she saw Matt walking towards her, and heaved her suitcase off the carousel.

'Is my gear through?'

Ellie shook her head. 'Haven't seen it.'

'Shit.' Matt scanned the information board. 'They said it had gone straight through. I'm going to check out the other carousels, just in case.'

He walked the length of the terminal building, scanning the spooling conveyor belts for the distinctive silver boxes that contained his photographic equipment. Reaching the last carousel, he spotted them just disappearing on the conveyor belt through the hole in the wall that led back outside. He sprang over a heap of unclaimed suitcases and started pulling his equipment off the carousel before it vanished altogether. As he did so, he realised that a second pair of hands was helping him shift the heavy boxes and turned to offer his thanks.

He stopped, startled. 'Alix!'

She smiled hesitantly. 'I thought you might need a hand.'

'I do, but be careful. Some of these boxes are very heavy.'

'It's OK, my nails won't break.'

'No, but my camera will.'

'Perhaps I'd better leave you to it. I wouldn't want to cause any damage.'

'Do you have to be so bloody sensitive?'

The words were out before he could stop them.

Alix put down the box she'd been carrying and walked away without a word, fighting to control her anger. She was determined not to let him get to her this time, but they'd barely exchanged three sentences before they'd been arguing. She should never have let Angela talk her into accepting this assignment. Ever since Matt had gone off with Sami in Lech she'd managed to avoid him, refusing any booking that came up with him as the photographer, no matter how prestigious. She knew the moment she came near Matt again all her old confusion would surface. She should have stuck to her guns and stayed away, but she'd talked herself into thinking she was over him. She'd been so busy working she'd barely had time to breathe, let alone think about a man who'd done nothing but make a fool out of her.

Almost as soon as the Après campaign had appeared in the press, Alix had been plunged into a breakneck schedule of planes, deadlines, early mornings and twenty-hour days as Angela had finally decided it was time to start using her. Alix wanted success – she needed it if she was ever going to realise her dream of financing her own design label – but she hadn't expected to find herself so exhausted at the end of each day that she was unable even to work on her design portfolio in private. She could have coped better with the punishing schedule and lack of sleep if she'd enjoyed what she was doing, but she was missing her work at Pavesi, much more than she had ever thought she would.

It was no wonder Matt had no respect for her. He'd seen her give up her talent to become yet another girl using her looks to claw her way up the ladder.

Now Alix realised that she hadn't stopped thinking about

Matt at all. For the last year she'd just pushed her feelings to the back of her mind and filled the vacuum they'd left with work. If she was honest, she had to admit she'd only accepted this assignment because it had given her the excuse she'd needed to see Matt again. She should have stayed away. She'd only been with him five minutes and already she was feeling rattled and self-conscious.

Her heart sank as she reached customs. She'd made her bed, and she was going to have to lie in it.

The travel-weary party landed in the capital of Burundi, Bujumbura, twelve hours later, just as darkness was falling. Ngome, Luke's friend and their minder, slid into the driver's seat of the dilapidated minibus that would take them overland to Goma, the border town between Rwanda and Zaire where more than a million Rwandan refugees had fled from the civil war that was tearing their country apart. They travelled through Burundi as fast and as silently as possible under cover of darkness, both Ngome and Luke unwilling to test their slightly questionable documentation with any of the ad-hoc militia who roamed the road leading north to Zaire. They'd been reluctant even to use their headlights, but the rutted dirt road had left them with little choice if they weren't to end up upside down in a ditch.

'Shit! Checkpoint ahead,' Luke muttered suddenly.

Ngome glanced at the wooden pole propped across the road on two oil cans, then peered through the cracked plastic of his dashboard to look at his mileometer. 'Should be the Zairean border. We've come about the right distance.'

'It's the border, all right. Look at the uniform those two soldiers are wearing.'

Ngome slowed the minibus and stopped a few metres in front of the checkpoint. 'They'll want dollars if we're going to make Goma before dawn.'

He pulled a wedge of money from the glove compartment and climbed out. Kip shifted peevishly on her uncomfortable plastic seat, slapping her wrist as a mosquito landed on her skin. 'I wish we could've flown straight to Goma from Nairobi. I didn't realise we were going to have to travel overland into Zaire.'

'There are too many Aid Agency flights into Goma at the moment.' Luke sounded irritable. 'They're having to circle for hours before they can land as it is. We'd never get a landing slot. I've told you this already.'

'You have not,' Kip snapped. 'Do you think I'd have come if I'd known?'

'Do you think I'd have asked you if I'd known you were going to be this petty?'

There was an embarrassed silence. Kip smiled tightly at no one in particular. 'That's what fourteen years of marriage does for you.'

Ellie stared out of the window at the African dusk, trying not to hate the woman sitting next to her. She felt as if she would have given the rest of her life for fourteen hours alone with Luke, never mind fourteen years. She wondered what it must be like to feel the security of knowing yourself loved. Kip had parents, a child, friends and family as well as Luke. Ellie felt the envy well up inside her.

Ngome swung himself back into the driver's seat and restarted the engine as the two guards ran to pull the wooden pole and oil cans out of the way.

'How did you manage that?' Matt asked.

'I told them I had to get to Zaire to bury my grandmother. They seemed very sympathetic, particularly after I showed them my documentation –' Ngome's teeth glowed against his dark skin as his face split into a wide grin. 'The green kind with pictures of Benjamin Franklin on them.'

Once they'd crossed the border, the rough road continued

as before, over mile after mile of huge flat African plains, the intense darkness relieved only by the pale yellow glimmer of their own headlamps. Despite the discomfort as the minibus jolted over the potholes and ruts in the road, the others soon fell asleep as Ngome drove on through the night. Luke stayed awake, staring silently out into the black night.

Dawn broke, the savage and magnificent beauty of the African sunrise reflected in Lake Kivu. Its clear waters gave no hint of the death and disease haunting its sandy shores.

Luke squinted at a low, hazy brown cloud in the distance. 'What's that? Looks like some kind of storm.'

Ngome's voice was expressionless. 'It's not a storm. Those are the refugees.'

Luke knew that in the past few weeks, a million Hutu Rwandans had fled their homes in terror from the Tutsi tribe advancing west across the country, and were now camped out in makeshift tents in Goma with no food or sanitation. Thousands of refugees were dying every day from cholera and dysentery in the camps. Aid agencies and American and French troops were working desperately to provide food and clean water, but it was a battle they were destined to lose. Luke and his team stared at the terrible vista, unbelieving. As far as the eye could see, the flat plains around the lake were filled with people, clustered on the barren, unforgiving volcanic rock that offered neither shelter nor food. The shores of the lake were invisible as people crowded the water like ants, their thirst too desperate for them to care about the risk of cholera. Many people were just sitting quietly beside the road. Children wandered through the crowds, crying for their mothers, and teams of skeletal labourers sweated in the early morning sun as they threw corpse after corpse into mass burial pits.

'I'm not sure I can cope,' Kip whispered.

'We have to try,' Alix said calmly. 'It's the only way we have to hand that we can help them.'

Nine

Alix stepped under the shower and turned her face up into the spray, gasping with shock as the cold water hit her. Slowly she began to soap her body, gratefully washing away the dirt and grime of the past seventy-two hours, suddenly acutely aware of the simple pleasure of being clean. Eventually she stepped out and wrapped a fluffy white towel around her body, savouring the fresh smell of soap and shampoo. A wicker basket filled with tropical fruits lay on the table next to her bed, and she picked up a guava and took a huge bite of pink, fleshy fruit. After the dried food and biscuits they'd been living on for the past three days, it tasted ambrosial.

She threw open the windows, breathing deeply as the heady fragrance of frangipani flowers and the Kenyan night filled her room. July was the African low season, and the elegant old hotel was almost deserted, many of its wooden chalets overlooking the hotel gardens closed for the summer. The paved paths leading towards the central lobby were half overgrown with grass, the outdoor tables and chairs neatly stacked beneath the hotel veranda. It had been raining, and the gentle breeze that ruffled the curtains carried with it the heady

369

scent of rich earth and vegetation. Alix leant on the window-sill and listened to the sounds of the African night, staring up at the dome of darkness studded with stars. Standing here, it was hard to believe the horrors that lay just a day's journey away. She felt utterly miserable and drained – by the terrible cruelty and suffering, by the wearying journey, and by the stress of being so close to Matt again.

After their argument at the airport, she and Matt hadn't spoken a word to each other for the entire journey from Nairobi to Goma. As Ngome had driven the minibus through the night, she'd been too aware of Matt's presence beside her to be able to sleep at first. The few inches of plastic seating between them was a no man's land neither of them could bridge. She'd stared out of the window, her nose almost pressed against the glass, not daring to look at Matt directly but sneaking tiny glances at his reflection. It had been like picking away at a scab, painful but irresistible. Eventually, she'd fallen asleep through sheer weariness.

Some hours later she'd jolted awake to find her head pillowed on his shoulder and feeling the gentle rhythm of his breathing beneath her cheek, had known he was fast asleep. Feigning sleep herself, she'd stayed motionless for an hour, breathing in the strong, male scent of him, allowing herself to imagine that this closeness was for real. Cramp had knifed her side, and pins and needless had numbed her arm and shoulder, but she hadn't moved, unwilling to surrender even a moment. She'd jerked away the moment he'd woken, angry at her weakness and too embarrassed to look at him all morning. But then they'd arrived in Goma, and her self-consciousness had taken second place to the scene that had confronted them.

It had taken Ngome two hours to reach *Children First*'s aid tent, less than half a kilometre away from Lake Kivu. They'd had to keep stopping to move the sick and dying out of the path of the minibus, forcing themselves to ignore the pleas from the hundreds of refugees pressing against the sides of the van, knowing there was nothing they could do to help. Kip and Alix had had tears coursing down their cheeks. As they'd reached the charity's tent, a tiny, bird-like woman of about sixty, dressed in stained white trousers and overalls, ran out to clear a space for them to park the minibus, clapping her hands to rouse the refugees drowsing in the shade cast by the tent.

Matt pulled back the minibus door and jumped down. 'You must be Mrs Bartholomew.'

The tiny woman had held out her hand. 'Please, call me Freda. It's a pleasure to meet you at last, Matt. Your father's told me so much about you. How is he, by the way?'

Matt had smiled. 'Resenting his age and the fact that he can't be here himself, but otherwise OK.'

'That sounds like Christopher. He never did like having to sit on the sidelines.'

'He asked me to give you this.' Matt had reached back inside the minibus and found his battered rucksack. He'd dug around in it for a few moments, then pulled out a small cardboard box. 'Morphine. He thought you might need it. I've some more at the bottom of some of my equipment boxes.'

Freda had taken the box. 'I don't want to know how you got this through customs, but thank you. We've been performing amputations without any kind of anaesthetic. This will help some of the worst cases.' She'd turned as a group of children started to swarm around the minibus. 'You'd better get on with your pictures before it becomes impossible to move.'

'Has Dad told you what we want to do?'

'Yes, he telephoned me when I was in Nairobi a few days ago.' Catching the hands of two of the children, she started to lead them back inside the tent. 'I hope it works, Matt. We need all the help we can get.'

Alix climbed out of the minibus as Luke and Kip started to unpack Matt's gear, watching as nurses wearing jeans and pink rubber gloves picked their way around contaminated diarrhoea and vomit and bloody needles. She wrapped a scarf around her face, trying to filter out the stench of sweat and excrement, but it was difficult not to vomit. Suddenly the argument she'd had with Matt seemed ridiculously trivial and she saw the risk he had taken by smuggling the morphine through Kenyan customs. No wonder he'd been afraid she'd drop one of his equipment boxes. The drugs hidden in them were worth more than gold to the people of Goma.

She'd watched as a dozen half-naked children followed Matt around the camp, their tiny hands clinging to the legs of his battered jeans so that he looked like a cross between Fagin and the Pied Piper of Hamelin. He never once shook them off or told them to go away, but stopped every so often to pick one of them up for a quick hug, letting them run their hands over his face as they curiously compared his white skin to the blackness of their own. Somehow he seemed at home in the barren, war-torn landscape; two days' stubble covered his jaw, his khaki photographer's waistcoat was damp with sweat, his boots scuffed and dusty – and Alix realised that the man she was seeing now was the real Matt Logan. He seemed so much more comfortable with himself, as if he'd suddenly rediscovered who he was, and she found herself relaxing with him. In the past, even when she'd been at her most angry, she'd been physically drawn to him, so strongly that it almost hurt; but now, for the first time, she'd actually found herself liking him as well.

Eventually Matt found the place he wanted to shoot his photographs, a small hill in the centre of a plain teeming with people, their makeshift tents stretching into the distance. Alix had changed into the dress Matt had chosen, now much the worse for wear, and picked her way carefully towards the hilltop.

As she reached Matt, a group of children ran past her,

throwing up a cloud of dry, choking dust. She started coughing as she tried to stop her eyes from streaming and causing her make-up to run.

Without speaking, Matt handed her a plastic bottle of tepid, but clean, water, and started to walk back towards his camera.

'Matt?'

He turned. 'Something wrong?'

Alix held out her hand. 'Truce?'

Matt took it. 'Truce.'

For a long moment, they stared at each other, her hand still in his. Despite their traumatic surroundings, she was acutely conscious of her fingers against his palm, her skin touching his. He was about to say something more, when Kip and Ellie arrived and they pulled apart in embarrassment. Matt retreated behind his camera, and Alix and Ellie spent the next eight hours standing in the blazing sun as he shot one roll of film after another. They hadn't had the chance to talk to each other again, but Alix hoped that their truce signalled a new beginning. She'd been wrong.

As she stood and thought about the shoot, everything she'd witnessed in the last few days, a breeze blew in through the open window, and Alix shivered. She slipped a simple white muslin dress over her naked body and raked back her damp hair from her face with her fingers. The moment they'd finished the pictures, the old strain between them had returned. On the return journey through Burundi, Matt had sat as far away from Alix as he could in the confined space of the minibus, studiously gazing through the window and barely speaking unless Luke or Ellie addressed him directly. He'd seemed withdrawn and tense, and Alix guessed he'd just wanted to get away from her once the assignment was over.

Suddenly she felt trapped by her hotel room. She didn't want to think any more, so she left the room and ran swiftly down the wooden stairs into the hotel gardens, heading towards the deserted swimming pool. She unfastened the iron gate, her fingers fumbling slightly with the rusty bolt, and darted down the steps towards the water. As she stared into the inky blackness, her senses seemed sharpened to the warm African night, the scent of the flowers in the gardens around her were more pungent, the noise of the cicadas drowned everything but the singing of her own blood pulsing in her veins. She felt a primal sense of life.

She pulled her dress over her head and stood naked once more, then dived into the water, swimming the length of the pool in a few strokes. She surfaced, her chestnut hair clinging wetly to her head, then dived again.

Finally she stopped and lay on her back and stared up into the darkness. It was useless to pretend she didn't care about Matt any more. She'd wanted him the day she'd first seen him in Giulio Pavesi's salon, and she wanted him now. She thought of him as he had been in Goma, so calm and in control, so compassionate, so strong in the face of all they had witnessed in the last few days.

She walked up the steps to the edge of the pool, the water glistening like a stream of pearls over her skin. Bending to pick up her dress, she suddenly spun round, her breath coming in gasps as she saw the tall, dark figure standing motionless by the iron gate. She held her dress against her body, her eyes locking with his.

Matt stepped forward. 'I'm sorry, I didn't mean to disturb you –'

'How long have you been standing there?' Shock made her words come out more aggressively than she'd intended.

'Only a few moments.'

'Well? Are you satisfied now? Spied on me enough?'

Matt sighed. 'I didn't know anyone else was here. Alix, do we really have to fight every time we meet? Can't we at least be friends?'

Alix's heart lurched with compassion at the hurt and exhaustion in Matt's eyes, the defeated set of his shoulders as he stood. 'I guess we could try.'

Matt smiled. 'I promise to keep a safe distance from you.'

Alix blushed. 'No, I'm sorry. It's my fault. Every time I see you I seem to say the wrong thing.'

'It's as much my fault as yours –'

She shook her head, droplets of water scattering over her thin bare shoulders. 'No, it isn't. It's mine. You seem to bring out the worst in me.'

'We bring out the worst in each other.' He moved towards her, and this time she didn't back away as he stopped in front of her. 'I wonder what our best would be like?'

Alix could feel the heat of his body through the thin muslin of the dress she was holding against herself, the electricity between them almost tangible as he moved closer. She stood motionless, terrified that if she moved or breathed she'd break the spell. Her heart hammered beneath her ribs as he bent to kiss her. As his lips were brushing hers he groaned and pulled away, slamming his fist against the iron gate in frustration. 'Oh, Alix, what are you doing to me? God knows I've tried to get you out of my mind, but I can't. I wish I could.'

She swallowed, fear and longing fighting for supremacy. Her life seemed centred on this second, on what happened next. She was twenty-four years old, and until this moment she'd never even been kissed by another man since her father. She closed her eyes. 'Please don't.'

Matt stared at her, confusion and disbelief in his eyes, and then suddenly he broke through the barrier between them, caught her in his arms and cradled her against him. 'Oh, God, Alix, have you any idea how long I've waited to hear you say that?'

He studied her face as if searching for an answer to a question he hadn't yet asked, then kissed her again, more slowly this time, his tongue slipping between her lips as he tangled his hands in her hair. Alix moaned softly as she felt his hardness press against her stomach, pulling him towards her as their kiss deepened. Her dress fell to her feet and Matt pulled away and stared at her, drinking her nakedness in with his eyes, desire darkening them as he took in her pink-nippled breasts, her slender waist, the small bush of russet hair between her thighs. He stood motionless, his breathing ragged as her hands moved lower to unfasten his Levi's and slid his jeans away from his body. They stood together without touching, so close that she could feel the hairs of his chest against her breasts, then Matt bent his head and kissed her forehead, her eyes, her cheeks, her nose, his lips moving across her skin and nuzzling the soft hollow of her throat. His fingers traced the outlines of her slender back and the gentle swell of her buttocks as his mouth sought and found her hard little nipples, then abruptly he caught her up in his arms, carrying her over to the soft lawn on the inside of the gate and gently laying her down on the grass.

'Are you sure?' he whispered. 'This is too important to get wrong. I want you to be absolutely sure it's what you want.'

'Oh, Matt, I've never been more sure of anything in my life.' She breathed in the mingled scent of desire and fresh earth and frangipani, and opened her arms to him as he moved against her, his tanned skin glowing against her own pale body as he moved over her, his hardness nudging insistently against her thighs. He held her breast in his hand, his soft dark hair silky against her throat, his tongue darting across its surface as she clung to him. His fingers probed between her legs and she shuddered as he caressed her tiny pink bud with a delicate, sure touch.

It began to rain gently as their bodies moved together in the moonlight. Alix stared up at him for a long moment as he held

376

himself up on his arms, poised between her legs. 'Oh, Matt. Don't ever leave me.'

Matt's smile was infinitely tender, infinitely soft. 'I will never leave you, Alix. I love you.'

And then he was inside her, feeling her tight, taut pleasure and following it with his own. He sensed her yield to him as he knew she had never done before, and realised for the first time how deeply he loved her. This woman was his life. He could no more imagine being without her now than he could consciously stop breathing.

He felt her shudder beneath him, the cool rain beating against his back, the rich warm earth against his legs. He could no longer tell where he ended and she began as his excitement pulsed in time with her own. She cried out as the waves of her orgasm crashed over her body, and suddenly he was part of the tide breaking against her, his own juices mingling with hers as they poured themselves into one another again and again until finally they lay spent on the wet grass.

'Oh, Matt. I never guessed.'

'Oh, Alix. You've always known.'

Ten

Matt lined the croquet ball up with a hoop four metres away, and gave it thwack with his mallet. The ball rolled smoothly across the green lawn, missing the hoop by a clear metre, and disappeared into the bushes.

'Hopeless,' Alix said. 'Four-one to me, I think.'

As she bent to position her mallet against her own ball, Matt slipped his arms around her waist and kissed her neck. Alix laughed and wriggled away. 'Nobbling the opposition isn't going to work. You're going to lose again anyway.' She hit her ball and watched complacently as it rolled neatly through the final hoop and clunked against the wooden stake on the other side. 'Five-one.'

Matt took the mallet away from her and hugged her. 'I surrender.'

Alix broke away and caught his hand in hers, leading him back towards the medieval farmhouse at the far end of the croquet lawn. 'To the victor, the spoils.'

'Strangely, I don't mind losing.'

Alix leaped nimbly over a small stream, the sun silhouetting her long legs against her dress. Matt stopped, wanting to hold the moment in his mind for ever. She was so beautiful.

378

Her eyes danced as she turned back to smile at him, her hair gleaming like gold in the sun. He could hear bees buzzing gently around the garden, the purl of the brook over the stones, the zither of crickets in the long grass curving around the pond to his right. A soft, warm breeze rolled over the Kentish Weald behind them, fluttering the curtains of the timbered farmhouse against its open lead-paned windows. Two American ladies in their mid-seventies were sitting drinking tea on a weathered bench to the side of the croquet lawn, their china cups chinking against their saucers as they chatted. In the distance, he could hear the faint murmur of Radio 4 and the clatter of crockery in the farmhouse kitchen. He watched Alix run up the first few steps of the wrought-iron fire escape leading up to their room, and knew he had never been so happy.

They hadn't been apart for a single moment in the three weeks since they'd left Kenya. They'd woken up in Matt's bed entwined around each other the morning after they'd made love in the gardens of the Norfolk Hotel, and had immediately made love again. Then they'd breakfasted on the basket of fruit in Matt's bedroom, taken the telephone off the hook, and made love for a third time. They hadn't needed to talk; their loving said everything for them. It had taken them until mid-afternoon to get out of bed. It was as if their need for each other was a physical thirst that had had to be satisfied before they could even think about anything else. Fifteen minutes before they were due to leave for the airport, Luke had hammered on the bedroom door and they'd stumbled out, laughing and giggling like teenagers, unable to keep their hands off each other.

'When did *this* happen?' Luke had asked, startled.

'About two years ago,' Matt said. 'It just took us this long to realise it.'

The five of them had been booked on a Kenyan Airways

fllight that afternoon to London, where they'd all been catching flights elsewhere: Alix had been due to travel on to Rome the next morning, Ellie had been flying to Delhi on an assignment for Gianni Versace at about the same time, and Luke, Kip and Matt had been heading on to New York a few hours later. They'd climbed into Ngome's minibus for the final trip to Nairobi airport, the others laughing and teasing Alix and Matt, who were barely able to peel apart long enough to climb into their seats. But even though she held on to him as tightly as ever, Matt had sensed Alix withdraw from him before they'd even reached the airport. She'd stopped responding to his gentle hugs, and as they'd taken their seats in the first-class section of the aircraft, she'd hidden behind the pages of a bestseller, pleading exhaustion. Matt said nothing, afraid that if he rushed her she'd shut him out altogether. Neither of them had discussed what was happening between them, or raised the subject of what they would do once they reached London: putting the magic into words might break the spell.

When the stewardesses had served dinner and dimmed the lights for the in-flight film, Alix threw down her book and turned to him.

'I don't want to go home to Rome,' she said suddenly. 'Not now, not after last night. I can't bear the thought of saying goodbye to you so soon.'

For a moment they were silent, then Matt stood up, opened the overhead locker and pulled out his rucksack. He dug around in it, extracting something Alix wasn't able to see, then he crossed the aisle and tapped Luke on the shoulder. 'Could you give these to Stephi for me?'

Luke stared at the rolls of film they'd shot in Rwanda. 'You playing hookey?'

'Something like that.'

As soon as they reached Heathrow and waved the others on

to their connecting flights, Matt stood beside Alix as she
called Angela Lindsay and told her she wanted to take a
month's break. Angela reeled off a list of prestigious
designers whom Alix would irreparably offend if she cancelled her bookings, and Alix turned to her lover, uncertainty
showing in her face. He kissed her as she took a deep breath
and told Angela she'd be in touch. When she put down the
telephone, her expression was half-defiant, half-terrified.
'OK, I've done it. What happens now?'

Matt had folded her in his arms, laughing. 'What happens
now, Alix, is that you and I –' his hand slipped beneath her
jumper and slowly started caressing her bare breast – 'get to
know each other better.'

He smiled now at the American ladies and ran up the fire
escape after Alix, thinking that they'd done exactly that.
They'd borrowed Ellie's canary-yellow MG BGT, which had
been sitting idly in a garage ever since she'd sold her mews
flat in Chelsea, opened a copy of Johansens' *Recommended
Hotels in Great Britain and Ireland* at random, closed their
eyes and selected Tanyard, the medieval farmhouse deep in
the Kent countryside where they were now staying. The fates
had guided them to one of the most beautiful places in
England. The farmhouse's half-dozen bedrooms, with their
latched wooden doors, low beams and uneven floors, looked
out over the most glorious and English views across the
Kentish Weald. Their room was on the top floor of the
farmhouse, its ceiling sloping down to meet the walls, its lead-
paned window so low that they could look straight out over
the pond and orchards from the wide double bed beneath it.
There was an air of peace and timelessness about the
farmhouse, as if they'd stepped outside the real world the
moment they turned into its drive and Matt had felt that here,
at last, nothing could reach them.

The past twenty days had slipped through their fingers like

pearls from a string. They'd explored the Kent countryside, visiting nearby Leeds Castle and Sissinghurst, driving over to Hever and Glyndebourne; Matt had even hired a light aircraft at Biggin Hill and flown Alix out over Dover and across the Channel. She'd been amazed to learn he'd qualified as a pilot during his years as a news photographer; he'd been equally startled to discover that she played tennis well enough to steal the much-coveted annual trophy from the regular members of a local club. There was so much to learn about each other, Matt didn't think they'd ever run out of questions for one another.

Nights had been devoted to discovering each other. Every evening, in the huge bed beneath the open window, a fresh breeze blowing across their naked skin, they'd made love. At first, the unrestrained passion which had consumed Alix in Kenya seemed to have vanished; she'd been desperately shy, insisting on the protection of darkness, reluctant to let herself go as if she'd suddenly become aware that this wasn't a dream any longer. Matt had responded to her need for patience, taking it slowly, never pushing her further than she wanted to go, reassuring her constantly that she was beautiful and loved. Gradually Alix had opened up to him like a flower in sunlight. He'd explored every part of her body, his tongue probing the soft delicate skin between her toes, his fingers stroking the cleft between her buttocks, his mouth sucking gently between her legs until she screamed his name over and over. Only when he was certain she was ready had he entered her, loving her so gently and so deeply that afterwards she'd cried quietly for hours in his arms.

It was then that she'd told him about her father. She hadn't been able to bring herself to say his name, but she'd described his visits in the middle of the night, the tainted kisses, the caresses she'd once thought were so full of love but which she'd learned were cruel and wrong. She told Matt about the guilt she felt, the terrible isolation she'd experienced thinking she was to blame. Matt had held her in his arms, kissing her tear-stained cheeks, reassuring her over and over again that it wasn't her fault, she'd done nothing wrong. Slowly, he felt she was starting to believe him. Every time he looked at her, he thought he couldn't possibly love her more, and yet each time he did.

He stopped at the top of the fire escape, gazing out across the rippling fields of grass and corn. It was their last day here together: tomorrow he had to return to his apartment in Manhattan and collect his gear together for his trip to Bosnia. He'd finally made the decision to go back to what he knew he was meant to do, his war photography. The trip to Rwanda had crystallised all the dissatisfaction he'd been feeling with fashion work, and being with Alix had put everything into perspective. He had to do what was right for him, whatever it took.

He'd contacted his old schoolfriend, David Cameron, who was now working as an international correspondent for the television news station, International News Network, and had married another INN reporter, Christie Bradley, after a stormy courtship. David, who was based in Rome, had put him in touch with the current crop of news picture editors, who'd welcomed Matt's return with heartwarming enthusiasm.

Perhaps he could spend a couple of days in Rome with Alix and drop by and see David before going on to New York to get his gear. He ducked into their bedroom, blinking as his eyes adjusted to the lack of sunlight, and slipped his arms around Alix's waist.

'How would you like an escort home?'

Alix hugged him. 'You mean it?'

'If you can spare another couple of days for me, I can think of a few reasons to be in Rome. I'm not going to see you for a month while I'm in Sarajevo, so we might as well make the most of this.'

'Oh, Matt. I can always spare time for you.'

Matt picked her up and carried her over to the bed. 'I was hoping you'd say that.'

Alix could still feel the delicious ache of Matt's love-making as the aircraft taxied to a halt at Rome's Fiumicino airport. She gazed out of the window, unable to believe that just four short weeks ago she'd left this same airport alone. Now she was returning with Matt.

Happiness spread through her limbs like warm water. She'd never even dreamed that this feeling existed, that loving and being loved could make you so content. Matt was the first person who'd ever made any attempt to know her, who'd seen who and what she was and found it worth loving. She'd been able to talk about her father for the first time in her life, and it had been like releasing a dam. She hadn't told him who her father was; there seemed no need for Matt to know his name. It was part of her past now. Matt was the future, and that was all that mattered.

They gathered up their bags and left the plane, shedding their jackets as the August heat hit them. It was a relief to reach the icy air-conditioning of the terminal building. They collected their luggage and walked briskly through customs. As they emerged into Arrivals they were met by a barrage of camera flashes and microphones as a horde of journalists surged towards them shouting questions.

'Signorina D'Alfonsi, is it true that you and Matt Logan are going to get married?'

'Matt, would you say you're an item?'

'Signorina, are you pregnant?'

'Alix, we hear that you're going to give up modelling so

that you can spend more time with Matt. Can you confirm that?'

Alix turned to Matt incredulously. 'How on earth did they find out?'

'I don't think you could call us a secret,' Matt smiled. 'You are one of the most photographed women in the world. I suppose it was only a matter of time before the paparazzi found out where we were.'

'But how did they know we'd be arriving here, today?'

'Angela probably told them.' He took her arm to guide her through the throng of journalists. 'She's never been one to pass up a chance of some good publicity. I'm sure she was behind that piece about us that Dempster ran in his column last week. I wouldn't worry about it.'

'I'm not. I don't really mind who knows about us, I'm just surprised they found us so quickly –' She broke off, unable to continue.

Matt was bending over their suitcases and missed the stunned expression on Alix's face as she saw the woman sitting on a plastic seat just beyond the customs barrier. Of all the people she'd expected to see waiting for her here, her mother was the last.

Joanna Cerreni stood up and smoothed the soft, pink tweed of her Chanel suit over her knees with pale, manicured fingers whose nail varnish was the same precise shade of baby pink. Her high-heeled Jimmy Choo shoes were the correct fraction darker and the pearls at her wrist and throat glowed creamily against her skin. She'd had her waist-length blonde hair cut in a style Princess Michael of Kent had later copied, and it gave her fine-boned face a delicacy and shape that belied her age. Her daughter was the international model, but Joanna, at forty-six, was still one of the most beautiful women in the world.

Alix felt sick as the woman she hadn't spoken to for eight

years walked towards them. In all that time she'd neither expected nor wanted to see her mother again, nor did she now. Instinctively she shrank against Matt.

Matt sensed her panic. 'Alix?' He spotted the woman walking towards him, and Alix felt her stomach clench and beads of sweat formed on her forehead as she saw the flicker of recognition in his gaze. His arm encircled her shoulders, but his eyes were on Joanna.

Joanna stopped in front of him, ignoring her daughter, a triumphant light in her blue eyes as she leant forward and kissed his cheek.

'Hello, Matt.'

Book Four

One

Piazza Capranica, Rome, Italy
Wednesday 23 November 1994
12.30 p.m.

'Alix, please, don't hang up –'

Alix felt the blood pulsing in her ears as she heard Matt's voice for the first time in three months. She gripped the receiver so tightly her knuckles whitened, her breathing so shallow she was unable to reply.

'Alix, won't you at least talk to me?'

Finally she found her voice. 'There isn't any point, Matt. It would only make things worse.'

'How do you know until you try? Alix, you haven't spoken to me for months, you haven't returned my calls, you haven't accepted my letters, you won't see me –' He paused, and when he spoke again she could hear his voice breaking up. 'What do I have to do to convince you that I love you?'

'Forget me, Matt. Go and find some nice, uncomplicated girl –'

'Alix, I don't *want* anybody else! Please, don't throw everything away because of something that happened years ago. I love you. I thought you loved me.'

Her eyes filled with tears as she replaced the telephone receiver. She knew it wasn't his fault. It had all happened nearly twenty years ago. He'd been barely sixteen when

389

Joanna had seduced him; if Alix was going to blame anyone, it should be her mother. Matt hadn't even known that she and Joanna were related. She'd never quite got round to telling him her real name; somehow, at Tanyard's it hadn't seemed important. Her life had begun when she'd met Matt, and nothing that had happened before then had seemed to matter. She'd tried to tell herself that the same applied to Matt when she'd discovered that he and Joanna had once been lovers. He hadn't betrayed her or been unfaithful, he hadn't even tried to keep it secret, he just hadn't known it would be of the remotest significance. And yet, every time she closed her eyes, she saw her mother's pale, slim, predatory body in his arms.

Matt had followed her when she'd fled from the airport in tears, trying to explain. She let him hold her as the taxi sped towards her apartment, but that evening, when he tried to kiss her in bed, she froze. She heard Joanna's cool, bitter laughter echoing in her head. In one moment her mother had snatched away all the confidence it had taken Alix so many years and so much effort to build up. Joanna had stolen the one precious thing in her life and reduced her to an ugly, unloved child again. Nothing Matt said or did now could change that, however much she wanted it to.

Matt had left the next morning. He hadn't wanted to go, but she'd insisted, telling him she needed some time to be alone. She'd watched him walk out of her apartment, knowing he'd never come back. When he'd returned from Sarajevo a month later, she got Angela to send her on one assignment after another that took her as far as possible from Rome. Matt repeatedly tracked her down, but she refused to take any of his calls and returned all his letters unopened. He'd only managed to reach her today because she'd come home unexpectedly after a booking with Yves Saint Laurent was cancelled and she'd forgotten to switch on the answering machine. She'd picked up the telephone without thinking.

In the last three months she'd learned to live with pain, blocking it out with work and cramming her days with so much activity she didn't have time to think. But at night she lay tossing and turning in bed, longing for Matt's arms around her.

She jumped as the buzzer on her intercom sounded. No one except Angela knew she was in Rome. She'd only got back yesterday evening –

The buzzer squawked again and Alix uncurled from the sofa, dashing the tears away from her eyes with one hand. She pressed the intercom. 'Yes?'

'Alix Cerreni?'

Her voice was wary as she heard her old name. 'I think you have the wrong apartment –

'Alix, it's Stephi.'

'Stephi! What are you doing here?'

The intercom crackled. 'Alix, could I come up to your apartment? I don't want to discuss it from down here.'

Alix opened the door before Stephi had a chance to knock, and just stared at her. She hadn't spoken to her father's former mistress in twenty years, but she'd seen her from a distance at a number of showbiz parties and product launches since she'd been modelling. She wouldn't have recognised the woman in front of her now. Stephi seemed to have aged a decade overnight. Her rich hair was heavily threaded with grey and her eyes red and swollen as if she'd been crying for days; deep lines scored the skin on either side of her mouth.

'Stephi, what is it?'

When Stephi spoke, her voice was raw with pain. 'Alix, it's your father. He – he asked me to come to you. He wants to see you.' Her eyes filled with tears. 'Please, Alix.'

Alix stared stupidly at the older woman. 'Stephi, I haven't seen my father for eight years –'

'I know. But he's sent me to ask you. He's dying, Alix.'

Stephi watched as Alix grabbed a jacket and locked her apartment, her face drawn as she followed Stephi down the stairs to the taxi waiting outside. She understood the shock Alix was experiencing. She'd felt the same herself only twenty-four hours earlier. Already it seemed like years.

She'd been half asleep when she answered the telephone to Roberto yesterday morning. She'd been so stunned to hear his voice on the other end of the line she hadn't been able to speak for several moments. When she'd finally pulled herself together, she'd crept out of the bedroom without waking Angela and taken the call in her study. His voice was so papery and weak that she could barely hear him. Even when he'd told her he was in hospital with kidney failure, she'd been too shocked for it to register. She'd told him she was coming and put down the telephone without even thinking what she'd say to Angela. Roberto needed her. That was all that mattered. He needed her and she would go to him.

The thought had sustained her through Angela's furious demands for some sort of explanation, through the frenzied packing, the drive to the airport, the ten-hour flight, the journey to the hospital. It had kept her going right up to the moment she'd walked down the San Giovanni hospital corridor and peered through the porthole window in the door to Roberto's hospital room. He'd seemed so old and frail, lost in the starchy white folds of sheets and pillows. She had always pictured him as the vital, larger-than-life lover of her youth. Now he seemed dwarfed by the sterile emptiness of the room. His bed was surrounded by the paraphernalia of illness – a kidney-shaped dish half covered by a white cloth on the bedside cabinet beside him, a glass of water next to it, the tall, sinister presence of the IV pole dripping fluids into his veins via tubes that tethered his hands to the bed.

'Do you want to go in?'

Stephi had turned to the nurse beside her. 'No. Not just yet. Perhaps when he wakes up –'

'If you're Stephi, he's been asking for you constantly,' the nurse had said, peering through the glass. 'You and his little girl. He'll want to know you're here.'

'In – in a while, perhaps …'

The nurse had regarded her sympathetically. 'It's a terrible shock, I know. Even though you know they're ill, it brings it all home to see them like that. You'll feel better in a while.'

Stephi had nodded silently and walked back into the waiting room at the end of the corridor, too shocked by Roberto's appearance even to cry. She'd stared around the tiny room, dimly registering the smell of stale cigarette smoke and the filthy carpet blotched with ancient coffee stains. She'd expected to feel many things – pity, anger, pain, sadness – but not this overwhelming sense of grief and loss. Her heart ached with what might have been.

As she passed the nurses' station on her way back to Roberto's room, she'd seen a chic blonde woman in her mid-forties walking towards her, dressed from head to toe in Chanel, a white leather Prada bag swinging gently from her shoulder. Stephi had known without needing to be told that this was Roberto's wife.

When they were level with each other Stephi had seen the absolute desolation on the other woman's face, and at that moment she realised that however much she'd loved Roberto, Joanna had always loved him more.

The woman had walked past, no trace of recognition in her eyes. Stephi had waited until the corridor was empty before pushing the door open. As she crossed the room she realised the man she had once loved so much had died a long time ago.

'Stephi. At last.'

'You only had to ask. I'd always have come.'

'I know.' There was a long silence before Roberto spoke again.

'Stephi, I asked you to come because I need you to persuade Alix to come and see me. Show her you've forgiven me, beg her to do the same. Will you talk to her for me?'

Stephi was puzzled. 'Of course, if it's what you want. But I haven't spoken to her since she was a little girl, Roberto. I doubt if she'd even remember me. Whatever your differences in the past, don't you think it'd be better if you contacted her yourself?'

'No, I can't –' Roberto broke off in a fit of coughing and Stephi waited for him to catch his breath, knowing there was nothing she could do. 'She won't listen. She wouldn't give me time to explain.'

'Roberto, what happened between you? Alix always worshipped you.'

Roberto's eyes held shame and pain. 'I did something terrible, Stephi. Something very wrong. I knew that, but I couldn't stop myself. I loved her so much –'

'Whatever it was, Roberto, it was a long time ago. It can be forgiven.'

He'd stared at her. 'You'll hate me, the same as she does. I wouldn't blame you. I hate myself.'

He'd stopped talking, and for a moment Stephi had thought he'd fallen asleep. Then he'd started again, slowly, as if the words were being forced from his lips. 'I don't know when it started. She was my little girl, but she was growing up so fast. She was a woman, too. I couldn't help myself. I loved her so much, Stephi. Too much. I didn't know how to stop.'

Stephi had stared at him in horror, suddenly understanding what he was saying. She'd wanted to run from the room, but something had held her to her seat. She saw the bitter self-loathing in his face and knew then that he'd punished himself since, a thousand times over.

And then he'd told her.

* * *

Stephi watched Alix now as she stared at her father through the porthole in his door. 'Have you – have you been to see him?' she asked without turning round.

'Not today. They told me he's too ill now to see anyone but immediate family. I thought that perhaps you might tell him I'm here –'

'You don't know what you're asking,' Alix said.

'I do.'

Alix stared at her. 'It's taken me ten years to even think of him without hating him. I'm not sure I'd be here now if it wasn't for the fact that he's dying. How can you even bear to be near him, knowing what he's done?'

'For the same reason as you,' Stephi said. 'Because I love him.'

Alix said nothing, and Stephi thought she was going to walk out. Then Alix turned towards her, her eyes bright with tears. 'When I was a child, I used to pretend that you were my mother. If only it had been true, how different everything might have been.'

The door opened and a nurse came out of Roberto's room. 'Signorina Cerreni? If you come with me, the doctor will see you now.'

Alix followed the nurse towards the nurses' station where a gaunt-looking doctor in his late forties was studying an array of charts.

'How is he?'

The doctor tried not to notice how attractive this young woman was despite her red eyes. 'Signorina, I'm afraid the prognosis is not good. Your father has acute renal failure in both kidneys. That means he is unable to process the toxins from his body, and they are slowly poisoning him. We have him on dialysis, but there is only a limited amount we can do.'

Alix clung to the edge of the nurses' station. He had told her nothing she didn't already know, but hearing it phrased in such cool, physiological terms suddenly brought it all home.

'Isn't there anything you can do? A transplant, something?'

'The chances of finding a suitable match are very slim. There are so many genetic possibilities that even within a close family unit, you could have an utterly different set of gene types –' He saw her confusion and tried to explain. 'With complete strangers, the chances of a match are even more remote. Your father is very ill. Even if we found the ideal donor in time, the chances of his coming through a transplant operation are not good. He might not even survive the anaesthetic. Then there is still the problem of rejection –'

'But it might work, mightn't it?'

The doctor nodded.

'You have to test me, Doctor. I'm his daughter. You have more hope of finding a match with a blood relative, you said so yourself. Surely I'm his best chance?'

The doctor looked at her strangely. 'I told your mother last week that her husband's only hope was a transplant and asked if you were a possibility. Of course, once she'd explained the situation –'

'Doctor, I haven't spoken to my mother once in the last eight years. Whatever you think she's told me, I can assure you she hasn't.'

Embarrassment and confusion were clear in the doctor's expression. 'I'm sorry. I thought you knew. I would never have said anything if I'd realised –' He saw it was too late to go back and desperately cast around for the right words to tell her. 'Roberto Cerreni is not your blood relative, Signorina. You can't give him a transplant because he isn't your father.'

Alix walked slowly towards Roberto's room and gazed through the window, trying to deal with the welter of emotions she felt. She'd come to her father to try to put the past behind her, to enable her to move forward free of the nightmares that had haunted her. Now she felt as if she had no past, and the thought was strangely liberating. Nothing could make what her father had done to her right, but for some reason knowing that he wasn't related to her made it seem less wrong. She realised Stephi was right. It was time to break the cycle of hatred and abuse, time to put the past behind her.

She opened the door and stood by Roberto's bedside. Whatever the biological truth, this man had been her father once upon a time. She wouldn't tell him she'd found out she wasn't his daughter. There wasn't much she could do for him, but at least she could spare him that.

She felt a sudden pressure on her hand and looked up to find Roberto's dark eyes, lucid and clear, fixed on her own. 'Alix.'

'Oh, Daddy.'

'I'm so – so thankful – that you came,' Roberto panted. 'I know I can never make up – for what I did. I don't blame you for hating me –'

'I don't hate you any more,' Alix whispered. 'I've wasted too much time grieving for the past already.'

'You can't despise me more than I despise myself. Alix – I –' Roberto broke off in a fit of coughing, blindly reaching out for the bowl on his nightstand.

The door opened and Doctor Donnatelli came into the room. He frowned when he saw that Roberto was not alone. 'Please, Miss Cerreni. Your father needs his rest –'

Alix squeezed Roberto's hand again. She stared down at him, suddenly certain that this was the last time she would ever have the chance to speak to him. She walked over to the bed, fighting years of conditioning as she bent to kiss his forehead, the first time she had willingly kissed him for more than ten years. He lay motionless, his eyes closed, his breathing painful and rasping. His skin felt soft and mossy

397

beneath her lips, every pore smelling of effort – effort to live, effort to stay alive long enough to tell her that he loved her, effort to accept the pain and the knowledge that he was about to die. She straightened up and smiled tremulously through her tears, finally saying the words she'd kept bottled inside her for so long.

'I love you, Daddy.'

Roberto heard the door shut gently behind her, and wondered if she knew how much he'd longed to hear those words.

Fernando Moreno. It all came back to him, where it had begun. They'd gone full circle. He hadn't thought about the Brazilian for years. Fernando had had something to prove that Roberto had never even begun to understand. The Brazilian had had to fight his way to the top, whereas Roberto had been given everything without even having to try. He'd met Fernando during his time in Brazil and flirted with his shady lifestyle because it had amused him. The rest of his life had been so well ordered, so respectable and dull. Fernando's set-up had been dangerous and therefore exciting. Moreno's tame priest, Father Lucio, had scoured the Brazilian *favellas* for the children of parents who couldn't afford another mouth to feed, persuading their parents to part with them for cash. Roberto had rubber-stamped the documents necessary for Fernando to export the infants to Paraguay and thence on to Europe. And Giulio Pavesi had been recommended to Fernando by Roberto himself as the person ideally placed to sound out wealthy, childless customers to whom the children could be sold. It had all been a game to Roberto. He salved stirrings of conscience with the knowledge that the children would be getting a far better life with their adoptive parents than they could ever have had at home. Roberto had never dreamed that one day it would be Fernando making the rules.

The memories overwhelmed him as sharply as if they had

happened yesterday. Again he saw Joanna standing at the bottom of the staircase of their home in Rio de Janeiro, seven months pregnant, clutching her stomach in pain and surprise as the baby had started to come eight weeks before its time. He could still smell the scent of the lilies on the tallboy in the corner of the entrance hall as she'd fainted and smashed into it and scattered them across the floor. Even now he could not bear their heady perfume. They had rushed her to hospital, where she had given birth to his son. He had lived for just three hours.

Roberto closed his eyes, heedless to the tears spilling down his cheeks as he saw again the perfect, tiny body they had shown him at the hospital, the tiny hands and feet, the minute fingernails, the long, soft eyelashes so similar to his own. He heard the echo of the doctor's voice as he told him that Joanna would never bear another child, that he should adopt as soon as possible if he wanted to save her from toppling over the edge into a twilight world from which she'd never emerge.

Roberto had known it would take years for them to complete the paperwork necessary to adopt a child in Italy. Joanna's doctor made it clear he hadn't got that long. In desperation he'd thought of Fernando. He'd gone to him and begged him to find a child they could pass off as their own, trying to ignore the strange light in Fernando's eyes as the Brazilian had realised that he had something Roberto wanted and would do anything to have.

Roberto had no idea where the baby girl had come from, but when Fernando had handed her to him three days later, he knew he couldn't have loved her more if she'd been his own. Perhaps that knowledge had been the first spark that had ignited Joanna's jealousy; perhaps it had been her pain at seeing him cradle another woman's child instead of her own. Robert knew only that he'd have given his life to protect his daughter then, and still would now. It had been for her sake that he'd continued helping Fernando even after he'd learned what they were doing at the Speretti Institute. It had been to protect Alix that he'd given up Stephi, the only woman he'd ever loved.

When he died peacefully half an hour later, his last thought was of her.

Two

Central Park South, New York, USA
Friday 2 December 1994
11.30 p.m.

Matt could still hear the main office echoing with shouts of congratulation and farewell as he slipped down the corridor towards the office that Luke still shared with his senior design assistants. Even though he'd built his costume jewellery company into a million-dollar business with over sixty outlets spread across America and Europe, Luke refused to move into the luxury suite his vice-presidents were always pressing on him in the hope that it would further their own corner-office aspirations. He maintained that the best way to run the company was from its nerve centre, where the jewellery was actually created, his only concession to his position being the fact that the office had one of the most beautiful views over the south end of Central Park that Matt had ever seen. Even in the midst of winter, the bird sanctuary was alive with movement and colour, an endless kaleidoscope of wings and water and grass just metres away from the dirt and noise of Manhattan itself.

Matt didn't bother to turn on the light as he eased his way around the shadowy outlines of the designers' desks, his eyes drifting towards the darkness outside, studded with the lights of a thousand homes and smeared with the drifting flicker of car headlamps. He knew his way around the office as if it was his own. He and Luke had collaborated on so many advertising shoots that it had become a standing joke between them that Matt should have had his own desk in the office.

He paused, glancing around the darkened room with a sudden sense of loss. In the three months since he'd gone back to news photography, he'd missed very few things about the fashion industry, but working with Luke was one of them. It was strange to return to New York now to celebrate an award he'd won for a magazine feature twelve months ago. Everything about Luke's office seemed at once familiar and alien, as if he was revisiting a street he hadn't seen since childhood. Nothing seemed to have changed, and yet there were tiny differences already that marked the time he'd been away – a new girl at the reception desk downstairs, glossy white magazine cuttings pinned over the yellowing newspaper articles he remembered on the cork board, a coffee machine that actually worked.

He felt his way towards Luke's cubicle to collect the leather jacket he'd left there earlier that evening. He didn't regret his decision for a moment. The photograph he'd taken in Rwanda had raised hundreds of thousands of pounds for his father's appeal for *Children First*. The pictures he took in places like Sarajevo could actually make a difference to the way the world reacted to a news story. He'd just been commissioned to go to a little-known Russian province, Chechnya, where there were rumours of imminent armed resistance against the Russian overlords. He knew that once he started taking pictures, Chechnya would be known to millions of people around the world.

If it hadn't been for his work, he wouldn't have been able to deal with losing Alix.

He opened the glass door to Luke's office and picked up his jacket, turning back to the darkened room without even breaking his stride. He was about to shut the door when he saw Ellie standing motionless at the window, staring down into Central Park. He put down his jacket and moved towards her, slipping his arm around her shoulder and joining her silent vigil without speaking. At last she turned towards him, her face gilded silver by the moonlight. Matt gently brushed her hair away from her forehead and smiled sadly.

'I guess the party was too much for you, too.'

Ellie turned back towards the window. 'I just needed to be alone for a while.'

Matt sighed. 'Yes, I know how you feel.'

'It's like everyone else has been invited to a party and you're just an interloper who fell through the doorway by accident,' Ellie said softly. 'There's an invisible barrier between you and the rest of the world that no one else can see. At least when you're alone you don't have to pretend any more.'

'And it would only take one person there with you to put it right,' Matt murmured.

Ellie smiled sadly. She knew Matt was thinking of Alix, but his words applied equally to her. If she had been there with Luke, nothing else would have mattered. She suddenly realised Matt probably didn't even know what had happened. 'Alix's father died last week,' she said quietly. 'The day you spoke to her.'

'I didn't know he was ill –'

'Nor did I. She telephoned me yesterday.' Ellie paused, her eyes searching his face. 'She's just found out that she's adopted, Matt.'

Matt was stunned. 'I have to go to her –'

'You can't do that, Matt. It would be too much for her to deal with right now. It's better if I go. Stephi told her that Roberto and Joanna Cerreni adopted her in Brazil, and Alix wants to go back there. I'm the best person to go with her.'

'Stephi? What does she have to do with this?'

'Stephi was Roberto Cerreni's mistress –' She saw Matt's look of disbelief. 'It was a long time ago now. Nearly twenty years. But she was the one he called when he was dying. It was Stephi who persuaded Alix to see him.'

Matt struggled to take it all in. 'Alix is going back to Brazil to trace her real parents? Is that wise?'

For a moment, Ellie didn't answer. She knew that going back to Rio was probably the most dangerous thing she'd ever done in her life, but she'd had enough of running. Her unknown enemy had been stalking her for too long. Every time she answered the telephone now she was afraid it would be him, waiting silently on the other end of the line for her to speak. So many of her letters had gone astray. And there had been the burglary, the South American face she'd been so certain she'd recognised from somewhere, although she couldn't quite place where. It had to end, one way or another. It was time she faced up to him. But she couldn't do that until she knew who he was, and there was only one place she'd find out. Brazil.

She realised Matt was still waiting for her to answer. 'It's what she wants to do, Matt. She has to come to terms with all this in her own way.'

'You will keep in touch?'

'Of course.'

Matt sighed, slipping his arm around her waist and drawing her head against his shoulder. 'Oh, Ellie. What will I do without her?'

Ellie shook her head wordlessly. Matt stared out into the darkness over Central Park. 'Still thinking about Luke?'

'I can't help it,' Ellie sobbed suddenly, burying her head in his shoulder. 'I've tried so hard to get him out of my mind, but I love him, Matt. God help me, I wish I didn't, but I do. I don't think I'll ever be able to stop.'

Matt cradled her in his arms, trying and failing to find something to say that would soothe a pain he knew was unreachable. Nothing would ever make it more bearable. You simply had to learn to go on living, to bury the pain so deep you were able to carry on despite the ache that never went away. He felt his own longing for Alix in his heart as he held Ellie, and knew that no matter how hard or how fast he ran, he could never escape. It would be with him until the day he died.

He heard a sound behind him and swung round. Ellie straightened up and dashed the tears from her eyes as he moved.

'Luke –'

Luke smiled. 'So this is where the party really is. And I thought all the best ones ended up in the kitchen.'

From the expression on his face Matt knew that Luke had been standing there long enough to have heard everything Ellie had said. He picked up his jacket and slipped past Luke into the main office without saying a word.

Luke didn't even glance at him; his eyes were on Ellie as she stood frozen beside the window. He'd always known she was beautiful, but he'd never stopped to think of her as a woman before. She'd always been something he'd admired and enjoyed looking at, like a painting or a piece of fine art, but he'd never thought of her in any more personal way. Suddenly her words had made him see her as a woman, and he realised how fucking beautiful she was. She gazed into his eyes and smiled. In that moment he wanted her just as much as she wanted him.

He crossed the room and caught her in his arms, kissing her with a passion a thousand times removed from Matt's achingly tender kiss. She felt her body respond to his touch as if he had sent a charge of electricity pulsing through her, her lips opening beneath his as her whole body became liquid in his arms. A sudden heat burned between her legs as desire shot

405

through her, her hands slipping beneath Luke's tweed jacket and under his shirt as if driven by a force of their own. Luke groaned and his back arched as she slid her hands upwards towards his shoulderblades. He kissed her fiercely, his lips biting and sucking her flesh as his mouth moved lower, nudging the soft collar of her blouse away from her shoulder and exposing one firm, high breast. Impatiently she forced his jacket over his shoulders, her fingers fumbling at the buttons of his shirt as he pushed his leg between her thighs and pressed her back against the wall. Suddenly he pulled back and ripped her shirt away from her body, gasping as he saw her half-naked before him, her skin glistening in the moonlight.

'Oh, God, Ellie, you are so beautiful,' Luke murmured, kicking off his shoes and moving towards her. 'I want you so much –'

He broke off as she smiled slowly and began to unfasten the black leather Versace jeans that sheathed her long legs. 'You were all I ever wanted.'

Luke slid his arms around her and buried his head between her naked breasts, his ebony skin gleaming darkly against her own. His hands slid down the curves of her body as he knelt in front of her, his lips moving across her stomach as he eased her jeans over her hips and down her legs, his mouth burning through the thin silk and lace of her panties. Ellie groaned and thrust her pelvis towards him, shuddering as he hooked his fingers in her panties and eased them away from her, his tongue burying itself in the black curls that crested her mound. His fingers gripped her buttocks as he thrust his tongue into her, her hands tangling in the tight mat of his hair as he found the centre of her pleasure and teased it gently with his mouth. His fingers probed the cleft between her buttocks and she felt them enter her from behind, pleasure driving at her from two directions so that she shuddered on the very verge of orgasm.

Abruptly Luke pulled away and stood up, shucking off his

trousers so that his cock sprang free, dark and turgid in the moonlight. Ellie groaned with wanting, pulling him towards her even as he laid her down on the floor beneath his desk, forcing her legs apart with his knee as he propped himself up over her, his dark eyes fixed on hers. She felt his cock nudge against her, searching blindly for her entrance, and thrust her hips up to meet it. He stared at her, and then suddenly he was inside her, filling her with his length in one swift, easy movement. She felt a deep sense of peace wash over her, then waves of desire as Luke stayed motionless within her.

'Oh, God, Luke, please –'

Luke smiled and shook his head, bending to silence her with a kiss before moving down to suck gently on her nipples, his cock huge and still within her. His tongue darted across the surface of her breasts. Finally he moved against her, a strange, sideways movement that intensified both her pleasure and her desperation. Her fingers clawed the carpet as she wrapped her legs around his waist and lifted her hips from the floor, feeling him slide a little deeper into her as she arched against him. She could see their bodies entwined in the light from the window, sweat glistening on their skin as Luke forced them to dance to the slow beat of passion she could feel gathering speed within her.

Suddenly Luke pulled out so that only the tip of his cock was still inside her, and Ellie groaned with frustration and loss. Luke laughed softly and moved inside again, and Ellie felt the beginning of a new pleasure start to ripple through her. She rocked against him as Luke withdrew almost to the edge again, then plunged back into her, a little deeper than before, repeating the slow, delicious, torturous movement again and again until she was almost screaming. Without once altering his rhythm, Luke knelt up between her legs so that he could see her body stretched on the floor in front of him. He reached for their discarded clothing and bundled it beneath her hips so that he could thrust even deeper, his cock sliding in and out of her with measured control despite the excitement she could feel pulsing beneath his skin. Ellie felt as if she were on an endless wave of pleasure, rising and falling, giving herself up to it in a sweet, exquisite gesture of surrender.

Slowly, almost imperceptibly, Luke's movements quickened, his thrusts becoming harder as he moved against her, his hands caressing her breasts as she arched towards him. Her breath came in quick, short gasps, desire flaming within her as she felt her orgasm peak, her legs gripping him tightly around his waist as she screamed his name over and over. Even as she came, she felt Luke still hard within her, his cock thrusting her beyond the point of pleasure. Her orgasm exploded like a series of fireworks blossoming in the night sky, rippling outwards from a centre that had become her whole existence.

Finally she collapsed on to the floor, shuddering slightly as her climax ebbed and flowed, feeling Luke still hard within her. Slowly he pulled out of her, cradling her body in his as she came back to him, and she lay in his arms, feeling the blood pounding beneath his skin as he held her.

She pulled away from him, twisting around and taking his cock in her mouth as he leaned back against his desk, his hands tangled in her dark hair while her mouth worked against him. Softly she tongued its tip, tasting her own musky juices and the slightly salty beads of his arousal as her mouth moved up and down the length of his cock, her fingers stroking his balls in firm, sure movements. She slid her hands down between his legs, the tips of her fingers gently probing his anus as her mouth moved in strong, knowing whorls along the length of his cock, her breasts rubbing against his thighs. She felt him shudder beneath her, his whole body growing taut as his own climax built. Her movements became more rapid, her teeth gently grazing the surface of his cock as he thrust his hips towards her. He groaned her name and arched his back, and she tasted the salty wetness of his climax as he came into her mouth.

He pulled her towards him and kissed her lips as he cradled her slender body, murmuring her name as he stroked her face and skin and hair. Even as her juices dried on his skin, he knew that he would never be able to hold her this way again. 'Oh, Ellie, Ellie. What have we started?'

Ellie buried herself in his arms, renewed desire already stirring within her as he rocked her body against his chest. 'I love you, Luke. I always have. Nothing can change that.'

He caught her head in his hands and turned her face towards him, sadness and pain mingling with the love and desire in his dark eyes. 'I have a wife, Ellie –'

Ellie touched his lips with her fingers to silence him. Slowly she moved over him and lowered herself on to him, taking his already stiffening cock in her hands and guiding him into her. 'I know. But tonight you're mine.'

Three

Islington, London, UK
Wednesday 7 December 1994
11.30 a.m.

Christie Bradley Cameron smoothed her heavy gold hair
away from her face and eased her way out from behind her
desk, grimacing as the edge of her stomach caught the wooden
top. She'd had nearly nine months to get used to the idea of
being pregnant, and still it took her by surprise. She felt as if
she was trying to manoeuvre a family-sized Volvo after
driving an MG BGT all her life. It was all very well for her
husband, David, to joke about the *Titanic* and three-point
turns, but he didn't have to steer his way around their tiny flat
unable to see anything from the waist down.

She smiled gently as she stroked her swollen belly, feeling
the child move within her. Apart from David, she'd never
imagined that anything would matter more to her than her
work as a reporter with INN. Now she couldn't imagine
anything more precious than her baby.

Christie had met David Cameron at INN nearly three years
ago. He was one of the news network's most respected
international correspondents, currently based in Rome but
with a brief that covered most of the world. They'd married
eighteen months ago and had adopted a two-year-old boy
called Sandy almost at once. His father, David's closest friend

and cameraman, had been killed on an assignment in Sarajevo when Sandy was a baby, and his mother had dumped her son in a foster home in order to marry again. Both Christie and David had tried to curtail their travelling for Sandy's sake and, secure in their love, the little boy had swiftly adjusted to the change in his life. He was the centre of their lives and, Christie knew, the new baby wouldn't change that.

Sandy would soon be home from nursery school, she thought as she picked up her notebook, her eyes skimming the words she already knew by heart. She'd been pursuing this story for nearly a year, chasing a lead she'd picked up in Buenos Aires when she'd been in Argentina the previous summer to cover the bomb blast at a Jewish community centre. In the following months, she'd travelled to some of the least accessible parts of Brazil and Paraguay trying to substantiate the rumours, but again and again she had only got so far before coming up against a wall of fear and silence. As her pregnancy had advanced, she'd been forced to conduct most of her investigations by telephone, the story still haunting her long after she knew she should have let it go. She was so certain she was close to breaking it.

In recent weeks she'd found herself returning again and again to her notes, staring at the list of names and dates and places as if she could force them to yield up what she needed to know by sheer strength of will.

She sank heavily into the armchair in front of the fire, her notebook propped on her knees. She had managed to trace the route used by the Brazilian baby-smuggling ring to Italy and from there on to the rest of Europe and the United States, impressed despite herself by its ingenious simplicity. The welfare centre run by the old priest, Father Lucio, in the Brazilian coastal town of Salvador had provided the perfect cover. No one had ever noticed that many of the baby 'orphans' he welcomed into the centre stayed just a matter of days before being adopted abroad, their departure invariably matched by substantial anonymous donations to the charity itself. Even if the connection had been discovered, there would be many who would argue that what these men had been doing had definite humanitarian merits – the babies undoubtedly had a better material chance at life in Europe or the States than in the *favellas* into which they'd been born. She'd discovered that the paperwork had originally been dealt with by Roberto Cerreni, the Italian Ambassador to Brazil from 1967 to 1970. His name had been on most of the adoption documents. She guessed he'd probably carried on pushing it through somehow when he'd returned to Italy, although she would never know for sure. She'd read in the paper that he'd died a couple of weeks ago. The only thing she didn't yet know was the identity of the mastermind behind it all.

She started as the telephone at her elbow shrilled, and picked it up. 'Christie Cameron.'

David's voice crackled over the international line. 'Darling, it's me. Just a quick call to let you know what I'm doing. I'm in Chechnya – I should make it to Moscow by tomorrow morning if the drive overland doesn't take too long. I'll have to overnight there, but I should be back in Rome by the day after tomorrow.'

'I can't wait,' Christie shouted. 'Did you get the armoured car out with you?'

'No, we had to leave it in Grozny. But don't worry, everything's fine.' He paused and shouted something to one of his companions that Christie couldn't catch. 'I have to go soon, darling, if I'm going to get to Moscow by morning. How are mother and baby?'

'I saw the obstetrician today. She says it's very mobile – just like its father. I'm still hammering away at the Rio story,' Christie said. 'It keeps me out of mischief –'

'Damn. I meant to tell you before, but I forgot. I was talking to Matt again last week – you remember his father used to work for the charity *Children First*? – and he suggested you might try speaking to a woman called Lucy Conto. Her brother ran a home for some of Rio's street children back in the early Eighties. I thought it had closed down after he was killed, but apparently Lucy took over. Matt thinks she's still there. If you look at the back of my cuttings file on Brazil, you'll find her number. I don't know if she can help you, but it might be worth a shot.'

'I'll give her a call,' Christie said, scribbling the name down in her notebook.

'Listen, darling, I have to go now. I'll be with you soon. I love you.'

'You too.'

Christie knew David would far rather she rested instead of chasing this story, but he had loved her too long to expect her to be any different. She sighed as she stood up and walked over to David's filing cabinet. The chances were that this Lucy Conto couldn't tell her anything she didn't know already, but she had a strange sense about this story. Her instinct told her there was far more to what was happening in Brazil than the baby-smuggling ring. All she needed was a name. She pulled out the file of clippings on Brazil and turned to David's notes at the back.

Perhaps Lucy would be able to give it to her.

Four

Speretti Institute, Pedro Juan Caballero, Paraguay
Thursday 8 December 1994
10.30 a.m.

Joel Aquila clutched his canvas satchel to his chest and nervously scanned the room, his sharp eyes missing nothing. His gaze flickered over the two narrow beds pushed hard against the peeling, grimy walls that were scarred with traces of old Sellotape and scraps of posters and photographs no one had bothered to remove. The scored blue linoleum was inadequately covered by a threadbare rug striped in garish shades of green and red, the barred window curtainless and forbidding. Soiled rags and blankets were piled up on the bed to his right, while the other was neatly made with worn, greying sheets and a thin woollen grey blanket. At the end of each bed stood a battered wooden chair, a pair of carefully folded pyjamas on the seat of the one nearest to him. Overhead, a single lightbulb hung naked from a coiled wire, casting strange shadows across the floor. The whole room had the faded, dismal air of an institutional waiting room whose occupants were always passing through, never staying. It was the most luxurious room Joel had ever seen in the whole of his eleven years.

He turned in alarm as he heard the bolt being shot home on the outside of the door. The doctor had already explained that they didn't like their guests to wander around until they'd had the result of the tests, just in case. He didn't feel ill, but after five years on the streets of Rio, he knew that didn't mean anything. He'd seen people who seemed perfectly well in the morning writhing in the grip of a fever by dusk, and dead less than twenty-four hours later. Cholera, dysentery, typhus. And AIDS, of course. You could never tell if you had that until it was too late. The doctor was right. It was better to be safe than sorry.

Joel's left upper arm was still bruised and sore from all the blood tests and injections he'd had, but the doctor had promised him the tenderness wouldn't last long. It would have gone by the time his new family came to collect him.

He dumped his bag on the clean bed and moved towards the window. Gripping the narrow bars, he squeezed his head between them and stared across the arid, empty red grounds of the Institute. From here, he could just see the deep green sea of the Paraguayan jungle over the six-metre-high stone wall that surrounded the Institute. It stretched as far as the eye could see, an endless emerald ocean. Along the edge of the jungle, a narrow red ribbon wound down through the hills, the only artery connecting the isolated Institute to the outside world. Joel knew without being told that anyone foolish enough to venture away from the road was unlikely ever to make it back. The jungle provided a far better deterrent to invaders than the guards patrolling the stone wall with their snub-nosed Uzi sub-machine-guns. Joel was bright for his eleven years; he wondered why such high security was necessary. The doctor said that some of the more superstitious peasants in the village of Pedro Juan Caballero at the foot of the hills believed the Institute was wicked, a nest of devils that would destroy them all. The guards and the wall and the arc-lights and security cameras were just to keep them at bay. It seemed a lot of trouble to go to because of a few foolish, frightened villagers.

Suddenly the bundle of rags on the other bed moved.

Joel stared at them, his eyes wide in his pale face. The doctor had dismissed the villagers as superstitious peasants, but what if they were right after all? What if this place was a nest of devils, or something worse? What if he'd been shut in here with something that wasn't human or – oh God – not even alive?

Frantically he looked for some means of escape. The window was barred, the doors locked. There was no way out. Whatever was in here with him, he would have to deal with it alone.

His heart pounding with fear, Joel stopped a metre from the edge of the bed, reached out and tugged the nearest edge of the rags. The small figure curled tightly on the bed didn't move. Joel felt relief flood through him: he wasn't dealing with the supernatural. Gingerly he poked the still form in the ribs and the child flinched and curled itself even tighter, drawing its legs up to its chest and encircling its bare knees with both arms. It was human and it was alive. That was enough for Joel.

He sat down on the edge of the bed and prodded the child again. 'Who are you?'

The child didn't move. Impatiently, Joel shook its shoulder. 'What are you doing, hiding under all those blankets and stuff? You scared me. I didn't realise anyone else was going to be here. I thought it was just me.'

'Usually they do leave you alone, the first night, anyway. They just didn't find the right person for me yet.'

'You mean they haven't found a family for you?'

The child sat up and swung his legs over the edge of the bed to face Joel. He was much older than Joel had first thought, perhaps eleven or twelve, and despite his obvious malnourishment, at least as tall as Joel himself. He wiped his wrist against his nose, which was swollen and red from crying, and stared at Joel defiantly. 'A family? Is that what they told you?'

Joel frowned. 'Of course. They brought me here, they gave me food, what other reason could they have?'

'You don't want to know.'

Joel felt the first stirring of alarm. 'Is there something the matter? Don't they want you after all?'

'You really haven't any idea?'

The boy rested his cheek against his knees and closed his eyes. 'They told you this was an adoption centre, right? An illegal adoption centre for people in Europe who aren't able to adopt the children they want there, but have enough money to buy a baby from somewhere else. That's why it has to be kept secret.'

'The doctor said lots of the people had plenty of money, but they were too old or too sick to be allowed to adopt children,' Joel said. 'And they don't all want babies, they want older children, like us, especially boys. Children who haven't got a home or family. Street kids no one will miss –'

'Oh, no one will miss us, all right. That's the whole point.'

'Look, if you're worried that you won't find a family, you needn't be,' Joel said reassuringly. 'The doctor said it sometimes takes a while. They need to make sure they've found just the right people for us –'

'Oh, there's a good trade in babies,' the boy said. 'That's how it all started, years ago. And it's true, they do still sell a few to desperate people who'd give anything for a child of their own. But do you really think anyone wants us? We're almost teenagers, we've been on the streets for years. We're pickpockets and thieves, vermin. Who'd take us in for free, let alone pay for us? Look outside! That wall, those guards, the guns, the watchtowers, the lights – the bars on the windows, the bolts on the doors. Do you really think that's to keep people out? Isn't everything on the wrong side? Shouldn't the guards be outside the walls?' He whirled round to face Joel, his eyes blazing. 'Isn't all this here not to keep them out, but to keep us *in*?'

Joel stared at him. 'But why? Why would they do all that if they didn't want us?'

'They want us, all right,' the boy said. 'They want to sell us, but not to families desperate for a child.'

'I don't understand –'

'They want our bodies, not us. They want our kidneys, our livers, our hearts, our lungs. We're no more than living, breathing spare parts. And they keep us here until they find a buyer who matches us and is prepared to pay the price. If they don't ask too many questions and if they sign enough cheques, they receive a little gift from the Speretti Institute. Made to measure.'

Joel felt the heat of terror sear through him as he stared at the boy and knew that he was right. 'No. That can't be it. It can't be true –'

'You don't have to believe me. Wait and see for yourself. Wait until Doctor Rochas comes back. Ask him about Judge Fernando. Ask him about Father Lucio. See how long you live after that.'

Joel was wakened from his fretful, exhausted sleep by water dripping on to his face. He sat up, startled, his eyes straining into the darkness. Directly overhead he saw a small iron plate, one corner peeling away from the ceiling and dark with rust. Joel rolled over on to his side as another bead of water dripped on to the bed, trying to block out the thoughts that filled his mind every time he closed his eyes.

His fear had taken him beyond panic, clearing his mind of every thought but the need to find a way out of this trap. He couldn't escape from the window – even if he'd been able to fit through the bars, he was four floors from the ground. Nor could he break down the door, which was solid iron and bolted

418

against him. His only chance lay in slipping away when they let him out for meals or to go to the bathroom. He'd worry about how to get out of the Institute once he'd got out of this room.

If he could just get back to the loading bay where he'd been delivered, perhaps he could get out the same way he'd got in – in the back of a truck. Once they'd reached the village, he'd find someone to hide him, try to get back into Brazil. Maybe he'd even make it back to Rio, hide out in the streets, or go to the woman who ran the charity that had helped him once before. Lucy Conto, that was it. He'd heard her brother had been murdered a long time ago, trying to help the street kids. She'd understand, she'd know what to do. He'd have to trust her.

If he ever got out of this place alive.

Another splash of water hit his pillow and suddenly he realised how stupid he'd been. Leaping off the bed, he ripped the mattress away and grabbed one of the wooden chairs. Working as quickly as he dared, he shoved it into the iron springs of the bed and stood on it, clutching the wall for support as the chair wobbled precariously. If he stretched, he could just reach the iron plate above his head. His fingers made clumsy by nerves, he grabbed the corner of the plate that was peeling away from the ceiling and pulled. It didn't move. Almost crying with frustration, he put his whole weight against the plate and suddenly felt it give beneath his fingers. The chair swayed, then toppled slowly on to its side, sending Joel crashing to the floor. He froze, waiting for the footsteps echoing down the corridor, the shouts of discovery.

Everything stayed quiet. His heart pounding, Joel put the chair back where it had stood and replaced the mattress. He shoved a few of the other boy's rags under the blanket and tried to shape them into the outline of a child's body. They wouldn't fool anyone who came right into the room, but if someone just looked from the doorway, it might buy him a little time.

Briefly he debated waking the boy, then decided he'd have a better chance on his own. He climbed on to the bars of the window and stood on the iron bedstead, reaching for the narrow gap exposed by the metal plate and praying he'd fit through it. He cursed as he found that he couldn't quite reach it. He'd have to jump. Mentally he counted to three, then threw himself towards the hole, hanging there as he scrabbled to find a purchase on the wall and haul himself up. He managed to get his head through the gap, fighting back tears as he tried to force his shoulders through. He wasn't going to make it. The gap was too small, he was never going to fit –

Suddenly he was through. He shoved his bottom backwards and reached down for the metal plate, still hanging from one side of the gap. He pulled it into place, and was plunged into darkness. He felt around, trying to decide which way to go. It was a sort of tunnel, perhaps a metre square. His room was the last in the corridor, which meant that there was only one way he could go if he wanted to get back above the main part of the Institute. He started to crawl along the floor, ignoring the pain in his hands and knees as his skin scraped against rough metal. Every ten metres or so he passed a small meshed window in the floor and peered through it, trying to gauge how far he'd come. The air-conditioning duct branched off a number of times, but Joel kept going, guessing that he had a better chance of finding a way down to the loading bay if he stuck with the main tunnel. He could get lost for ever if he disappeared into the maze of passageways on either side.

Suddenly he smelt the stench of gasoline, and looked down to find himself directly above the loading bay. He almost cried with relief as he saw the truck standing deserted in the garage. If he could only get on board before someone came.

Quickly he worked at the metal plate covering the duct that

420

ended in the garage ceiling, praying that it would come loose. He felt it give and gingerly eased it away, his heart pounding. He waited, his ears straining for sound, then dropped to the floor, skidded towards the truck and threw himself underneath it, his breath sounding so loud in his chest he wondered why the whole building couldn't hear it. Forcing himself to count slowly to a thousand, he eased his way out from beneath the truck and slid carefully under the tarpaulin in the back. Wearily he closed his eyes, fear and shock suddenly catching up with him. If he could just get safely to the village, get back to Rio, reach Lucy, she'd figure out some way to stop it.

He was asleep by the time the engine started.

Five

Avenida Presidente Vargas, Rio de Janeiro, Brazil
Monday 12 December 1994
3.30 p.m.

Fernando Moreno replaced the telephone, his hand shaking with fear and anger. The idiots! They should have told him the moment it had happened. He might have been able to do something about it then. Instead, they'd waited for four days while they blundered about trying to find the child on their own. He could be anywhere by now.

Fernando pushed his chair back from his desk and paced anxiously towards the window, trying to assess the damage this might cause. After President Collor de Mello's impeachment and resignation two years ago, Fernando was somehow managing to cling to power under his replacement, Itamar Franco, but he knew he was walking a tightrope. People were tired of watching their elected representatives sucking the country dry while they endured rocketing inflation and mass unemployment. One whisper of corruption on any level would mean instant dismissal from the government, perhaps even criminal charges.

And letting this insignificant boy escape from the Institute could be all it would take.

He knew his own supporters were restless, no longer sure of their own future as Fernando's wavered. His defences were already crumbling; there were too many desperate to save their own skins for him to be able to survive much longer. It was only a matter of time before some of them decided to cash in what they knew about him in return for immunity against prosecution or a heap of dollars in a foreign bank account. If someone started to piece the jigsaw together and this boy started talking....

Fernando opened his filing cabinet, reaching behind the neglected paperwork for the quarter-full bottle of Glenfiddich at the back. He poured himself three fingers of Scotch and replaced the bottle, his confidence returning as the fiery liquid hit the back of his throat.

The threat was there, but he was probably being over-cautious. The boy was almost certainly dead by now, lost or starving somewhere in the dense jungle that surrounded the Institute. Fernando drained his glass and paced back to his desk. Even if the boy *did* survive, he could probably ride out the rumours for long enough to transfer his funds out of the country and arrange his own escape from Brazil. All he needed was time.

The telephone on his desk rang and Fernando snatched it up before his secretary next door had a chance to answer it. 'Yes?'

'Massimo Luca here.'

Fernando tensed. Luca was officially Rio's Chief of Police; unofficially, he specialised in damage control: intelligence and elimination. Fernando had once counted Luca amongst his allies; these days, it was impossible to be sure of anyone. He played for time, wondering what Luca knew. 'Massimo, it's good to hear from you. It's been too long. How's your wife?'

'Fine, fine.' The Chief of Police paused, clearly not wanting to be drawn into conversation. 'You remember that girl you wanted to find a while back?'

Luca suddenly had his full attention. 'She's here?'

'Yes. She arrived at the airport last night. Her details just came up on the computer.'

'You're sure it's Ellie Cassidy?'

'Of course.' Luca sounded impatient. 'I'd had her name flagged, as you asked. You were right, she has an American passport now. Her details were processed at Immigration along with the other non-Brazilian passport holders. The information was on my desk six hours after she arrived in this country.'

'Was she alone?'

'No. Travelling with an Italian girl, Alexandra D'Alfonsi.'

The name meant nothing to Fernando. 'No one else?'

'No.'

Fernando thought quickly. Ellie Cassidy posed a greater danger than anyone else at the moment, including the boy from the Institute. When he'd first seen Ellie's picture two and a half years ago, his immediate reaction had been to kill her, but doing so might precipitate the precise scandal he'd been trying to avoid. His position had been far from secure even then. He had still had a measure of control in Rio, but he'd been uncertain of his reach beyond Brazil. He hadn't been able to risk stretching as far as Europe or the States, where Ellie seemed to spend most of her time. It would have involved too many people he didn't know, and couldn't trust, to arrange her death. Instead, he'd opted to play a safer, longer game. He'd had one of his men check her apartment in London to make sure that there was nothing that could be traced to him – a diary, letters, anything – and then embarked on a campaign of subtle intimidation: phone calls to her hotels, tampered mail. He'd made her feel he was right behind her everywhere she went. He'd guessed that, sooner or later, she'd come back to face him.

'Where's she staying?'

'I don't know. I've told you all I can.' Luca paused, and when he spoke again, Fernando couldn't miss the chill in his voice. 'Don't call me again, Moreno. You're not the safest person to know any more.'

The line went dead. Fernando replaced the receiver, his fears forgotten as adrenalin surged through him. Death had cheated him of Roberto Cerreni; it seemed he'd waited too long to be revenged on his old adversary. He'd never really wanted to destroy Roberto, anyway; knowing that he had the power to do so had always been enough.

But Ellie Cassidy was a different matter. She'd eluded him for long enough, but she was within his grasp now. He just had to find her.

Six

Alix stood up as the old priest padded back into the room, his bare feet making no noise on the cold stone floor. In a few moments, she would meet the one man who could tell her who she was, and for the first time in the five days since she and Ellie had left Rome, she felt a flicker of doubt. Until now, the need to know who she was had driven every other thought from her mind. Now, suddenly, she was afraid of what she might discover. Roberto Cerreni had kept his silence for nearly thirty years. He had clearly thought it best that Alix should not know the truth.

She had never had the chance to speak to Roberto again after that evening when she'd finally been able to forgive him. He had died hours after she had left him, almost as if he had been clinging to life just long enough for her to reach him. Neither she nor Stephi could bear to go to his funeral. Instead, on the day he'd been buried, they'd both got quietly drunk at Alix's apartment, crying and laughing as they'd talked about the man they'd both known, the vital, larger-than-life presence of Alix's childhood.

Afterwards, Alix had told Stephi that Roberto hadn't been her father. She'd guessed from Stephi's calm reaction that the

426

older woman had already known. It was from her father's former mistress that Alix had finally learned all that Stephi knew: that she was the child of Brazilian peasants, that she'd been brought to Roberto when she was a day old by a priest called Father Lucio to replace the son he'd lost. More than that, Stephi hadn't been able to tell her.

Alix had known that she had to find out the rest of the story. She had to know who her parents were – their names, where they'd lived, if they were still alive. For all she knew, she might have brothers and sisters living somewhere in Rio, she might have a ready-made family waiting out there for her. She'd had to go there.

At once she'd thought of Ellie. Some time ago, her friend had told her the truth behind the official PR version of her life, according to which she'd been born into a wealthy Brazilian family and moved to America as a child. Ellie had never revealed exactly how she'd survived on the streets of Rio, but Alix had guessed. She'd heard enough about the dangerous, amoral city to know that there were few ways a girl as vulnerable and beautiful as Ellie could have stayed alive for so long. And she knew that her own quest would take her into some of the poorest and most dangerous quarters of the shanty towns. She couldn't do it alone.

As soon as Alix had told Ellie what she'd been planning, Ellie had insisted on coming with her anyway. They'd arrived in Rio five days ago, but it had taken them this long to track down the priest who'd been involved in her adoption. The church that Ellie had remembered from her childhood had been burned down in a fire several years previously, and Father Lucio had been taken in by a community of monks living in an ancient monastery in the hills above the city. Eventually a district nurse had been able to tell them where he was.

They followed the old monk now as he shuffled through the

cloisters and across the stone square at the centre of the monastery. A low fountain shaded by lime trees chattered quietly at its centre, the sound of the water echoing around the silent courtyard. On the other side of the cloisters a white-robed figure glided between the columns, carrying a wooden bucket of water. The monastery had a timelessness that Alix felt must have remained unchanged for centuries.

Alix turned as she felt a gentle touch on her arm. 'Are you absolutely sure you want to do this?'

'Would you want to know, if it were you?'

Ellie hesitated, then nodded. 'Yes. If there was a chance of finding out who my father was –' She paused, choosing her words with care. 'Alix, you have to be prepared for the fact that Father Lucio might not know who your parents were. It's a long time ago now – there must have been so many children who passed through his hands. He's an old man, in his eighties. And he's very ill. Even if he did know once, he might not remember now. And anything he does tell you, however much you might want to believe it – it might not be true.'

'But if it is –'

'It still might not be what you want to hear,' Ellie spoke softly. 'Alix, the people who gave their children to Father Lucio must have been very desperate, and very poor. Your parents aren't sitting in a cottage with roses round the door waiting for their long-lost daughter to return. They may not even be alive. If they are, they won't be the sort of people you're used to. You don't know what life here is like. Your mother may have been a teenage prostitute who doesn't know who your father was. She could have been raped by her own brother. Anything.'

Alix glanced back across the courtyard as a bell slowly began to chime the hour. 'Whatever it is, the truth has to be better than not knowing. Ellie, can you understand what it's like to suddenly not know where you came from, who you are? I feel as if there's a whole part of myself missing. However much it hurts, I have to know what that part is.'

'I never knew my father,' Ellie said. 'I don't even know if my mother did. She died when I was four. I have never had a past. You have to face the fact that you may never be able to find yours either.'

'But I have to try.'

Ellie knew better than anyone the risk Alix was taking in delving so far back into her past. She had recognised Father Lucio's name the moment Alix had telephoned her in New York and told her Roberto's story. The old priest's name had triggered a thousand memories in her mind – her mother carrying her into the tiny church in Nova Esperancia for the baptism of yet another unwanted brother or sister, the anger and frustration she'd felt when Father Lucio had let her mother die and had taken the baby that had cost her her life. Whatever truth was waiting here for Alix, Ellie couldn't let her face it alone.

She felt the cool reassurance of the .38 revolver tucked against her breasts beneath her white silk blouse. When Alix had called her she'd known that fate was finally drawing her back to Rio, back to her roots. She'd run from her nameless enemy for too long, but she'd realised when Alix had asked her to come with her to Brazil that it was time to settle the score. She was going to find out the real name of the man who'd watched her being raped and then murdered David, the man who'd called himself Colhor when he'd paid to fuck her two years later. This time it was she who had the advantage of surprise: he didn't even know she was here. She was going to track him down, and then she was going to kill him.

She gave Alix a smile of reassurance as they stopped outside a small wooden door at the far end of the passageway. Their ancient, taciturn guide opened the door to Father Lucio's cell and stood back to allow them in before quietly shutting it behind them. Her eyes travelled the tiny oblong room, taking in the plain whitewashed walls, the simple wooden crucifix above the door, the narrow window through which a single block of yellow sunshine fell across the stone floor. Ellie sat down on a small wooden stool to the left of the door as Alix took the chair next to the narrow iron bed. The old man lying in it turned slowly to face her as she sat down, his eyes filmy with age as he tried to focus. Ellie could hear the rasp of his breath as he struggled to sit upright.

'They said – they said you wanted to see me.' Father Lucio's voice was faint.

Alix glanced across at Ellie for encouragement and took a deep breath. 'Father Lucio, I need your help. I think you may know who my parents are. You arranged my adoption.'

The old man stared at her, fear and guilt plain on his face. Then he turned away, shaking his head. 'I don't remember. It's too long ago. There were so many –'

'My father – the man you gave me to – his name was Roberto Cerreni. He was the Italian Ambassador to Brazil. Surely you can remember? He adopted me when I was a tiny baby.'

'I never dealt directly with anyone.' Father Lucio's voice became irritable. 'I just supplied the children. The Judge arranged the paperwork –'

'Please. Think back. It would have been the autumn of 1970. The – the adoption wasn't planned. You would have had to find me quickly. My – the Cerrenis – took me straight back to Rome. Please, try to remember …'

The old man shifted uneasily in the bed, trying to equate this beautiful young woman with the dirty, scrawny babies he'd traded like so much scrap metal. Despite her obvious distress, this girl was dignified and poised, and she had an air of authority about her. It was partly the way she carried herself, her chin tilting slightly upwards with determination as if she was used to battling the world for what she wanted; but there was something else, too, some steely resolve at the core of her that made him glad she didn't know the whole story of what he'd done. He found that he was moved, despite himself, by the pain he saw in her eyes. They were very unusual eyes – wide, thick-lashed, the colour of molten gold. Unforgettable eyes.

Cerreni, she had said. Twenty-five years ago. Cerreni. *And those eyes* ...

With a sudden, terrible fear, the old priest knew exactly who she was. He turned his face towards the wall. 'I don't know who you are. Leave me alone. Go away. I can't remember.' Spittle flecked his lips. 'I can't remember. I can't remember.'

Alix had been so certain this man would hold the key to her past, that somewhere in the confusion of his mind lay the information she needed, and now she was as far from knowing the truth as she had ever been. Tears of disappointment and frustration filled her eyes as she felt Ellie's gentle arm slip round her shoulders.

'Alix, you tried, but he doesn't know. He obviously can't remember so far back.' Ellie glanced towards the bed as they reached the door. 'Perhaps it's better this way. Roberto didn't want you to know. He must have had his reasons.'

'I can't bear it, Ellie. I'll never know now.'

Alix leant her hot forehead against the cool stone of the monastery wall. Ellie felt a stab of pity as she watched her. She'd never known her own father, but at least she hadn't had to grow up and discover she'd been living a lie. Ellie stared out across the tranquil courtyard, thinking about what the old priest had said; and then she remembered. 'Alix, maybe there is someone else who can help. Father Lucio mentioned something about a judge arranging all the paperwork. He can't be that difficult to find. He must have been quite influential to have been in a position to process the kind of documentation that Roberto would have needed to get you out of the country and into Italy. And he would have moved in the same circles as Roberto. There can't have been many judges in that position. There must be some sort of record of them –'

'Of course! I should have thought of that before.' Alix was already pacing towards the monastery door. 'I'm going to find my parents, Ellie, if I have to spend the rest of my life looking.'

For the next two days they searched through the microfilmed newspapers and public records at Rio de Janeiro's central library. They widened their search to include the six months prior to the Cerrenis' return to Rome, reasoning that the date Alix had always considered to be her birthday might not be accurate. Several times they thought they'd found the judge they wanted, only to discover that he'd been posted abroad or was out of office at the time that Alix had been adopted. Alix was scanning yet another screen detailing government appointments in October 1970, when suddenly Ellie shouted exultantly and kicked back her chair. 'I've found him!'

Several people turned to stare at them, and Ellie covered her mouth with her hand, trying not to laugh. 'I've found him, Alix,' she whispered again. 'The judge responsible for processing adoption and expatriation documents, from September 1966 to July 1974. He moved on then to greater things, but he's the man who would have dealt with your papers. He's the one you want.'

'What's his name?'

'Fernando Moreno,' Ellie said as her friend peered over her shoulder at the screen. 'He's a Finance Minister now. I don't know what he looks like, there isn't a picture, but we should be able to find him now that we know his name.'

Seven

Ellie lay naked on her bed and gently tossed the revolver from one hand to the other, enjoying the feel of the cool steel against her palms. She felt an unexpected excitement as she lay back against the pillows, gently tracing the line between her nipples and stomach with the revolver, allowing her hand to slide lower so that the gun barrel slipped into the wetness between her parted thighs. She imagined David's killer on top of her, fucking her even as she slid the gun from beneath the pillows and held it against his head, just long enough for him to feel the terror of knowing he was about to die before she pulled the trigger and blew his brains away. Her stomach tightened with desire and her breasts tingled as she rubbed the gun across her clitoris. She wanted his death with a visceral, primal longing that came from deep within her soul.

Moments later, her body exploded in an orgasm that was sweeter and more intense than any she had ever experienced.

It was several minutes before she realised that someone was knocking impatiently at the door and calling her name. She sat up, her dark hair tumbling across her breasts as she hastily slipped the gun into the top drawer of her bedside table.

'Who is it?'

'Ellie? Is that you?'

'*Matt?*'

Ellie grabbed the pale blue bathrobe lying on the end of her bed and slipped it on as she ran to open the door. 'What the hell are *you* doing here? How did you know where to find us?'

'Angela told me which hotel you were staying at,' Matt said wearily. 'Can I come in?' He squeezed past her.

'Matt, what is it?'

'I need to speak to Alix,' Matt said. He sounded exhausted, but his voice held a note of urgency. 'Is she staying here too?'

Ellie hesitated for a moment, before crossing the room and picking up the telephone. She watched Matt's face as she dialled Alix's room. His eyes were red-rimmed and raw from lack of sleep, his jaw covered with two-day-old stubble, and his clothes looked as if they'd been slept in. His fear for Alix reawakened her own as she waited for her friend to answer. 'She said she had a headache and wanted to go to bed for a couple of hours. She's probably still sleeping ...' Her eyes followed Matt as he paced edgily up and down. 'Matt, why are you here? I told you I'd get in touch if there were any problems. I don't think Alix will even agree to see you –'

'Is she answering?'

Ellie frowned. 'I don't know where she can have gone, unless she's in the bath ...' She paused, then depressed the button on the base of the receiver and dialled the switchboard. 'Perhaps I've got the wrong number. Hello? Can you tell me the number I should be dialling for Alexandra D'Alfonsi's room? Oh, I see. Yes. No, no message, thank you.'

She turned to Matt, confusion in her eyes. 'The receptionist said she saw Alix go out over an hour ago, she doesn't know where.'

'We have to find her, Ellie. She doesn't know what she's getting into.' Matt dug around in his canvas Billingham bag and pulled out a folder. 'After you told me that Alix wanted to

434

go to Rio to trace her parents, I called an old schoolfriend of mine, David Cameron. He and his wife adopted a little boy about eighteen months ago. I was going to arrange for Alix to meet them, I thought it might help if she talked to someone who'd adopted a child and heard the other side of the story –' He broke off, aware he was digressing. 'Anyway, David wasn't there, but I got chatting to his wife, Christie. She's a journalist with INN. When I told her about Alix and mentioned Rio, she suddenly realised it fitted in with a baby-smuggling story she's been chasing for months in Brazil. As soon as I told her Alix's real name – Cerreni – we knew for sure. Roberto Cerreni was involved in more than just the adoption of his daughter. Thousands of babies from the *favellas* have been sold abroad in the past twenty years. When I spoke to her then, Christie knew Cerreni's name and that of the priest who found the children, but not the name of the man behind it all, a Brazilian judge.'

'Why didn't you tell us this before we came out here?'

'I couldn't get hold of you – that must have been the day you were travelling here from Rome. Anyway, what good would it have done? What Roberto Cerreni did was illegal, but he probably did it from the best of motives. Knowing the truth wouldn't have helped Alix.' He started to leaf through the contents of his folder as he talked. 'But then Christie rang me back two days ago. A little boy called Joel turned up at a children's shelter in Rio and spoke to one of her contacts, a woman called Lucy. Joel told her the name of the Brazilian behind the whole scam –'

'You didn't need to come all the way here to to tell us,' Ellie interrupted. 'We've already managed to track down the judge who processed all the paperwork. He should be able to tell Alix what she wants to know; if he can't remember himself, he may have kept some sort of record –' She stopped suddenly as she caught a glimpse of the glossy 10" by 8" in his hand. 'Matt, show me that photograph.'

'What's the matter?'

'*Give me the photograph.*'

Ellie snatched it away from him, her skin turning ashen as she studied it. 'Colhor.' She said nothing for a few moments, studying the face of the man she'd hated for nearly half her life. 'Who is he?'

'I was coming to that. There's more to this baby-smuggling ring than children. This man has been trading in human spare parts: organs for transplant. Kidneys, mainly. His thugs pick up street children no one's going to miss – either lure them with promises of a new life abroad, or just bundle them into the back of a van – and take them to a clinic just across the border with Paraguay. They're kept there until a suitable client is found, then they're killed in cold blood and their organs are shipped abroad. Christie thinks this man is responsible for the deaths of hundreds of children, though proving it is going to be harder. There are so few witnesses left alive.'

'His *name*, Matt.'

'It's the Judge. Fernando Moreno.'

Ellie stared at him in horror. 'Oh, God, Matt. I've just realised where Alix must have gone.'

Unselfconsciously she shed her bathrobe as she pulled a silk jumper over her head and started to tug on a pair of Levi's. 'We were going to go to Moreno's office tomorrow. I've never seen his face before, I had no idea who he was. Alix was impatient to see him, but I didn't think she'd try to talk to him alone.'

'We have to reach her first,' Matt said urgently. 'God knows what that man will do –'

Ellie opened the drawer of her bedside table and drew out

her gun, checking that the chamber was loaded before sliding it into her canvas tote bag.

Matt stared at her in disbelief. 'Ellie, would you actually use that?'

Ellie coolly returned his gaze.

Matt shivered. 'Jesus, Ellie –'

'We'd better go. That is, if you're still coming.'

Neither of them spoke as they ran down the stairs and through the hotel lobby. Matt flagged down a taxi as they emerged on to the Copacabana promenade that separated the hotel from the crowded stretch of white sand, then sank back against the torn plastic seat as Ellie gave the driver directions.

He tapped his fingers against the arm-rest as the taxi slowed behind a queue of heavy traffic. Since Christie had called him in New York with the news, he had been racing halfway across the world to get to Alix before it was too late. He hadn't even stopped to pack an overnight bag, leaving Christie trying unsuccessfully to telephone Alix and Ellie in Rio to warn them, while he travelled. The flight from New York to Brazil had seemed to take for ever. He'd sat bolt upright in his seat in an agony of impatience, unable to sleep, trying not to think what would happen if he was too late. He'd had no idea what he'd do or say once he'd reached Alix; he hadn't even known if she'd agree to see him, given the way she'd acted for the past few months. But he'd been determined to force her to listen to him if he had to lock her in her hotel bedroom and shout through the door.

Matt knew he should have hated Alix for the way she'd treated him, shutting him out of her life yet again; but when he'd discovered the danger she was in, the pain and anger had instantly dissolved. He'd realised that he loved her more than his own life. It wasn't an easy feeling to live with. It made him vulnerable; but it also made him happier than he'd ever thought possible.

437

He stared desperately at the traffic in front of them. 'How much longer?'

'Fifteen minutes. Maybe if we walked –'

'How far is it?'

'I don't think it's far, but it's a while since I've been here. Things might have changed.'

Matt watched Ellie's face as she stared at the city, and realised for the first time that she was going through a difficult time herself. She'd never confided the truth about her background to him, but he'd pieced most of it together from the bits she'd let slip over the years, plus what Alix had been able to tell him. The rest he'd filled in for himself. He knew about the telephone calls she'd been getting for the past couple of years, the tampered mail, her fear that she was being stalked. He saw now that she'd brought the gun with her to Rio without even knowing about what had been happening at the Speretti Institute. She must have a score to settle of her own. He sensed her loneliness and reached out to take her hand, wanting to share her pain. 'It's a long time since I've been here, too.'

'You've come to Rio before?'

'When I was about twelve or thirteen, I was here with my father. I've never forgotten it. There was a terrible mudslide up in the hills, and I ended up helping with the rescue. I pulled a little girl out of the mud, she can't have been more than four or five. I've often wondered what happened to her.'

'Elizabetta Ferreira.'

'Yes, how did you –'

They stared at each other.

'Oh, my God,' Matt said quietly. 'All this time, and we never knew.'

Fernando Moreno contemplated the young woman before him. He could see that beneath the fatigue and stress, she was exceptionally beautiful. Her current air of supplication made her seem younger than the twenty-five years he guessed her to be, but she had walked into his office half an hour earlier with a grace and poise that had impressed him despite himself. She seemed strangely familiar, although he couldn't quite think why. She still hadn't given him her name. His eyes ran over her face, noting the rich copper hair caught into a loose chignon at the nape of her neck, the skin so pale it was almost translucent, the high cheekbones and firm, wide mouth. He felt himself harden as she moved and the light from the window behind him fell across her and revealed the small, high breasts beneath the pale pink silk shirt she was wearing. Automatically his eyes shifted to take in her endlessly long legs and the slender shape of her pelvis. In other circumstances, he might have been tempted to fuck her. As it was, he already knew he was going to have to kill her.

'My dear, you are making some very serious allegations against me,' he said eventually. 'Despite everything you've told me, I really don't see what you have to support them. The dying words of a senile old man –'

'Father Lucio told me that you arranged for identity papers and the approval of overseas adoptions for a number of children in the late Sixties and early Seventies.'

'Naturally I was involved in the processing of such details. It was part of my remit as a High Court judge. It is a great leap of conjecture to suggest that I was actually responsible in any way for finding these children.'

'I realise I may never be able to *prove* your involvement. That's not what I'm trying to do,' Alix answered. 'Senhor Moreno, all I want to do is find out where I came from, who my parents were. I'm not interested in anything else, I'm not after revenge, just the truth.'

'Even if I was involved in the – humanitarian – arrangements you suggest, how could I possibly remember them all?

This Father Lucio didn't suggest I knew the families of these children, did he?'

'No –'

'In that case, I really don't see how you think I can help you.'

Alix stared at him. He must have seen hundreds of children pass through his hands, signing documents without even knowing their names. Even if he received some kind of financial recompense from the adoptive parents, there was no reason why he should remember – or even have known – the origins of the children he passed on. But he must have known Roberto Cerreni personally. His had to have been a particularly special commission. Surely, even if most of the children he dealt with were anonymous credits to his bank account, he would know where the child he gave to the Italian Ambassador had come from?

'Senhor Moreno, I wasn't adopted by just anyone. My – my father – was Roberto Cerreni. I can't believe that you wouldn't remember him –'

Fernando stared at her in shock. He stood up suddenly and moved towards the coffee percolator at the side of his office, desperately trying to collect himself. He could remember as clearly as if it were yesterday the warm October evening when Roberto Cerreni had come to him and told him of Joanna's miscarriage, the terrible knowledge that there would never be any more children. He had sat and watched Roberto's misery, savouring the knowledge that, for once, he had had something the mighty Italian Ambassador, with his perfect wife and perfect career and perfect life, wanted.

Cerreni had asked – begged – him to find them another child, a baby the same age as their own would have been if it had lived, one they could pass off as their own when they returned to Rome. He had offered everything he had, but Fernando hadn't wanted his money. It had been worth it just to see the proud Roberto humbled, to know that the Italian would be indebted to him for the rest of his life.

And now he had that same cherished daughter in the palm of his hand.

He smiled at Alix. 'My dear – Miss Cerreni – can I get you a coffee?'

He could feel the girl's eyes on him as he switched the coffee percolator on. He vividly recalled the trouble they had had finding a child that the Cerrenis could pass off plausibly as their own. Joanna had been so fair and pale. Father Lucio had been unable to locate a baby in the *favellas* who could possibly be presented as her child. Time had been running out, and they still hadn't found a child for Roberto.

And then he had thought of Annabel.

'Sugar? Milk?'

'Neither, thank you.'

Fernando added three spoonfuls of sugar to his own cup. He hadn't known Annabel long, barely a few weeks, before she'd been stupid enough to get pregnant. He hadn't wanted the child, but her parents had insisted. Her father had been a wealthy coffee plantation owner, so Fernando had reluctantly agreed to marry her. When Roberto had come to him, she'd been eight months pregnant.

He remembered how he had watched dispassionately as Father Lucio and his driver had held her down on his own bed while the nurse he'd bought for a few hundred dollars had induced the baby. He had listened to Annabel's anguished screams as she gave birth to the tiny girl, without feeling a shred of remorse or regret. It had been Annabel's mistake. She'd forced it on him, and he had simply taken what was rightfully his.

He'd known that no one would ever believe her story even if she'd been stupid enough to repeat it. Annabel had committed suicide only weeks after her baby had been stolen from her, her mind destroyed by grief. Fernando had barely thought about her since then.

He stared into Alix's eyes, and suddenly the reality hit him.

He was looking at his own daughter.

His overwhelming feeling as he watched her was of distant curiosity, as if he had just unearthed a toy from his childhood long since lost. This was his daughter, the child he would have had if he had chosen to live his life another way. He had felt nothing for her then, nor did he now. He studied her carefully, knowing he would never see her again. He could find little of either himself or Annabel in her – except for her huge, translucent gold eyes. When he stared into them, it was like looking into a mirror.

Alix put down her empty coffee cup and stood up. 'You don't intend to tell me anything, do you, Senhor Moreno? If you won't help me, I'll have to find someone who will. I've got this far. It's just a matter of persistence.'

Fernando met her gaze and realised with mingled fear and admiration that his daughter had inherited more from him than his eyes. She might not recognise it for what it was, but she possessed the same steely determination that had driven him all his life. He knew she wouldn't let the matter rest until she had discovered what she wanted to know.

Or died in the attempt.

He shook her proffered hand. 'In that case, Miss Cerreni, I must wish you well. I hope you don't regret your decision.'

He watched as she left his office, with her regal, gliding walk. She was very self-possessed for one so young. He felt a brief, unexpected flicker of regret as he picked up the telephone and issued his instructions. He knew she would head towards the Justice Ministry on the Avenida Rio Branco where he had worked for so many years. It was the logical place to go – it was what he would have done. It was a shame that she had to die, but he couldn't allow her to ask any more

442

questions. Not now that he was so close to freeing himself for ever from the secret in his past.

He turned as the door to his office opened, ready to snap at his secretary, but her name died on his lips. Slowly he replaced his coffee cup on the desk, his eyes never leaving the gun levelled directly at his chest.

'I do hope you can think of a good reason why I shouldn't blow away your balls and force them down your throat before I kill you,' Ellie said calmly. 'Because I can't.'

Eight

Rio de Janeiro, Brazil
Monday 19 December 1994
5.00 p.m.

Fernando felt no fear as he led Ellie and her companion out of his office, only anger at himself. Massimo Luca had warned him that she was in the country a week ago, but he'd been stupid enough to underestimate her yet again. She'd been harder to find than he'd expected, although now he understood why. She'd been changing hotels, not because she'd been afraid of him, but because she'd been scouring Rio for someone who could help her friend find her real parents. Fernando knew he hadn't given the matter the attention he should have done. He'd been too preoccupied with the problems at the Speretti Institute, and anyway he'd calculated on having the advantage of surprise. He felt the hard steel of Ellie's gun against his ribs and knew he'd have to be very lucky to be able to make any more mistakes.

They left the building, Ellie tucking her arm through Fernando's for the benefit of the security guards, the gun concealed beneath the jacket she'd folded over her arm. As they emerged into the street, Fernando paused for a moment, then turned left into Avenida Presidente Vargas.

'Are you sure this is the right way?' Matt said.

'I won't just kill you if you're wrong, Moreno,' Ellie

444

warned. 'By the time I've finished with you, you'll be glad to die.'

'It's the quickest way to the Justice Ministry in Avenida Rio Branco. That's where I would have gone,' Fernando said. 'I arranged for one of my men to follow her from here. There's a small back street between my office and the Ministry. I told him to – to deal with her there.'

'You fucking *bastard* –'

Ellie held Matt back with her free arm. 'For Christ's sake, Matt. We need him alive.'

'Which street?'

Fernando hesitated.

Ellie shifted the gun. 'Answer him, Moreno.'

'The one just past the Air France office. You can cut through that street and it brings you out into a tiny square – I don't know what it's called. She'll have to go through the square when she turns off this road. It's the only way.'

Matt started to jog towards the Air France office, his pace quickening into a run as he swung down the narrow street just beyond it. Startled pedestrians dodged out of his way as he raced past them, his heart pounding with exertion. Sweat ran down his forehead and he wiped it away with his sleeve, searching the street in vain for any sign of Alix. He cursed as a group of ragged street children blocked his path, a couple of them waving newspapers in his face to distract his attention while the others skilfully picked his pockets. Several alleys opened up in front of him, all of them shadowed and deserted, and Matt stopped running. He had no idea which way she would have taken. He could hear Ellie's voice several metres behind him as she forced Fernando to walk in front of her; even if Moreno was bringing them the right way, they were already at least ten minutes behind Alix. If one of his men was following her, they'd never reach her in time. She could already be lying in some gutter –

He shouted at the street children. 'Hey! Have you seen a tall, white lady with red hair go past?'

One of the children broke away from the group and held out his hand, palm upwards. 'How much, mister?'

'Have you seen her?'

'How much?'

'OK, OK.' Matt dug in his pockets and discovered that they'd already cleaned him out. He undid his watch strap and held the Breitling above their heads. 'You find her for me, you get to keep this.'

'Follow me, mister.'

The children swarmed down the alleyway to Matt's right and he followed them, shouting at Ellie and pointing towards the street he'd taken. Two of the boys grabbed his hands and started pulling him along, shrieking words of Portuguese he didn't understand. For a moment he wondered if he was being led into a trap, then they were standing in a square and he saw Alix's red head disappearing down another alley on the other side. He shouted her name, but she was too far away to hear. He turned as Fernando and Ellie reached the square.

'Moreno, is your man with her now?'

Fernando shrugged. Ellie whipped him around the side of the head with the butt of her gun, and Matt flinched despite himself at the savagery of the blow. 'Answer him!'

Fernando reeled, blood pouring from a cut above his ear. 'I can't see. It's too far away.'

Already Matt was running towards Alix. Ellie forced Fernando to kneel on the cobbles with his hands clasped above his head, the street children shouting and dancing around them. Alix turned as she heard the clamour, her expression changing to one of amazement. 'Matt –'

Matt saw the man materialise from the shadows behind her at the same time as Ellie. The sunlight glinted on the killer's knife as he moved towards her. The man was almost at her throat when Matt threw himself headlong against her in the most important rugby tackle of his life. At the same moment, Ellie pulled the trigger of her gun and fired.

The bullet glanced harmlessly off the wall of the church behind them. The man was already disappearing down a side street as Matt pushed himself up from the cobbles, his eyes feverishly searching Alix's face as she lay, stunned, beside him.

'Alix, are you hurt? Did he touch you?'

Alix shook her head, too shocked to answer. Matt stood and helped her to her feet. 'Are you sure you're OK?'

'I'm sure –'

Her reply was lost in his kiss. Matt wrapped his arms around her, pulling her towards him as her mouth opened beneath his and he tasted the sweetness of her. She stiffened, and relief that she was unhurt was suddenly replaced by fear that she'd push him away from her again before he had a chance to explain. He broke their kiss and stepped backwards, holding her face between the palms of his hands as he stared deeply into her eyes. 'Alix, I love you. I always will. I'm not going to leave you, you must know that. You have to trust me. Please.'

For the first time Alix noticed how exhausted he looked, how drained. It wasn't the two-day stubble or the crumpled clothes, but the expression in his eyes. She could see the love there, and behind it the dread that he'd lose her again. He looked like a man who had risked everything on one last, final roll of the dice, and suddenly as she looked at him she didn't see Joanna or Roberto's shadow falling across his face, but her own. The only thing that stood between her and happiness with Matt was her own fear.

She smiled. 'Do you think you could kiss me again?'

It was several moments before they were aware of the clamour behind them. Matt remembered Ellie and Fernando and took Alix's hand as he led her back towards the square. Ellie's shot had summoned a dozen policemen to the plaza, and they were now trying to push their way through the knot of people in the centre of a growing crowd of street children, tourists and shopkeepers. Alix and Matt followed them and reached a small clearing in the centre of the crowd. Fernando was kneeling on the cobbles, his hands still above his head, while Ellie stood in front of him, her gun trained on his forehead. Four or five policemen surrounded them both, half of them pointing their guns at Ellie, half at Fernando, uncertain which of the two they should apprehend.

'Get this girl away from me,' Fernando said to the policemen nearest to him.

Ellie didn't move or speak.

Fernando didn't take his eyes off Ellie's face. 'My name is Fernando Moreno. I'm the Minister for Finance. This girl is a whore and she's trying to kill me.'

One of the policemen started to move towards her, and Ellie's finger tightened on the trigger. 'Another step and I'll blow his brains out.'

The policeman stopped. Fernando glared at him. 'Ignore her. She's bluffing –'

'I don't think so.'

He glanced up at Alix. Her expression held nothing but contempt, and Fernando felt an unexpected surge of admiration. She was his daughter, all right. She played to win, although she probably didn't realise it yet. If and when she decided to take control of her life, there would be few who could stand in her way. He thought with a flicker of regret what a good team they could have made.

And he'd given her away to Roberto Cerreni, his enemy, a man he despised.

Matt stepped forward and held out his hand. 'Come on,

448

Ellie. It's over. You have to let the police take over now. We can put him away for ever. He's not worth it.'

Ellie's hand wavered. She hadn't thought beyond this moment, to what would happen when she actually found the man who'd destroyed her life. From the corner of her eye she saw the police guns trained on her and realised that, in their eyes, at this moment she was the criminal. She stared at Fernando, thinking how much evil this man had wrought, how many innocent lives he'd taken. She remembered David and suddenly knew that when Fernando had killed him, he'd killed her too. She'd been living a half-life ever since, too afraid to let go and share herself with anyone for fear of losing them again. The only man she'd been able to care about wasn't even hers to love. She'd been running all her life, and at the end of it, she had nothing: no home, no family, no one to love; with Fernando behind bars, she wouldn't even have anyone to hate. Nothing. She lowered the gun, her vision blurred by tears.

Fernando scented triumph and started to rise. Ellie saw him smile, that same smile she'd seen the day he'd watched his men rape her and killed the man she'd loved.

Her finger tightened on the trigger and she fired.

Nine

Brompton Oratory, London, UK
Friday 3 February 1995
11.30 a.m.

Alix and Matt led the way out of the church. The rest of the mourners fell in behind them, discussing the memorial service and each other in muted whispers. Alix blinked in the pale, wintry sunshine as she emerged on to the steps, holding tightly to Matt's arm for support. Her face was pale but composed as she glanced at the mourners clustering near the church steps. She recognised the faces of a dozen people she'd never met: David Cameron, his arm around his wife, Christie, their tiny new son sleeping peacefully in her arms; Cindy Crawford and her estranged husband, Richard Gere, who'd buried their differences to come together for the service; Claudia Schiffer, Alastair Blair, Iman and David Bowie, Rod Stewart and Rachel Hunter. CNN camera crews chatted with their opposite numbers from INN and the BBC; journalists from newspapers and fashion magazines jostled with photographers from Reuters and *Hello*!

'I think Ellie would have been pleased.' Alix's smile was sad. 'So much attention. If only she could have been here to enjoy it.'

Matt squeezed her hand. 'I think she is.'

Luke broke away from a group of journalists and came

over. He hugged Alix for a moment without speaking, his loss suddenly too painful for him to find the words. 'Oh, God, Alix, I do miss her.'

'I can't believe it's six weeks since she died. I keep reaching for the telephone to call her, and then I remember.' Her voice trembled. 'If it wasn't for me, she wouldn't even have been there, she'd still be with us now—'

'Alix, you've got to stop thinking like that,' Matt said. 'Ellie had her own reasons for going back to Rio. What she did had nothing to do with you. It was part of her own battle with Fernando.'

'I know. But it's hard sometimes.'

'I'm just glad you were there with her,' Luke said. 'I would hate to think of her dying alone …'

Alix shivered. She'd known even as she'd cradled Ellie on the cobbles in the square in Rio de Janeiro that it was too late to save her. She'd clung to Ellie's hand as they'd waited for the ambulance, begging her to hold on, too numb to feel anything as she'd stared at Fernando's lifeless body a few feet away from her. Ellie's shot had killed him instantly, but the police bullets that had slammed into her body almost at once had left her cruelly alive for several minutes. Alix had watched helplessly as her breathing became shallow and rapid, her skin filmed with sweat. She'd never regained consciousness. Death had come a few moments later, before the doctors had even reached them.

Alix couldn't have coped with the next forty-eight hours without Matt. Even though he was weighed down by his own grief, he'd taken charge of everything. He'd arranged for Ellie to be buried up at the monastery in the hills where she and Alix had found Father Lucio, knowing that she'd find peace at last in the quiet, tranquil gardens high above the city. The two of them had been the only mourners at the simple funeral. They'd held each other in shared grief as they'd watched the

451

coffin being lowered into the ground, their love-making that night filled with tender sadness. The next day, they'd flown back to England and Matt had taken Alix to stay at his parents' home in Sussex.

It was at East Lambrook Manor that Alix had finally started to put the past behind her, finding unexpected solace in the company of Matt's father. At seventy-nine, Christopher Logan was an older, wiser, version of his son, the altruism which he and Matt both shared tempered in his case by years of experience. Alix had spent hours wandering through the wintry gardens of the estate with him, talking about the past: her childhood, her feelings towards both Joanna and Roberto, her mingled confusion and relief at discovering she was adopted. Once, Christopher had asked her if perhaps Joanna's feelings towards her had stemmed not from personal dislike, but from jealousy and grief that Alix had supplanted her own, lost, child in both her own life and her husband's affections. Christopher hadn't pushed the point, but for the first time Alix had felt pity for the woman she still thought of as her mother. She doubted that she and Joanna would ever be close, but perhaps now that Roberto was dead and Alix knew the truth about her birth, she and her mother would be able to call some sort of truce. She hated to think of Joanna alone with her grief.

This memorial service had been intended as their final goodbye to Ellie; the next time she and Matt entered a church, it would be for their wedding. Christopher had been delighted when she and Matt had announced their intention to marry in the spring; even Caroline had expressed her pleasure, spurred perhaps by the fact that Matt's elder brother, at fifty-one, had still not provided her with a grandson and heir for East Lambrook. With Roberto, all Fernando and Father Lucio all dead – the old priest had died in his sleep the day before they'd buried Ellie – she would never know who her real parents were; but it had ceased to matter. She had Matt, and

Christopher and Caroline had already made her feel as if she was part of their family.

'Alexandra –?'

She pushed her thoughts aside as Edouard Chambrun came towards her, trying to mask her shock as she saw the ravages grief had wrought. He looked nearer eighty than the sixty she knew him to be. She guessed that without his lover his life had ceased to have any real meaning.

The story of the Speretti Institute had made headlines across the world the week after Ellie's death. Roberto Cerreni, Father Lucio and Fernando Moreno had been beyond retribution, but Giulio Pavesi had been destroyed by the revelation that he'd been part of the scandal, albeit innocent of involvement in the horrific organ trade. It had soon become clear that he'd only acted as a go-between for Fernando and his wealthy, childless customers, but the knowledge of the gruesome truth behind the Institute had been enough to wreck his mind. Alix knew that criminal charges had been waived on the grounds that Pavesi was not fit to stand trial, but his own conscience had imprisoned him in a twilight world of madness without hope of parole. But it was Edouard's loss that made Alix's heart twist with pity.

'I'm so sorry, Edouard.'

The man took her hand and squeezed it wordlessly between his own.

'Is he any better?'

'No.' He smiled with sad dignity. 'But that is my grief, not yours. It would be unfair of me to burden you with anything further. Tell me, my dear, what will you do now?'

'I won't go back to modelling,' Alix said. 'It was never something I really wanted to do, and I went into it for all the wrong reasons. I don't know what I will do yet, but I think I might work on my designs for a while, and then look for a

453

place at one of the New York houses – Ralph Lauren, perhaps, or Donna Karan.'

'Would you consider working with me?'

'For you?' Alix stared. 'But Signor Pavesi –'

'Giulio will never work again,' Chambrun said. 'Even if he recovers his mind, his reputation has been destroyed. But there are hundreds of people whose livelihoods depend on the House of Pavesi. Everything is already in place. It just needs someone with your genius, my dear, to make it live again.'

Alix was stunned. 'I don't know –'

'I wouldn't expect you to work at the House of Pavesi. If you joined us, we would become known as the House D'Alfonsi. I would sign everything over to you; there's nothing left for me there now.'

Alix turned to Matt. 'Matt?'

'It's what you've always wanted,' Matt said softly. 'Your own design house.'

'But what about us?'

'I'll leave you to think about it,' Chambrun said. 'Please say yes, my dear. Don't waste your talent. I would never forgive myself.'

They watched the man walk stiffly towards his waiting taxi.

'We don't have to live in New York,' Matt said. 'I can always move to Rome, you know. It has an international airport, I could reach places like Sarajevo and Chechnya from Italy more quickly than I could from New York.' He tilted her chin towards him with his index finger. 'The future is about us, Alix, not about what we do or where we live. If this is what you want to do, then do it.'

'I love you, Matt Logan.' She lifted her head to kiss him, then paused. 'There's just one thing –'

'What?'

'I'm going to have to work on some sketches of my own

before I can start work on the first collection of the House D'Alfonsi. Some maternity outfits.'

Matt stared at her in disbelief.

Alix smiled radiantly. 'I'm pregnant.'